The
Secret of the Ancients

The Displacers Series

Book 2

Simon Brading

First published 2015

This edition published 2025

Cover design by Andrėja Dikšaitytė

www.forgottenscriptorium.com

ISBN: 978-1-917470-51-3

As always, JJH.

PROLOGUE

Jamaica, 1718.

The man ran wildly through the tropical forest, fleeing for his life. Sunlight streamed down through the scant breaks in the canopy overhead and, despite it being midday, it was dim and shadowy and the trees had a sinister aspect that just added to his fear. He was panting, gasping for breath and soaked in sweat; the heat and humidity were draining his energy rapidly and he had to stagger to a halt. Suddenly dizzy, he clutched hold of a nearby palm tree and rested his forehead against it for support, trying desperately to recover enough strength to carry on.

'I'm… too old… for this sh…' He looked up as the sound of shouting and cursing reached him. 'Sugar! They're faster… than I… thought.' He closed his eyes, letting his thoughts drift; reaching, trying to find that particular state of mind…

He sighed and opened his eyes again. It was no good, the men chasing him were too close, there were too many distractions and he was far too tired to concentrate properly. It wasn't going to work.

He shoved himself away from the tree with a groan and struggled on, his legs burning with the effort, heading for the sounds of waves crashing on the nearby beach.

The man looked to be about forty years old and was dressed in eighteenth century style clothing, all dirty now from his reckless race through the forest - a rough white cotton shirt, brown trousers and black boots. His hat had fallen off at some point revealing light brown hair that was plastered to his forehead and he had a few days of scraggly growth on his chin, giving him an unkempt look. There was a long, wicked looking knife tucked into a royal blue sash around his waist finishing his period, piratical look, but his foul language as he stumbled over bushes and tripped on tree roots was all too modern and certainly didn't match his clothing.

He thought back to how he had gotten into his current mess. Not returning to where he knew he wasn't welcome would probably have been a good idea in hindsight, but his curiosity had gotten the better of him. As always.

He'd shown up in Port Royal at night and arranged to meet some old friends of his, members of the crew of the Mermaid, Captain Smith's ship. In the dark he hadn't seen the wanted posters, hadn't noticed that his likeness was posted everywhere, hadn't realised that everybody in the town knew who he was and that the vast majority of them wouldn't hesitate to turn him in. He'd only had a few minutes to speak to his contacts, Bosun Brown and Captain Smith himself, in a shack on the edge of town before some men from the crew had run in to warn them that there was a mob approaching. Brown and Smith had slipped off into the night; he had told them to go, not wanting them to be associated with him and put them into danger, and he himself had run off into the forest, hoping to make it through to the coast and the safety of the sea.

That safety was now so near. Only a few metres away the trees were starting to thin out and through them the shore and the beach could be glimpsed, the ocean sparkling blue, invitingly, in the blinding midday sun. The sight spurred him on and sent a last surge of adrenaline through him that quickened his pace and gave him hope; a hope that lasted scant seconds and then was dashed to pieces when his left foot went into a rabbit hole, hidden in the undergrowth.

His ankle twisted badly as he was brought up short and he fell sideways, crashing heavily to the floor. He howled in agony as a surprisingly sharp root drove itself all the way through his calf and the noise sent the birds in the nearby trees flying in a sudden burst of colour, screeching in alarm.

He clasped his hand to his mouth, biting into the flesh around the base of his thumb in an attempt to take his mind off the pain and stifle any further screams. He lay as still as he could, struggling to calm his breathing and the pounding of his heart so that he could listen to see if his cries had been heard.

There was a brief hush as the forest seemed to hold its breath with him and the only sound was the crash and hiss of the waves on the sand of the beach, tantalisingly close. For just a moment he thought that he had lost his pursuers, but all too quickly there were renewed shouts - it seemed that they had only paused to listen and work out which way all the noise had come from before continuing to close the net on him.

He gritted his teeth against the pain and frantically tugged at his foot, eventually pulling it free from the hole. Next, he tried to slip the root out of his calf, but he couldn't stop himself from screaming as a fresh spike of agony shot through him. He gulped in deep breaths, blinking rapidly, fighting against the darkness that was encroaching on his vision and threatening to overwhelm him. He instantly realised that the root wasn't going to come out very easily and if he tried to drag it out by force he would most likely lose consciousness, something he could in no way afford to do, so instead he used his long knife to first cut away his trouser leg and then carefully chop the root from the tree. It took very little time because thankfully the knife was very sharp and soon he managed to free himself, leaving a couple of inches of wood sticking out of both sides of his leg. The sight was rather comical and a giggle escaped him before he could stop it.

'Come on, idiot, you don't have time for that!' He growled at himself, letting his anger at his own weakness strengthen him and used the burst of energy it gave him to stand up on his good leg, using a nearby tree to pull himself up.

There was a bottle of the local moonshine in his pocket and he pulled it out and took a swig of it. His eyes watered and he gasped as the strong drink burned his throat, but it served to clear his head a little. He took a deep breath and steeled himself then poured some of the liquid on the wound to disinfect it and clean away some of the blood. It stung and he winced, but it was nothing compared to the pain of the rest of his injuries and hopefully it would stop him from getting some nasty tropical disease.

Satisfied that he had done as much as he could to prepare himself and realising he was fast running out of time, he tried putting some weight on the leg. He bit back another scream as it buckled beneath him and he had to grab at the tree to prevent himself from falling over, scraping his palms against the rough bark. There was no way he was going to be able to walk on the leg, but he had no time to look for anything to use as a crutch, so he started hopping hesitantly towards the beach that was so close, but yet still so far.

A few minutes later he was out of the forest and crossing the ten metre wide beach of beautiful white sand towards the ocean. He was disappointed that he couldn't stay and enjoy the scenery, but he was fairly certain that if he did it would be the last thing he ever saw in this world.

The sand was making it impossible for him to hop; because all of his weight was on one foot it was sinking in too deep for him to make any noticeable progress in his weakened state. Desperate, he put his other leg down, testing it again to see if it would take at least some of his weight, but pain instantly shot through him and he fell to his knees. He had no energy left to scream and just gasped as black spots swam before his eyes. He shook his head, trying to clear it and started to crawl slowly forwards.

He was only a few feet from the water and his hands were already sinking into damp sand when the men burst from the trees behind him.

He lurched to his feet, or foot, and turned to face them. The sweat pouring down his face wasn't just from the heat anymore and his face was slowly turning white as blood loss and exhaustion took its toll. He stayed there, swaying, barely managing to stay upright, facing the men who had been hunting him like an animal.

They had stopped on reaching the beach and spread out in an extended line in front of the trees, making sure that they were blocking all possible escape through the forest. Not that he could have run anyway. They were large men, pirates, thugs, mostly bare chested and bare footed, a very bloodthirsty-looking lot who wouldn't hesitate to jump into a fight, but they just stood there watching him, instead of immediately descending on him like the vultures they were.

'Hiya, fellas!' The man put on a brave face and grinned at them, but they just stared back at him and waited with a patience that was not in the slightest bit typical of them.

It wasn't long before a familiar, powerful voice rose over the sound of the waves and the reason for the delay became clear.

'Well, well, well. Lieutenant Andrew Berry… Sorry, it is still Lieutenant, isn't it? The Royal Navy haven't promoted you, have they? Or drummed you out yet?'

Out of the shadow of the trees emerged the leader of the pirate crew. Dressed impeccably in black trousers, a white shirt, long black jacket and shiny black high-top boots, he looked like he'd just been out for a stroll instead of on a manhunt through the jungle. On his head was a large tricorn hat and sticking out from his chin was what gave him his name: a huge, bushy, black beard.

'Oh, hello, Edward, fancy meeting you here!' Andrew tried to look cheerful and unworried, but he knew that he hadn't got much energy, or time, left. His blood was staining the sand below him in a trail leading back to his adversary and he was feeling weaker by the second.

He had hoped that the pirate lord wouldn't have been with his men, that they would just capture him and take him to their captain, giving him more chances to escape, but no such luck. However, the wet sand beneath him now was firmer than the dry sand had been and he was able to hop on his good leg, edging backwards towards the water while making it look like he was just keeping his balance.

Blackbeard wasn't fooled, though, and he grinned widely. 'Where are you going, Mr Berry? I don't see any British longboats waiting to carry you away this time. Or are you waiting for an albatross to swoop down and carry you away?' He pantomimed looking around, up and down the beach and then squinted into the sky with an overtly suspicious look. His men laughed evilly at his clowning.

Suddenly, Blackbeard's whole demeanour changed and he growled in fury. He began to walk slowly down the beach towards Andrew, taking his time, savouring the moment. His men, like the faithful hounds they were, followed closely behind, closing the trap around Andrew, ready to pounce at a single word from their master.

'I forbade you from ever coming back to Port Royal, Andrew, how dare you disobey me!' Blackbeard stopped and held out his hand to one side. 'Slow match!'

One of his men produced a length of slow match, a slow-burning rope, and blew on it to make the tip glow before handing it to his captain. Blackbeard, ever a master of the theatrical, used it to light three fireworks, little things that he always had woven into his beard in order to strike terror into his opponents and make him look even more fearsome. They fizzled into life, spitting sparks and casting his eyes into deep shadows.

He casually threw the smouldering rope over his shoulder and resumed his advance towards his prey.

Andrew had continued to creep backwards and his feet were now in the ocean up to his ankles. He could feel the familiar tingling beginning, but he knew he wasn't nearly deep enough yet and needed to buy more time. Luckily, he still had one final card left up his sleeve. He just had to find the opportunity to play it. 'Don't you want to know why I came back?'

Blackbeard was now only a few steps from Andrew, but he stopped and stood with his hands on his hips, his curiosity piqued. 'Please, I'm dying to know why anyone would willingly sentence themselves to die horribly in a cage for my amusement.' His sneered, his sarcasm almost palpable.

'Because I thought you needed a shave.'

Andrew still had the bottle of alcohol, and while Blackbeard had been distracted he had slipped his hand into his pocket and popped the stopper. He whipped it out and threw the liquid in Blackbeard's face where it got in his eyes and began to soak into his beard.

'What on earth…?' Blackbeard blinked, taken by surprise, and wiped the liquid from his eyes. 'Why did you do that?' He gave Andrew a puzzled look and for a second he didn't seem quite sure what to do, but then the shock and the anger was back, amplified this time into full fury. The pirate lord opened his mouth, probably to order his men to grab Andrew, but it was almost pure alcohol that was running through his beard and when it finally reached the fireworks there was a *whoosh* and suddenly his beard was just *gone*. He cried out in horror and clutched at his face.

It was the closest shave that anyone had ever had and the skin that was revealed was milky white compared to the rest of his face. It also revealed the reason why he grew his beard so long; he had a very weak chin that did absolutely nothing to inspire fear. Indeed, Andrew had to stifle a laugh as he noticed that Blackbeard actually bore quite a strong resemblance to "Mr Bean".

'That's a good look for you, actually.' Andrew smirked at him, returning the pirate's sarcasm. His confidence had returned in full and he knew he could take time to enjoy the moment now; he had made it far enough into the water and he could feel the sand shelving steeply beneath him.

'I'LL KILL…' Blackbeard charged forwards with his arms outstretched, reaching out to grab him, but with a cheeky grin Andrew threw himself backwards into the ocean. There was a huge splash and he was covered by the water.

'…for a beer!' Blackbeard was standing on the beach, ankle deep in the water, his trousers rolled up to his knees. His facial hair was intact and he was smiling at the lovely ocean view, wriggling his toes in the sand and enjoying the fish nibbling at his ankles. He turned and scowled at his men, who were just standing around. 'You men! Come on, crack open those barrels of grog! What are you waiting for? And you lot, build up a fire and start roasting the pigs!'

He watched, making sure his orders were being obeyed before turning back to the sea. An idle thought crossed his mind: wasn't there something he had been about to do? He couldn't for the life of him remember…

He shook his head and smiled. 'Come on lads! Last one in is a rotting corpse!' Laughing he stripped off his jacket and shirt, throwing them up onto the beach, before running into the water, his hat still on his head of course.

Andrew fell heavily off his armchair and screamed as the branch moved in the wound. Blood was spreading slowly across the floor of his living room as it seeped from his leg and not for the first time he was glad to be in Spain and have a tiled floor. He struggled to pull his phone out of his pocket and rang the emergency number that was programmed into the phone of every member of the Honourable Society of Displacers.

While he was waiting for the doctor to come he laid his head back against the cool floor and went over the Displacement in his mind.

He smiled through the pain.

'Totally worth it… Ow.'

CHAPTER 1
ANSWERS

It was a fateful, stormy day in May when Sam Vives had suddenly found himself not where he was supposed to be. He hadn't understood at the time what was happening to him, and he still didn't really, but he was hoping that was going to change soon.

Outwardly Sam wasn't special in any way, he was just a normal fifteen year-old boy with brown hair and brown eyes, but he had a gift, a gift that was promising to give him unlimited adventure and also put him in considerable danger. The first time it had manifested it had sent him to eighteenth century Jamaica, made him the captain of a pirate ship, the Mermaid, and almost got him killed. Several times.

During his short time in the past he had had several incredible experiences, some of which he still couldn't quite believe, including commanding the Mermaid in a ship to ship battle and one particularly notable duel with Captain Bonny, a friend he had made while he was there, that he liked to think of as the "*second* greatest swordfight in modern history".

It hadn't all been fun and games though; he had had to deal with the infamous Blackbeard and his bizarre competition, as well as a murderous young man calling himself "Jack Swallow", who had tried to kill him at every step. Sam had won the competition and defeated Swallow, a loss that he hadn't taken well. The young man had sworn vengeance and Sam had found himself with a mortal enemy, even though he still hadn't known what was really going on - most of the time he'd thought it was just some kind of dream.

When he made it back home, he had told his Uncle Andrew what had happened. He had fully expected that he would say that he was mad, but to his surprise, not only had he believed him, but he also had an explanation for what had happened. He told Sam that he was a "Displacer", like he himself, and that they were capable of travelling through time, although usually with a lot more control than Sam had demonstrated.

Andrew went on to tell him a little bit more about how they did what they did and why, but hadn't gone into too much depth because it was extremely complicated. He had promised to explain everything as soon as they had more time and he could do it properly and carefully.

It was a promise that Sam was still waiting impatiently for him to fulfil.

However, despite being none the wiser about how he could use his newfound powers, he could already feel a change within himself, he felt more confident and far more sure of himself.

The first time he really noticed this difference in himself was only a few days after his "Displacement" to Port Royal. He was walking home through the park near his home after school on Thursday. It was late and he was on his own, having stayed after classes for his weekly piano lesson, and he wasn't really paying much attention to the world around him because he was too busy daydreaming about the adventures he was going to have - something that he liked to do very often. This time he was envisioning himself as a knight in shining armour, jousting with the evil black knight for the hand of a beautiful, golden-haired maiden, although what he was supposed to do with just a hand he didn't quite know. Being a healthy, but fairly innocent teenager, meant that most of Sam's daydreams involved heroic deeds, battles, a lot of sword fights and awkward romantic encounters that were very hazy in the details, apart from the kissing, which he'd done a bit of in Port Royal, but were nonetheless quite exciting and very distracting. He was caught up in rehearsing his speech to the maiden in his head with lots of thees, thous and wherefores, so he didn't realise that there was a very large boy standing in the middle of the path, blocking his way, until he was right on top of him and had to jerk to a halt so as not to walk into him.

He looked up and found himself face to face, or rather face to chest, with Rafa Sánchez.

Rafa was Sam's other nemesis, a bully who had made Sam's life miserable for years. Fortunately, though, unlike Swallow he didn't actually want to kill Sam, even though he did threaten to do so on a regular basis. However, Rafa was worse than Swallow in one very important way and that was that Sam had no way of avoiding him; Rafa was a student at Sam's school, in his class and also in the fencing team with him. His favourite pastime was using Sam as a punching bag and consequently Sam tried to avoid him as much as possible. He had managed to outwit the bully many times in the past, but he still had the scars to prove that it wasn't always possible to do so and it was small consolation that he had finally grown too big to be stuffed in a locker.

Sam took a few slow paces back to better see the boy who had bullied him for so many years. Something about the situation, the way the tall bully was standing with his arms crossed, blocking Sam's way, glaring down at him, was very familiar and Sam chuckled when he realised what it was - when he had first arrived in Port Royal he had been confronted by some pirate thugs who were trying to prevent him from getting to a meeting with Blackbeard. They hadn't been particularly clever and he had easily confused them, allowing him to just walk right past. However, he knew that the same tactics he'd used with them weren't going to work this time; Rafa wasn't exactly top of the class, being a bit on the dim side, but he more than compensated with a kind of cunning intelligence, like a wild animal, and wouldn't take his eyes off of Sam long enough for him to get away.

'Vives. I told you to watch your back.'

Sam smirked, mockingly. 'And yet here you are standing in front of me.'

Rafa snarled. 'Always the smart-arse. Well, nobody's laughing and in a minute you won't be *able* to anymore.' He slammed his fist into his palm and started to advance threateningly.

It was curious, but Rafa and his threats just didn't seem scary anymore, especially when compared to what Sam had been through in Port Royal; he was nowhere near as big as some of the pirates that Sam had faced and comparing him to Blackbeard himself was laughable.

Something clicked in Sam and his face hardened as he realised that he was never going to be scared of Rafa again.

The bully's step faltered as he saw the change in Sam's attitude; he might have been a bit of a dull brute, but it appeared he was still perceptive and could tell when someone wasn't cowed. He stopped, still a couple of paces away. 'On second thoughts, I've had a long day and I don't feel like taking out the trash right now. Count yourself lucky, Vives, you get to walk away in one piece. For now.'

Rafa closed the last of the gap between them and tried to knock into him with his shoulder as he went past, but Sam had been waiting for something like that and simply swayed away. The big boy stumbled slightly when he didn't meet the resistance he'd expected, but kept walking without looking back.

Sam smiled as he watched the boy go; it seemed that his life was just getting better and better! Now, if only Uncle Andrew would give some sign of life.

In fact, it wasn't until the middle of June, almost six weeks after Andrew had made his promise, that Sam finally got to talk to his uncle.

Thankfully, though, the time had passed fairly quickly; school was winding down for the summer holidays and he'd had exams, a couple of fencing matches and a weekend away with his family up the coast with his paternal grandparents. He'd been so busy that he hadn't actually had much in the way of free time to have a decent talk to his uncle before then, anyway, even if the opportunity had arisen.

Sam had seen Rafa around quite a few times after his encounter with him in the park, but the bully had always been with some friends, all as brutish as him. They moved as a pack, watching him, following him wherever he went. It seemed that Rafa wasn't willing to face him one on one anymore and was looking for an assured win - typical bully behaviour. They took to waiting for him somewhere they knew he'd be, like after school or fencing practice. However, unfortunately for Rafa, this strength in numbers had meant that Sam could spot them a mile off and he had easily avoided another confrontation.

After school finished for the summer there were no longer any opportunities for Rafa and his gang to wait for Sam at the end of the day. However, the trouble with schools in Spain is that usually the students are all from the same neighbourhood and Rafa lived just a few streets away from Sam. This meant that there was always going to be the possibility of a chance encounter and Sam was going to have to stay on his toes, even during the holidays - he'd already seen them lurking in wait for him in the park a couple of times.

The holidays did, however, mean that Sam finally had time to go and see Andrew when he called.

It was a hot, clear and bright afternoon just after lunch when Sam walked up to Andrew's door at the appointed time and rang the bell. He waited for a minute or so and was about to ring again when the door opened to reveal his uncle.

Andrew looked terrible; there were dark circles under his eyes and his light brown hair was messier than usual and seemed to have more streaks of grey in it. However, his smile when he saw Sam improved his aspect considerably.

'Sorry to keep you waiting, Sam. I'm not very mobile right now, as you can see.' He brandished a cane in his right hand while holding onto the door with his left to balance. He had all of his weight on his left leg and his right one barely resting on the floor. 'Come on in.' He stepped awkwardly to one side and motioned for Sam to enter.

Sam walked in and closed the door behind him. He smiled mischievously at his uncle. 'What happened? Is that a common side effect of being a Displacer or did you fall over in your old age?'

'You shouldn't be so cheeky to a cripple!' Andrew laughed. 'No, actually, I had a bit of an accident a couple of weeks ago - fell over when I was running through a forest...' He waved his hand in dismissal, as if his injury was nothing. 'It's a long story. Maybe I'll tell you all about it later, but for now we have stuff to do. Can I get you something to drink? Tea?'

'In this weather?'

'Best thing for it!'

Sam shrugged. 'Er, OK then, I suppose...'

'Good man!'

Andrew hobbled away, moving so slowly that Sam had plenty of time to have a good look around before he followed.

The knick-knacks that he'd been curious about on previous visits were scattered haphazardly around the hallway as usual, but with his new perspective on things he saw them in a much different light. Items that were clearly of some era past, obviously souvenirs of Andrew's Displacements, just like the handkerchief and double-headed coin that were in a box on his own desk, were sitting on every surface with no evident order to them. The only thing that they had in common was that they all looked fairly new, despite their age or the period they came from. For example, the collection of what looked like Roman or Ancient Greek pottery, bowls stacked on top of dishes as if they were ordinary crockery, was all completely intact and painted in bright colours as if it had just come out of the kiln - usually when Sam had seen those kinds of things in museums they were in glued-together pieces, the colours faded or gone more than a thousand years before. Among the bits and pieces, he spied the carved wooden box containing the coins that Violeta, his seven-year-old sister, had played with on his last visit here. He now knew that they were real and he wondered briefly if Andrew had discovered the bite-marks on the large gold one yet.

He wandered towards the kitchen, but hesitated at the door which Andrew always had locked. Out of habit, he tried it, but as always the handle didn't turn. He shrugged and continued, before stopping again at a shallow, glass-fronted cupboard at head height on the wall that was filled with small statuettes of all shapes and sizes. He didn't have a clue what most of them were, but he thought one was an Ancient Egyptian statue of Anubis, a couple, which were fairly rude in nature, were African and at least one was Oriental. It was just as well that Violeta was still too short to reach them because, if her dolls were anything to go on, he didn't think any of them would last very long in her hands.

Andrew poked his head out of the kitchen and chuckled, noting Sam's curiosity. 'You've always been fascinated by my collection and now you're one of us I can actually tell you how I got them, if you want.'

'I'd love that, thanks!'

Andrew smiled and disappeared back into the kitchen, but a second later he reappeared. 'Oops, forgot! How many sugars d'you want?'

'One, please.'

Andrew vanished again and Sam heard the clinking of a spoon against china as he stirred the teas vigorously.

Sam tore himself away from the statues with some reluctance. He was glad that one day he would hear the stories behind them, but today he had other priorities. He walked down the hall to join Andrew in the kitchen and leant against the counter. He watched Andrew pouring milk into the black tea.

'You don't know how lucky you are, Sam.'

'Being a Displacer?'

'No.' Andrew handed Sam a mug. 'I only had two pyramid bags left! We almost had to drink that awful stuff they sell here in Spain!'

Andrew grinned and Sam humoured him with a grin in return, although for him a cup of tea was a cup of tea, no matter what kind of teabag it was made with. He preferred coke anyway.

'Would you mind carrying mine for me? If I try to hop around with it, it'll end up everywhere.'

'Of course.'

'Thanks.' Andrew limped out of the kitchen, along the corridor and into the living room.

The living room was in the same condition as the hallway - every available surface was littered with an assortment of odds and ends from every era of human history, only in here there were dozens upon dozens of books competing for space with them.

There was a television, but it had books piled up in front of it obscuring more than half of the screen, the sofa was covered with more of them and only two of the three armchairs were available for the use for which they were originally intended. All of which were placed around a coffee table that didn't have much room left for coffee.

Andrew sat down in one of the armchairs and motioned for Sam to take a seat opposite him in the other.

Sam put Andrew's tea in a rare empty spot on the table within easy reach of him and then sat down. He leaned forward in his seat and looked at his uncle expectantly.

Andrew smiled at him. He blinked. 'Oh, yes! Would you like a biscuit? Got some nice Jammy Dodgers…'

Sam shook his head. 'No thanks, I've just eaten.'

'Suit yourself.' Andrew took a biscuit from an old tin, half-buried under books on the table and started nibbling at it, sipping at the tea. 'Ah! That's the stuff! Can't beat a good cuppa!'

Sam took a sip from his tea, more out of politeness than anything else. He realised that it wasn't as bad as he'd feared, but he had more important things on his mind than tea. He put it down again quickly and again stared at Andrew.

Andrew chuckled. 'I can see you're impatient for answers! Well, now that the civilities are out of the way I suppose we can begin.'

'If you wouldn't mind.'

Andrew laughed at that. 'That's good! You've been bursting to blurt out all your questions since I let you in! "If you wouldn't mind" indeed!'

Sam just shrugged and waited.

'I'm sorry, I'll stop playing with you.' Andrew took a quick sip of tea while he gathered his thoughts. 'Well, let's start at the beginning. I realise I might have told you some of this already, but it's best to go over it again just in case. Do you remember what I told you about driving a wedge into a time-line?'

'"Displacing" someone.'

'Exactly. Now, in science fiction on television or films, time travel usually works by the person turning up as they are with the clothes they have on, speaking how they normally do, acting like modern-day idiots and boom, hilarity ensues. Displacing is very different, thankfully. We insert ourselves into the time-line and don't just plonk ourselves down on top of it, we are added in, so to speak. What language were you speaking in Port Royal?'

'Spanish, wait, English…' Sam frowned. 'Uh, actually I don't know.'

'It's not too surprising that you didn't realise, seeing as your mother is English and you're pretty fluent in it. You were probably speaking English because most of the people you met there only speak English.

It doesn't matter, though; not only does the time-line adapt to us, but we adapt to it. How else would you expect to go to ancient Egypt or Rome or even old England and be able to talk to anyone? You'd need a lifetime of study before you could do anything worthwhile.'

'So, does that mean that you can speak the languages of everywhere you've been?'

Andrew shook his head. 'I'm afraid it doesn't work like that. I wish it did! It would make the modern world a lot easier; think of the fortune I could make translating books from all sorts of weird languages! No, unfortunately we don't bring that sort of thing back with us after a Displacement. We speak the language like we were born to it while we are there, because for all intents and purposes we were, but lose the knowledge when we come back.'

Sam thought about this for a second while he sipped at the tea, which seemed to be growing on him after all. 'I'm fairly sure I knew stuff about how to sail ships and use swords that I don't anymore. There's also a lot of other stuff I remember doing that I have no idea how I knew what to do. It's all very confusing. Do you understand what I'm saying?'

'Of course.' Andrew smiled encouragingly and motioned for him to continue.

'One other thing that's been really bothering me is why everyone accepted me as the captain of the Mermaid. After all, I'm just a kid.'

'You're a bit on the young side, and the short side as well, but they would have seen you differently than you are, seen you as being older and bigger. They probably gave you more space or didn't quite look you in the eye, right?'

'I did get the feeling that sometimes they were talking to my hair, yes. Their eyes kept sliding upwards.'

'Don't worry, I'm sure you'll grow up and that'll no longer be a problem!' Andrew laughed. 'They would have seen what they expected see - an adult. A handsome, suave, authority figure… a bit like me.' He gave Sam another one of his cheeky grins before leaning forward to pick up the tin of biscuits. He held them out to Sam. 'Sure you don't want one? They're very good!'

'I'm fine, thanks.' Sam shook his head. 'So what about Swallow? Why was he just a weedy young man, then?'

Andrew took another and waved it in the air as he continued. 'The short answer is that he wasn't; Displacers see each other as they are in their present, so you saw him as he is right now and he would have seen you as you are. To everyone else he would have looked a lot different.'

'That would explain a lot. He was giving me the evil eye from the moment he saw me. I thought it was only because he thought I was a rival, but he must have seen that I was just a boy and not a captain like everyone else did.'

'Correct, but that's not the only reason he would have known what you are; we can feel other Displacers when we get near them - we get this knot in our stomachs, like excitement or nerves. You'll be feeling it right now actually, but you've been here long enough to get used to it, so you don't even know it's there.'

Sam frowned; now that his uncle mentioned it, he *had* felt something like that when he'd arrived, but had dismissed it as just excitement at continuing with his training. 'So that's why I felt the way I did every time I was near him. I assumed it was me reacting to him being a... well, not a nice person.'

Andrew laughed at Sam's refusal to call someone a bad name, even Quentin, who had tried to kill him. 'Right. What you were feeling was your powers reacting to his - it's one of the ways we find new members, actually.'

Sam absentmindedly reached out to take a biscuit, even though he didn't really want one, and munched on it as he took a moment to think. 'OK, so our appearances change to match what people expect of us, but that doesn't explain everything, like, I remember this one time Quentin shook hands with Caesar; Caesar tried to crush his hand and he just stood there and took it, no problem. How was that possible for him? He's not exactly strong.'

'It was possible because when you're in the past you don't just *look* different, you *are* different. For example, in your fight with Bonny you were leaping around like a champion gymnast, and in your fight on the French ship you were obviously stronger than you are now because you were waving around a heavy cutlass as if it were nothing. You were accepted as a captain not just because you looked like one, but because you *became* a ship's captain. Which means that you had all the knowledge, experience and abilities that implies - all the things that you needed to know so as not to just crash your ship into the first rock you encountered.'

'That would have been a bit embarrassing.'

'Indeed!' Andrew chuckled again, obviously enjoying his role as a teacher. 'And Quentin would have been different as well - something more in keeping with the role he was playing, like one of the big thugs that Blackbeard had on his crew. He certainly would have been a lot less geeky and weedy than he is in the present! He would have to have been adapted to his situation in order to survive, exactly like you were, not only with the knowledge he needed, but physically as well.' He sipped at his tea, thinking. 'Swallow told you he had to work his way up to first mate over the course of a year, right? He must have started as an ordinary sailor or close to. He would have had to be strong enough to fit in with Blackbeard's crew, stronger, actually, because they wouldn't let a weakling command them. Actually, you were extremely lucky to go right in at the top, as the captain; it's not usually that easy.'

'Why did he spend a year there, though? Couldn't he just come back here and keep trying until he got the character he wanted?'

Andrew laughed. 'This isn't TV or the theatre, Sam - you can't just read for the role you want until you get it. Once you have visited a time-line and become someone, then that is who you will always be when you are in what would be the lifetime of that person. The people will know you as that person and will remember what you have done every time that you go back. And every time that you leave they will forget you all over again.'

'You told me that before, and I think it's a real shame. I had so much fun and I know that the people around me did too. I'd like it if they could remember it all.'

Andrew suddenly turned serious. 'That's another thing; you must stop thinking about this as just a bit of "fun". I may laugh and joke with you about it here, now, when we are safe and not even planning a mission, but this is deadly serious. Not only is our job extremely important, but you could very easily die if you treat it as a game and do something silly just for the fun of it.'

'Sorry.'

Andrew put his head in his hands and sighed. 'No, *I'm* sorry. It's been a disastrous couple of years and I really don't want anything else bad to happen, especially not to you; I'm not sure I could take it.'

He looked up again and Sam could see the pain of his memories in his eyes.

Andrew sighed. 'Alright, so you already know that you can bring things back with you as long as you're holding them in your hands - you have a couple of nice souvenirs already, and you may have noticed a few of mine.' Andrew waved his hand at the items that covered every surface. 'But we also bring back other "souvenirs" that we aren't so fond of. This is one I got from my last trip.'

Andrew rolled up his trouser leg to reveal his calf and the huge scab from where the branch had stabbed into him. The whole of his lower leg was one big bruise that was yellowing as it healed.

It looked absolutely revolting and Sam was suddenly glad he hadn't taken a biscuit as his stomach turned. More importantly, though, it served to finally hit home how dangerous time travel really was.

Andrew saw Sam's discomfort and rolled the trouser leg back down as he continued. 'As I've said before, you can be killed, but any injury you pick up will also follow you back here. There are no saved games, you have no extra lives and you cannot restart the level if anything goes wrong - this is real life, in real times, with very real dangers. You can always escape by Displacing back, but you need a certain amount of concentration to do that; it's not very easy to do if you're being eaten by a lion or hanged from a tree.'

At this last Andrew winced and rubbed his neck as if remembering a past trauma, but then he suddenly broke into a smile, 'of course it's not all doom and gloom. You'll see the wonders of the world, both ancient and modern, visit cultures long disappeared and speak with people that you've only read about in the history books and it's far more likely that you'll get run over by a car outside this flat than it is that you'll be killed in a battle or die of the plague! And don't forget about the skills and the knowledge that you get naturally every time you Displace somewhere, that'll usually be enough to keep you safe.'

'If you say so…' Sam looked doubtful, but he didn't think he would mind a bit of danger if it was always going to be as much fun as it had been in Port Royal. 'So, can I go wherever I want, or is it random?'

'You can go more or less anywhere, anywhere there are people anyway, because we have to have someone to Displace. Which means no dinosaurs, sorry!'

'OK, no dinosaurs. Got it. And, *damn*, by the way…' Sam considered for a second, remembering the things he had daydreamed about over the last few weeks. 'So, what about the future? Can I go get a book with all the sports results for the next few years?'

Andrew groaned. 'Oh, god, John is going to love you… No, you can't go to the future and pick up a sports almanac or stop your kids from going to jail or do any of the other "cool" stuff you've seen in the movies. A Displacer needs a reference to home in on and because the future hasn't happened yet there *are* no references, we have nothing to aim for, even if it were possible.'

'Again, *damn*!'

Andrew chuckled, shaking his head. 'I think you'll find there are more than enough exciting things to see and do in the past to keep you busy for a lifetime. Several lifetimes in fact.'

Sam grinned. 'I can't wait!' He sipped at his tea as he thought back over what Andrew had told him so far. 'So, is that what I have to do to Displace? Aim for something?'

'In a nutshell, yes. You already know you went to Port Royal because you were daydreaming about pirates and that's basically how it works - you concentrate really hard and think of where you want to go and that's where you go. How to concentrate properly is one of the things I'll teach you.'

'When?'

Andrew laughed. 'Soon! Don't be so impatient!'

'OK.' Sam pouted, but he figured that he could wait, as long as it didn't take his uncle another six weeks to get around to seeing him again. He frowned as something occurred to him. 'OK, so if I went to Port Royal because I was thinking about pirates, then why was I in the right place at the right time to stop Swallow? Was it just a really big coincidence? Or does that kind of thing happen all the time?'

'That's a very good question.' Andrew nodded. 'And the short answer is that I don't know. And no, it's completely unheard of for two Displacers to end up in the same place unless they do it deliberately.'

Sam was surprised at this. 'Really?'

Andrew shrugged and gave him a wry smile. 'Yep. Never happens and I don't know why it did to you. I don't have all the answers, none of the Displacers do. It's not as if we have an instruction manual. Well, we *do* have one but it's just a bit of a joke; John made it up for an April Fools prank one year. He aged it and everything then told everyone that he'd found it in the archives, fooled a few of us with it for quite a while. Not me obviously, just some of the others... He'll probably send you a copy if you ask him. Or even if you don't... Anyway, what I'm trying to say is that there are a lot of things that we don't know about our own abilities that we're still trying to work out, even after a few hundred years.'

'Can you at least tell me who Swallow is? And please don't tell me that "Jack Swallow" was his real name.'

'No, it's not and he used to be one of us, actually.' Andrew sighed. 'His real name is Quentin Price. Displacing usually runs in a family and he comes from a prominent family of Displacers, the latest in a long, and until now, distinguished line of them. '

'But nobody in my family are Displacers, are they?'

'There are… always exceptions to a rule.' Andrew looked somewhat reluctant to comment any further and Sam was left slightly puzzled when he hurried on. 'Quentin had big expectations heaped on him from a very early age and I'm afraid his father was a bit, shall we say, *overbearing*, which didn't help.'

'So, why did he try to kill me? And why was he after Blackbeard's diamond in the first place?'

'Ah, and now we get to the very heart of the matter!' Andrew finished off his tea and placed the mug down on the table before looking back up at Sam and clasping his hands together. 'Our whole reason for being, well, what *we* believe to be the reason we have our powers, is to keep the time-line *correct*. If John was here he'd tell you that our mission is to "put right what once went wrong".'

Andrew paused, looking at Sam expectantly, and blinked in surprise when he said nothing. 'You've never seen *Quantum Leap*? Oh, thank god! That quote's not exactly true anyway; we don't put right what went wrong, it's more that when something that was once right goes wrong we make sure that it doesn't stay that way.'

This confused Sam more than it helped him. 'I don't understand.'

'That's OK, neither did I at first.' Andrew smiled reassuringly at Sam. He reached out and took yet another biscuit. He bit into it and chewed as he continued, his words slightly muffled as a consequence. 'Contrary to popular belief, the past is not set in stone. Occasionally it begins to drift a bit and what actually happened, what should happen, starts to change. It's usually only small things, but they can create ripples which spread dangerously. For example, let's say that on one specific day, for some reason a man decides to walk a different way to work instead of the way he always goes. Big deal, nothing could possibly go wrong there, right? But that change of route means that the coin which falls out of his pocket doesn't drop onto the pavement that it was supposed to, a passing child doesn't bend down to pick up that coin, the child doesn't use that coin to buy a pie at a nearby shop. This means the child isn't in the shop to overhear the plot to blow up Parliament being planned in the back room, so he never tells his father about it. His father, who by the way, just happens to be a guard at the Palace of Westminster. So men are never sent down into the tunnels below the Houses of Parliament… And suddenly the 5th of November has a whole new meaning and the history of England as we know it is changed forever.'

'Wow… Like the butterfly effect in chaos theory.'

'Indeed! Very good! That's an extreme case of course and thankfully it's not often that serious, but even the most minor change needs to be corrected, otherwise the whole fabric of time might fall apart. So, our job is to keep everything nice and tidy - we can feel when time starts to bend and distort from how it should be and we do what we can to prevent it. Sometimes we don't manage and the repercussions can be felt through the ages, but the world hasn't ended yet, so we're not doing too badly!'

'And what has that got to do with Quentin?'

'Ah, yes. We, the Displacers, protect the past in order to secure the present. Quentin is one of those renegades who manipulate the past to affect their present and future.'

'What would he have changed by taking the diamond?'

'Most likely nothing. Not everything is essential to the time-line otherwise we wouldn't be allowed to bring back any souvenirs.' Andrew spread his arms with a grin to indicate the artefacts he had spread around the room. 'The diamond could probably have been taken out without consequence and it's actually almost certainly lying at the bottom of the sea right now, lost forever, like a lot of pirate treasure. Our theory is that Quentin just wanted it for the money. What *would* have changed things, though, was if Blackbeard's first mate became the heir and not your Mr Smith. That would have had an enormous impact on things.'

'So, I didn't spoil anything by winning?'

'We have to be careful sometimes not to make things worse, but we looked into it and we're fairly sure that's the way it should have turned out.'

Sam nodded. 'I'm glad. Smithy was a good man, he deserves it.'

A shadow of something like regret crossed Andrew's face, but it was gone in an instant before Sam could remark on it. He slapped his thighs decisively and stood up awkwardly, leaning on the armchair as he picked up his walking stick. 'You have a lot to think about, and I have some work I need to do, so let's call it a day. I really don't want to start with the rules or anything now anyway; they're far too complicated to rush and not just a bit boring.'

He laughed, but Sam frowned up at him, disappointed. 'But you haven't told me anything useful! Like how I concentrate! How I can control it!'

'That's the most complicated thing about all of this, and don't worry, we'll get to that tomorrow. Do you think you can clear a trip to the beach with your parents?'

'The beach? What on earth for?'

'You'll see!' Andrew grinned.

Sam left Andrew's block of flats and walked slowly up the pavement towards his home, just a few streets away.

Lost in his thoughts and bent over in the heat of the early summer sun, he didn't notice the figure step out of the deep shadow of a doorway across the street and it wasn't until he was almost home that he felt the presence of someone looming up behind him. He knew who it was instantly; there was only one person that would be following him up the street - Rafa. He was most likely alone, though, otherwise he would have attacked already and had his friends drag Sam into a secluded spot in which to hurt him. Whether the bully was alone or not, Sam knew he couldn't allow him to stay behind him; Rafa would think nothing of taking him by surprise and hitting him in the back.

He set his face into a scowl and turned, crouching slightly and raising his fists, ready to face the bully down again, determined to fight if necessary.

There was nobody there.

Sam straightened up and relaxed. He looked from side to side, but didn't see anyone. He frowned and turned, taking the last few steps to get to his front door.

He looked around one last time and then went in.

Quentin Price watched his prey from the cover of a bus shelter across the street. Now was not the time to do anything impulsive, a real chance to take a proper revenge would come soon enough, he just needed patience.

CHAPTER 2
DR LIVINGSTONE, I PRESUME

As soon as Sam left, Andrew washed the mugs then made his way to his study and switched on his computer. He sat down and connected to Skype, looking to see who was online. As usual, John, who worked from home, was available. He shrugged. He'd been hoping for someone a bit more reliable, or a bit less annoying at least, but he needed help so he rang him anyway.

While he waited for the call to connect he went over his conversation with Sam in his head, thinking about how the boy had looked throughout. All in all he thought that Sam had taken it pretty well; there had been no sign of greed at the thought of possible riches and there had been no recoil from the talk of responsibility and danger. In fact, all he'd seen in him was a genuine love of adventure and a keenness to begin that was normal for someone his age.

His thoughts were interrupted as the call went through and the inanely smiling face of John appeared.

'Wotcha! How's it going with the kid, Mr Miyagi?'

Andrew sighed. 'Afternoon, John…'

John was slouched down in his chair in his study, surrounded by film posters and memorabilia. His "day job" was as a web designer and programmer and he seemed to spent most of his time in this one room in his house, which made it easy for him to fulfil his duties as a Displacer and unfortunately made him Andrew's "go-to guy" for urgent or last minute jobs.

'So, how is Daniel-san doing? Is he waxing on and off yet?'

'I'm not entirely sure what that means in his case, but no, today we've just had a cup of tea and a chat…'

'Boring!'

'…and tomorrow we're going to start work on the basics.'

'Yay! Well, let me know if he makes the jump program.'

Andrew didn't reply, he just cringed inside. Sometimes he hated talking to John; it was always a mismatch of one movie reference and quote after another. His current favourite source was *The Matrix*. Not Andrew's favourite film. 'OK, will do. Anyway… the reason why I called is I need your help; I can't Displace right now and the Elders have a job for us. Can you do it?'

'The old and venerable ones call and I respond! I can, yes, no problem. But what on earth were you doing back in Port Royal anyway? Didn't you learn anything last time you went up against Teach?'

'I had to go back to check that everything was alright after Quentin's little visit.'

'And?'

'Everything was as it should be, but there were some anomalies that I'll share with the whole group during our next conference call.'

'Fair enough. So what's the job?'

'Are you up to date with your malaria shots?'

Africa. 10th November 1871.

The jungle was untouched, pristine, wild. At least it was until the explorers got there and started making one hell of a mess of things.

Two European men led dozens of native porters through the trees. The man in the lead was sweating profusely, but smiling, enjoying himself immensely. He was wearing brown trousers, a dark brown leather jacket, which was very impractical in the heat, and a sweat-damp fedora on his head. He was using a machete to cut his way through the underbrush, swinging it easily, enthusiastically, rhythmically, in time to his own singing.

'Ba ba da dah. Ba ba dah… Ba ba da dah! Ba ba dah dah dah!'

The tune was recognisable the world over. But only if you were alive after 1981.

The other man, Henry Morgan Stanley, was following a few metres behind, safely out of reach of the swing of the machete. He was wearing more typical nineteenth century explorer garb - a khaki suit with a pith helmet. He called out to the man in the lead. 'Are you sure you know where you're going, Dr Jones?'

'Yes, Mr Stanley, of course I do! And, as I keep telling you, please, call me Indy!'

John stopped chopping and tipped his hat to Stanley. He readjusted the bullwhip hanging from his belt and muttered to himself as he turned away. 'Damn thing keeps getting caught on the bushes, it's so impractical. Honestly, sometimes I think Hollywood just makes things up as they go along...'

'I'm sorry?'

He raised his voice to call over his shoulder. 'Nothing, Mr Stanley, nothing! We're almost there, by the way. Just a bit further!' He started chopping again.

Once Stanley had dropped back to the group of bearers, John stopped cutting and quickly checked to make sure that nobody was watching him. He pulled a small hand-drawn map out of his pocket and opened it up. He'd memorised the local geography from Wikipedia before Displacing and jotted it down as soon as he had arrived so that he wouldn't forget; it was a distinct advantage at a time when most of the African continent hadn't been mapped out yet. He'd also read relevant passages from Stanley's diaries as part of his preparation and knew exactly when and where the explorer would be and exactly where he should have his famous meeting with Livingstone.

All that knowledge added up to making it an easy enough mission to complete and it would have been quite pleasant, if it hadn't been for the conditions in the jungle - it had been a hard month of disgusting insects, snakebites and amusing intestinal problems caused by bad water and a diet of mostly meat. None of that had really bothered him though; it was just part of the job of a Displacer and he'd been in far worse situations. Besides, Lake Tanganyika was just up ahead and home was finally in sight.

He folded the map and put it away, took a swig from his water bottle to cover the real reason for his pause and rolled his shoulder before swinging the machete again. Fortunately he had a strong right arm, otherwise he'd have had to give up long ago and they would never have made the rendezvous on time.

An hour later they broke out of the trees and found themselves on the shores of a massive lake.

John stood there, smiling, taking in the sight of the massive body of water and luxuriating in the cool breeze that had sprung up as soon as they had cleared the jungle. He could see several groups of animals spread about the shoreline, drinking their fill; they were mostly zebra and antelope, but there were also a few yellow specks in the far distance that he thought might be a pride of lions. Out on the water itself there were a few scattered fishing boats, but they were barely visible, just black dots in the vastness of the lake.

Stanley came staggering out of the jungle behind him. 'My word, is this the Atlantic already?'

'Not quite, Mr Stanley. This is Lake Tanganyika.'

'It's huge! Remarkable! And you say that Dr Livingstone is here? Wonderful!'

Stanley started to walk the wrong way around the lake.

John looked at him exasperated and then face-palmed, shaking his head. He sighed. 'Mr Stanley… Are you sure you want to go that way?'

Stanley stopped and looked around myopically, he didn't seem to have noticed the small village only a few miles away in the opposite direction to which he had started walking. He shrugged. 'Well it does seem that one way is as good as the other, we could just go the other way around, I suppose. Oh my! It looks like there's a village over there! What a stroke of luck! I do hope they have tea.' He started to walk along the shore of the lake with the bearers strung out in a long line, following him silently, as patiently as ever.

John watched the explorer go with a faint smile.

Despite appearances, Stanley wasn't as incompetent as he seemed. He'd lost his maps and notes and had his compass broken in an unfortunate accident, an unseasonable mudslide, which had logically put his whole expedition in peril. To make matters worse, all of his tea had been destroyed at the same time, something which would have caused many an Englishman to throw in the towel and flee back to civilisation.

Under those desperate circumstances it had been completely understandable that someone who was already so far out of his depth was therefore thrown into utter confusion.

In the distance smoke was rising from the cooking fires of the village, quite obviously marking it; there was no way that Stanley could go wrong now and John was sure that even if he couldn't find Dr Livingstone in the village on his own, then somebody would get the two of them together eventually.

He was positive that Stanley would be fine, but even so, he almost followed just in case. He shook his head and laughed at himself for worrying so much. 'Honestly, sometimes I don't know how we even had an Empire.'

He closed his eyes, took a deep breath and…

…came awake with a smile.

To John a month had passed, but to Andrew it seemed that he had merely closed his eyes then opened them up again a minute or so later.

'Well?' asked Andrew.

'I came, I saw and I presumed, Dr Livingstone. Easy-peasy. Like bullseying Womp Rats back home!'

'Uh, OK… Does that mean it went without a hitch then?'

'Yes, I managed to point him back in the right direction while letting him make the decisions. You know, the S.O.P.' He chuckled. 'Funny story: I found him wandering along the Zambezi all right, just in the wrong direction. I'm pretty sure he would have got to the rendezvous on his own, eventually, but it might have taken a few more years than it should have.'

'By which time Livingstone might very well have been dead already.'

'Exactly. So crisis averted.'

'Good. Thank you for doing this for me, John, I know you had that trip to Babylon planned.'

'You're welcome, and don't worry, I can put it off for another month. Babylon isn't exactly going anywhere.'

'Sorry.'

'Anyway, if you ever need help with the young Padawan just give me a call. By the way, have you told him about the little top-secret prophecy the ancient and wise Elders think he's going to fulfil?'

'Not yet, he's under more than enough pressure as it is.'

John grinned. 'Now that's a conversation I'd like to sit in on! I wonder how he'll take it… Anyway, if you'll excuse me I have a date with a *Raiders* DVD.'

'Haven't you seen that enough times already?'

'Sacrilege!'

Andrew chuckled and shook his head. 'Enjoy yourself, you've earned it. Bye for now.'

'See ya!' John signed off.

Andrew was just about to disconnect and turn off his computer when Skype notified him of an incoming call. He answered immediately and smiled when the smiling face of Anne Barclay filled the screen. 'Good afternoon, Anne!'

'Good morning!' Behind her loomed the spectacular view from her corner office of the skyscrapers of Manhattan, the city where she had been born, shining in the early morning light.

Anne was one of the few American Displacers and Andrew had been seeing her for a few months. She was a decade younger than he was in real life, but among Displacers that meant less than nothing. They were still not very serious, but that was mostly because her work took her all over the globe and she wasn't often in Europe. Unfortunately, because of the sometimes extreme time difference between them, that also meant they didn't often get a chance to talk.

Andrew glanced at the clock in the corner of the screen. It was ten in the morning for Anne. 'You don't usually ring me so early in the day. To what do I owe the pleasure?'

'Oh, nothing much really. I just saw you were online and wanted to find out how you're doing.'

'You had no ulterior motives for ringing?'

'Of course not!'

Andrew grinned. 'You just thought you'd ring, even though you're at work and never call me at this time.'

'Well, there are unusual circumstances, right? You're injured, so of course I'm going to call you as often as I can!' she protested. 'And besides, I was already thinking about you because Lisa and Julia called me last night for a girly chat. They asked me whether I'd heard from you and if you were feeling better.'

'Is that right?' He raised an eyebrow and smiled knowingly; the two women had obviously seen Anne as a source of information on Andrew and his mission in Barcelona and decided to pump her for information.

'I had to tell them I didn't know how you were, because I hadn't spoken to you in a while.'

'Yes, it must be all of, what, two days since we last had a conversation?'

'Exactly! That's much too long!' Anne smiled and batted her eyelids. 'So, tell me. How are you, darling? How is your leg?'

'Not bad.'

'Is that true? Or is it just some of your typical limey stiff-upper-lippiness?'

Andrew chuckled. 'Caught me! It's a bit sore, but nothing that can't be sorted with a good cup of tea.'

She laughed. 'The British remedy for all ills!'

'Indeed! Along with Vicks VapoRub, of course, but, even though my grandma always swore by the stuff, I don't think it's going to help much in my case.'

Anne laughed again, but Andrew could see that she was itching to turn the conversation towards the real reason for her call.

Although it was fun to make her squirm a little for trying to be so sneaky, he didn't want to go too far with teasing her, so he decided to put her out of her misery and broached the subject himself. 'Oh, by the way, just in case you're interested, Sam and I finally met today for a nice little chat and I'm going to be starting his training in earnest tomorrow.'

'Really?' She tried to put on an innocent face, but failed dismally and grinned cheekily instead. 'I hadn't meant to bring it up, but seeing as *you* have, then why don't you tell me how it went and what you think of him?'

Andrew grinned back. He didn't mind her prying and he certainly wasn't upset that she hadn't called purely out of concern for him; he knew that everybody was curious about Sam and was rather surprised that it had taken them so long to start pestering him. 'He's a good kid, I'm sure he'll be fine.'

Anne frowned, turning serious. 'But you're worried.'

'No, I'm not.'

'Come on, I know you too well! I can see it in your face.'

'OK, then, yes, maybe I am just a little bit.'

'More than just a bit from the looks of things. You know that you really don't need to worry, right? You won't lose Sam like Ralph did Quentin; he's a completely different person.'

'Even so...'

Anne interrupted him. 'Don't, Andrew! You have to have confidence in him! You can't wrap him in cotton wool and hide him away from our world, you have to let him learn and make his own mistakes. Anything else might damage his chances, might stop him from fulfilling whatever potential he might have, regardless of whether it's him in the prophecy or not.'

Andrew nodded reluctantly. 'Yeah, I know.' She was right, up to a point, but too many mistakes had been made in recent years and there was too much at stake to not take every possible care.

She smiled. 'You'll be fine. Just believe in yourself. And him.'

'I will.' Andrew smiled back. 'Thank you.'

'You're welcome. Now tell me more about him, what's he like?'

Andrew settled back in his chair and forgot about the pain in his leg for a while as he lost himself in discussion with the woman who, until Sam had come along, had been the only thing that had been keeping him going.

CHAPTER 3
THE BEACH

Summer in Barcelona is hot, but made more than bearable by the presence of a coastline full of beaches, not all of which are constantly filled to the brim with tourists.

Sam was used to spending quite some time on the beach in the school holidays. Whenever they could, his parents would take Sam and Violeta up the coast to spend a few days at their grandparents' beach house in Blanes and he'd also spent many days on the city beaches with boys from school, playing football and just generally having fun. It was not really too unusual then for Uncle Andrew to want to take him to the beach and his parents readily agreed. Sam was fairly sure that they were actually quite glad to get him out of their hair for a while.

Sam met Andrew at his flat in the early morning and they drove north up the coastal motorway to one of the quieter beaches near a town called Sant Pol de Mar. Sam was quite happy not to be going to one of Barcelona's beaches; during the last few years, the sea in the city itself had become more and more polluted and the beaches far dirtier because too many people were not cleaning up after themselves and he didn't want to have to worry about dodging cigarette butts instead of concentrating on what his uncle was teaching him.

Andrew parked the car and they went down towards the sea. Sam carried the bags because Andrew had enough trouble just walking with his cane. They chose a patch of beach in among the rocks that was as far away from anyone else as possible, something that was usually quite hard on the Catalan coast, even in June, which was why they had come so early.

They set out the towels and stripped down to their swimming trunks. Andrew turned away to take off his t-shirt and trousers, folding them neatly to put them in his bag, which gave Sam the opportunity to see his body for the first time. He stared at it, horrified; the recent wound in his leg wasn't the only sign of injury that his uncle had - his entire torso and much of his legs were covered in a network of old scars and there was barely a patch of skin left untouched. There were small burns, hundreds of thin scratches on his forearms and five jagged parallel lines over his ribs that might have been claw marks from an animal. The worst by far, though, were the dozens of long thick lines crisscrossing his back that looked like they were from a whipping.

Sam had never heard of anyone being injured so much and surviving and he shuddered before he turned away to resume getting changed, not wanting to be caught staring.

Quickly they were both down to shorts and Andrew raised his eyebrows at Sam's garishly colourful board shorts, but said nothing.

Sam just stood looking at Andrew, expectantly, with his hands on his hips.

Andrew looked back at him blankly for a few seconds, then faked realisation. 'Oh, right! Of course, you're right! We need sun cream!'

Sam wanted to shout at his uncle, but he saw the grin on his face and knew he was being toyed with. He grabbed the cream from his bag and settled for playfully tossing it just a little bit too hard at him. They hadn't spoken much in the car because Andrew had seemed to be in a very thoughtful mood and Sam hadn't wanted to interrupt him, so he figured that a few more minutes wouldn't make much difference.

Andrew finished putting cream on and put the bottle away. 'Oh, all right then! We'll get started if you want.'

Sam was dripping with sarcasm when he replied. 'Thank you.'

'Are you sure you don't just want to lie here for a while? Get some sun? You're looking a bit pasty…'

Sam just gave him a blank look in reply.

Andrew grinned. 'Fine then, suit yourself. Come on.'

Sam followed him as he limped down to the water with difficulty, leaning heavily on the cane which kept sinking into the sand.

He stopped just short of the water and turned to face Sam. 'Look, sorry I've been playing with you, but there is a point to my being so annoying; you really need to work on your patience.'

Sam laughed. 'It's been more than a month since I went to Port Royal, believe me, I have been patient.'

'That's exactly what I mean - a month is nothing, Sam.' He sighed. 'I think there's something that you haven't quite grasped about your new circumstances. Do you remember I told you yesterday that when we return from a Displacement nothing changes about us, apart from any injuries we've suffered on it?'

'Uh-huh.' Sam nodded.

'Well, that whole thing about "nothing changes" also means that it doesn't matter if we spend fifty minutes or fifty *years* in the past - when we return we are still *exactly* the same age that we were when we Displaced.'

'Ok...'

Andrew smiled wryly and shook his head. 'I can see that you still don't get it. OK, then, let me ask you a question - how old do you think I am?'

Sam looked him up and down, then smiled slowly. 'You're about fifty, aren't you?'

'Cheeky bugger! I'm forty-two, thank you very much! Well, actually, that's not true. Yes, I was born forty-two years ago, but I'm actually two hundred and seventy-six years old. And I'm nowhere near as old as some other Displacers have been when they reach my age.'

Sam opened his mouth to comment, but then closed it again when he realised he had no idea what to say.

'Yes, I had about the same kind of reaction when I first found out.' Andrew chuckled, but then suddenly became serious and Sam could almost see the weight of all those years bearing down on him. 'Sam, you have to understand that the biggest change to your life since becoming a Displacer is not that you're going to have dozens of adventures or that you are going to be in a lot more danger than you would have been, although both of those things are certainly true. No, the biggest change that you're going to have to deal with is that you no longer have just the *one* lifetime to live and unless you do something silly and get yourself killed you have not decades, but *centuries* ahead of you. There is no rush anymore, Sam! You don't need to do everything all at once. Be patient, please, take your time and make sure you do things right. And for god's sake don't go rushing into anything and getting yourself killed. That would be...'

He trailed off and a look of intense pain crossed his face as his eyes became unfocused and he stared out at the ocean, but before Sam could say anything the smile returned and he reached out to put his hand on Sam's shoulder. 'Anyway, as I said - try to be patient; you have all the time in the world. Literally. You don't even have to work out exactly what that means to you right now either. Give it a few years to sink in, or maybe a decade or two!' He squeezed Sam's shoulder and jerked his head in the direction of the sea. 'For now, let's see about teaching you how to control your powers, shall we?'

Sam nodded eagerly. 'Yes, please!'

Andrew huffed with laughter. He shook his head and muttered to himself. 'I don't know why I even bother; teaching patience to a teenager is like debating the merits of Rimsky-Korsakov with the Sex Pistols... Now *that* was completely pointless.' He turned away and hobbled a few steps into the water until it was around his ankles. 'OK, come over here.'

Sam went and stood next to him, uncertainly. 'What are we doing? You're not going to make me do anything silly, like a rite of passage or a hazing ritual or something, are you? Because there are people around and *whoa*!' He stopped talking and looked down as he realised that he could feel the cold water on his feet, the sand between his toes and... something else.

'There it is!' Andrew grinned. 'You feel that, don't you?'

'Yes!' Sam didn't need to ask what he was supposed to be feeling because he remembered it all too well from that day in the rain back on the ship - the tingling sensation that he'd naively thought was acid rain. 'How come I haven't felt this before?'

Andrew shrugged. 'When you came to the beach last year your powers hadn't been activated.'

'OK, but I've also had a few showers since I came back from Port Royal, wouldn't I have felt it then?'

'Well, you weren't looking for it. It's also not as noticeable in the shower because it's running water and it already makes you kind of tingle. OK, let's go all the way in.' He took a few hopping steps further into the sea, then, when he was deep enough, he threw his cane back onto the beach and dove headfirst into the water, coming up about ten metres further out. He lay on his back, sculling in the gentle waves, head tilted back, basking in the sun and waiting for Sam to join him.

Sam waded out slowly, with a bit more dignity than his uncle, feeling the tingling sensation travelling up his body at the same rate as he submerged himself in the cold water.

He was soon deep enough to be buoyed by the water and had to start swimming to make any progress and after a few easy strokes he stopped next to Andrew and began to tread water.

Andrew lifted his head slightly and glanced at him out of the corner of his eye while he bobbed up and down. 'So? What do you feel? I bet your whole body is tingling now, right?'

Sam nodded. It felt like his skin was vibrating. It was a bit strange, but it wasn't at all unpleasant.

Andrew lay his head back again and stared up at the sky as he continued. 'One of our number, who fancied himself a bit of a poet when he was young…'

Sam interrupted, grinning. 'It was you, wasn't it?'

Andrew waved him off with a smile. 'That's not important right now. Anyway, this unknown, unappreciated genius said that we "immerse ourselves in the flow of time" and that is why being in water helps us like this. However, it might well just be because the feeling of being in water is so similar to the feeling we get when we Displace. Whatever the reason, it's an easy way of getting into the past or back again and it's especially helpful if you are hurt or there's too much going on to concentrate properly.'

'OK.'

'Right now, if you started thinking about a time and a place that you wanted to go to, you'd start to Displace. We don't really want you to do that, so instead I want you to think about your family. Think about being at home, think about Violeta touching your toys and books without your permission, think about eating your mother's wonderful cooking.'

Sam stopped treading water and let himself float next to his uncle. He closed his eyes and pictured his life at home.

The tingling feeling instantly drained from his body, like liquid poured from a glass, leaving him a bit cold and with a slightly puzzling feeling of loss. He opened his eyes and frowned. 'It's gone, the feeling's gone. Now I just feel wet and a bit cold.'

'Good, that's exactly what's supposed to happen. We call it "Calming". When you have a shower or go out in the rain or go swimming you don't want to be Displacing every time you start thinking about your history homework or whether Atilla the Hun was a pretty cool guy, so if you keep your mind "Calm" and focused on where you *belong* then that is where you stay.'

'Where I belong? Like where my home is?'

'Yes, but it's more than that. You belong in this time-line, in this here and now. You *are* Sam Vives. As long as you keep that knowledge inside you then you're fine. Then Displacement can become a *conscious* act; you get to *choose* when and where to go instead of it happening randomly, like it did to you last month.'

Sam nodded. It all made perfect sense to him, as if it was something he already understood but hadn't known how to explain.

'Right, now relax again. Concentrate on the feeling of the water, let that tingling feeling build up again. Tell me when you've got it.'

Sam closed his eyes again. He relaxed and let himself float, gently moving his hands back and forth to keep his head just out of the water.

Andrew waited patiently, watching Sam as he looked inside himself.

After about a minute, Sam could feel that he was ready. 'OK. Got it.'

'Sure?'

'Yes.'

Andrew was seriously impressed with the speed at which Sam was picking things up, but he continued without commenting on the fact. 'All right. This time think about Rafa. Think back to one of those times a few years back when he caught you after school, or shut you in a locker. Imagine how it would really surprise him; the look on his face if suddenly there were two of you there to stuff *him* into the locker.'

Sam chuckled, 'That would be fantas… Hang on, the feeling's gone! Why?'

'Because that is the first and most important limit to our abilities; we cannot Displace within our own lifetime.'

'Why not?'

'It's because of the whole identity thing. You are already in the time-line because it's yours, so there can't be another. And you can't go back to a time that you've already been to for the exact same reason. If you wanted to, you could go back to Port Royal immediately *after* you left and continue being the intrepid Captain Samuel James Vives Hudson of the Mermaid, but you can't go and be a spectator at that "contest" of yours because you're already there. Nor can you go to another part of the world at the same time to do something else. Got it?'

Sam nodded.

'OK, good. Let's practice Calming again before we move on because this is really important.'

Andrew got Sam to concentrate on his family and life at home several more times, banishing the tingling sensation and reinforcing his sense of self. Sam found that each time was easier than the last until it was becoming almost second nature.

After about an hour, Andrew said that they had done enough and they got out of the water. Sam ran to fetch Andrew's cane for him and they went back to the towels and sat down. They were shivering slightly, but they started to warm up quickly enough in the sun.

Andrew pulled out some drinks from a small cooler and they sat watching the waves, sipping at cokes.

It was approaching mid-morning and quite a few more people had arrived while they had been in the water. Some of them were within earshot, so Andrew made sure to keep his voice down as he talked. 'Soon you won't have to consciously keep concentrating on your family or home in order to stop yourself Displacing by mistake; you'll start to get a certainty of who you are and where you belong that will anchor you in place, even if you're distracted.'

Sam nodded. 'OK. Fine. That's all great. Now I know how *not* to Displace, so how about teaching me how to control it when I *do* want to?'

Andrew raised an eyebrow. 'Aren't you tired? Usually after their first Calming lesson all anyone wants to do is fall asleep.'

Sam shrugged. 'I feel fine. What's next?'

Andrew stared at him. So far he had been surprised and not just a little impressed by the kid and he found himself wanting to see how much he would be able to do, whether he would make the "jump program", as John had put it, and master both of the technical aspects of Displacing, something that not even Quentin had been able to do.

These were the two things that enabled a Displacer to travel in time and get back again and they were the most important things, as well as the hardest, that a Displacer had to master. The rest of the training was more a matter of experience and was easy in comparison.

He shrugged and smiled. 'Alright, then, we might as well. So, the next step is to try to find that tingling sensation when you're not in the water, we call it "Preparing."'

'Preparing. OK, how?'

'It's a bit like meditation in a way. John would probably tell you to "free your mind."'

'He sounds like a lot of fun, I can't wait to meet him!'

'If you're into films and video games then I suppose he could be.' Andrew shrugged. 'Anyway, let's get back to it, shall we?'

He began to speak in a low voice, gently, hypnotically, melodically. As if he was directing meditation. 'Close your eyes and take a deep breath, just like before. Shut out your surroundings, get rid of all distractions. Concentrate, try to breathe into your whole body. Send your awareness through it and feel every part of you. Recall that tingling feeling you felt in the water and start imagining it in your fingers and toes; they're the easiest. Then when you have it there, let it spread out to the rest of your body until you feel like you did when you were immersed in water.'

Sam listened and did what he was told. He concentrated and tried to shut out everything. He was not exactly sure how to really do that, but was amazed when he immediately spiralled dizzily down into his own body and the world around him completely disappeared, except for the sound of Andrew's voice and his own heartbeat.

Andrew watched Sam closely. He nodded in approval when his nephew's frown of intense concentration softened as he relaxed. 'This is a very difficult exercise, so don't be worried if you can't do it the first time; some Displacers have been known to be unable to do it on their own and have to resort to immersion in water. They Displace in the bath and need to find water to get back...'

'OK, got it.'

Andrew blinked. 'Sorry, what?'

'Done, what do I do now?'

'Done?'

'Yes.' Sam nodded without opening his eyes, desperately trying to keep hold of the sensation, which was making his body feel like it was twitching and jumping.

Andrew stared at him, mouth open. He closed his eyes and reached out with his mind. He could feel it was true. 'Oh my god...'

'What? What's wrong?'

'Even if it wasn't your first time that shouldn't only take twenty seconds! Hell, I can't do it in less than thirty if I'm not distracted, and I was talking to you the whole time!'

'Maybe I'm not doing it right?'

'Oh, you are, I can feel it, you're bloody buzzing with energy. Make it go away, please, Calm yourself before you end up god knows where.'

Sam concentrated for a second and felt the sensation wash away, once again leaving him feeling strangely empty and somewhat disappointed.

'Bloody hell! What are you, kid?' Andrew laughed, not believing what he was seeing. 'Do it again.'

Sam closed his eyes and concentrated. He was starting to feel a bit like a performing animal and the thought crossed his mind that there had better be a biscuit in it for him if that were true.

There it was, that was it. Now all he needed to do was grasp it and...

Andrew had his eyes closed and he felt it when Sam did. 'That was only about twenty seconds, it's got to be some kind of record.' He shook his head in wonder. 'OK, relax, shut it down, that's enough for today.'

Sam concentrated briefly and the tingling went away. He opened his eyes and smiled as he met the shocked gaze of his uncle, but then his vision blurred as the world swam around him and darkness closed in from the corners of his eyes. He clutched the sides of his head and squeezed his eyes shut again as dizziness threatened to overcome him. 'Whoa!'

'He's only human after all! Here, eat this.' Andrew threw a chocolate bar onto Sam's lap. He waited until Sam had opened it and taken a huge bite before continuing. 'When you Displaced to Port Royal I bet you slept a lot the first day, didn't you?'

'A couple of days, give or take,' Sam mumbled with his mouth full.

'That's pretty typical for a first time; your body didn't know what had hit it. Don't worry, it'll get easier and you probably won't sleep as long next time and even less the times after that. Displacing does take a lot out of you, though, and you should try to eat something as soon as you arrive to keep your blood sugar up or you'll feel the consequences in the days after. Fruit will do, but chocolate is best - just don't tell your mother I told you to eat more chocolate or she'll kill me. Also, you've got to remember that the first time you sleep it's going to be very deep and it'll take a lot to wake you up, so make sure you sleep somewhere safe. My first time in the Amazon I went to sleep against a tree and woke up in a cocoon hanging from a branch. That was a bit of a shock, I can tell you.'

It was Sam's time to stare at Andrew with his mouth open; he could never be sure when Andrew was being completely serious because he was always joking around, but something told him that this time he was.

'Close your mouth and chew; you don't want to attract flies!' Andrew smiled. 'Just go to bed early tonight and you'll wake up in the morning as usual, no problem. You didn't actually Displace, so you didn't use as much energy as you did going to Port Royal and won't have to explain to your parents why you slept for two days. Oh, one last thing before I forget - although I don't think you're ever going to have much trouble Preparing, if it's an emergency and you don't have time or can't concentrate, then remember that you can always just immerse yourself in water, like Quentin, your friend "Jack Swallow", did when he was cornered on your ship. That will instantly bring you back once you think of home, even if you're in danger or distracted. It's like an ejector seat.'

Sam finished the chocolate bar and put the wrapper in his bag to recycle later. He yawned and belatedly covered his mouth with his hand. 'Oops, excuse me!' His eyelids felt heavy suddenly and he could barely keep his eyes open.

Andrew laughed. 'Don't worry about it! Why don't you take a nap while we work on our tans? I'll wake you up in a couple of hours to take you home.'

'Sounds like a good…' Sam didn't even manage to get the full sentence out before he fell into a deep sleep.

Andrew leaned on his elbow and watched Sam snoring gently with his mouth hanging half open.

It was incredible, what the boy had done that morning, unprecedented. As far as he knew, nobody else had ever had Sam's ease with Displacing, except maybe for Quentin, and Sam would have to be tested to see how the two of them actually compared.

Was there something special about this latest generation or was it just a coincidence that two so exceptional Displacers had turned up at the same time? That was a matter for the Elders to investigate; it was part of their job after all, but it seemed more than likely that something was happening, because even Rachel, his own niece, had tested higher than anyone else ever had and had held the record until Quentin had come along and blown it away.

The Honourable Society of Displacers had fragments of a prophecy that they had collected over the ages in the attic of its headquarters in London. Painted on pottery, written on papyrus, carved into stone and bones, it made vague promises about a Displacer with special powers and naturally many of the Displacers had been positive that it referred to Quentin.

Unfortunately, it wasn't very clear about what he was supposed to do and the Displacers as a whole had watched Quentin very closely, waiting for him to give them the answers to the riddles in the prophecies that had puzzled the Society for hundreds of years.

The pressure and the expectations had most likely been one of the main reasons why he had abandoned the Displacers - he had reacted badly, the praise had gone to his head and he had become arrogant and demanding and ultimately had "gone over to the dark side", as John had put it.

The Society had been devastated, thinking that they had lost their one chance at fulfilling whatever the prophecies hinted at, but then

Quentin had been forgotten when Sam had come along and defeated him in his first ever Displacement.

However, what Sam had done in Port Royal had raised far more questions than it had answered, not so much because he had demonstrated abilities far above what he should have had, although that was puzzling in itself, but rather that it should have been impossible for him to have interacted with Quentin in the way he had.

Normally, Displacers had to have the *exact* same destination in mind and Displace at the *exact* same time in the present in order to end up in the same time-line together and if they didn't get it *exactly* right then they wouldn't be able to do what Sam had. For example, if the two had only been in the same *time* and not the same *time-line*, then when he'd gone back to Port Royal to have a look around he would have found the first mate of the Queen Anne's Revenge was Blackbeard's successor, not Smithy - Sam wouldn't have been able to affect any changes Quentin had already made. What had happened, therefore, was just too unfeasible to be purely coincidence and had the Elders scrambling to find out what was going on and whether it was some talent of Sam himself or some external force at work.

And Andrew was sure that, when they found out what the boy had done that morning, many Society members would lose no time in saying that it proved it was Sam who the prophecies referred to.

Andrew felt sorry for his nephew; someone so young should not have the hopes of so many people, the whole world, piled on him. It was probably just as well that he still had no idea of what was already expected of him.

'All in good time,' thought Andrew, laying down on his towel and closing his eyes. 'For now, please let him enjoy himself a little, while he can.'

Sam dozed in the passenger seat the whole way home and when Andrew pulled up outside Sam's flat he had to shake him to wake him up. 'Sam, we're here.'

Sam snorted as he came awake. He looked around bleary eyed and it took him a while to realise where he was. He stumbled out of the car and stood on the pavement, fumbling in his bag for the keys.

Andrew wound down the passenger side window and leaned across speak to him. 'Go on, get some rest, but make sure you keep practising. Only Calming though. Don't practice Preparing; we don't want anything happening by mistake, because then you won't be able to do anything at your lesson next week.'

'Do I really have to wait a whole week before we meet again?'

'Yes! Patience, remember?' Andrew laughed. 'Besides, you have to have time to recover and practice what you've learnt today; you're good, Sam, but you're not that good. Yet. Also, I have some help coming and she won't be here until Wednesday. Please give my regards to your parents and see you next Thursday!'

With that, Andrew drove away, heading for the garage in the basement of his block of flats.

Sam was feeling excited but frustrated at the same time. He had this whole new world, an eternity of adventures available to him, beckoning him, but he was forbidden from enjoying them yet. A week wasn't too long though and he resolved to spend it practising hard; he had quite enjoyed seeing the look of shock on his uncle's face when he had Prepared so quickly and wanted to make sure that he continued to surprise him.

He watched Andrew's car turn the corner then went inside, so lost in thought that he didn't see the four boys sitting on a bench across the road playing cards and watching him maliciously.

Andrew sat in his study and rubbed his leg. He'd taken the bandages off to go to the beach, believing that the salt water would do the wound good, then put them back on when he got home and now it itched like hell and he was having trouble getting to the right spot to scratch. He grabbed a ruler from a nearby desk and stuck it beneath the bandages, finally getting to the right place. He sighed in relief and leaned back in his chair, eyes closed and scratching furiously.

'Ahem.'

Andrew was interrupted by the sound of Ralph clearing his throat. He opened his eyes and peered from under his eyelids at the wall in front of him.

Every single one of the computer monitors were on and occupied and twelve people were watching him scratch himself with varying degrees of patience and amusement.

'I'm sorry.' He sat up and uncrossed the leg to place it on the floor out of sight of his webcam. 'Uh…Where was I?

'Port Royal.' Ralph, unsurprisingly, wasn't one of the more patient members of the group and certainly wasn't amused.

'Oh, yes. Thank you, Ralph. Sorry. Anyway, I went back to Port Royal to have a look around in the wake of Sam's Displacement.'

Ralph tutted and shook his head. 'That was very foolish of you after what happened last time. You should have sent someone else.'

'Foolhardy maybe, but not foolish; I thought it was a worthwhile risk to take. I know my way around well enough and I had the contacts to get the information I needed. I thought that I had a good chance to get in and out without attracting too much notice. Besides, I didn't think that you were going to volunteer to go in my stead.'

'I might have, but at least I wouldn't…'

'So, what did you find out, Andrew?' Anne quickly interrupted and steered the conversation back onto course before the two rivals started flinging insults, something that had ruined more than one meeting.

'Quite a lot actually, despite the personal cost. I'm very glad I went and I think that the Elders will be extremely interested in what I found out.' Andrew gave Ralph a pointed look before he continued. 'I spoke to Captain Smith; he still had the diamond, as he should have, Quentin hasn't gone back to try to reclaim it. And he is still Blackbeard's heir, although we all know how that ends up…'

There was a chorus of sad yeses from most of the people there.

'…but the most intriguing thing is that he has a dim recollection of serving under a "Captain Vives."'

'That's impossible!' The Indian woman in the top right hand corner screen leaned forwards until her face filled the entire screen.

'Normally, I would agree, Lisa, but it seems that Sam may be just a little bit more special than we thought. Everywhere I went I saw evidence of Sam's visit. I spoke to Bosun Brown as well and his recollection of Sam was even stronger than that of Smith.'

'The anomaly…' said John in an ominous voice.

'This is *still* not the Matrix, John…'

There were chuckles at that.

'If this is true, then it seems to go a long way to confirming our suspicions about Sam. Could he really be who we have been waiting for?' This came from an older, almost completely bald man, James Hudson, an Elder, who also happened to be Sam's grandfather.

'It's too early to say, James. While the results of his maiden voyage into the past were unusual, to say the least, that in and of itself is not conclusive.'

'I still find it ridiculous and faintly offensive that we are putting so much stock in the boy, just because of a few scraps of ancient writings that we are not even sure have been translated properly.'

There were agreeing noises and nods from a couple of the people at Ralph's words, mostly the ones who had supported him in the election for the leader of the Displacers years before, an election that he had lost and Andrew had won.

Andrew snorted. 'You didn't seem to have any problem with that when it was your son who everybody was piling their hopes and praises on.'

Ralph spluttered and was about to answer back, but he was interrupted by Anne, who injected a bit of realism into the proceedings.

'Gentlemen, please! As always this will be a matter of contention until definitively proven either way. There is no doubting that the boy is special, Andrew's preliminary findings show that without a doubt, but we will just have to wait and see exactly how special he is until he has been tested fully, or done something to clear up the matter.'

Andrew nodded. 'Indeed, thank you, Anne. In the meantime we should start digging through the archives to find any relevant references we may have missed. James, can you organise that, please?'

'It will be a pleasure.'

'Thank you. Well, if there is no other business? Anyone? Then, thank you all, and Rachel, I'll see you at the airport on Wednesday.'

The blonde-haired girl in the bottom left screen nodded. 'Looking forward to it!'

'And don't forget my tea bags!'

Rachel sighed and rolled her eyes. 'Don't worry, I won't.'

Andrew waved as he signed off, then instantly grabbed the ruler and started scratching his leg furiously.

CHAPTER 4
REST AND RELAXATION…

Over the next few days Sam took Andrew's orders to heart and rested as best as he could, or at least as much as he could stand.

The evening after he had gone to the beach he went to bed at seven and didn't wake up until ten the next morning, starving hungry. His sister and mother looked at him a little bit strangely when he walked out of his bedroom so late in the day, but, aside from a grin from Violeta, they offered no comment. They didn't even say anything when he ate two bowls of cereal and five pieces of toast; what is normal for a teenage boy isn't necessarily normal for anyone else - he was active and usually ate a lot and they probably just figured that it was the summer holidays and there was no reason for him to get up early.

After breakfast he wasn't sure what to do with himself. Andrew had told him to practice Calming, but that involved getting wet and he didn't think his parents would look very kindly on him being in the shower for hours and besides, they would probably get the wrong idea about what was taking him so long. He didn't feel like going to the beach again either; he'd had enough sun for a while. He could have gone to the pool, but he didn't want to go on his own and he didn't really like the chlorine very much.

In the end he decided that he'd just take the day off and do stuff that was unrelated to Displacing, stuff that he would normally do during his summer holidays; he was still feeling tired and Andrew had said not to push things.

He flopped onto the sofa and switched on the television, flicking through the channels for a few minutes before eventually settling on something that he usually liked. He watched for a while, but he just wasn't enjoying it; it didn't seem the same, it seemed artificial, superficial - the programming during the day had always been bad, but he'd never realised quite how bad until now. It wasn't holding his interest at all and his thoughts kept wandering back to the beach and his lessons and how alive he'd felt with the tingling sensation running through his body. After only half an hour he turned the television off again and wandered out of the room.

He stood in the corridor, looking from one end of the house to the other. His father was at work and his mother had gone out a little while before, taking Violeta to see some of her friends at a nearby play centre, so he was alone in the flat. Usually he would take full advantage of the chance to lounge around and play a computer game or his music at full volume, but for some reason he didn't feel like it.

With a sigh, he went back into his bedroom and stood in the middle of the room, searching for inspiration. He couldn't believe how frustrated he was that he couldn't Displace - it was like getting a remote control car for your birthday, but then finding out that you didn't have the batteries, and that it was a Sunday and the shops were all closed.

His eyes alighted on the souvenirs on his desk, the coin and handkerchief from the eighteenth century, a period of history he knew next to nothing about, and he smiled as an idea occurred to him - he might not be able to use his abilities, but he could certainly do the next best thing and get organised for when he could and make a list of all the things he wanted to do when he had the chance.

He sat down at his desk and pulled out a fresh sheet of paper. Pirates had been an excellent start, but there were plenty of other things to see, even if dinosaurs and the future were off the table.

The ideas started to flow as soon as he put pen to paper and very soon the page was completely covered, so he grabbed another, and another. When he ran out of ideas he went through his textbooks and began searching on the internet. Suddenly, he found he had a reason to be interested in history and he laughed when he realised that what had always been one of his weakest subjects at school was now the most important to him and might well end up being his favourite.

Finally, he leant back and reread the locations, times and events scrawled on the pieces of paper strewn about his desk; if he only got to go to half of these places, do half of these things, he'd be more than happy. In fact, when he thought about it properly, he knew he'd even settle for only doing a tenth.

Unfortunately, the whole exercise had only served to make him more excited, restless and eager to begin and he threw his pen down on the desk and stood up. He glanced out the window at the cloudless blue sky and realised that he should really be outside enjoying himself instead of cooped up, trying to rest. He decided to go and see if any of the boys from school were out and about - he was tired, but he could still kick a ball around in the park or something and call it resting because it wasn't Displacing and, besides, it would take his mind off of things.

Five minutes later he walked through the open metal gates and into the park. It wasn't much of a park, by British standards anyway; it was little more than an open space with a dirt floor where the local kids could play. It had a couple of five-a-side football goals and a few basketball hoops, all desperately in need of repair. To one side there was a small, fenced-off space with one of those fun bouncy rubber floors, swings, a climbing frame and some other little things to keep young children occupied. It was a popular place during the evenings, where parents could come, dump their little monsters into the play area and sit back on the benches surrounding it to talk with friends and generally catch their breath. It was also a focal point for most of the tough kids in the neighbourhood too, but they usually just came out at night and weren't so interested in playing games. There were a half-dozen or so boys kicking a ball around between the goals and Sam stopped to look at them. He recognised one of them from his school, he was from the year above and he saw that most of the other boys were bigger than him as well, but they had uneven team numbers and he thought they might still let him play.

However, before he could go up and ask if he could join in, a huge slap on the back knocked the wind out of him and made him stagger, almost sending him sprawling.

He took half a second to curse himself for his stupidity at not realising that of course Rafa would be waiting for an opportunity for revenge, then he spun on his heels to face his attacker, intending to face him down the same way as he had last time.

This time the bully wasn't alone, though, he had brought friends. The park was only a couple of streets away from Sam's home and that had been more than enough time for the four boys, who had been waiting patiently for him across the street from his house, to catch up with him.

Cold washed through Sam, making him feel almost exactly like he had the day before when he had Calmed when floating in the sea and he broke out into a sweat that the heat hadn't yet managed to provoke. However, he knew that he couldn't show his fear, so he straightened and forced a smile, trying to look unafraid.

Rafa smiled and growled at him. 'Vives…'

Sam interrupted him with a sigh and not just a little false bravado. 'Yes, I know - you told me to watch my back and I didn't.'

Rafa's mouth closed with an audible plop; Sam had stolen his words. He evidently didn't have anything else prepared to say and there was a brief pause as he tried to work out what to do next.

Sam faced the four boys. Without looking away from Rafa he took in the situation around him from the corner of his eyes. The football game was going on normally; the boys either hadn't noticed what was going on or, more likely, were ignoring it as nothing to do with them. No help was going to come from them and likewise there were no adults on the benches or walking by to appeal to. He was on his own.

For the first time Sam realised that his newfound "superpower", although exciting and life-changing, was going to do absolutely nothing to solve his day-to-day problems; even if he did manage to Displace now he wouldn't escape because he would just return to this exact time and place, still facing these four bullies, just a lot more tired.

The boys with Rafa shifted impatiently, wondering what he was waiting for and Rafa glanced at them. Sam could almost see the wheels turning in Rafa's head as he tried to think of something clever to say that would allow him to regain the face he had lost with his henchmen because of Sam's cheekiness - not what they had been expecting from someone who was supposed to be afraid of him. In the end he failed to come up with anything and just settled for getting directly to the point. 'Get the bastard!' He snarled and pointed at Sam, just in case the boys didn't know who he was referring to.

Sam ran.

He had been ready for the order and managed to dodge their reaching arms. He did everything he could to get around them to one of the two exits and from there to home and safety, but even with his head start they easily blocked him at every turn. He jumped low fences and ducked behind trees and around any obstacle he could find, the same tactics that he had used when Swallow had ambushed him in his cabin on the Mermaid, but even though they were bigger and slower than him there were four of them and he could never quite get clear of them.

Everywhere he ran they cut him off from escape, but his twisting and turning was gradually wearing them down and causing confusion.

He saw his chance when two of them tripped over each other, leaving a small gap and he tried to jump one of the benches and get through it, but he was more tired than he thought from his trip to the beach and misjudged. He caught his foot and went sprawling.

He cried out in pain as he fell heavily, skinning his knees and elbows and grazing his cheek, his shorts and t-shirt providing no protection from the rough ground. He scrambled to get up, but one of the boys shoved him onto the floor again and punched him. He knew that they wouldn't let him get back on his feet, so he rolled into a ball to protect himself from their attacks, a tactic Rafa had helped him perfect over the years.

The boys laughed and gathered around to hit him a few more times for their own gratification, but they had beaten and humiliated him, proving their superiority and that, along with the sight of the blood coming from his wounds and his already considerable pain, seemed to be enough for them.

Rafa put in one last vicious kick to Sam's thigh, then leaned down to taunt him. 'I'll see you around, Vives. It's a long time until school begins again, so keep watching your back.'

Sam just groaned and lay still as they stepped over him and strutted away, still laughing.

Nobody came to help him. The boys playing football continued to ignore him, concentrating on their game. They knew Rafa too well and they didn't want to become a target themselves.

Sam slowly picked himself up and flopped down on the bench that had so recently betrayed him to nurse his wounds, feel sorry for himself and get his breath back.

Half an hour later he limped home, bruised and battered. He went straight into the bathroom and cleaned himself up as much as possible, putting antiseptic cream on anything that was bleeding. He came out of the bathroom and tried to sneak to his bedroom without bumping in to anyone, but walked straight into his mother, who had evidently been waiting for him right outside the door.

'Hi, Mum.'

She noticed the scratches straight away. 'What happened to you?'

'I fell over playing football, it's no big deal.'

'Let me see.' She inspected his knees and elbows and then looked at the scrape on his face. 'You'll live.' She frowned at him. 'Is there anything you want to tell me?'

Lots… 'No, the game just got a bit rough, that's all.'

She nodded, but Sam could tell she didn't believe him. 'Alright, then. Leave those cuts to air for now, but put plasters on them for bed; I don't want you bleeding all over the sheets.'

'OK.' Sam went around her and hobbled down the corridor towards his room.

She called after him. 'Dinner is in two hours!'

'OK, Mum!' He went into his room and closed the door. He laid down on the bed, wincing at the pressure on his sore limbs and stared up at the ceiling.

He hated secrets. He'd thought he had enough of them already; hiding Rafa and the bullying from his parents, but now he had a new secret and it was so much bigger.

He almost felt like some kind of secret agent leading a double life, like James Bond, that is if James Bond was a wimp who got stuffed into lockers at school and beaten up on playgrounds. Things at school were going to change though, and soon, he could feel it. Even after only one Displacement he could feel a change in himself, he was more confident. Rafa had seen that in him too, which was why he'd had to bring friends this time.

Sam smiled, then winced when his cheek hurt. Maybe he could displace to China and learn kung fu or something - that would surprise the heck out of Rafa. For now, though, he'd stay indoors, away from danger, and wait for his next lesson with his uncle.

CHAPTER 5
A SAFE PLACE

The next week was incredibly boring and passed far too slowly for Sam.

It was a bit cowardly maybe, but, for safety, he barely left the flat and when he did go out he made sure to be with a group of friends or his mother, like when she went shopping or took Violeta to the park or the library. It was just as well, because every time he looked out of the window he saw Rafa and his friends sitting on the bench across the road, playing cards or hunched over Nintendos. They didn't seem to have anything better to do with their time than wait for him to show himself and continue to torment him. Sam actually thought it was quite sad that they were choosing this as the most interesting thing to do with their lives right now instead of enjoying their summer holidays and he almost felt sorry for them. Not sorry enough to go out and let them chase him around again, of course, but still, he wondered what the situation had to be like for Rafa at home for him to want to sit in the street outside Sam's house rather than be there.

He did his homework for Andrew as conscientiously as he could under the circumstances. He went to the beach a couple of days with his friends, arranging to meet outside his house so as not to be alone and then taking the bus as a group. They were shadowed the whole way by Rafa and his gang, but they didn't dare try anything with the other boys surrounding Sam. He also managed to persuade his mother to take him and Violeta to the swimming pool a couple of times. It was easier to practice there than in the sea because he could be on his own while his mother was with Violeta; the beach was already too crowded for him to concentrate properly. Every successive time he tried Calming it came easier and he was now positive that nothing unexpected would happen next time it rained.

Eventually, Thursday rolled around again and with it his next lesson, which he would have at Uncle Andrew's flat. The only trouble was that Rafa was still lurking outside on the street with his friends, waiting for a chance to catch Sam alone. He couldn't ask his mother to walk with him without telling her why and he considered asking Andrew to come and walk with him, but rejected the idea because he knew that his uncle was still having trouble getting around.

He realised that there was nothing else for it, he was just going to have to make a break for it. He lurked behind the street door of his building, in the shadows, looking out through the glass at the boys and waiting for them to become fully engrossed in a video game together. As soon as he saw them cheering and laughing he opened the door and slipped out. He was halfway down the street before he heard them shout and start after him. He broke into a run and fled around the corner, quickly losing them in the back streets. He was fairly sure that he'd left them far behind, but didn't stop running until he was standing at Andrew's door, panting hard.

He rang the bell and waited nervously, looking up and down the street for any sign of the bullies. 'Come on, come on, open up...'

He was relieved when he got the familiar feeling in his gut that spoke of the approach of another Displacer and the door opened behind him. He spun around to greet his uncle, already beginning to step into the flat, but stopped short when he found himself face to face with a girl instead.

She was blonde with blue eyes and slightly taller than him; only by a couple of inches, but enough that he had to look up at her. In the heat, she was wearing a pair of faded blue jeans shorts and a green tank-top that showed off her developing figure and athletic build in a way that made Sam's heart race. She was pretty, while not quite being beautiful, but there was something about her that grabbed him and wouldn't let go and he wondered if that was what love at first sight felt like. He was going to dismiss the pounding in his heart and the heat in his cheeks as just the after-effects of his run down the street, but unbelievably he thought he saw a reaction in her as well - her mouth parted slightly, almost in a sigh and her breath hitched, but then the moment was gone and her eyes narrowed to slits as she stared down at him.

'You must be Sam.' She spoke to him in English and Sam was flustered for a second, not because of the unexpected change in language - he always spoke to Andrew in Spanish - but because of the way she looked him up and down frankly before gazing intently into his eyes. 'You're shorter than I thought you'd be.'

She smiled at him and his heart flipped. 'I, uh… yes... um... Hello?' He wanted to say more, to sound less like a bumbling idiot, but the words wouldn't come.

There had been brief moments in Port Royal when he had felt something akin to this, like when he had danced with that girl at his victory celebration, or found himself just a little too close to Captain Bonny, but the feelings he'd had back there had been nowhere near as strong as this; for some reason *this* girl was making his brain completely switch off.

She smirked, seeing how flustered he was, and raised an eyebrow. 'Well? Are you going to come in, or not?'

Sam came out of his stupor and jerked into movement. She stood aside and he went past her, catching a whiff of her musky perfume. He turned around as she closed the door and was about to ask her who she was, but a voice called out from deeper in the flat, forestalling him.

'Sam! Come on in! I'm in the sitting room!'

He turned and walked down the hall to the sitting room, overly conscious of the girl following him and her eyes boring into her back.

He found Andrew in the sitting room in one of the armchairs, rubbing his leg and grimacing in pain. 'Sorry I didn't come to let you in; the leg's feeling a bit worse than usual today.'

'That's OK. Is it getting any better?'

'Yes. But slowly… too damn slowly.'

The sitting room was slightly tidier than it usually was; the books were in neater piles and there was actually room to sit on the sofa, not just on the armchairs. Sam felt vaguely offended; Andrew had tidied up for the girl, but hadn't been bothered to do so for him.

'I see you've met my niece, Rachel.'

The girl, Rachel, walked past Sam, almost brushing up against him, and he again caught her scent. She sat on the sofa, crossing her legs in an elegantly fluid motion and smiled up at him.

Sam smiled back at her, a little unsettled; her open appraisal was still making him very nervous. 'More or less, she knows who I am, but she didn't exactly introduce herself.'

'Now, now, Rachel, manners.'

'Sorry, Uncle Andrew. Hi, Sam, I'm Rachel, Rachel Evans.' She reached forward and held out her hand.

Sam took it and twitched as something like an electric shock passed through his body. She didn't react at all, though, so he dismissed it as his imagination.

At her touch the clouds seemed to lift from his eyes and his head started working again. He smiled at her, almost himself again, and shook her hand, surprised at how strong her grip was, but how soft her skin felt.

The moment seemed to go on forever as he gazed into her deep blue eyes and he didn't realise that he was still holding onto her until she raised an eyebrow and pointedly looked down. He hastily pulled his hand back, his cheeks burning.

'Pleased to meet you, Sam.' She grinned knowingly and he looked away quickly.

'Rachel is a Displacer as well, of course,' said Andrew. 'She's here to help me with you for the next few weeks.'

'Months?' suggested Rachel hopefully.

'We'll see. I'm guessing your mother might want you back at some point, though.'

'I wouldn't bet on it.'

Andrew chuckled. 'Yes, you're probably right.'

Sam frowned as he struggled to keep up with the quick exchange in English and thought that maybe his mastery of the language wasn't as good as he had thought. Yes, he spoke it with his mother most of the time, but her fluency and vocabulary had suffered over her years in Spain and the speed at which these two were speaking was in a whole different order. Plus, what he spoke with his mother wasn't always strictly English, it was more Spanglish, often mixed with Catalan for good measure.

Andrew noticed his difficulty. 'Sorry, Sam, Rachel doesn't speak Spanish, so we're going to have to work in English from now on. You'll get used to it quickly enough, don't worry, and it'll be good for you. Besides, you'll need it with the other Displacers, so it's as well to practice. Just let me know if there's something you don't understand.'

Sam nodded. 'OK.'

'Good man! Anyway, as I was saying, Rachel has kindly agreed to help me with your training. At the moment I can't Displace because my leg is still hurting too much, so she'll be taking care of the practical side of things while I give the explanations.'

'When do we start?'

Andrew turned to wink at Rachel. 'I told you he was keen.'

She smiled and nodded, not taking her eyes off of Sam, who was still feeling very uncomfortable under her gaze.

Andrew saw his unease and grinned. He took pity on him and changed the subject. 'Why don't you sit down? Would you like a cup of tea before we start? Rachel brought a suitcase full of tea bags with her, so thankfully I'm stocked up for a little while.'

Sam dragged his eyes away from Rachel and went to sit down on the spare armchair. 'I'd rather just get to work, please.'

'Fair enough. Rachel?'

'Ready when you are.' She closed her eyes and shook her head as if loosening her neck. Sam watched as she took a deep breath and sort of settled into herself.

'Right then, Sam, I need you to concentrate. Rachel is going to start Preparing.' Andrew spoke quietly so as not to disturb her. 'You should start to feel a build-up of energy soon; it will be similar to the sensation you've been experiencing when you do it yourself, but it will come radiating out of her instead.'

Sam took a deep breath and waited, watching the girl, trying to ignore the way her shorts had ridden further up her legs when she had sat down. It took about a minute, but finally he began to feel a vibration in the air. It was almost a static charge, like a storm was approaching. It built up over another minute until it felt like his skin was itching. He noticed his arm hair starting to stand on end and he could feel the energy starting to build in himself in sympathy. He felt like leaping from his chair and into who knows what…

Andrew knew that Sam still lacked some control and had been keeping a close eye on him. He put a stop to things before they could go too far. 'That's enough, Rachel, thank you.'

Rachel opened her eyes and almost immediately Sam felt everything go back to normal. He found that he was breathing heavily, sweat had beaded on his forehead and it was almost a physical desire that he was feeling. 'Whoa…'

'Quite,' said Andrew with a slight smile.

Sam shifted in his seat. Impossibly, he was even more uncomfortable than he had been before. He made sure not to meet Rachel's eyes as he took a deep breath, thinking of other things and trying to calm himself down.

Andrew and Rachel watched him. They shared a knowing smile; they knew exactly what kind of effect this had, especially on a teenage boy, whose body was going through some pretty strong changes of its own already. Discreetly, they gave him a few seconds to sort himself out.

'Right, well, you should have felt your body,' Andrew chuckled. 'Sorry, your *powers*, that is, responding to Rachel's. Now what you're going to do is Prepare at the same time as Rachel and then latch on to her energy in order to do a controlled Displacement to what we call a "safe place". Not only is this a good exercise, but it will also render it impossible for you to Displace again for a month or so and we'll be able to train properly without having to worry about you going anywhere unplanned.'

'What's a "safe place"?' Sam asked.

'It's one of those locations in time that we have already determined is free of any possible distortion. It's a place where it doesn't matter if you create a presence in the time-line, because you'll never need to go there to mend it.'

Sam wasn't sure he fully understood, but he got the gist and nodded. 'OK…'

'Anyway, this time when you Displace you won't need to concentrate on a destination, because Rachel is going to do that for the both of you. It'll be like riding a tandem bike; the two of you are pedalling, but Rachel is in the front seat and deciding where to go. Got it?'

Sam nodded; Andrew used out-of-date metaphors for everything, which sounded silly but always made sense. He let out the breath that he'd been unconsciously holding and unclenched the fists that he hadn't even noticed he'd curled.

Andrew raised an eyebrow at him. 'You ready for this?'

'Yes.' With the prospect of a Displacement ahead of him Sam was certain that he would be able to concentrate; his desire for adventure would far outweigh his desire for… other things. He was sure of it.

'Come over and sit on the sofa with Rachel then.'

Sam eyed the girl, who hadn't stopped watching him and still had a disconcerting smile on her face. He reluctantly stood up and moved to the sofa, sitting down as far away from her as he could.

Andrew laughed. 'You'll need to get a bit closer than that! Don't worry, she hasn't got anything too contagious. Just fleas.'

'Oi!'

Andrew laughed again and she stuck her tongue out at him, which didn't do much for Sam's composure.

Sam nervously moved a bit closer to her. Rachel had other ideas, though, and shuffled towards him until their legs were touching.

'Right, now join hands,' Andrew said.

Rachel held out her hands in front of her.

Sam lifted his hands and hesitated, biting his lip; this was starting to get a bit intimate and he was no longer quite so sure that he'd be able to block out the distractions and concentrate well enough to Prepare.

Rachel rolled her eyes at his uncertainty and just grabbed his hands. She pulled them roughly towards her until their forearms were resting on their legs, then looked at Andrew questioningly. 'Wembley?'

He nodded. 'That'll do. Whenever you're ready.'

She immediately closed her eyes and Sam could feel the energy start to build up. Again, Andrew spoke gently.

'OK, Sam, relax, feel the energy build and feel your body building up its own energy in sympathy…'

Sam closed his eyes. He could feel the energy building in Rachel, but he wasn't responding to it as much this time; just as he'd feared, the physical sensation of holding her hands was seriously interfering with his concentration. He opened his eyes and glanced at Andrew to see if he had noticed and found his uncle watching him, stifling a laugh behind his hand.

Trying not to disrupt the girl's concentration, he adjusted his position in a vain attempt to get more comfortable, then took a deep breath, closed his eyes and tried again.

Rachel was literally buzzing with energy now and it was strong enough that it washed away all other competing sensations, forcing all his distractions out of the way. It was contagious and he could feel his own body, his own *soul* responding to it as it spread through his hands before moving to the rest of him.

He could feel himself vibrating, could feel Rachel vibrating, could feel the two vibrations coming into synchronisation, complementing each other until…

'Rachel, he's there. Now.'

'ENGLAND!!! ENGLAND!!!'

The incredible noise of thousands of people chanting at the same time hit Sam like an almost physical force and he opened his eyes with a start to find himself standing high in the terraces of a football stadium behind one of the goals. He was surrounded by a solid crowd of people with red and white hats and scarves, waving British flags and shouting at the top of their voices. There were more flags hanging from the stands to one side of him underneath huge, distinctly old-fashioned floodlights, these ones of several different nations with the cross of St

George in pride of place in the middle. The pitch below, a bright vibrant green despite the overcast day, was empty except for the goals at each end - the game was evidently yet to begin.

'What the... where are we?'

'Can't you guess?' Rachel laughed at him.

'ENGLAND!!! ENGLAND!!!' The crowd continued to chant, the noise deafening.

Sam chuckled and shook his head. 'OK, I guess we're here to watch an England football match. Can you tell me a bit more, though, please?'

'Well, this is one of the most significant points in history, a seminal event that marked the lives of countless millions of people and is still talked about to this day in hushed tones in the homes and pubs of England...' She made a grand gesture, as if presenting some kind of masterpiece. 'We are in Wembley stadium on July 30th, 1966 with ninety-seven thousand other people and England are about to play Germany.'

'And why the hell is that so special?'

Rachel stared at him, expecting him to be joking, but quickly saw that he wasn't. 'Oh, god, that's right, you're only half English... Well, this is the most important match in English football history.' She leaned in to him, speaking directly into his ear so that nobody else could hear her. 'Spoiler alert. In just over two hours England will win the World Cup for the first and only time in their history.'

'Couldn't we have gone to 2010 to watch Spain beat Holland? Now that was a good match.'

Rachel sighed. 'Two things. First, *this* is history at its finest, that's not, and second, have you forgotten what Andrew told you about Displacing in your own lifetime?'

Sam blushed. He realised that he really didn't like looking stupid in front of Rachel and tried to cover. 'Oh, right, sorry, it must have slipped my mind with the Displacement and the noise.'

'Don't worry about it!' She waved away his mistake as if it were nothing and began craning her head to search the crowd. 'Besides, we're not here for the football. Not this time anyway.'

'We're not?'

'No, we're going to leave before the game starts. Who knows, one day you might want to bring someone special here to watch it...'

She glanced sideways at him and smiled and Sam's already pounding heart did a somersault. He idly wondered what would happen if he had a heart attack right there and then.

She squeezed his hand, which Sam hadn't realised she was still holding, and turned away again to point down the terrace. 'Today I brought us here for them.'

Sam looked in the direction she was pointing.

He would never normally have been able to pick any specific person out of the thousands in the stadium, but he felt drawn to someone and he searched for them down where Rachel had indicated.

His eyes locked onto a young man a few rows below them, part of a group of three dressed in sixties-style clothing just as he and Rachel were. He had his arm around the shoulder of a young, stunningly beautiful woman, with waist-length chestnut hair and long eyelashes. Accompanying them was another young man, who was joyfully shouting along with the crowd, but looked vaguely out of place to Sam.

He could feel that all three of them were Displacers, but it was the first young man who really caught his attention and for some reason he was strangely familiar.

Sam blinked as he realised who the man reminded him of. 'Hang on, is that Andrew?'

'Yes.'

'He looks so young!'

'He is, he's about twenty-three years old, I think.'

'How is that possible?'

Rachel shook her head and grinned sardonically. 'You still haven't quite worked this all out yet, have you? There are more than a dozen Displacers in this stadium right now, in fact everyone who was born after 1966 is probably here.' She jerked her head in the direction of the trio below them. 'Andrew himself came here to watch this game about twenty years ago with his best friend and his wife.'

'His wife? But Andrew isn't married!'

Rachel grimaced. 'He was. And at the same time he never has been.'

'What? That doesn't make any sense. How can both of those statements be true?'

Rachel looked like she was on the point of bursting into tears. She watched the three friends below them, laughing together as if they didn't have a care in the world. She sighed. 'Andrew really should be the one who told you about this…'

Sam could see that she was reluctant to continue and that she was choosing her words carefully.

'Andrew's wife, Susan, was a Displacer as well, obviously. They met when they were in their early twenties and immediately fell madly in love, as you can see. This was actually one of the first times they

Displaced together. John, who you'll probably meet soon, is the man standing next to them and he was the one who introduced them.'

'They look happy.'

Rachel nodded. 'They were. Very.'

Sam watched them, still finding it hard to believe that the scruffy youth in dire need of a haircut was his uncle and that he had been married.

While John chanted with the crowd, the couple were leaning in close to speak to each other, alternately pressing their mouths to each other's ears, laughing and occasionally sneaked a quick kiss.

'Why haven't I ever heard of her? Did they get divorced?'

'Susan died during a Displacement.'

'That's terrible… But even so, Andrew never speaks of her and I've never seen a photo.'

Rachel turned to look at Sam. 'Andrew really hasn't told you any of this?'

'Told me what?'

'Dying during a Displacement is the worst thing that could ever happen to a Displacer because it becomes like you never existed. You disappear from the time-line, you're erased, forgotten, and everything you ever were, or did, just vanishes. That includes all photos and videos and even diary entries or newspaper articles that were about you. The only people who are able to remember you are the Displacers you met.'

'But why can't someone just go back and prevent it from happening?'

'Unfortunately, that's impossible; anything that a Displacer does whilst in the past becomes fixed and can't be changed, either by another Displacer or by the natural drift that we believe we exist to correct. By extension, that means that the death of a Displacer in the past can't be undone either, because it was a change made by them.'

'So, he can't do anything to change her death, despite being able to change just about anything else he wants to… That's horrible.' He looked at the woman a few steps below him. She seemed so alive, so happy, it was hard to believe that nobody apart from a very small group of people knew that she had even existed. 'Who was she?'

Rachel turned to face him, looking at him seriously. 'Haven't you ever wondered why everyone calls Andrew your uncle?'

Sam shrugged. 'I just figured he was an old family friend or something, that it was an honorary title.'

'He really is your uncle. Susan is your mother's younger sister, your aunt. Which makes us related, I suppose, but distantly and not through blood. I'm your aunt's husband's niece.'

'But my mother doesn't have a sister!'

'As I've been saying; she did, but never has.' Her voice almost cracked with emotion as she continued. 'Susan disappeared completely from the time-line when she died. You lost an aunt, Andrew lost a wife and your mother lost a sister, who she now doesn't even know she had. It's a tragedy that has happened far too many times over the years, to too many good people.'

'When did she die?'

'About four years ago.'

'Four years? Then why can't I remember her? I would have easily been old enough.'

'Because four years ago you hadn't gotten your powers as a Displacer yet. I was lucky, in a way, I got my own powers the month before she died. You...'

Rachel was interrupted and had to stop speaking when the England fans around them started singing at the top of their lungs and Sam took the opportunity to study the woman talking with Andrew a few rows down from them. She was as real as everyone else around them and he knew that if he went up to her he would be able to touch her and talk with her. He was finding it very hard to assimilate the fact that, to all intents and purposes, she had never existed.

Once the crowd had quietened down a bit Rachel continued. 'You still call Andrew your uncle and your mother probably still feels like she's related to him in some way, but none of you quite know why. It's all part of being a Displacer; the time-line can't erase Andrew or what he means to your family, so it provides an excuse for him being there, in his case being an honorary uncle instead of a real one.'

'Why can't we just go down there and tell them what's going to happen? Give them the chance to change their own futures.'

'Even if we did do that, as soon as we left they would forget they'd ever met us; we're in the same time as them, not the same time-line, which means that's not actually them, it's just their shadow, the trace they leave of themselves in the past.'

'Oh, right. Of course.' Sam sighed. He was beginning to see that Displacing wasn't just about fun and games after all and he didn't like it one bit.

'But that's not the worst thing. The true tragedy is that *we* get to come here and meet her and talk to her, but *he* can't.' She stabbed her finger at them, pointing almost angrily at Andrew, tears coming to her eyes finally. '*He's* already bloody here. Down there with her. He can't Displace to *any* time in her lifetime because it's *his* lifetime as well! He can't even go to any of her Displacements to see her because he's there with her already!' She wiped the tears from her eyes and took a deep breath to calm herself. 'Anyway, it's up to Andrew to tell you the details of how she died if he wants to, but I thought you had a right to know that you had an aunt.'

There was a huge cheer from the crowd and Sam spotted the teams marching out of the tunnel to the dressing rooms and onto the pitch below; eleven men in red English strips and eleven in white German ones, about to do battle, overseen by a single man in black.

'It's time to go, but I have one thing I want to do first.' Rachel brandished some scissors, opening and shutting them.

'Where did you get those from?'

'I stole them from the girl in front of me - I learnt pickpocketing from a thief in Baghdad, it comes in handy every so often. Be right back.' She grinned and then slipped through the crowd, moving easily through the press towards the trio of Displacers below. She sneaked up behind them and stood behind Susan for a few seconds then turned and made her way quickly back to Sam, putting something in her pocket.

Sam looked at her quizzically.

'A little something for Andrew - I'll show you when we get back.' She stood next to him. 'You know how to get yourself home, right?' she asked.

'Yes.'

'Do that now, I'll wait and make sure you've gone, then follow you.'

'OK.'

Sam closed his eyes and shut out the sound of the crowd around him. Thankfully, it was so constant it was like white noise. He woke the energy inside himself, feeling it building and filling his whole body. He thought of home, his family, his poor mother who had unknowingly lost a sister, he thought of his uncle…

…and woke up in Andrew's sitting room.

He opened his eyes and looked at Andrew with sympathy.

Rachel opened her eyes at the exact same time. She immediately released his hands and frowned at him. 'How the…' She turned to Andrew. 'Five seconds… FIVE BLOODY SECONDS it took him to get back here! What is this guy?'

Andrew smiled at her. 'I told you he was a natural.'

'Natural is one thing, but that…' she waved a hand at Sam. 'That is something else entirely!'

She shook her head and gave Sam one of her appraising looks before looking down. 'Oh, right! Here, I got this for you. To add to your souvenir collection. From a proper football team.' For the first time Sam saw that she had a red and white England scarf dangling from her right hand. She folded it up before holding it out to him. 'I'm not sure you're going to get much use out of it in this country, though!'

He took it and turned it around in his hands, feeling the softness of the wool. 'Wow, thank you!'

'My pleasure!'

'How did you get it?'

'I have my methods…' She winked. 'But don't worry, I didn't steal this like I did the scissors!'

She stroked his hand and gave him one of the smiles that made his insides melt before turning to Andrew. 'We saw you there with Susan. I thought you would have told Sam about his aunt already.'

The grin disappeared from Andrew's face and he winced as he remembered a painful past. 'There was never a good time and when you said "Wembley" it was already too late.' He shrugged. 'This way was as good as any for him to find out, really.'

'It shouldn't have been left to me to explain, though.'

'I know, I'm sorry.'

There was a brief silence as Andrew stared into nothing, lost in his memories.

Eventually, Rachel broke the silence. 'I brought you a souvenir as well.'

She opened her hand. Lying in it was a lock of chestnut brown hair.

'Is that…?' Andrew could barely speak as he gazed down at the hair, he reached out and gently took it from her. He lifted it to his nose and breathed in its scent. His eyes started to cloud and his voice trembled as he spoke, 'I need some more tea, anybody else want tea? I'm going to go and make some tea.'

He stood and made his way out of the room as fast as he could, but not quite fast enough to prevent Sam from seeing the tears begin to stream down his face.

They watched him go in silence.

As soon as the door closed, Sam turned to Rachel. 'How the hell did you get that without her noticing?'

'Easy enough for a ninja like me. Come on, let's get out of here; we'll give Andrew some time to himself.' She stood up and went to the door, making sure that the coast was clear before going through. Sam followed her to the front door and they went out.

CHAPTER 6
THE SHOWDOWN

As soon as they got out of the flat and onto the street Rachel started marching quickly down the road with a determined look on her face.

Sam made sure the door was closed, then had to run to catch up with her. He walked beside her as they crossed the road and went into some side streets.

'Do you know where you're going?' asked Sam.

'I'm not going anywhere. I just want to walk.'

'Fair enough.'

He walked beside her in silence, letting her work off whatever was on her mind. Eventually, after several minutes, she slowed down and her face softened. She sighed. 'I'm sorry, I just had to clear my head.'

'It's alright.'

'No, it's not, I need to stop letting my emotions get the better of me like this. But it's hard; we've lost a lot of people in recent years.'

'Really? How?'

'We don't know the specifics in most cases, because, obviously, when people die Displacing on their own we have no way of knowing what happened. We only know what happened to Susan because Andrew was there and he barely survived to tell us.'

'What did happen?'

'Now, that *really* isn't up to me to tell you. Andrew will do that when he's ready. It's enough for you to know that Displacing is dangerous at the best of times, but there are some people out there, a group of them, we think, who are working against us. And that makes it a hell of a lot more dangerous than it should be.'

'You mean, like Quentin?'

'Yes, especially Quentin. Andrew said you had met him.' There was a look of almost pure hatred in her eyes as she all but spat out Quentin's name, which made Sam inch away from her involuntarily. 'He's one of them and he's one of the worst; he's vicious, sneaky, and malicious. The others are nowhere near as bad as he is.'

'Others? Are there many of them?'

'We are sure that there are at least five of them, including Quentin, because we've had four poached from under our noses just as we were about to recruit them, but there are probably a few others who we don't know about. Oh, and there have always been rumours of a leader, who is not Quentin, by the way, but nobody has a clue who it is or has even been able to confirm if he really exists.'

'And what does the group want?'

'Money, power...' Rachel shrugged. 'The usual things that unscrupulous people want. But instead of getting it in the traditional manner, they manipulate the past to create a favourable present for themselves. It's actually harder than you would think; you can't just go back and buy shares in Apple, for example, because as soon as you came back to the present the purchase wouldn't exist anymore. They have to do little things, bring back small items, stuff that they can carry in their hands, like artworks or the diamond you stopped Quentin from getting. Or they influence people like governments and kings to shift the balance of power to their advantage... By the way, do you know we're being followed?'

'What?' Sam looked over his shoulder. Scurrying along about twenty metres behind them was one of Rafa's friends, trying to be inconspicuous, but failing dismally.

'Do you have a fan club already?' asked Rachel, grinning. 'Can I join?'

'Oh, god, don't they ever give up?' Sam sighed, embarrassed. He hadn't wanted to tell Rachel about Rafa because he didn't want to look weak in front of her. 'I have a bit of a bully problem, but it's OK, there's only one of them today.'

'Think again.'

From out of a side-street, a bit further back, ran another of the goons, pointing in Sam's direction. He was followed closely by Rafa and the fourth goon from the group and they all hurried to catch up with their friend. There was a huge smile on Rafa's face that Sam didn't like.

'Did these guys do that to your face?'

Sam involuntarily reached up to touch the skin on his cheek, which was pink and raw after the scabs from his run-in with Rafa had fallen off, a move that also exposed his skinned elbows to her.

Rachel's eyes narrowed as she took in his wounds. 'That would be a yes.'

'Yes! OK? They beat me up and I would really like to start running, please, so they can't do it again!' Sam nervously tugged on her arm, trying to get her to start moving.

'Nonsense! I want to meet your friends.'

Rachel gently shook off his hand and Sam reluctantly followed her as she strode purposefully off the pavement and into a small square. It was one of those squares that are so prevalent in Barcelona, with a drinking fountain and a couple of benches, which always have a congregation of pensioners and pigeons. She stopped and looked around the space, empty in the summer sun, and nodded in satisfaction before turning to face the fast approaching youths.

'You really don't, they're not very nice…'

Rachel waved away Sam's words, smiling confidently at him, then looked up at the boys as they stopped in front of them, forming a line - a solid wall of thuggery.

They stood with their arms crossed, glowering at Sam and Rachel, trying to look intimidating.

Their tactics worked on Sam and he almost took a step away, but Rachel seemed to be completely unafraid and wasn't backing down. This didn't do much to settle his nerves; she still had no idea what she was getting into.

'Who's the piece of skirt, Vives? Is she your girlfriend?' Rafa stared at Rachel, looking her up and down and grinning lasciviously. 'She's far too good looking for the likes of you... I think you should introduce us and we'll see if she wants to be with a real man.'

He blew a kiss at Rachel, who just sneered at him in return.

Sam started to translate for Rachel, who hadn't understood Rafa's Spanish. 'He said…'

She interrupted him with a smile. 'It was probably something inane about me being too good for you and that I should go home with him, right?'

'Er, yes. How did you know?'

'I know his type.' She tilted her head to one side and looked at Sam quizzically. 'You're not afraid of him, are you?'

'Not usually, not anymore. I can handle him one on one, no problem. And by that I mean that I can run faster than he can, but if you hadn't noticed it's not just him to be afraid of…' Sam gestured at the boys who had surrounded them.

Rachel looked around the boys with interest, as if seeing them for the first time. They smiled, leering at her.

'There's two of us and only four of them - it should be interesting. Now do you want to get them out of your hair, or are you going to be a wimp your whole life?' She shook her head and smiled wryly. 'Wow, I feel like Marty McFly talking to his dad in the past… OK, then, why don't you just take Biff and I'll deal with the rest.'

'Sorry?!?' Sam looked at her incredulously, he couldn't believe that this girl was suggesting they take on four bullies, all of them larger and heavier than they were.

Rachel explained it to him again, slowly, as if to a little child. 'I'll deal with these three…' Rachel pointed at each of Rafa's friends in turn, 'while you take care of that big oaf,' she stabbed her finger at Rafa. 'Do you need me to draw a diagram for you?' She grinned.

Sam was bemused; she actually seemed to be enjoying herself and almost looking forward to the prospect of receiving a beating.

Rafa was getting impatient. He was looking back and forth from Sam to Rachel as they spoke, but had no idea what they were saying. He didn't do well in English classes, in any class for that matter, but English was his worst by far; he could barely manage to ask for ice cream, he certainly couldn't follow a full conversation. 'Enough already, Vives, we're going to pound you into the floor while your girlfriend here watches and then we'll take her home with us and show her the good time that you're obviously not equipped for.'

The four boys laughed, enjoying the moment. They could see that Sam was frightened, which was giving them confidence.

However, they were completely ignoring Rachel, which meant they hadn't yet seen the almost bloodthirsty look on her face.

While his friends started to close in, Rafa reached out to grab the front of Sam's shirt and lifted his fist to strike.

Suddenly, Rachel dropped into a fighting stance and turned to face the three goons. They halted their advance and stared at her, incredulously, before they started to laugh.

Their laughter was cut off abruptly as Rachel exploded into motion and leapt at them.

She spun like a whirlwind, moving between them from one to another, striking out on all sides with fists and feet.

The youths tried to fight back, but they were unable to make contact; next to her it looked like they were moving in slow motion and she hit them over and over while ducking and weaving around their clumsy swings. She didn't do much damage to them with her attacks, though, instead, to Sam it looked more like she was trying to show them her superiority and frighten them into backing away.

Sam and Rafa shared a glance. For once they were united in something - amazement.

Even though Rachel's strikes weren't hard enough to do much individually, the damage started to add up due to the sheer number of them that she was landing. The three thugs were soon struggling to draw breath, both because of the energy they were expending and the result of being hit in all the right places by the incredibly accurate girl. As they tired, their attempts to retaliate became wilder and began to prove more dangerous to each other than to her and several times one or other of them believed he had a clear shot at her only to miss and hit one of his companions, delivering far more damage in one blow than she ever had.

Eventually, they had had enough. An unspoken agreement between them and as one they broke away and ran into the street, narrowly avoiding being run over by a passing car.

Rachel wasn't even breathing heavily and she laughed as she watched them go. As soon as they disappeared around the corner she turned back to face Sam and Rafa, who were frozen like statues, staring at her with their mouths open.

She smiled at them sweetly. 'OK, your turn, boys.'

Sam snapped out of his daze first and looked up at Rafa. He pushed away the hand that was still weakly holding him by the neck of his t-shirt and stepped back, raising his own hands in a poor imitation of Rachel's fighting stance.

Rafa blinked and looked at Sam in turn.

A second later he broke into a sprint, desperately trying to catch up with the rest of his gang, his tail firmly between his legs.

Rachel came to stand beside Sam and together they watched the bully run away. She was laughing, 'Now, that was fun!'

Sam turned to her. 'How...? What...?'

Rachel just grinned, enjoying his confusion. She raised an eyebrow.

Finally, Sam found the right words. 'How did you do that?'

'I told you I was a ninja.' She looked around, spotted a nearby bench and led the way to it. 'You have a lot to learn, Grasshopper. Come on, let's sit down and talk.'

They sat down and Sam swivelled to look at her. Her breathing was already completely normal, her clothes were unruffled and her hair was still in place - it was like the fight had never happened.

He waited for her to start speaking and tell him just what the hell had just happened, but she just sat there, smiling faintly watching the traffic go by as if it were the most important thing in the world.

'Well?' he prompted finally.

She laughed. 'You have no patience!'

'What is it with you people and patience?' Sam growled. 'Andrew's always doing this to me as well; making me wait for answers. It's really annoying!'

'That is because you haven't grasped the most important thing about Displacers yet.'

'And what's that?'

'We're incredibly patient.' She grinned at him.

'Oh. Ha, ha.' Sam looked away, sulking.

'Seriously now, we *are* patient, but there is a good reason.'

'Yeah,' Sam grumbled. 'Andrew told me how old he was and that I should be patient because I'm going to live for, like, a thousand years or something.'

Rachel laughed. 'Not quite *that* long, but yes, we tend to think in lifetimes instead of years.' She turned to look at him finally and gave him one of the smiles he liked so much. 'So, how old do you think I am, then?'

'I don't know, sixteen? Seventeen maybe?'

She nodded. 'In absolute, traditionally counted, real-world numbers I am sixteen, yes, and I will celebrate my seventeenth birthday early next year. However, including today's I've done seventeen Displacements since I turned fifteen and if you add it all up I'm actually closer to thirty. I could have been a lot older, but I've had to do quite a few short missions for Andrew that didn't take much more than a week each and haven't had a chance to go on some of the longer trips that I've got planned yet.'

Sam was shocked and for a moment he didn't quite know what to say. Some of his teachers were around thirty and he tried to reconcile how he looked at them and how adult they seemed, with how he saw this girl, a girl who he was very quickly growing to like. He found that he just couldn't do it and with no just a little horror he realised that it would also make her closer to his mother's age than his.

'You look pretty good for a thirty year old.' He forced a smile, trying not to think of the age difference between them and how it would probably mean she would never look at him the way he all of a sudden wanted her to.

'Thank you!'

She laughed as if she didn't have a care in the world, just like someone his age would.

Most of his worries evaporated and his smile became genuine, but he frowned as something occurred to him. 'I thought you said you'd been Displacing for four years?'

'I got my *powers* four years ago, yes, when I was twelve, but the Society has some pretty strict rules about children Displacing and wouldn't let me do anything until I was fifteen, apart from some training missions and a few joyrides to safe places, like the one we've just been to, always holding hands with members and for less than a day at a time.'

'You got your powers at twelve? Is that normal? And how come I got mine so late?'

'Pretty much, yes.' She grinned and looked him up and down critically. 'It's fairly closely linked to puberty - boys typically get their powers later, usually around 14, but since you're such a late bloomer...'

'That doesn't matter; you know I'm going to be taller than you in a year or so!'

'Size isn't everything, Sam, darling. Has nobody ever told you that?' She batted her eyes at him and he just had to laugh.

'OK, so you've got a bit of a head start on me, but I'll catch up, don't you worry, after all, I can Displace twice a month.' He stuck his tongue out at her and it was her turn to laugh.

'You have a good point, but don't overdo it; I don't like older men.' She winked and patted him on the cheek before sticking her own beautifully pointed tongue out and crossing her eyes.

'Anyway...' Sam shook his head in exasperation. There was no winning an argument with her, even a silly one, but he didn't care; it was just too much fun being around her. 'So, you've lived, what, twelve or thirteen years in the past? What have you done with all that extra time?'

'Andrew doesn't often allow me to have a Displacement for myself, but when he does I like to study stuff - martial arts and things. I lived in a Shaolin Temple for just over two years, which was a bit of a laugh actually, spent another three years with a guy in Okinawa, which was the most incredible experience of my life, and I even ran around with the SAS for about six months. Oh, yeah, and believe it or not, I actually got to spend a few months studying with Bruce Lee in Seattle, which was pretty memorable, as you can probably imagine!'

'Wow, that's so cool!' Sam made a mental note to seriously expand his list of things he wanted to do in the past; Rachel had done things that hadn't even occurred to him and the light in her eyes, her enthusiasm and the smile on her lips as she recounted her experiences just made him want to get started having his own adventures even sooner. He hoped that he would get the chance to Displace with her again, but next time for much longer, so that he could get to know her better...

His train of thought was interrupted when Rachel gave him a half-smile, raising an eyebrow and he blushed as he realised that he had been staring at her in silence for quite some time. He looked away and found a particularly interesting pigeon to watch as he turned his mind back to the conversation. 'Um. So you learned martial arts? How? I thought we didn't bring that kind of stuff back with us?'

'We don't bring back the skills that we get when we Displace, like the languages that we know innately when we arrive and the things we need to know, but we do get to keep anything we spend time learning - exactly like if we'd spent the time learning it in the present. It's the same as the memories of a Displacement; you wouldn't forget the things that you did in the past or the conversations you have, so why would you forget the things you read or learn? And thankfully that includes muscle memory. Of course, every time I learn a new style or technique or something I have to spend hours practising it here in the present, because you don't get to bring your body back with you. Hours in the gym during a Displacement don't mean squat back here!'

'That's pretty handy...' Several new possibilities sprang to life in Sam's mind. There were so many things he could learn and not just martial arts like Rachel - even though he didn't like football very much he could train with Pelé or Maradona and come back to play for Barça, or he could study with one of the great fencing masters and become world champion.

'It's not all fun and games, though, Sam,' said Rachel with a frown, anticipating his thought processes. 'Apart from the very real risk of dying and being erased from history, just think of what it will do to your relationship with your family. Let's say you Displaced for a few years each time, you could easily accumulate twenty, twenty-five years of experience in total over a year here in the present, which wouldn't be at all excessive. What do you think it is going to be like to be sixteen in body, but older in actual years than your parents? They will still treat you like a child when in your mind you will be anything but. And just think how many times you'll have to go through puberty!' She said this with a laugh, although Sam could see she was being serious. 'You really should learn how to take care of yourself as soon as possible, though, it'll help you with your bully problem and keep you safer in Displacements.'

This was something Sam could agree on and he nodded enthusiastically. 'And it's also really cool.'

They shared a grin.

'Speaking of cool, I keep meaning to ask. What's with all the awful names we have for everything? "Calming", "Preparing"... Even "Displacers" isn't exactly the coolest of names for a group of superheroes.'

Rachel chuckled and shook her head. 'Yeah, it's really not! I certainly wouldn't go around boasting that I'm a Displacer, or put it on a t-shirt. John's actually been trying to get them to change the names of everything for about twenty years, but apparently it's tradition or something. Apparently the name and the terms have all been around for a few hundred years, ever since the founding of "The Honourable Society of Displacers".'

'That makes sense; they probably sounded quite cool in the 18th and 19th century.'

'Probably! Anyway, if you were going to change the name of the group, what would you choose? All the good names have been taken by films and comic books. Same with our abilities - do you want to shout "flame on!" every time you Prepare?'

Sam smiled wryly. 'Yeah, I suppose you're right.'

She grinned. 'I'm sure John does something like that in his mind every time he Displaces, though.'

'"By the power of Grayskull!"'

'That's a good one! You watch classic cartoons too?' Rachel laughed. '"To infinity and beyond!"'

'What about "Puppy Power!"'

Rachel guffawed. 'I'm *sure* that's the one! John as Scrappy Doo, that's actually quite apt... I'll have to tell everyone about that! I think you're going to fit in very well with our little "Band of Merry Men", Sam.'

'Nah, that name will never catch on, it's too obvious.'

'It was worth a try.' Rachel grinned and stood up. 'Come on, we should be getting back to Andrew; he's probably had his cup of tea by now and be back to normal. He'll want to continue with his lectures.'

'Oh, good…' Sam stood and followed her along the road, jogging to catch up with her purposeful stride. He smiled, content; this was turning out to be even more fun than he'd thought it would be.

CHAPTER 7
PRACTICE

Andrew didn't have any more lectures planned for that day, or if he did he wasn't in the mood to give them. He just told Sam to go and continue practising Preparing.

Sam reluctantly said goodbye to Rachel and left the flat, already looking forward to coming back. He wasn't too upset that he wouldn't have any more lessons that day, though, because he had a lot to think about; he had big plans to amplify his list of future Displacements and wanted to jot down his ideas before he forgot them.

He was almost all the way home before he realised that he wasn't at all worried about being ambushed by Rafa and he was hopeful that he had seen the last of the bully, at least until school started again in September. He didn't think that Rafa was going to be back any time soon, unless somehow he found an entire army to back him up, but even that didn't worry him too much because apparently he had all the time in the world to learn how to fight and if he managed to get half the skill that Rachel had, then he would have no problem defending himself against the sluggish bullies. He resolved to take her advice and get some training as soon as he could; like she had said, it would help him survive in the past and would also make his life a whole lot better in the present. Also, there was the added bonus that she might agree to accompany him if he went on a Displacement like that...

However, his excitement over the ever-growing list of things that he planned to do with his future in the past was dampened somewhat by the things that Rachel had said about his outgrowing his family. He didn't want to believe that his relationship with his family would somehow be soured by his experiences as a Displacer, but he could see how it might be and, just in case she was right, he spent the rest of the day with them. He played games with his mother and Violeta in the afternoon, helping colour in Violeta's drawings, and then in the evening, when his father came home from work, he sat on the sofa with him and watched Star Wars for what must have been the ninth or tenth time, saying the words together, waving around toy lightsabers and sharing a bowl of popcorn.

Playing and having fun with his family made Sam realise that things had gotten far too serious for him recently and a few hours of being just a child again really helped him to relax. That night he got the best night's sleep that he'd had in a long time, and it wasn't just because of the Displacement that day - in fact he wasn't feeling nearly as tired as he had when he had gone to Port Royal; going tandem seemed to use less energy, especially if you were in the passenger seat. Also, not having to worry about Rafa was such a relief that, for the first time in years, he was able to let go of the fears that had always been in the back of his mind.

Andrew was back to his normal self the next day when Sam turned up at his flat. He said nothing about his wife and the circumstances of her death and instead concentrated solely on his tutelage of Sam. He seemed to be fine; the world knew nothing of Susan and it appeared that ignoring it was his way of coping with it.

Sam spent that day, the next, and the ones after that, practising Preparing and Calming and listening to Rachel and Andrew telling stories about their Displacements.

It was a very enjoyable time and it passed very quickly, with many cups of tea in pleasant company and comfortable walks with Rachel, getting to know her better.

About two weeks into Sam's training, Andrew brought out a set of three ring binders, two blue and one red. He placed the blue ones on the coffee table before opening the red one and showing Sam the first page. It was covered with dates and places with their distinguishing features, all neatly set out in rows and columns - like a spreadsheet, but on paper. 'Most old-school Displacers like me put together a collection of something like historical flash cards which are pages full of information, dates, places - whatever works for them in order to be able to focus on a point in history to Displace to. It's not essential to make these anymore; nowadays you can just go to a Wikipedia page, read it and then Displace without much problem, but most of us like to do it this way.'

Andrew flicked through the binder. There was page after page of his neat writing, all organised by year, starting with the year he was born and working backwards through time. 'Raw data is usually enough to get to a specific place and time, but it can be imprecise, so we use the experiences of other people in the Society to narrow it down.' He pointed to an entry where he had made extensive notes based on information he had received from someone called Richard Peterson. 'We used to have regular discussions, talks by the Elders - nice social evenings that would familiarise our members with important time-lines to make it easier for them if they were ever called to go to those periods. We don't do that anymore and it's a real shame because they used to be good fun, but there's no call for it because nowadays we have access to computers and databases with all the information we could possibly need. It's far too easy, in my opinion,' he wrinkled his nose as if detecting a bad smell. 'And John's even working on an App, for god's sake.'

He rolled his eyes and the two teenagers exchanged an amused glance. He saw them and laughed. 'Yeah, yeah, I know - I'm old and out of touch. But I'm not too much of an old fogey to recognise that, no matter how much I dislike it, this easy access to information is actually making our lives a lot easier - in the past if you didn't have enough details to Displace then you might have found yourself in the right time, but with a long walk or a lot of borders to sneak across.'

He put down the red binder and picked up one of the blue ones. He handed it to Sam, who looked through it as Andrew continued.

'These two contain a private record of all my Displacements - where I went, who I was, what I did and as close as I can get to the exact days I was there. Above everything else, the dates are the most important information to take note of because you need to know if it is possible for you to go to a specific time and place if it is required of you. As I said, these are my personal records, but we also have to write a second report for the Society's records which are stored in the archives in London. We tend to make those reports much more impersonal, just a cold record of what we did and when, less who we met and what fun we had, if you know what I mean - send the facts to the society and keep the memories and feelings for yourself. You should start to write your own accounts if you haven't already.'

Sam's eyes flickered over the titles on the pages. Andrew had made what looked like hundreds of Displacements and seen so many famous episodes in history - here was the storming of the Bastille, there was the death of Julius Caesar… and so many battles! Hastings, the Battle of Britain, Agincourt, Bunker Hill, the Somme… So many things that Andrew had witnessed that Sam had heard about at school or seen in films.

Too soon, Andrew closed the folder with a loud snap, making Sam jump and leaving him wanting for more. 'Anyway, enough stories for now, it's time for more practice. Come on, let's see if you can bring that time down even further.'

'Not possible,' said Rachel with a smile.

Andrew's experiences were fresh in his mind as Sam settled in and closed his eyes. He was getting a bit tired, he'd already done this five times that day, but looking at the things that Andrew had done had given him fresh energy and an increased desire to complete his training as quickly as he could and get Displacing for himself.

His mind drifted back to Andrew's reports as the familiar sensation started spreading through his body and he remembered the last one that he'd seen; the Battle of the Somme. He'd heard so much about the trenches of World War One in history class, seen them so many times in films and he wondered what it had been like to actually be there. He decided to ask Andrew about it later when they had finished working; he'd like to hear a firsthand account.

The tingling feeling infused his limbs and then his torso before finally spreading to his head. He frowned. Somehow, subtly, it felt different this time.

Suddenly, Andrew's voice was crying out with some urgency, 'Sam! Calm…'

'…yerself, laddie!' The voice was gruff and had a thick Scottish accent attached to it. It definitely wasn't Andrew's and it could be barely heard over the constant din of explosions that assaulted him.

Sam opened his eyes with a start and saw that the world around him was coloured in shades of brown.

Disorientated and shocked by the awful noise, for a second he thought that he was looking at a sepia photograph or something, but quickly realised that he wasn't even in Andrew's flat any more. He groaned; if he kept Displacing by mistake he was going to start making a name for himself that he really didn't want. That was the least of his worries at that moment, though, because it seemed that he had been thrust into the middle of a battle in World War One.

It was early morning, the sun was just coming up and the smoke that was everywhere was being blown around by a biting wind. He was wearing a drab brown tunic top, had a heavy metal helmet on his head and an antiquated rifle made mostly of wood clutched tightly in his hands. He was leaning against the bare earth wall of a trench, standing on spongy, waterlogged and rotting wooden boards. It was muddy, filthy, and the smell was awful; a mix of unwashed bodies, open latrines, mould and rotting wood, all with a bitter chemical undertone that made Sam gasp for breath and his eyes water. He wiped his eyes with his waterlogged sleeve, trying to clear them, but that only made them stream more; his clothing was impregnated with something sour that stung them. To either side of him were long lines of men, packed shoulder to shoulder against the wall; soldiers, evidently from a Scottish regiment because they were all wearing kilts along with the same brown tunic and metal helmet that he was and all had the same type of guns, which looked like little more than toys to Sam's eyes. They all seemed fairly calm and stoic, despite the deafening thunder of the big guns that was making Sam twitch nervously, and some of them even appeared to be sleeping standing up.

Sam glanced down and saw that he too was wearing a kilt - he'd been wondering why his legs were so cold. He self-consciously pushed the strange garment back down as the wind lifted it and shuddered as the gale swirled around parts of him that weren't used to being left so unprotected from the elements. He shivered and shifted his weight, feeling his socks squelch unpleasantly in his sodden boots. His tunic and the shirt below it hung heavy and damp against his skin and there was a fine drizzle in the air that was numbing his hands and his face.

Suddenly, the gunfire stopped and there was silence aside from the ringing in his ears and the chattering of his teeth.

'Keep yerself calm, laddie. Not long to wait now. The shelling's stopped and it'll be our turn soon, you'll see; it's the same dance every time.'

Sam turned towards the sound of the voice and looked at the man beside him. He was leaning casually against the muddy wall, a roughly rolled up cigarette dangling from his mouth. He couldn't have been more than twenty-five years old, but the worry lines on his face that were ingrained with filth and the dark black bags under his eyes made him seem much older. Lank ginger hair poked out from under his helmet, greasy and stained brown with mud. On the surface he didn't look nervous, but Sam couldn't tell whether it was because he wasn't afraid or whether he was resigned, although there was a slight tremor in his hand that betrayed his tension as he reached up to pull the cigarette out of his mouth and offered it to Sam, holding it between two fingers with cracked and bleeding nails that had been bitten to the quick. 'Want a drag? It'll help calm ye.'

'No, thank you. I don't smoke.'

'Suit yerself.' He shrugged and put the cigarette back between his lips. 'Ye should start, though; it'll do ye good, put hair on yer chest.'

While taking up smoking was in no way a good idea in Sam's mind, the man's advice to calm down certainly was, and that was what he tried to do. He closed his eyes and concentrated, feeling the tingling sensation begin and start to spread. He only needed a few seconds…

Whistles sounded from all around and the man slapped Sam hard on the arm, instantly breaking his concentration.

'Come on, laddie, up we go and sharply now, ye dinna want tae git shot fer cowardice!'

Sam opened his eyes and saw that the men had begun scrambling up the walls of the trench, scaling the long ladders that were spaced out along the line.

Sam followed the men up the nearest ladder, clutching his rifle in one hand and climbing with the other, doing his best to not look upwards, and emerged into the weak sunshine of the battlefield.

He assembled with the other soldiers in a rough line, several men deep, standing shoulder to shoulder on the flat ground in front of the trench, waiting for the order to advance.

Nervously, Sam looked around. The regiment he belonged to were only a small part of what was now a long, unbroken line of men that stretched into the distance on both sides and that was only hazily visible through the mist of the early morning and the smoke that was left over from the shelling.

Sam had a feeling that he really didn't want to be there very much longer. He took a deep breath and closed his eyes again, but before he could Calm himself and get home the whistles sounded once more and he was jostled on all sides and forced to walk as the line started to advance slowly.

The man who had spoken to him before was still beside him. He took the remains of his cigarette out of his mouth and threw it down, grinding it into the mud with his next step, then spoke to Sam out of the side of his mouth as they advanced. 'What's yer name, laddie?'

'Sorry?'

'Yer name! Come on, talk tae me, it'll take yer mind off things.'

'Sam, it's Sam.'

'Pleased to meet ye, Sammy, I'm Jock. Ye just arrived, right?'

'You could say that.'

'Och, rough luck having an offensive yer first day, but at least ye haven't been hanging around getting bored like the rest of us poor fools. Small mercies, aye?'

'I suppose.'

They advanced very slowly towards a destination that Sam couldn't see - visibility was still very poor. It was almost peaceful and would have been a nice stroll if it weren't for the holes in the ground and the complete lack of any birdsong or other life in fact. He was even starting to warm up as he walked forward; it was hard work moving with his boots caked in mud and alternatively slipping or sticking in the soft earth.

Suddenly, the quiet was shattered once more by the booming of explosions and all along the line men and mud were thrown into the air. Sam jumped and glanced nervously from side to side.

'Steady, laddie, dinna fash yerself. If it's yer time, it's yer time.'

'But why are we just walking like this? Surely we would be less of a target if we ran?'

Jock nodded. 'Aye, that we would, but this is the way things are done. The generals like their wars to be nice and civilised, they like their dying to be done all neat and tidy like in lovely rows. Because that'll show Jerry what fer.'

Sam was appalled and he itched to run, to anywhere. He could find a hole and hide in it until he could get himself home.

Shells were exploding everywhere now. Thankfully, they weren't the huge explosions that Hollywood films always portray, but they were enough to do serious damage to the line of men and the sound of screams filled the air.

'I have to go, I have to go,' Sam muttered. It would be so easy to die here - death just seemed to be reaching out a hand at random and picking whomever it pleased. It could so easily be him next. He could feel his control over himself slipping away. His breathing was coming rapidly and he couldn't stop his eyes from darting around, like a wild animal trying to find the way to escape. His hands tightened on his rifle until the wood of the stock creaked under the pressure and his legs shook with every step he took, his muscles trembling uncontrollably.

Jock glanced sideways at him, concerned, his face more creased than ever. 'Stop talking like that, laddie! Ye'll get yerself in trouble!' He jerked his head back urgently, indicating for Sam to look over his shoulder. 'Keep walking, but tek a gander behind us.'

Sam glanced behind. Following the thick line of soldiers was a much smaller, sparser line of men wearing caps instead of helmets. They had pistols held at shoulder height and were watching the men like hawks. 'Who are they?'

'They're the bloody officers. They have orders to shoot anyone who retreats, it's bad for morale, ye ken? Now face front before ye attract attention to yerself!'

Sam hastily looked to the front again. This was getting worse by the second, somehow he needed to find some peace to Calm himself and get out of the hell he had found himself in.

The explosions were coming more and more often now in an almost constant thunder that shook the ground beneath his feet and threw fresh smoke and dirt into the air, further obscuring his vision. Suddenly they came to thin lines of barbed wire, strung across their path, but the men in the lead were ready and tossed blankets over them so that the advance could trample over them without stopping.

Over the sound of the shelling began a new, even more terrifying sound, one Sam knew very well from old war films; machine guns were chattering as they opened up from the German trenches and they quickly added considerably to the already high death toll. The line of allied soldiers started to thin as more and more bodies fell from it, but each time a gap opened it was closed by the men behind so that a solid wall was presented to the enemy that they couldn't possibly miss.

'FIX BAYONETS!' came the cry from the officers stalking behind and Sam watched bemused as his own hand, seemingly by itself, pulled a long straight knife from his webbing and attached it to the end of his rifle. The click as it went into place was echoed by thousands of other bayonets along the line of men; a signalling of intent, a stiffening of resolve, and Sam found himself straightening slightly, walking taller despite his terror. The motion of fixing the bayonet had been very familiar somehow and had brought about an automatic reaction in him; discipline and training that he had never had, recalled by a body that was his, but not his at the same time.

Men continued to drop from the line into the mud all around him, but somehow Sam was suddenly unafraid. That half-remembered training had asserted itself and his vision had narrowed so that all he could see was the line of spiked helmets that was now visible, poking above the German trenches about a hundred metres away. He slid down into a huge, muddy shell hole with a pool of stagnant and stinking water at the bottom and scrambled up the other side, striding determinedly ahead.

Jock was still there with him. 'This is it, laddie, time for the crunch.' The man's face was set in a determined grimace, just like Sam's now was. 'Let's take it to them!'

Sam nodded, confident now that everything would be fine.

Then his world turned upside down.

When Sam opened his eyes he was lying on the ground, flat on his back, looking up at a grey sky with eyes that didn't seem to want to remain focussed on anything.

He couldn't quite remember what he was doing there. He had a vague impression in his mind of a girl with golden hair, but wasn't sure what she had to do with him lying in the open air. He thought that perhaps there had been a picnic, but he couldn't for the life of him remember coming out on one with her, although someone was definitely barbecuing somewhere nearby, and not doing it very well, because there was an awful stench of burning and a lot of smoke in the air, making his eyes water.

Several men ran past, spraying him with mud and water, interrupting his chain of thought. They were strangely dressed in brown shirts and funny skirts and holding long sticks and he frowned; they shouldn't be playing hockey this close to people having lunch, it was dangerous - someone could get hurt. He wanted to call out to them, to scold them, to get them to stop or move somewhere else, but all that came was a cough and they were gone before he had found his voice.

He tried to relax again, thinking that he would quite like to go back to sleep, but there was something nagging at the back of his mind that wouldn't let him rest, something about the situation that didn't seem right, or that he wasn't quite understanding and he got the impression that there was something urgent that he had to do, something very important.

Calm.

He smiled as the word floated into his mind; that was it - he needed to be calm. In which case he had nothing to worry about, because he was already calm. Calm and happy.

There was a ringing in his ears that was almost completely blocking out any sound, but some noises were getting past it - loud bangs like fireworks and the shouts and screams of what appeared to be hundreds of people having a lot of fun.

He yawned and closed his eyes with an annoyed sigh; if only everyone would just quieten down a bit, he'd be able to go back to sleep until that girl got back from wherever she had disappeared to...

The ground shook as a shell hit the ground only a few metres from Sam, rocking him and showering him in mud and other things. His eyes shot open and the world snapped back into focus as the terror and urgency came rushing back. This was no picnic, this was a war and he had to move, he couldn't stay where he was or when he was, he had to get home, however he could.

He tried to sit up, but his left arm wasn't working for some reason, so he rolled onto his side and looked around. He was lying on the slope of the shell hole that he had just crossed, so he was safe from the machine gun fire for the moment and at least a bit protected from the shelling, but he was still in mortal danger. Jock was lying next to him and he started to reach out to him for help, but froze, horrified. He was staring up at the sky, unblinking, and he wasn't in one piece anymore. Sam closed his eyes, shutting out the sight, but it was too late, the image was already burned into his mind.

That was when the pain finally hit him.

He collapsed back into the mud, clutching his unresponsive left arm. He'd broken bones before, but he didn't remember it hurting this much; the pain was almost paralysing in its intensity.

His hearing was starting to come back and he slowly became aware of the sound of screaming, loud in his ears, coming from very close, and he looked around for the source. Obviously it wasn't coming from the unfortunate Jock, but he found that there was nobody else nearby. Mystified, he took a deep breath to ask who it was and call out for help, but the screaming abruptly stopped. He realised that it had been him screaming all along and he could feel his throat rasping from the effort.

He closed his eyes, forcing himself to breath normally and when he had regained a little of his composure, he tried to move again, to claw his way out of the hole and make his way back towards the trench and safety, but there was no strength in his legs and he just slipped back and sank into the mud. He kept trying, over and over, and barely managed to get his head out above the level of the ground before collapsing, utterly exhausted.

He looked out over the battlefield towards the German lines. The British were still advancing and he wanted to cry out to them, to get them to stop before it was too late, before they died like Jock. He wanted them to retreat, to run to come and help him, take him back to the safety of the trenches - he no longer cared about being shot as a coward, he just wanted to get away, to escape.

A series of explosions went off close by, showering him with more dirt. His situation was very precarious up on the edge of the hole and, realising that there was no way he was going to make it all the way to the British lines on his own, he pushed himself backwards. He slipped a few feet down the slope and curled up in a ball, right back where he had come from.

More explosions went off around him, shaking him, making him slide further down the slope, juddering his arm and sending a fresh wave of pain through him that almost caused him to pass out again.

He was panicking now, terrified, in real danger of losing his mind, of losing control. Becoming almost delirious with the fear and the pain. Tears were streaming down his face and he could feel his throat cracking as the screams came from him again, unbidden.

Part of him still couldn't believe that this was actually happening, still expected it to be a nightmare that he would wake up from at any second. That part of him was telling him to just give up, to lie back down and close his eyes, but the other part of him knew that that was the worst thing he could do and that there had to be a way out, if he could only find it.

'RETREAT!'

The shouts of the officers and the noise of their whistles could barely be heard over the incredible din of the battle. A few men in caps appeared at the edge of the hole, already making their way back to the British lines. They barely paused as they waved frantically for the rest of the men to come, so desperate were they to get to safety themselves. Seconds later the other soldiers started streaming by, running headlong back towards their own lines, all discipline gone. There were more of them alive than Sam thought possible; somehow they had lived through this hell. A couple of them fell into the hole, missing Sam by inches and splashing face-first into the water at the bottom of the shell hole before picking themselves up and scrambling up the far side, chased by gunfire and artillery.

He lifted his good arm and tried to call out, tried to catch their attention, tried to get them to help him, but they were too preoccupied with their own safety and either didn't see him or didn't want to stop.

The last of them disappeared from his sight behind the lip of the shell hole and once again he was alone with Jock.

They had left him.

He didn't blame them; he wasn't sure that he would have stopped either, but with them went his last hope of getting to safety.

Sam rolled over onto his back and looked up at the dark clouds overhead, blinking against the smoke and the drizzle in the air. The shells continued to hit the ground all around, shaking him. A particularly close explosion rocked him, sending fresh agony through him and igniting sparks behind his eyes. His vision darkened momentarily and he put his hand to his head. It came away covered in red, a splash of unwelcome colour in a monotone world. He gasped for breath, fighting to remain conscious, but found it difficult to take in air because of an unpleasant pressure on his right side.

He felt helpless. He just wanted it all to stop, wanted to go home, but there was nothing he could do to change his situation and again that voice in the back of his head was whispering to him to just give up. There was no rest; the shells were falling all around, constant, and he knew that at any moment one of them could drop right on top of him. He would never feel it coming, it would just be the end. He would die. He was terrified of being killed and desperately wanted to live, but at the same time he almost welcomed the prospect; he wanted the torment to end and saw no other way out.

But then the shells from the big German guns began to move further away, chasing the British back to their lines, giving him a moment of respite.

Some of the dust settled from the air and he gasped as a fresh breeze wafted over him, the cold of it a welcome stimulus, serving to sharpen his mind where before it had only numbed his limbs. Some of the irrational fear fled and a shred of reason forced its way in, giving him a new purpose - he mustn't die here on a battlefield in a time that wasn't his own; his family would forget him as if he had never existed and Andrew would have another dead family member to mourn. And Rachel...

Rachel.

It was the thought of Rachel, more than anything else that spurred him to keep trying and not give up.

He closed his eyes, attempting to block out the noise and relax so that he could concentrate, but it was no use, he couldn't do it; there was just too many distractions. He couldn't Calm injured in the middle of a battle. He couldn't get home.

The world around him began to fade as his vision closed in and the noises became dull as he began to fall into unconsciousness. The blood pouring from his head was pooling beneath him on the earth, wetting his cheek along with tears of frustration and anger.

It would be so easy just to give in and listen to that part of him that was insisting that it wasn't worth trying, to go to sleep and let the pain just wash away.

The heavens opened up and the rain started pouring down in earnest, soaking him completely in seconds and that sparked something in him. His thoughts leapt into sharp focus, just for an instant, but long enough for a memory to come to the forefront in his mind: Andrew had once said something about emergencies, that there was a way you could get back if you were in trouble or too much pain…

Water!

His eyes shot open and he lifted his head just enough to look down at the bottom of the deep shell hole; it was partially filled with water and getting deeper by the second in the downpour, but would it be enough? Whether it was or not, he had to try, because it might well be the last hope that he had.

He rolled onto his stomach, almost passing out from the pain as his left arm shifted and the broken bones rasped together. He cried out, both with the agony and the effort, as he started to crawl on his belly, digging his good hand into the mud to pull himself to the bottom of the hole.

He reached out his arm and put it into the filthy water, immediately feeling the tingling sensation begin.

All of a sudden, the noise from the explosions and the shooting stopped and shouts rose from behind him, from the enemy lines. He couldn't understand them, but they were definitely coming closer - the German infantry were counter-attacking.

It was suddenly even more urgent that he get out of there and he summoned all his remaining energy to lunge forwards and, screaming from the pain, he flopped face-first into the water.

The pool wasn't more than a few feet deep, but it was much more than he had expected and he plunged under the surface, immediately became fully submerged, his heavy clothing dragging him under and the sucking mud keeping him there. He panicked and his lungs burned as he weakly struggled to lift his head out of the water, but he didn't have any strength left.

If he'd had any breath he would have laughed; after everything, he was just going to drown, without getting home.

Home. The word echoed in his mind, evoking the concept of self that he'd worked so hard to reinforce over the last couple of weeks.

HOME!

He shouted it in his mind and…

‘…yourself! Don’t Displace!’

‘Too late!’ screamed Rachel, leaping to Sam’s side. Her terrified face was the last thing he saw before he toppled from his chair and everything went black.

CHAPTER 8
THE VISITOR

Sam woke up to the sound of beeping, the smell of disinfectant and a dull ache, seemingly throughout his whole body. He opened his eyes to see a plain white ceiling. It was too bright and he gasped as a sharp pain shot through his head.

His parents appeared in his field of vision, leaning over him with concerned expressions.

'Sam, you're awake!' His mother reached out, but hesitated before touching his cheek and instead took his hand in hers, taking care not to disturb the various tubes and wires that were coming from it.

He looked around, instantly recognising the fact that he was in a bed in a hospital room. 'What happened?'

'Andrew said you were hit by a car, a hit and run.' His father reached out and patted his arm, concerned, but forcing a smile.

'A hit and run…?' Sam frowned up at them, puzzled, but quickly realised what Andrew must have done. 'Oh yeah, right.' There was no way Andrew could tell his parents the truth, or that they would believe him if he did. Sam still didn't like lying to his family, though, but it seemed that he was going to have to get used to it, especially in this case. The thought of a lifetime of lying to his parents made him suddenly uncomfortable and he shifted in the bed. He groaned as the movement caused the general ache to graduate to pain. 'Ow.'

His mother bent down and kissed him on the forehead. 'You should try not to move, darling; you need to rest. You have a concussion, a few cracked ribs and your left arm is fractured. The speed the car must have been going it could have been a lot worse, but you're alive and you're awake, that's all that matters.'

His father released Sam's arm and put his hands on the rail of the bed. As always he was slightly uncomfortable with showing his feelings. 'The cut on your head was quite deep and you lost a hell of a lot of blood, which is why you're hooked up to a drip and on a monitor.' He scowled. 'To make matters worse, Andrew didn't manage to get the number plate of the car, so the police are saying that they can't do anything.'

Sam smiled; his father was understandably upset that his son had been hurt and was in hospital, but what was really making him angry was that somebody was going to get away with what they had done - his father, ever the lawyer.

He struggled to lift his head to look down at his body, but didn't have the strength. His mother read his intentions, though, and she pressed the button on the remote control to adjust the bed, tilting him up so that he could see.

His left arm was in a cast up to the elbow and he also had bandages tightly wound around his chest. The injuries were serious and it was going to take him a while to recover, but at the same time he was relieved; nothing was missing, which was more than he could say for poor Jock.

From this new position he also noticed for the first time that Violeta was there as well. She was standing beside his bed and was doodling on his cast with her crayons, her tongue poking out of one side of her mouth. He reached across and ruffled her hair. She made a noise and pushed his hand away in mild annoyance, but didn't stop drawing.

He smiled at her then looked back at his parents - they were putting on brave faces but he could see that they had been very worried about him. 'I'll be fine! Don't worry about me, I just need to get some rest, I'm pretty tired...'

Much as he liked having his family there, Sam realised that he really was very tired. Not only was he injured, but he had also Displaced so he needed to sleep properly, not just be unconscious.

'Of course, darling, we'll be right here.' His mother motioned towards a cheap looking sofa and a couple of armchairs that were lined up under the window opposite the bed.

'There's no need to stay, I'm old enough to sleep on my own!' Sam tried to smile at them, but he couldn't find the strength to do even that. 'It's not as if I'm going to go anywhere...'

His eyes closed and he fell into a deep sleep.

Andrew was finding it very hard to explain to his fellow Society members exactly what had happened to Sam.

The trouble was that it was completely unprecedented and if he hadn't witnessed it himself he wouldn't have believed it. One second they were running through Preparing drills with Sam and the next he was falling from his armchair, dripping wet mud onto the floor, with blood pouring from a deep head wound, a broken arm and cracked ribs. He'd even brought a loaded Lee-Enfield rifle back with him, the strap tangled around the hand of his wounded limb. It had clattered to the floor, the bayonet coming dangerously close to spearing Rachel in the foot.

None of that was particularly unusual; Displacers often brought souvenirs and injuries back with them - the unusual part, and the bit that was the hardest part to believe, and explain, was the fact that it had happened only two weeks after Sam's previous Displacement.

Every single one of the screens were active; it seemed that word of Sam's misadventure had gotten around and the Displacers were curious. Rachel was perched on the arm of his chair, lending support, but she was only a junior member and didn't have much to say in the meetings.

As usual it was Ralph Price who was the most critical of Andrew's every move and predictably took the opportunity to attack. 'Once again you bring us news of your failures, Andrew.'

'And once again you fail to see the true significance of today's event, Ralph.' Andrew snapped back, not feeling like playing nice for once; he was sick and tired of the constant criticism from Ralph, especially seeing as in this case it was completely unwarranted. Added to that he was worried about Sam and could feel a headache coming on from the stress.

'I think that most of us have indeed grasped the significance, Andrew, but it is still hard to believe that you have lost control of the situation again.'

'Ralph, now is not the time,' Lisa broke in sternly, 'Andrew, you said that the boy was hurt?'

'Yes, he's in Barcelona Hospital right now. He lost a lot of blood from a deep cut on his head, but the emergency services managed to transfuse him before anything bad happened. Apart from that he has only minor injuries, nothing long term or life threatening.'

'Thank heavens for small mercies.' She sighed in relief. 'Then we should be more concerned with his mental health than his physical injuries; having a Displacement go this badly so early in his career may well dissuade him from ever trying again.' Lisa's concern was shared by many of them; they did not want to lose such a promising member of the group at so difficult a time, and especially not Sam, who might well hold the hopes, and the fate, of the Society on his shoulders.

Andrew tried to assuage their doubts as best as he could, 'Sam is a lot stronger than any of you think - he has put up with a lot at school and he dealt with himself very well in Port Royal.'

'That doesn't take away from the fact that you now have two strikes against you. One more…' Ralph glared at Andrew, it was no secret that he had wanted the leadership of the group and had taken it very badly when Andrew had been chosen over him.

Andrew didn't rise to the bait this time and just ignored him. 'We are not even close to seeing the limits of Sam's abilities. You have all received the test results - he is in every way remarkable. I feel that it would not be in our best interests to coddle him or try to protect him, beyond what we would normally do for a burgeoning Displacer. I will try to keep him as safe as possible, obviously, but not at the risk of holding him back - I believe it is worth allowing him to make his own way, within limits.'

The Displacers weren't too sure about whether Andrew's plan was the best for Sam and it looked like there was going to be some debate, but then one voice rose above the others, drowning them out with the authority and experience behind it. 'I think that's a good idea, but at least *try* to stop him from participating in any more wars, please. At least for a few more years.'

Andrew nodded. 'I'll do my best, James, but if he's as bloody-minded as his grandfather then you know I'm going to have trouble doing that!'

James chuckled. 'I'm sure you'll be able to keep him in line.'

Andrew shook his head and smiled wryly. 'Yeah, because looking after him has been *so* easy up till now…' There were some laughs at that and Andrew took the opportunity to close the conference call. 'OK, then, I'll be in touch after I've spoken to Sam and found out exactly what happened to him, but for now, that is all. Thank you for connecting.'

He nodded at them. As head Displacer he could dismiss them like this, even if they had more questions that they were dying to ask, or if, like Ralph, they wanted to attack him some more. One by one the screens went black as the Displacers signed off, until Anne was the only one left.

Rachel patted Andrew on the shoulder and smiled. 'I'll give you some privacy.'

'Thank you.'

She left, closing the door behind her.

'Hi, Andrew.'

'Hello yourself.'

'You have to take care, you know; Ralph has been talking behind your back. He's been trying to convince people that you're not the one who should be leading us.'

'He's been doing that for years.'

'Yes, but it's never been as important as it is now and, because of the trouble you're having with Sam, people are starting to listen.'

'Hmm.' Andrew didn't like it, but she had a point. As always.

'He is wrong, though; you are exactly the sort of leader we need right now. Ralph would just lock Sam away and smother him in bubble wrap until we need him, but you will get him through this, I'm sure of it, and he'll be better off for it.'

Andrew grinned lopsidedly at her. 'Thank you for the vote of confidence, I sincerely hope you're right.'

She smiled back at him. 'Don't let it distract you. You know you're doing what's right and I'll make sure that everyone else knows it too. Take care, keep up the good work and I'll see you soon!' She blew a kiss to him.

'Bye, Anne.'

The screen went blank leaving Andrew sitting on his own with a silly smile on his face.

Sam came awake slowly. He had no idea what had woken him, but he was fairly sure that something had and he was getting the feeling in his stomach and the back of his mind that he got when another Displacer was nearby and he thought that perhaps Andrew or Rachel had come to visit him.

The hospital room was completely silent, though. There was no beeping, so he figured that he was no longer attached to the machines and it was obvious that his family weren't there - he hoped they'd taken him seriously and gone home to carry on their lives while he slept.

The curtains were closed and the room was fairly dark, but there was just enough sunlight coming through the small gap in the middle and around the top of the curtains for him to be able to make out the dim shadows of the furniture, balloons, flowers and what looked like a bowl of apples on the table next to the bed. One of the shadows next to the window moved and his eyes shot to it. There was a crunch as someone bit into an apple.

'Hello?' It came out as a weak croak and he coughed; his throat was dry, still sore from screaming and his voice had no power to it.

'Andrew really isn't taking very good care of you, is he?'

'Dad? Is that you?'

There was an all too familiar chuckle from the shadow. 'Not quite.'

A hand reached up and pulled the curtain open a few feet, revealing the source of the voice.

Sitting on the chair by the window was "Jack Swallow", the man who Andrew had called Quentin Price, the renegade Displacer who had tried to kill Sam in Port Royal.

'Hiya, Sammy, how've you been?' He took another bite of the apple, and smiled, speaking around the mouthful. 'Thanks for the apple, by the way, they're delicious, you should try one.'

Sam shifted in the bed, suddenly frightened. 'What are you doing here? How did you find me?' He tried desperately to keep his voice level and not show his fear; he didn't want to give the man the satisfaction, but to his chagrin it cracked again.

Quentin grinned mockingly as he stood up and moved towards the bed. 'Good news travels fast.' He reached out with his hand towards Sam, a gesture that reminded him of Darth Vader from the Star Wars film he had watched with his father the other night. He looked very much like he was going to try to strangle Sam… but instead he picked up a bottle of water from the bedside table and casually offered it to him. 'You're sounding a bit dry there, you should drink something. Then we can have a nice chat.'

Sam took the bottle warily and automatically tried to open it, but realised that he couldn't with one arm.

Quentin laughed when he saw the difficulty that Sam was having. 'Silly me, I'd forgotten you were helpless.' Quentin took the bottle from him and opened it before handing it back.

Sam took a few short sips. It hurt to swallow, but the water was a relief and when he spoke again it was with an almost normal voice. 'Thank you.'

That surprised Quentin and he barked out a laugh, 'I try to kill you and you thank me for handing you your own water?'

Sam shrugged. 'Manners are easy, life is hard.'

'Don't I just know it, and you're finding that out as well it seems.'

Quentin leered down at Sam and the only thing he could do was stare back up at him - there was no way he could fight back if Quentin tried anything, nor could he run, like he had done on the Mermaid. He wasn't even sure that he'd be able to reach the button that would call the nurse before Quentin stopped him. The only thing he could do was try to keep him talking and hope that someone came along before anything bad happened.

The same mad glint was in the man's eye that had been there in Port Royal and he seemed just as highly strung - his knuckles were white as he clutched the metal safety rail at the side of Sam's bed and he never quite stopped moving, his eyes darting around and his weight shifting from one foot to another as if he were dancing to music only he could hear. His eyes were red as if he hadn't been sleeping and his hair was longer and scruffier than it had been, it now covered his forehead, but still didn't quite hide the ragged white line there - a souvenir given him by Sam.

There were many things that Quentin could blame Sam for, his humiliation in Port Royal principal among them, but that scar was a permanent reminder of his failure and he was obviously paranoid about it if he was trying to cover it. With the already delicate balance of the disturbed young man's mind, Sam feared that it might be enough to cause him to do something rash in order to gain his revenge. Like attack his enemy in a hospital in the present day.

Quentin tutted and shook his head as he made a show of surveying Sam's battered body. 'You know, you really should let us train you instead of that washed-up old man; it would be a lot safer for you.'

'You tried to kill me and now you ask me if I want to join you?'

Quentin shrugged. 'You were a rival back there. Right now you're not.'

Sam nodded in understanding and sipped at the water, taking a few moments to try to calm his nerves. 'Thank you for your kind offer, but I think I'll stick with Andrew.'

'Your loss.'

Sam finished the water then leaned over to place the empty bottle on the nightstand. The remote control for the bed and to call the nurse was there, but it was just out of reach. He wasn't sure he'd be able to get to it with his body as it was and it would be all too easy for Quentin to stop him. He decided not to try; it was better not to provoke him. He settled back onto his pillows, taking his time to make himself comfortable before speaking. 'So, did you really come to offer me a job, or are you here to finish what you failed to do in Port Royal?'

'That was what I had originally come here to do, of course, but then I saw you lying there, so pathetic, like a wounded bird...'

'A Swallow or a Sparrow?'

'Very funny! Like a wounded Sparrow with a broken wing.' He grinned and rapped his knuckles on Sam's cast, making a hollow noise. 'I decided that it would be much more satisfying to leave you alive for now, because when I kill you in the past it will hurt your friends so much more.'

Sam blinked at the man, astounded that he could talk about killing someone so casually with a smile on his face. 'So, if you're not going to do anything to me now, then why are you still here? Aren't you afraid someone's going to walk in? Maybe Rachel's around; I'd love to see her kick your arse.'

'I bet you would!' He laughed, 'Well, I came all this way to see you, I wasn't about to leave without at least saying hello, without at least letting you know that I'm thinking of you…' He grinned maliciously.

'That's lovely. Thank you.'

'You're welcome. But you're right, I suppose I should be going. Running into Andrew wouldn't be pleasant and you never know what might happen. There is, well let's just say "unfinished business" between us and it wouldn't be a good idea to air it out in such a public place.' He chuckled and threw the remains of his apple into the bin on the way towards the door.

There was something Sam had been curious about since Port Royal and, despite his fear that the man would change his mind and turn on him, he knew that it might be his only chance to ask, so he called out, stopping Quentin before he could go. 'If you don't mind, I have one question before you go.'

The young man paused and turned back. 'Really? And what is that?'

'What the hell was that parrot for?'

Quentin grinned. 'It was really boring in Port Royal sometimes and I was always messing around. That day I'd done the dead parrot sketch for the crew of the Queen Anne's Revenge. Needless to say, they didn't get it.'

'Probably because it wasn't a Norwegian Blue.'

He laughed. 'That must have been it! That Jamaican amazon was the only one I could find and the line about "pining for the fjords" probably didn't make quite as much sense. Of course, after you turned up things got very interesting very quickly and I no longer needed to find ways to entertain myself.'

'And the food you were throwing at it?'

'Oh, that! You really didn't get that?'

Sam shook his head.

'That was something Johnny Depp's character did in *The Lone Ranger* - I thought I'd mix a few metaphors, if you know what I mean. Of course, if I'd known you were such a noob and had no idea who or what I was then I wouldn't have bothered!'

He laughed and Sam waited for him to finish before smiling and speaking quietly. 'You're a bit nuts, aren't you?'

The grin vanished from Quentin's face in an instant and was replaced by an ugly snarl as he lunged forward until his face was an inch from Sam's. 'I'm not crazy, boy, I'm smart! I got out of that ridiculous club before they could get me killed on their stupid crusade and if you're smart, you will too. But if you do decide that you just can't bear to leave them, then make sure you don't get in my way, because unfortunate things happen to people who get in my way, Sammy boy. Just ask Andrew.'

Sam shrugged and smiled sweetly. 'I've beaten you once, I'll do it again.' He found that he wasn't at all impressed by Quentin's tirade and realised that he didn't feel threatened by the man anymore. He was almost certain now that Quentin had never actually meant to do anything to him. Killing someone in the past was one thing, they would just come back to life when you left and even if you were caught and locked up you could just go home as soon as you were on your own. Doing so in the present, on the other hand, was a completely different matter; you had to worry about troublesome little things like the police and being charged with murder. Even Quentin wasn't crazy enough to risk anything in the present.

Quentin growled angrily and was about to respond, but he was interrupted when the door opened and an elderly nurse walked in.

She smiled when she saw them and came over to the bed smiling widely. 'Oh! You're awake at last! And you have a visitor, that's nice!' She winked. 'He really shouldn't be here, but I'll allow it for now. I just have to check your blood pressure. Don't mind me!'

She said all of this in Spanish, of course, which Quentin didn't understand and he watched her nervously until she started putting a blood pressure cuff on Sam's good arm and pumping it up. When he saw that she wasn't paying any attention to them he put on a fake smile then leaned down to whisper in Sam's ear. 'If I were you I'd give up on Displacing; it's very dangerous. You never know who might be lying in wait for you in the past and next time there may not be any foolish first mates around to take the knife for you. Be seeing you, Sammy boy. '

Without waiting for an answer he stormed out of the room.

Sam watched him go. He discovered that his whole body was under tension and his arm was aching because of it. With a conscious effort he forced himself to relax. He took a deep breath and winced as his ribs twinged.

The nurse finished what she was doing and stood looking down at him. She patted him on his good arm. 'How are you feeling? Can I get you anything?'

Sam realised he was starving. 'I'm a bit hungry, am I allowed to eat?'

'Of course! I'll get you something as soon as I can. In the meanwhile, do you want an apple? You've got a big basket of them here.'

Sam eyed the basket warily; even though he wouldn't put it past Quentin to have done something nasty to them, he didn't think that he had. 'OK, I'll have one, please.'

'Such a nice, polite boy,' the nurse handed him an apple, ruffled his hair and then left.

Sam looked at the apple, inspecting it for all the usual childish prank stuff like marks or spit. Finding nothing, not even a mark from a syringe, he polished it on his chest and bit into it. It was delicious and didn't last very long.

Later that day Sam was flicking through channels on the television, trying to find something even half worth watching, but it was all daytime television - lots of minutiae about the lives of fake celebrities and the opinions of annoying people who thought they knew everything, but were really just idiots. He wished he had his laptop or something to write with; he could be using the time constructively expanding his lists of possible adventures or writing his report for his latest adventure, although he had to admit that his enthusiasm for Displacing had waned quite a bit after his most recent experience.

Eventually, he turned off the TV and threw the remote on the bedside table, disgusted with it.

Thankfully, right at that moment Andrew and Rachel walked in and Sam's day brightened up immediately, especially when Rachel smiled at him. 'Hi, Sam.'

'Hi, Rachel. Andrew.' Sam smiled at Rachel then nodded at his uncle.

'You're very lucky to be alive, young man,' Andrew said, frowning down at Sam.

Rachel hit Andrew on the arm, exasperated. 'For god's sake, don't be such a killjoy! Of course he's alive; it's Sam! He can't...'

Andrew coughed, interrupting her and she didn't finish her sentence, instead she shook her head at Sam in amazement. 'Two weeks! Two bloody weeks! Nobody can Displace again so quickly! That was amazing!'

Sam shrugged. 'Maybe it was because we went tandem to Wembley; it wasn't me doing it.'

She shook her head vigorously. 'It doesn't work like that, does it, Andrew?'

Rachel looked to Andrew for an answer, but he didn't reply; he hadn't heard her question because he was staring down at Sam's arm and at the plaster cast in particular.

'What are you…?' Sam looked down at his cast. There, in one of the few blank spaces left by Violeta's artwork was written "With Love" in strange handwriting along with Quentin's name; he'd signed Sam's cast while he'd been asleep.

Andrew had gone almost as white as the hospital sheets. He reached out to touch the signature, as if he was checking that it was real. 'That's his signature, how did you get that?'

'He was here.'

'Who?' Rachel looked down at the cast and saw what they were looking at. 'Oh my god! What was he doing here?'

Sam shrugged. 'I'm pretty sure he only came to try to frighten me off and wasn't here to kill me.'

Rachel shook her head. 'I wouldn't be too sure of that.'

'Well, he did tell me that he wasn't going to kill me in the present, that he was only going to do it in the past.'

'You spoke to him?!?' Andrew was almost hysterical.

'He was waiting for me to wake up, sitting in that chair and eating one of my apples. They're delicious, by the way. Who brought them?'

'I did! I'm glad you like them.' Rachel beamed.

'Thank you!' Sam smiled back at her.

'Will you two stop with the chitchat, this is serious!'

Sam put on an apologetic look. 'I'm sorry, Uncle Andrew, I promise I'll behave.'

Rachel stifled a laugh, but Andrew deliberately ignored her as he continued. 'So, what did he say?'

'He said that he and you had unfinished business and that I had to ask you what happened to people who got in his way. What does that mean?'

'No idea.' Andrew made a show of shrugging and Sam got the distinct feeling that he was hiding something, but his uncle moved on before he could press him. 'Anything else?'

'He didn't say much more, actually. I think he took my interference in Port Royal very personally and just wanted to say hello and make a few threats.'

Andrew shook his head and frowned in concern. 'But for him to come here, that's not just taking it personally, that's something else entirely, it's the behaviour of someone rather unbalanced.'

'Yes, he's nuts! We already knew that!' agreed Rachel.

Sam laughed. 'That's exactly what I told him!'

'Really? To his face?'

Sam nodded with a grin.

Rachel guffawed and shook her head in wonder. 'Wow, he must have loved that!'

'He was a little bit annoyed, yes.'

'Yes, thank you both.' Andrew interrupted them, annoyed that they weren't taking things a bit more in earnest. 'Seriously though, I think Sam has to be a bit more careful from now on. Even though Quentin is unlikely to try anything in the present, he will *definitely* do anything he can to get his revenge on Sam if they meet up again in the past.'

Rachel frowned. 'How likely is that, though? I mean, Port Royal was a fluke, right? Or are we thinking that…?'

Andrew broke in sharply. 'Yes. It probably was just a fluke, but we need to be prepared in case it wasn't.'

Rachel opened her mouth to reply, but again Andrew gave her a pointed look, telling her not to say anything more.

Sam looked back and forth from one of them to the other. He knew there was something he was missing, but he was too groggy to figure out exactly what it was and he was too tired to even ask, not wanting one of Andrew's long explanations, during which he would definitely fall asleep. He filed his suspicions away for a later date and eagerly leaped on what Andrew had said. 'Well, maybe I should pay a visit to some of those martial arts teachers Rachel studied with? Then it wouldn't matter whether he attacks me here or in the past; I'd be able to take care of myself.'

Andrew thought for a second before nodding slowly. 'That wouldn't be too bad an idea, actually, and I know Quentin - he's not the kind of person to have wasted many Displacements, if any, on training himself physically. He's just not that way inclined. He's not a very active person.'

'He was a bit clumsy when he was trying to kill me on the Mermaid.'

Rachel laughed. 'Because he's a geek! For his first solo Displacement he chose to go and watch the filming of the original Star Trek series!'

Andrew was indignant. 'There is nothing wrong with being a geek! John is a huge geek and look at all he has done for the group.'

'Like making us laugh…'

'Even so, young lady, maybe you should try using your brain a bit more often instead of just your muscles; you might find you accomplish a lot more.'

Sam was grinning at Rachel, enjoying her being told off by Andrew. She noticed and slapped him lightly on the arm.

He winced and rubbed it. 'Ow!'

She gestured at Sam and looked at Andrew, as if she'd proved her point. 'See? He's a wimp! Even if Quentin does fight like a girl, Sam here still needs toughening up.'

Reluctantly, Andrew agreed. 'OK then, we'll get Sam some training so he can look after himself.'

'Yessss!' Rachel jumped up and down in excitement and pumped the air in victory. 'Ooh! Ooh! I've been wanting to go to this one place in ancient Korea… I could take him there in a couple of weeks!'

Despite wanting nothing more than to spend time in the past training with Rachel, Sam wasn't particularly convinced about Displacing again so soon, especially not to somewhere potentially dangerous. He didn't really want to admit it, even to himself, but he was scared. If he had to, he would confess his fears to Andrew later, when they were on their own; his uncle had been his confessor for years and the only person he had ever confided his bullying problem to, he would understand. The last thing he wanted was for Rachel to know, though, so he decided not to say anything about it at that moment. Instead, he lifted his injured arm. 'I'm not going to be able to Displace that soon; I've got a broken arm, remember?'

Andrew smiled. 'No need to worry about that; it's not strictly your body when you Displace - you won't have a broken arm in the past. As long as you're not in too much pain to be able to Prepare then you'll have no problem.'

'Oh. Good.' Sam forced a smile, as if he was happy that there was no excuse for him to postpone his next Displacement.

Andrew looked at Rachel a bit sceptically. 'This place you want to go to, is it going to be dangerous?'

Rachel shrugged, shook her head and grinned at him cheekily. 'How dangerous could sixth century Korea be?'

Andrew just raised an eyebrow.

Rachel sighed. 'Alright, maybe we'll start with some simple boxing and work our way up to Ninjas and Samurais. He will be ready to Displace in a couple of weeks at the same time as I am, right?'

'If it wasn't just a fluke.' Andrew sounded doubtful.

'You know it wasn't. Come on, admit it, you think he's the one, right?'

Andrew shook his head. 'We still don't know for sure.'

'Of course not, but you've got a feeling, haven't you?'

He sighed. 'Yes... I suppose so.'

Sam frowned, not only because he didn't like the fact that they were discussing him as if he wasn't there, but also because he had no idea what they were talking about. 'What is it you think I am? The one what?'

Andrew looked down at him. He waved away Sam's question. 'I'll tell you later. Right now you've got to get dressed; your mother will be here soon to take you home. Come on, let's get you up.'

Andrew motioned for Sam to get up and went to pull the sheets back, but Sam clamped his arm down on the sheets, stopping him from doing so. He looked at Andrew and then at Rachel. She was grinning knowingly and waiting expectantly.

'Uh, Andrew, I've got no pants on...' Sam was now a bright shade of red.

Andrew looked around at Rachel and then back at Sam. 'Oh...'

'You're so dumb sometimes, Andrew.' Rachel patted Andrew on the arm. 'I'll be outside, call me when he's decent. Just don't tell him about how we had to undress him and put him in the shower when he came back from the wars.'

She walked out, giving Sam a wink.

He looked up at Andrew questioningly.

Andrew shrugged. 'The arm and the blood we could explain, the mud would have been a bit harder - we had to get it off before the ambulance arrived, and I couldn't cope with you on my own.'

Impossibly, Sam went an even brighter red. 'Oh, god...'

CHAPTER 9
DOUBTS

The next few days went by far too slowly and far too uncomfortably for Sam. He was mostly confined to bed, taking painkillers and drifting in and out of consciousness, not quite fully aware of the time that was passing. The only times that he did leave his bed were either to eat, which he did listlessly, not talking or interacting much, watched by his anxious family, or when he stood in the shower staring at nothing, a plastic bag taped onto his cast to keep it dry, washing away blood that seemed to keep coming back, over and over and over. His parents thought it was just the pain and the pills that were responsible for the dark circles and the haunted look in his eyes; they had no idea what he was going through. As far as they were concerned he had only been in a traffic accident, they had no notion of the psychological damage that had been done to him - less than an hour on a battlefield had been enough to give Sam shell shock. Unlike the other men, who had already been in the trenches for some time and had been somewhat inured to the appalling conditions, he had in no way been prepared for the impact of the experience on his mind.

The full reality of what had happened to him had finally struck Sam when he had gotten home and the terror he had felt returned to haunt him. It hit him full force; he couldn't think, he couldn't concentrate and everything was like a dream. He'd been told to sleep as much as he could, but he preferred to be awake with the pain because in his sleep was where Jock's dead eyes awaited him. They stared at him, burning into his mind as he sank into clinging mud to the sound of screams, the chatter of machine guns and the crump of shells exploding.

On the fourth day his mother knocked gently on his bedroom door and poked her head around the door to tell him he had a visitor. Seconds later, Andrew walked into his bedroom with a big smile.

'Hey, kiddo! I brought you some biscuits; I know how much you like Jammy Dodgers!' The smile faded quickly when he saw the empty look in the boy's eyes. 'How are you doing, Sam?'

For the first time in days Sam felt something beyond fear. He sat up in bed and focussed all his pent up anger and anguish on his uncle. 'You told my family I got hit by a car! You lied to them, and now I have to as well! I can't talk to them about any of this!'

'Shh! Keep your voice down!' Andrew hissed, waving frantically. He came over and sat on the side of the bed so that he could speak quietly. 'I wasn't exactly going to tell them the truth, was I?'

Sam glared at him in silence for a few seconds, then he deflated, flopping back onto his pillows. 'No, I suppose not.'

'Look, a lot of Displacements are rough and dangerous; we go to some pretty turbulent times in history and we get hurt all the time. It's part of the job. Adults don't have to explain themselves as much when it happens, but you're still living with your parents - I had to make up something and the only way to explain your injuries was with a traffic accident. I'm sorry we have to lie to them, but I did what I had to do.'

'Didn't the doctors know you were lying?'

'Yes, of course they did. Your injuries weren't exactly consistent with a car crash and you slept for two days after you regained consciousness, which isn't exactly normal either. There would have been a lot of questions if it wasn't for the friendly doctors that the Society have on hand to diagnose what we need them to and then do the paperwork so everything seems normal.'

'You have doctors...' Sam stared at him with his mouth open. 'And the police? Are they "friendly" too?'

'Yes, the local police are taken care of. Otherwise they'd be out wasting time looking for a car and a driver who doesn't exist.'

Sam shook his head, wincing as his headache came back with a vengeance. 'I really don't like this. Any of this.'

'I know and I'm sorry, but it's a necessary part of our lives as Displacers; we have to hide what we are so that we can be free to do what we have to.'

Andrew looked at his nephew with not a little sympathy. Sam had never liked hiding his bullying problem from his family, but had done it because he hadn't wanted to worry them. This, though, was very different; he was having to actively tell lies to them. However, while that would undoubtedly trouble Sam in the years to come, Andrew doubted that it was why he had such a haunted look on his face that his annoyed expression couldn't quite hide; the pain in his eyes went far beyond what could be due to his physical injuries or the lies and Andrew recalled what Lisa had said about having to worry about Sam's mental health. He spoke in a soft voice. 'Do you feel like telling me what happened?'

Sam swallowed. He didn't particularly want to relive his experience, he did it enough in his nightmares, and for a moment he considered refusing and sending his uncle away, but he knew that he was going to have to talk about it at some point; as Andrew had said, it was all part of the job. He nodded reluctantly.

Andrew smiled encouragingly. 'World War One, right?'

'Yes.'

'Why didn't you come back straight away?'

'I couldn't; I got there just as they started an attack. They herded me along with them and I didn't get a chance to get myself home.'

'You went over the top? Oh god…'

'Yes.'

Sam told him everything that had happened on the Displacement, reliving it in his mind. His voice caught as he described how the bodies of the men around him had been flung into the air like rag dolls and when he told Andrew about Jock's death he felt the tears start to fall.

When he finished he turned his head away from Andrew and buried his face in the pillow.

Andrew sat there in silence, aghast. No adult would come through a battle like that unscathed, and countless thousands hadn't, he could only imagine the effect it would have on a fifteen year-old boy from the relatively peaceful world of the present. He couldn't help thinking that Ralph was right: he had failed Sam yet again. He tried to find something positive to lift Sam's spirits. 'Uh, good thinking with the puddle at the bottom of the shell hole.'

Andrew waited for a response, but Sam didn't move. 'Um... but you know that you could have jumped straight into it when you passed it the first time, right?'

Sam's voice was small and muffled by the pillow. 'I'm tired, could you leave me alone, please?'

Andrew kicked himself; he hadn't known what else to say, so he had just said the first thing that came into his mind. He had known it was a mistake as soon as it was out of his mouth. 'Yes, of course.' He sighed then stood up and went to the door.

He paused with his hand on the doorknob and looked back at Sam. The boy hadn't moved. His sobbing had stopped, but he still had his back turned and was pointedly ignoring him. Andrew didn't know what to do, he was so used to being the person that Sam turned to when he was in trouble that this new rejection puzzled him. And it hurt.

'We'll go back to practising in a few days when you've had some rest. It'll take your mind off of things.'

There was no reply from Sam and Andrew grimaced, he *really* wasn't very good at this kind of thing. 'OK, then, let me know if you need anything. I'll see you soon.'

With one last look at Sam, he left, closing the door quietly behind him.

As soon as the door closed, Sam rolled onto his back. He listened to the sounds of his uncle saying goodbye to his family, heard Violeta's laughter as Andrew told her a joke or did a magic trick for her. He found himself smiling for the first time in days when the front door banged shut with Violeta's usual enthusiasm, sending a slight shock throughout the house.

He regretted his harsh treatment of Andrew; despite how much it had hurt to describe what had happened, he did feel a little bit better for having shared it with somebody. He was not nearly his usual self, but it felt surprisingly good to have gotten it off his chest, as if keeping it bottled up inside had made it into more than it was. That wasn't to say that it hadn't been the worst thing he'd ever experienced, because obviously it had been, but that didn't mean it had to cast a shadow over the rest of his life.

He sat up, clutching his ribs as a spike of pain shot through him, taking his breath away, then slowly got out of bed and limped across the room to sit at his desk. He took a clean piece of paper from a drawer, then picked up a pen and held it over the page.

He took a deep breath, preparing himself mentally, and then started to write.

He didn't have many technical details to make note of. He had no idea of the exact date or the place, he didn't even have a clue as to what battle it actually was that he had taken part in, so instead he wrote down all that he could remember: the sights, the sounds, his feelings, everything that he had told Andrew and a few things that he hadn't recalled until now.

After about an hour he put aside his pen and shook his aching hand as he looked at the finished result - two reports: one as complete as he could make it for him to keep and one for the Society with just the bare details. Somehow, the act of putting it down on paper made the Displacement seem less personal, less like it had been him there; it was now a part of history, in the past.

All part of the job, as Andrew had put it.

That didn't make everything alright again, though; it would take more than just a single conversation with Andrew and then a written report to do that, but it was a start.

He hid the reports then stood up from the desk, took another deep breath and left his room to re-join his family.

Andrew's visit, combined with no longer needing to take so many painkillers, served to bring Sam almost completely out of his misery. He became more his usual self and over the next couple of days he spent more time out of his room than he did in it, getting back into a more normal summer holiday routine of video games, television and meals with his family. His arm would be in plaster for a few more weeks and he still found it hard to get enough sleep as a consequence, but it was no longer a reminder of the shell hole and the brief moment that he had given up on life. Instead, he often found himself staring at the signature as if it could tell him something about his new mortal enemy; he couldn't quite believe that someone hated him so much as to vow to kill him and actually mean it.

More than a week had passed since the accident before he finally felt ready to continue his training. He had very mixed feelings about it, but eventually the possibility of adventure and a sense of responsibility won out over his remaining fears.

Rachel opened the door to Andrew's flat. She carefully folded him into a hug before holding him at arm's length by the shoulders and searching his face. 'Hi, Sam. How are you doing?'

He shrugged and looked down at the floor. 'Not bad, considering. Better than before anyway.'

'Good, I'm glad. Are you ready for this?'

'I'm not really sure.'

'Well, just remember, I'm here for you.'

Sam lifted his head and smiled at her, shyly. 'Thank you.'

She nodded, returning his smile warmly, then led him into the living room where, of course, tea had been set out.

Andrew was sitting in his usual armchair. He looked up as Sam came in and grinned. 'There you are! You took your time coming back, anyone would think you'd had an accident or something! Come on, we've got a lot of work to do if you're going to be ready to Displace with Rachel next week.'

Sam knew he was only joking, but it wasn't quite what he had wanted to hear and Rachel realised that. She rolled her eyes at Andrew, giving him a disapproving look, before reaching out to take Sam's hand. 'There's no hurry, Sam. We'll go when and if you're ready. It's your call.'

Sam smiled at her as once again the small physical contact with her helped to settle him immensely.

She squeezed his hand in reassurance and went to sit down on the sofa while Sam took a seat on the free armchair.

Andrew pushed a mug of tea across the table to him along with a plate of biscuits. 'Is your arm alright? You're not in too much pain to do this?'

'No, I'm fine, it doesn't hurt very much right now. It's more itchy than anything else.'

'Good! Let's get down to it then - I want to go back to practising Preparing today; let's see if we can't bring that already impressive time down a bit more.'

'OK.'

'But Sam, as Rachel said, there's no hurry; we've got all the time in the world. If you need a break or anything, just say.'

'OK.' Sam nodded. He could do that, he could Prepare; it was only training, it wouldn't take him anywhere dangerous.

He took a deep breath, closed his eyes and started to concentrate, exactly as he'd done hundreds of time before. However, unlike every single one of those hundreds of times, this time he found it impossible to clear his mind. He tried over and over, but the more he forced it the worse it became, like a pressure building up inside him, an almost claustrophobic instinct that was just telling him to get out, to get away, to go.

So he did.

'I'm sorry, I can't.' He leapt to his feet and ran to the door, throwing it open to crash against the wall and almost running down the hall in his rush to escape.

He was hyperventilating, gasping in air, as he walked up the street. Black spots were starting to swim before his eyes and he was finding it hard to focus. He had to make himself stop and he leaned against a wall, resting his forehead against the cool brick. He closed his eyes, trying to bring his breathing under control and his heart rate down, trying to shut away the terror that had surged up inside of him again.

A hand came down on his shoulder and he jumped in shock, spinning to confront the threat, his one good hand already coming up to cover his head. He fully expected to find Rafa standing there, ready to take advantage of finding him on his own; that would be just his luck, but instead he found the sympathetic face of Rachel.

She said nothing as she took hold of his hand and pulled it down from its defensive position. She gently led him to a nearby bench, guiding him to sit next to her, then wrapped her arms around him.

Sam leaned against her, drawing strength from her, feeling his pounding heart slowing and his ragged breathing calming. Eventually he lifted his head to look at her.

She released him and leaned back on the bench. She stared at him, not breaking eye contact.

There was a long silence and Sam started to feel uncomfortable under her scrutiny. He had to work hard to resist the urge to look away. 'What?'

'Your mother says you're moping, feeling sorry for yourself.'

'Wouldn't you be?'

Rachel shrugged. 'I've taken worse beatings than you have and lived to tell the tale.'

Sam looked away. 'It's not just the broken arm….'

'Then what is it? Talk to me. Or would you rather talk to Andrew? Shall I go and get him?'

She started to get up, but Sam stopped her. 'Please. Don't go.'

She sat back down and looked at him expectantly.

Sam took some time to sort out his thoughts, staring into the distance but seeing nothing. Rachel's insistence and his unexpected unwillingness to disappoint her was forcing him to think about why he had run out on the training session, making him reconnect with feelings that he had been trying to bury and deny. He realised now that he had only told Andrew the physical facts of his Displacement; the Society weren't interested in his feelings so he hadn't told Andrew about them, nor had he put them in his report, he had kept them to himself, bottled up inside. However, it was those feelings that had been eating at him for the last week and had caused his panic attack; they were what was most important to him and it was obvious now that more than anything else he needed to cope with them. And if that meant sharing them with someone who could help him come to terms with them, just like he had shared his bullying problems with Andrew, then that was what he had to do.

The words started to come, hesitantly at first, but quickly gained momentum until they were rushing out, as if they'd only been waiting for a chance to escape or his permission. 'I was absolutely terrified. Death was all around and there was nothing I could do to influence whether I survived or not, I had no control whatsoever. At first I wanted to run away, but I couldn't; I had no choice except to keep moving forward with the rest of the men, walking blindly into the guns. But then when we got closer and the orders started to come, the Displacement gave me the skills I "needed" - I fixed my bayonet like I'd done it hundreds of times before, I stood up straighter and had courage in the face of the enemy. It was training which was completely useless in the end, though; hundreds, maybe thousands of us died marching across that field without ever even getting within sight of the Germans. Worse, though, when those orders came, I also got the discipline of an infantryman. It was as if I lost control of myself; my mind closed off and I turned into a good little soldier, one who was no longer worried about being sacrificed for absolutely nothing.'

Rachel nodded. 'It sounds to me that you got the authentic World War One experience. I read through Andrew's notes on his own time there when you got back and, even though he was an officer back at headquarters and only ever saw the front line when it was quiet, I still got a sense of how horrific things were. Millions of men died for absolutely nothing, because generals thought it was a good idea to attack heavily fortified enemy trenches, just so they could draw a new line a few centimetres forwards on a map. I'm really not surprised you've been affected this much by it.'

She reached out and put her hand on his shoulder, trying to comfort him, but he turned to look at her with red-rimmed eyes and shook his head.

'You haven't heard everything yet. That was bad, yes, but it wasn't the worst of it. There was a moment, after I'd been hit, when I was lying in that hole with Jock... dead... right there beside me, that I...' He had to pause as the words stuck in his throat and it all came rushing back to him again. He pressed his hands against his eyes, trying to stop the tears from coming again. 'I *gave up*, Rachel. I accepted that I was going to die there and I lost all hope. I just laid there and *welcomed* an end to the nightmare.'

Rachel listened to him in silence, aghast at what he was saying, finally understanding why he was finding it so hard to continue, finding it so hard to explain something that no fifteen year old should have to feel, but that unfortunately so many did, even today, in so many places around the world. She found herself fighting back tears in sympathy with him, waiting for him to continue, wondering what she could possibly say to him.

She didn't have to say anything, though, because when he took his hands away from his eyes they were shining, not with tears, but with a sudden realisation and an inner strength that she hadn't seen in him before, in anyone before.

'I didn't stay there, obviously, and I'd almost forgotten why, but it's coming back now - I was on the point of giving up, I *had* given up; I'd closed my eyes and stopped struggling. But then I thought of you. It was you; *you* brought me back. I remembered you taking on those bullies; the way you wouldn't back down, the way you stood up for me and I realised that you would never let me live it down if I gave up and died there.'

She laughed. 'Too true. I would have kicked your arse from here to the Sagrada Familia!'

Sam chuckled as well. It was the first time he'd laughed for days, the first time he'd felt even remotely like laughing; Rachel just had that effect on him. He wiped his eyes with his sleeve and sat up straighter.

Rachel turned serious. 'Well, you've seen one of the worst events in human history now and you survived. And you can be pretty sure you won't have to go blindly into anything like that again because we know what you can do now, we know that you can Displace every two weeks.' She patted him gently on the shoulder. 'Now, how about we go back in and you try again? And next time you Displace I'll be there holding your hand and we'll see about you learning to take care of yourself, OK?'

'OK.'

They stood up, but there was one last thing that Sam wanted to say. 'You know, Quentin told me that I'd be better off leaving Andrew and letting his group train me.'

Rachel laughed and dismissed the notion out of hand. 'He lost to you in your first ever Displacement! What the hell is he going to teach you?'

Still laughing, she led the way to Andrew's door and they went back in.

Sam sat on the sofa next to Rachel for his next attempt, drawing comfort from her presence, using it to help him focus. His eyes were closed, but he could still feel Andrew watching him, feel his worry, his uncertainty; Andrew would probably call this a make or break moment, or something equally dramatic.

He realised that, in the end, this was just the same as facing a bully; if he stood up to the doubting voices lurking in his head they would back down.

He forced down the doubts and concentrated, beginning to Prepare. There was still some reluctance, something telling him he shouldn't be doing this, but he'd made up his mind now; there was no way he was giving up on the potential to have so much fun in so many interesting times. No way he was going to disappoint Rachel. He reached for that place inside him, pushing aside the fears that tried to stop him.

He managed to Prepare on his very first try.

Andrew nodded. 'Again.'

Sam had no more problems after that.

CHAPTER 10
TRAINING

The days couldn't go by quickly enough for Sam; he was impatient, and not a little nervous, to see whether he really could Displace again, or whether some mental block would kick in when he knew it was for real and not just practice. He still had misgivings about Displacing again and the fear was still in the back of his mind, but he also knew that he had to do it or he would regret it for the rest of his life. Also, Rachel would probably make him regret it as well, or worse, refuse to ever see him again.

He went to Andrew's flat every morning and met with Rachel and Andrew to continue his training. He tried, fairly unsuccessfully, to get his head around the bewildering array of rules of what was and wasn't possible, as well as making sure he could Prepare and Calm on demand. They only met up for a few hours each day, though, because they didn't want his family getting suspicious or wondering what he was getting up to, although, he was fairly sure that if he just told them that Rachel was his girlfriend they would be fine with him being gone longer.

Rachel walked him home every day after training and they got to know each other more without having to worry about Andrew listening to them. After their conversation on the street, he had become much closer to her and those all too short walks quickly became his favourite part of the day. They began to discover feelings for each other that went beyond the purely professional and Sam found that for the first time in his life he didn't feel awkward talking to a girl.

During those brief conversations they became so engrossed with each other's company that they often had no eyes for anything else but each other. Which was why Sam was so shocked and reacted so aggressively when he found himself suddenly face to face with Quentin on the doorstep of his home.

'You! What are you doing here?' His hands curled into fists automatically and he crouched slightly, preparing for a fight, glaring at his enemy. He was even more glad that Rachel had accompanied him home now, because with a broken arm he wasn't sure he would be able to fend Quentin off.

'Your friend here was just telling me how sorry he was to hear about your accident. I didn't know you had an English friend.'

Sam blinked and straightened, taken aback. He looked away from Quentin to find his mother and Violeta standing behind him in the shadows of the doorway.

'Mum?'

'Oh, hi, Sam!' She smiled and Violeta waved. Thankfully they had both completely missed Sam's hostility towards the young man.

'Has he never mentioned me? I feel mildly offended!' Quentin laughed gently and smiled, almost charmingly at Sam's mother. 'His English teacher brings me in for conversation classes all the time.' Quentin now turned his charm towards Sam. 'Hi, Sam, how's the arm?'

Sam wanted nothing more than to wipe the smirk from Quentin's face, but with his family standing there he couldn't, so he gritted his teeth and forced a smile. 'Fine, thank you. Much better.'

'Good, good!'

Sam glanced quickly at Rachel to see how she was handling the encounter, expecting her to be on the verge of leaping to attack. To his surprise she looked perfectly calm and had a smile on her face, as if she were meeting with a friend.

'Would you like to have dinner with us, Mr Price?'

Sam's attention shot back to his mother, horrified at her inviting his worst enemy into their house; he could hardly remain civil for a few seconds in the street, he didn't think he'd be able to sit through a whole meal. He mused that sometimes it was a real drawback to have an English parent, with her outmoded way of being polite.

Thankfully, Quentin seemed to know it wouldn't be a good idea either and he shook his head, pantomiming regret. 'Oh, that's very kind of you, Mrs Vives, thank you, but I'm afraid I can't; I just came round to see how Sam was before I caught a flight back to England.'

'Oh? You're leaving Barcelona?'

'Yes, I've got a new job.' Quentin winked at Sam.

'What a shame! I've noticed such an improvement in Sam's English recently, due to you I suppose. It's a pity he's losing such an obviously talented teacher.'

Sam seethed as his mother beamed warmly at the man who had tried to kill him only a couple of months before.

'Yes, it is a bit of a shame, I agree; I have the feeling he could have done great things under my tutelage.' Quentin was obviously barely stopping himself from laughing and he coughed to cover that fact before continuing. 'Well, I should be on my way. It was a pleasure to meet you, Mrs Vives, and you too, Violeta.' The malicious young man smiled condescendingly down at the girl and it was all Sam could do to stop himself from jumping on him and pummelling him to the floor.

'Good luck with your new job! I hope it goes well for you.' Again, Sam couldn't believe his mother wasn't picking up on the man's wickedness; she was usually such a good judge of character.

'I'm sure it will. Thank you.' Quentin nodded then turned his back on Sam's mother and grinned at Sam again. He held out his hand.

Sam's mouth dropped open. He was astounded at the gall of the man, but was forced to play along in front of his mother. He reached out and shook Quentin's hand. It was cold and clammy and he released it as soon as he could.

'See you around, Sam.' Quentin nodded and gave Rachel a leer that Sam's family couldn't see before walking casually off down the road.

Sam's mother exhaled in relief as soon as he was out of earshot. 'What a horrid young man, I don't know how you stand him.'

Sam and Rachel slowly turned and looked at her. They stared at her for a second before they laughed. By the time they looked back to the road, Quentin had gone. They shrugged and turned back to her.

Sam smiled at his mother. 'And here I was thinking you liked him.'

'Oh, god no!' She shuddered. 'He's a smarmy git with a puffed up sense of his own importance, but I was brought up to have manners and be polite, like you were Sam. I wasn't about to say any of that to his face!'

'Thank you, Mrs V, you've restored my faith in humanity!'

Sam's mother laughed. 'So, Rachel, how about you? Are you going to stay for dinner?'

'Er, no, thank you, Andrew is cooking…' Rachel didn't look at all enthusiastic about the prospect.

'OK, another time then, but don't leave it too long, alright? You know you are always welcome here.' Violeta tugged on her skirt and she looked down at her. 'Well, I should get this little monster inside; it's time for her snack. See you soon, I hope!'

'Bye, Mrs Vives. Bye, Violeta!'

Sam and Rachel waited for her disappear into the foyer of the block of flats with her daughter in tow and for the door to close before turning back to each other.

'A "new job"… do you think he was talking about another mission?'

Rachel frowned, thoughtfully. 'I don't know… Maybe.'

Is he stupid enough to say something like that to us if it were true?'

'Stupid, probably not. But arrogant enough? Definitely. Whatever, I should get back to Andrew and tell him about this. The Elders need to know.'

'I suppose so. Well, I guess I'll see you again tomorrow.'

'Indeed.'

There was silence for a few seconds as they just stood there, looking at each other. Rachel smiled slightly, but Sam didn't quite know whether that was an invitation or not, so in the end he just turned away to open the door.

'Bye.'

'Bye, Sam.'

He smiled as he entered, letting the door swing closed behind him.

Rachel walked quickly away, heading back to Andrew's flat.

Sam watched her go through the glass pane in the door, hidden in the shadows. He wasn't sure; it was probably just wishful thinking, but he thought that he had caught a flash of disappointment on her face before she had turned away and he cursed himself for his shyness.

A few days later Rachel declared that she was ready to Displace. It was a Saturday afternoon and they were in Andrew's sitting room, having tea, again, and taking the time to discuss possible time-lines for them to go to. Rachel was next to Sam on the sofa while Andrew sat in an armchair idly rubbing the leg that was very nearly healed, but still, in his own words, 'itchy as hell'.

'How do you know?' Sam asked her.

Rachel thought for a second before shrugging. 'I dunno.'

Andrew cut in with a laugh. 'It's impossible to explain, really, we just do. And you should have known too, before going to the war - you should have felt ready.'

Sam took a deep breath and glared at his uncle, feeling quite angry suddenly. 'Maybe I would have done if I you'd told me that I was supposed to feel something!'

Andrew grinned sheepishly and ran his hand through his hair nervously. 'I was going to... but nearer to when the month was up... I guess I thought I had that long at least... there's just so much to teach you... um...'

Rachel rolled her eyes. 'What budget Hugh Grant here is trying to tell you is that we thought we had at least another couple of weeks until you were ready to Displace. Nearer to the time we were going to introduce to you the fact that one day you were going to wake up, or be walking down the street and the feeling inside of you would change from being a passive thing to something more *alive* somehow.'

Sam thought about it, turning his gaze inwards towards that place where he liked to picture his powers as a Displacer residing - somewhere deep in the pit of his stomach. 'I guess... yes, I suppose it does feel a bit different, like its tugging me towards something.

Andrew nodded. 'Yes, the past. It's pulling you towards the past. It means you're ready too.'

Rachel grinned and clapped her hands together in glee. 'Yes! Then let's do this! No time like the present, right, Sam? Where shall we go? Do you fancy Chinese? Japanese? Maybe a bit of Thai?' She winked and Sam smiled back at her.

They spent the next ten minutes talking about a few of the ideas that Rachel had for Sam to learn how to defend himself, but Andrew adamantly refused to let them go to anywhere he considered even remotely dangerous and ruled them all out.

Sam didn't admit it, but he was actually quite nervous about some of the more "interesting" prospects that Rachel had in mind and in the end he was quite happy when they agreed on New York as a compromise; it was on the list of places that he would like to visit in the present, so he figured that going there in the recent past would be just as good. Unfortunately, she wanted to go there to do some serious boxing training, so he didn't think he'd have much time for sightseeing, unless running through the streets counted.

Even with everything agreed, Andrew still had his doubts. 'It's too soon, Rachel, I'm really not sure about this. He should be safe for another month at least, you can do this next time. Just take him somewhere safe, like the opening day of Disneyland in 1955.' He looked at Sam with a keenly happy expression on his face. 'That would be fun, right, Sam?'

Rachel sighed and shook her head. 'Come on, Andrew, we're only going to New York, it's perfectly safe!'

'It's New York! Of course it's not safe! And in the eighties…'

'You worry too much, Grandad.'

'Someone has to.' Andrew turned to Sam with a sigh. 'Go on then. But at the first sign of trouble you make her bring you back, OK? I'm counting on you to be the sensible one, alright?'

Sam grinned cheekily, 'I'm not sure that you should; I want to have fun!' He turned to Rachel. 'Come on, let's go already!'

Rachel laughed and held out her hands.

Sam took them, then turned his head to wink at Andrew. 'Only joking, I'll take care. See you now!'

He looked Rachel in the eyes, nodded and closed his eyes.

When he opened them again he found himself standing hand in hand with Rachel in a lush green jungle-like forest.

'I've never actually been there, but I've seen a few photos and I'm pretty sure this isn't Manhattan…'

He looked her up and down. She was wearing a short tunic-like shirt with a rope belt, sandals and had bare legs. It was not exactly suitable clothing for a city. When he looked down he was relieved to find that he was wearing trousers, although he also had on a tunic and sandals.

Rachel winked. 'No offence to Andrew, but honestly, who wants to box? It's a bit boring when there are so many cool martial arts to study. No, this isn't New York, this is one of my little secrets.'

'So you lied to him.'

She grinned. 'Blatantly and unashamedly.'

'Good; I wasn't really looking forward to all the montages and stuff.'

Rachel laughed. 'That's pretty funny, kid! Come on, I want to introduce you to someone.'

They started walking through the trees.

'Where are we then?'

'The Kongoseki mountains, Kunigami district. In Okinawa.'

'Okinawa? As in Japan?'

'Yes.'

'I guess that explains the clothes then.'

'Yes, you look a bit like Luke Skywalker.'

'Cool!'

They grinned at each other.

Suddenly Sam stopped. Rachel walked a few more steps before she realised he was no longer following her. She turned around and found Sam waving his left arm around.

'What?'

'Oh, nothing! Just that this is so cool!' He ran his hand up and down his arm, squeezing, feeling for a break that wasn't there.

Rachel shook her head and gave him an exasperated look. 'Noob.' She turned her back and started walking away.

Sam trotted to catch up with Rachel. He walked along beside her, still twisting his arm in the air. His mind was telling him to stop waving it around like an idiot before he hurt himself, but it was perfectly fine; there was nothing wrong with it, it was as it had been before the accident.

'Ow!'

'What?'

'I hit my arm on a tree.'

'Serves you right. Now stop acting like a fool in case someone sees you.'

'See me? Here?' Sam looked around at the completely empty forest.

'You never know who is going to be waiting behind the next tree in this forest. Isn't that right, Master Hamato?'

'Yes. It is indeed, Rachel-san.' Two steps away from Sam a small Japanese man slipped out from behind a tree.

'What the…!' Sam leapt backwards, tripped over a tree root and fell on his arse. He started to struggle to his feet, but his attention was caught and held by the two people standing in front of him and he froze where he was, watching mesmerised as they faced each other and bowed slowly, eyes locked and unblinking.

The man looked to be about seventy years old, but Sam couldn't be sure if that was even close. He was wearing a plain grey kimono, the colour of storm clouds in winter, and a pair of the funny wooden platform shoes that you saw in Japanese samurai movies. There was nothing funny about the long sword he wore through the sash at his waist, though, and Sam had a quick thought: there seemed to be a lot of swords involved in Displacing. Not that he was complaining; as far as he was concerned, the more swords the better.

The moment stretched on. They were as still as statues; neither of them moving a muscle, neither of them blinking, the only sound in the forest coming from the insects and birds.

There was a buzzing noise in Sam's ear and he felt a sharp pain at his neck. He winced and slapped at himself, turning his head to look for the offending insect. 'Ow! Mosquito!'

In that instant Rachel and the man flew at each other.

Sam couldn't say who had attacked first, it looked simultaneous to him, but Rachel told him later that the man, Master Yoshi Hamato, had moved the little finger on his right hand and according to her that was a blatant provocation. Hamato in turn told him that it had been Rachel who had attacked first, but that his own foot had sunk a millimetre into the soft floor of the jungle, which may count as an initiation under the unwritten rules of such duels; he said this with a smile and a wink at Rachel, though, so Sam took it with a pinch of salt.

In the end it didn't really matter which of them had attacked first, because neither of them had the advantage as they closed to fighting distance in a heartbeat.

Sam had been astounded by Rachel's speed and ability when she'd fought off Rafa's bully friends, but he realised now that she had actually been holding back; she was a flurry of movement, twisting, turning, kicking and punching, raining blows from every angle. Even so, she was doing absolutely nothing to perturb the man, who barely moved yet managed to evade everything she threw at him.

With a grin, Rachel accelerated, throwing two or three attacks at a time with multiple limbs, but still the man just subtly twitched and swayed and her blows missed by millimetres each time. At no time did she lose control, though; she seemed to anticipate his dodges and used the lack of resistance to flow into her next move.

'Enough.'

The voice was so quiet that Sam had his doubts that he had really heard it, but Rachel instantly froze in mid kick. A half-second later she was as she had been, facing the man with her arms at her sides and not even breathing heavily.

'You've gotten slower, Rachel-san, but not too much. It is acceptable.' The man nodded. He then turned to glance sideways at Sam who was still gawping at them from his position on the ground, looking back and forth from one of them to the other with his mouth open. 'Who is your friend and does he know he is sitting on that anthill?'

'His name is Sam Vives and I shouldn't think so for one second.'

The meaning of their words finally got through to Sam and he leapt to his feet. He twisted and turned, finding that his legs and lower body were covered in little black ants. He started brushing frantically at them, trying desperately to get them off.

Rachel and Master Hamato were laughing at him as he jumped around.

'Well, he has energy at least,' said the old man, shaking his head.

Rachel made her way over to Sam and started to help him. 'Don't worry Sam, they don't bite.'

'Oh, good.'

'Yeah, if I'm not mistaken, these ones only burrow beneath your skin.'

A couple of hours later they were sitting in the living area of Master Hamato's home. He lived alone in a large wooden cabin in the middle of nowhere. It was surprisingly well made and clean if sparsely appointed - it consisted of just three rooms: two small bedrooms, and the larger living area, all floored with straw tatami that smelled fresh and clean. There was also an outside bath around the side of the cabin that was little more than a large squat wooden barrel that had probably had sake in it at one point.

The trek to the cabin had been a long and gruelling walk through the jungle forest. Rachel and Hamato had chatted almost the whole way there as they clambered over huge tree roots and went up hills and down others. There were a couple of streams to hop across and at one point they had to go along the top of a small waterfall, jumping from stone to stone across the rushing river, less than two feet away from a drop of about half a dozen metres or so.

Sam felt like he was in the scene from Avatar when the guy gets lost and is taken on a trek through the night-time forest. He stumbled over everything that he possible could, getting tired very quickly and making an incredible amount of noise, whereas Rachel and Master Hamato moved so silently and were so sure footed and confident that they had no trouble keeping up their conversation about philosophy the whole way. They never stopped talking and the old man didn't get out of breath.

Eventually, they had descended a short hill with loose stones, which Sam all but rolled down while Rachel and Hamato strolled ahead as if on a walk in the park, and encountered the cabin sitting in a clearing surrounded on all sides by the jungle.

They were having tea. Sam reflected that tea, along with swords, also seemed to be a big part of Displacer life for some reason. In this case it was green and not Andrew's usual PG Tips, which was a nice change.

'Sam-san, I can see by the way you move that you have not studied martial arts before, but that you have had some training.'

'I fence a bit, if that's what you mean?' Sam made a couple of motions in the air with his right hand; a quick circular parry and riposte.

Hamato's eyes narrowed slightly as he sized Sam up. 'Hmm, yes, I see now. That will help you a little bit. A very little bit.'

'When do we start?'

'We already did on the walk here.'

'Really?'

Rachel shared a sly smile with Hamato. 'Can I tell him, please?'

Hamato smiled and assented with a small nod, then sipped at his tea as Rachel turned to Sam.

'We're only about a hundred metres from where we first met Master Hamato.'

'What?!?'

'The walk here was a test, to see how you would cope with certain things, your balance, your stamina, whether you are afraid of heights…'

Hamato flicked a chopstick at Sam unexpectedly and he barely managed to bat it to one side before it hit him on the head. He was about to protest, but the old man forestalled him. 'Your reactions.'

Rachel laughed. 'He did the same thing to me when I first came here.' She turned deadly serious suddenly. 'And now Master Hamato will use all of that information to decide whether to train you or not. We might be going home in a few minutes if you didn't shape up.'

She turned to the old man and they waited for Hamato to speak.

Sam found himself holding his breath. It was suddenly very important to him that he win Hamato's approval and he realised that it most likely had something to do with the girl who was sitting uncomfortably close to him; he was pretty sure it was her approval that he actually wanted and training with Hamato would be a good start to getting it.

Hamato took another sip of his tea. And then another. Slowly he put the cup down and looked at Sam. His was suddenly stern and it felt like he was looking into Sam's soul as he declared in a hard voice, 'I will train him.'

The look on Hamato's face reminded Sam of the one Yoda had when Luke told him he wasn't afraid to train on Dagobah. He swallowed as he felt a chill pass through him and wondered what he had gotten into.

Hamato led them out of the back door to where there was a lean-to sheltering the bath. There was also a vast array of weapons hanging from the outside wall of the cabin. Sam recognised a few of them from films, but most were a mystery to him and some looked more like farm implements than anything else.

Hamato indicated the weapons. 'In your time here, Sam-san, you will learn to wield every single one of these objects, but your greatest accomplishment will be when you can use something that is not a weapon as if it were one.'

He held up the pair to the chopstick that he had thrown at Sam earlier. He held it out to Rachel and indicated a straw dummy set up outside in the yard about twenty metres away.

Rachel bowed as she took the chopstick from him then whirled in place and hurled it. It hit the dummy with a thunk and stuck there, more than half of its length buried in the centre of the dummy's head.

Hamato sighed. 'Not bad. A bit off centre.' Rachel bowed her head in shame as Hamato continued. 'Any idiot can kill with a sword, you just stand there and swing it until you hit something. To kill with a chopstick or gouge someone's eye out with a spoon, *that* takes skill. So, first you will master the weapons, then you will master yourself.'

Sam rubbed his hands together eagerly. 'OK, then, which one first? The sword? The sai? The nunchucks would be cool!' He gazed longingly at the rack of weapons.

Hamato chuckled and shook his head. 'No, no, no. First… you run. Your body is your first and most important weapon, without it all of these are useless. You will run until you can run no longer. And then you will run some more. You know the way, Rachel-san. Hajime!'

Rachel bowed to the master, indicating for Sam to do the same and then she led him away at a trot.

Sam spoke as soon as they were hidden by the trees and out of earshot of the cabin. 'Does Master Hamato know what we are?'

'He knew that there was something different about me as soon as he saw me. I don't think he knows *exactly* what we are, but he does know that we're the good guys.'

'And how did you find him?'

'I didn't; he found me. I had heard stories of a wise man living up here, rumours of a martial arts master hiding away from the world, and I followed them. I camped up here for three months, searching the forest, hunting and doing my own training. In all that time I didn't even find his cabin. Then I woke up one morning to find him sitting a couple of feet away from me, brewing some tea over a fire that he'd managed to build and light without waking me. It's hard to sneak up on me, I can tell you, it's even harder to follow me without my knowing, and he'd been doing it since the day I walked into his jungle. He asked me what I wanted and I told him that I wanted to train with him. He agreed and I spent the next three years with him.'

She glanced at him as he ran beside her and sighed as she sized him up. 'Now stop talking, you're going to need to save your breath.'

Sam wasn't unfit by any means and he'd come to the past mentally prepared to train, but after only ten minutes he was starting to breathe heavily and after half an hour he was on the verge of collapsing.

'How long are we going to keep running for?' Sam just about managed to gasp out.

'Until Master H tells us to stop.' Just like on the walk earlier, Rachel wasn't having any trouble breathing whatsoever and she looked at him sideways with a grin. 'That Rocky montage isn't sounding too bad now, is it?'

'Huh,' Sam huffed. He was somewhat amused, but just didn't have the energy or the breath to reply.

'Just keep running, Sam, you can do this.'

Rachel's encouragement gave Sam renewed strength, but it didn't last long and it was a full hour before Hamato appeared. He stepped out of nowhere into their path, and held up his hand for Sam to stop.

Sam immediately collapsed to the floor taking in huge gulps of air. He'd been on the point of throwing up for the last few minutes, but he hadn't been able to bear the thought of doing that in front of Rachel and had only just managed to control himself.

Rachel kept jogging on the spot, still not out of breath and barely sweating.

Hamato turned to her. 'Four laps, top speed.'

'Yes, Master.' Rachel went sprinting off and was lost from sight in between the trees in seconds.

Now that Rachel had gone, Sam took the opportunity to get rid of the contents of his stomach.

Master Hamato watched him impassively, waiting for him to finish.

Eventually, Sam wiped his mouth and stood up unsteadily, wobbling, but determined not to fall.

Hamato nodded. 'Good, you have determination at least, that will make up for your lack of conditioning. Come, there is work to be done.'

Sam smiled weakly and followed him, sure that his training was about to begin in earnest. Would it be weapons training first or unarmed combat? Perhaps some super-secret ninja technique.

It was none of those, in fact; in true "Daniel-san" fashion, Sam spent an hour sweeping the floors and dusting the surfaces inside the cabin. When that was done he was sent to fetch water to fill the bath and top off the drinking barrel. The river was a good quarter of a mile away and it took him about a dozen trips to do the job, carrying two very large and very heavy wooden buckets at a time. While he was doing all this he was taunted by the sight of Rachel and Hamato training, laughing like two old friends, using all of the weapons that he wanted to be learning and generally looking like they were having a lot of fun.

At midday, Sam helped Rachel with the food. She showed him what needed to be done, taking him through the jungle, checking Hamato's animal traps and finding fruit and vegetables. Then it was back to the kitchen to clean and prepare it, while Hamato sat and soaked in the bath that Sam had just filled.

While the food was stewing he walked with Rachel to the waterfall that they had crossed on the way to the cabin - it was actually just a little bit upstream from where Sam had filled his buckets earlier and not the hour away that the roundabout route had made it seem.

Sam stood on the edge of the river next to the falls and took in the view. The cascading water fed a deep blue pool that was ringed by vibrant green trees and bushes, shading it and making it seem very cosy and secluded. It was truly beautiful and the constant sound of the waterfall was somehow soothing and Sam could almost feel the worries and doubts he had brought with him drifting away.

Rachel took her sandals off, throwing them down onto the bank of the lake below, and hopped across the rocks until she was in the middle of the drop.

She beckoned to him with a grin. 'Come on!' She dived headfirst, dropping the six or seven metres like an arrow and landed in the water with barely a splash.

Sam kicked off his sandals and chucked them after Rachel's, then very carefully went out onto the stepping stones; he felt very weak and somewhat shaky from the morning's exertions and really didn't want to injure himself on the very first day. He stood on the rock that Rachel had jumped from and looked down. It seemed like a much longer drop from there than it had from the riverbank.

Rachel had surfaced and was floating on her back, looking up at him.

'Come on, Sam! Don't be a chicken!' She laughed happily and sculled backwards away from where he would hit the water.

Sam swallowed nervously, but just like before, there was no way he wanted to look bad in front of her, so he stepped back from the edge, took a deep breath and leapt.

'Oh, shh….!'

His shout was cut off abruptly as he hit the water and plunged feet first into the depths. When the bubbles cleared he saw that he was a good few metres under the surface and he struggled to swim upwards, but seemed to make no headway because his clothes were weighing him down and he was exhausted from all the exercise and the Displacement. He was starting to panic and was just about to run out of breath when he finally broke the surface. He gasped for air and trod water, waiting for his heartbeat to go back to normal.

Rachel was watching him from a few metres away, smiling, and Sam realised that he had been safe all along; she had been standing by to rescue him if he hadn't made it to the surface. He splashed her, annoyed that she had let him think he was going to drown and she laughed.

'How are you enjoying yourself so far, Sam?'

'Well, I'm getting good at cleaning and fetching water, my legs can barely hold my weight anymore and I vomited whatever I had in my stomach when I got here, so… I'm having a lot of fun, thanks!'

'You're toughening up your body before you begin the real training. You need to. I went through much the same thing the first time I did any training, but it was a lot worse than just cleaning and fetching water, maybe I'll tell you about it some time. Trust me, if you just leapt straight into all the good stuff you'd just end up getting hurt right away and have to give up. Anyway, if you don't feel like putting in the hard work, you know you can always go home whenever you want.'

'Let's see how I feel tomorrow when I wake up; if my body hurts as much as I think it will, then I may go home, or I might just use some very foul language and tough it out.'

'That's the spirit!' Rachel laughed then swam to the side of the pool, she got out and began to take off her clothes. She threw her rope belt onto a nearby bush and then started to pull her tunic off over her head.

Sam watched her nervously. 'What are you doing?'

'Well, our clothes are clean, well, clean-ish anyway, and we want them to dry. You take yours off over on the other side of the pool. Go on, I promise I won't peek!' She grinned widely and Sam wasn't so sure that she was being totally truthful.

He swam to the other side of the pool and got out and moved behind a bush to take his clothes off. He was still wringing them out when there was a splash as Rachel re-entered the water. He finished hanging them on a bush and then realised that he was going to be in full view of her when he got back into the pool.

'OK! Don't look!'

Rachel laughed. 'I won't!'

He checked to make sure that she had her back to him, then ran and jumped into the water with a whoop.

Now that he was no longer being weighed down and had to struggle to stay afloat, the water was quite pleasant. It was warm and he could feel his muscles being soothed. He closed his eyes and floated, enjoying the sensation.

'You're doing well, actually, so don't worry.' Rachel was floating beside him. 'When I came here it wasn't my first training Displacement; I had already been doing martial arts for years and I spent the three months before Master Hamato agreed to train me working out and getting fit in this time-line. You've been thrown into the deep end, with no training and almost no fitness, of course you're going to struggle. It's remarkable that he agreed to take you on, either he saw something in you, or he might only be doing it as a favour to me... Come to think of it, that's probably it; after all, we both know there's nothing special about you!'

She grinned at him and Sam chuckled. 'I feel very privileged...'

'You should be! He hasn't trained anyone else but me in forty years.'

They lay there, side by side, the only noise coming from the waterfall, looking up at the clear and incredibly blue sky.

Eventually, Rachel broke the silence between them. 'We should start getting back, dinner will be almost ready.' She swam to the side of the pool and started to climb out.

Sam watched her for a second before he realised that she was naked and he shouldn't be staring at her. He blushed and swam to where he had left his own clothes, climbing out and putting the bushes between the two of them as quickly as he could.

Rachel smiled to herself as she dressed. She knew that Sam had watched her and she had sneaked a glance herself as he had climbed out; it was only natural, but he had looked so embarrassed about it. In some ways he was so grown up, but in others he was so shy and innocent that she had to keep reminding herself that there was a world of difference between them; he was still only fifteen, in body *and* in mind - he lacked her more than a decade of experience in Displacements. Even so, she couldn't help but like him. However, she had to admit there was more to it than just that; despite what she had said about Hamato only agreeing to train Sam because of her, she knew that the old master wouldn't have done that - he must have seen the same thing in him that she did.

After lunch Hamato gave Sam an axe and directed him to a few fallen trees. He showed him how to chop them up then went off to work with Rachel.

Sam chopped wood until his hands were red raw, carrying piles of it to the back of the cabin every so often and stacking it up against the wall. Whenever he could, he sneaked glances at Rachel and Hamato training, while trying not to make it obvious that he was and also trying not to chop off his own foot as he did.

They went to bed early that first night, very shortly after a dinner of the leftovers from lunch. Sam found that he was sharing the spare room with Rachel, but he was far too tired to worry about the sleeping arrangements or whether he was going to disturb her with his snoring. They rolled out the futons that Hamato had stacked in the cupboards and Sam all but fell face-first onto his. He was instantly asleep, so he didn't see the fond look that Rachel gave him as she tucked him in.

Hamato woke them before dawn. Sam was as stiff as he had known he would and could barely move. He wanted nothing else but to stay where he was, but Hamato threatened to kick him out of bed if he wasn't up in ten seconds, so he summoned all his willpower and struggled to his feet. After he'd rolled away the futons with Rachel, who was as bright and cheerful as if she'd spent the day before at home in front of the television, Hamato told them to run again. Sam ran on his own, allowing Rachel to go at her own speed; he'd done the circuit with her enough times the day before to not get lost.

He started slowly in the half-dark, shambling along through the early morning mist as if he was an extra from a zombie series, but as he got warmer his muscles started to loosen up and his stride lengthened. He still wasn't able to go very fast, but at least he wasn't in real pain anymore. After half an hour or so, the sun came up and warmed him further at the same time as it revealed the beautiful countryside around him.

He wasn't feeling nearly as bad as he'd thought he would be and when Rachel passed him for the second time he was able to lift his head enough to watch her go by. She was running with such grace and beauty that it took away what little breath he had left and that, more than anything, made him decide that he wasn't going to go home, at least not right away.

The next few weeks passed quickly with the days being much the same; Sam doing hard physical work while Rachel trained with Hamato. His conditioning improved slowly but steadily - every day he could run further and faster and, while by no means could he keep up with Rachel, he knew that he wasn't doing as badly any more. The work was becoming easier and he was developing hard places on his hands and feet, as well as muscles that he didn't know existed; one time Rachel walked into the bedroom and laughed when she caught him checking out his burgeoning abdominal muscles.

The sixth week after they had arrived, Sam was nearing the end of his run when Hamato suddenly appeared in the middle of the path in that way he had of just materialising somewhere and motioned for him to stop. Sam staggered to a halt and stood, trying to control his breathing, waiting for the old man to say something, but instead he just motioned for Sam to follow him and led him back to the cabin.

That was the day that Sam started his training in earnest.

The weeks turned into months and Sam spent most of his time punching and kicking, working on basic techniques against the straw dummy outside the cabin, whether it was pouring with rain or swelteringly hot. It was boring and repetitive, but Sam didn't mind one bit because he felt like he was finally doing something constructive. Of course there were still the daily runs and Rachel still lapped him, but instead of doing so five or six times like she had the first couple of weeks, he was now only being passed a couple of times.

And there were the daily baths.

Sam still wasn't exactly comfortable being naked around Rachel, but he was getting more used to it, especially seeing as Hamato habitually walked around naked after his own bath. Sam remembered reading somewhere that nudity in Japan was seen as being something fairly normal, so he resolved not to make such a big deal of it, and Rachel certainly didn't.

One morning, about five months into the Displacement, Sam did the maths and realised that if he'd been living in the "real" world then it would have been November 1st and he would be celebrating his sixteenth birthday.

In that moment, he finally understood what Rachel had been trying to tell him after the football match: here he was spending all day every day in the single-minded pursuit of something and would be doing so for months, maybe years. He would have experiences that his parents would never know he'd had and he would grow, both mentally and physically. However, when it was all over he would go home and instantly be back in his old body, his family wouldn't know that he was any different, wouldn't know that in his mind he was no longer a fifteen-year-old boy. They would continue to treat him exactly the same as they always had and, despite any changes he'd gone through, he would have to act, at least around them, how he always had.

It was worrying and he hoped he would be able to deal with it when the time came, but at the same time it was an interesting philosophical question; he would have birthdays in the past that he would celebrate again with his family and friends, but which time would be real? Was he sixteen now? Or would he turn sixteen five months after he got back?

He didn't know the answer, but what he did know was that when he told Rachel it was his birthday, she had crawled over to his futon and kissed him.

While it wasn't his first proper kiss, it was the first one that actually meant something to him and all of his worries about his parents vanished with it as he realised that there would always be someone by his side, like his uncle, or hopefully Rachel, who knew what he was going through.

She kissed him for a full few seconds, which seemed like an eternity to him, but before he could truly begin to appreciate it her lips were gone and she was smiling at him.

'Come on, time to go running.'

Rachel jumped to her feet, but it took Sam a few extra seconds than he usually needed to compose himself enough to be able to get out and help Rachel roll the futons up.

A few months after Sam's birthday Hamato seemed satisfied with Sam's progress and he graduated to harder techniques. He also got to pick up a weapon for the first time, even though it was only a wooden sword - a practice weapon called a "bokken". About the same time the weather started to change and while it never got very cold in the jungle, the water in the river came from the mountains and was freezing. It was especially cold under the waterfall, which brought about a new phase of training - for reasons which Sam couldn't quite fathom, Hamato made them stand under the waterfall for hours at a time, practising techniques while the water beat down on them. He and Rachel would come out shivering and go straight into a run to warm up.

Shortly after he began training with the sword, Sam started working on his throwing. For a couple of hours each day he used both hands to chuck various things at the straw dummy outside the cabin. It was frustrating at first and he had to spend a lot of time searching for wayward "shuriken", especially when he was practising with his left hand, but he made progress. It was one of the few things, along with how to cook and clean, that Hamato trusted Rachel with teaching him and she got so exasperated with his ineptitude one of the first days that she threw her hands up and shouted that he "threw like a girl". From that day on they could barely keep a straight face while they were training and ended up laughing and messing around a lot of the time. Hamato didn't seem to mind, though, and he turned a blind eye to their clowning as long as Sam improved, letting them have their fun and blow off steam, which meant that throwing practice quickly became one of their favourite activities.

According to Hamato, Sam was making remarkable progress and about a year into the Displacement he made him begin sparring with Rachel. For the first time Sam had an opponent; up until then it had always been the dummy or the air that was receiving his novice techniques, but from that point on he had something real to aim at, something that moved. Something that hit back. Hard.

Up until that point the only pain he had had to deal with had been sore muscles, blisters on his hands and feet, and a few cuts and scrapes from the trees and rocks that he brushed against in passing, but with this new regimen he discovered bruises in a big way. From the start, Hamato refused to let Rachel hold back very much and Sam would barely be able to think about a technique before he found himself on the ground or wheezing for breath after being punched.

It was a soul-destroying couple of weeks and Sam came the closest to giving up that he had since the very beginning. He kept going, though, both because he wasn't willing to see all the hard work he'd put in so far go to waste and because he couldn't bear for the time with Rachel to end.

Then, one day, somehow, he began blocking some of the attacks. He wasn't sure whether it was because he was finally learning something or if it was some instinct of self-preservation, but it gave him hope and he redoubled his efforts.

In the following days he was blocking more and more of Rachel strikes until it became rare for her to hit him at all and not long after that he found that he was able to use the time those blocks bought him to retaliate. Initially, his feeble attacks got nowhere near their target, but he came closer and closer each day as he got more and more competent, until finally, miraculously, he managed to hit her with one of his kicks. It was only a scrape, nothing more than a soft rub against her ribs, but he was so astounded with this unexpected success that he failed to see Rachel's counterattack coming.

He woke up ten minutes later with a wet cloth over his eyes, but a big smile on his face.

From then on Sam's abilities grew exponentially. The blocks started to come by instinct; his mind recognising what she was going to do almost before she did it, just by the movement of her eyes or the shifting of her weight. He still couldn't stop all of her attacks, but it was enough to make sparring bouts last for minutes before he was knocked down instead of seconds. He was also able to keep up with Rachel on their morning runs, although in the first months he ended them in far worse condition than she did.

His seventeenth birthday came and went and still they worked, training every day and adding a weekly run to the top of nearby Mount Yunaha and back. They also spent an hour each night before bed alternately talking about philosophy and ancient wisdoms, or meditating; Hamato insisted that they develop spiritually as well as mentally and physically. If nothing else, the hour gave them time to rest their stressed bodies and, when not meditating, they used the time to stretch while they were talking.

As the years passed, Rachel grew into a beautiful young woman and, while she didn't get any taller, she filled out in ways that Sam found very interesting. Sam in turn became a lean young man with a mature look about him and finally got his growth spurt to become almost an inch taller than her.

Sam had initially thought it was strange to be fighting someone he was attracted to, giving them bruises and receiving them in return, it definitely sounded counterproductive as far as relationships go, but it created a certain camaraderie between them and the two of them became very close. However, Hamato kept them so near their limits of endurance that they had no energy left for anything physical to develop between them. The only time they really had to themselves were the daily baths, which they spent talking and sneaking the occasional peek at each other, although by that time they were so familiar with each other's bodies that there was no real need to be surreptitious about it. The birthday kiss was never repeated, but Sam had the sneaking suspicion that Rachel was interested in him - she was just holding back for some reason. He held out hope that she would reciprocate his feelings for her, but to his disappointment nothing ever happened.

They got to know one another to such an extent that they could anticipate so well what the other was thinking and going to do, that the fights between them got longer and longer and they began to go whole training sessions without either of them being able to land a single blow.

They found themselves laughing more and more each day as well, as they got to understand and appreciate the other's sense of humour, while Master Hamato stood watching them train with an almost permanent scowl on his face. He chided them for their irreverence and lack of seriousness and made them do extra work as punishment, but then smiled when he thought they weren't looking.

They ran, trained, ate, bathed, slept, and then did it all over again. They fought on the rocks over the waterfall, they fought on fallen tree trunks, they fought on top of the mountain. They fought with swords, staffs, sticks, spears and shuriken. They fought blindfold and in the dead of night. They fought while sitting, and kneeling, and with a hand tied behind their backs. They fought and fought until one day, after they had been in Okinawa for more than three years, Master Hamato told them that they had fought enough and ordered them to stop. That in itself wasn't unusual, but the emotion in his eyes was, and Sam wondered what was going on.

Hamato beckoned to Rachel and, suddenly very serious, she went over to face him; apparently, she knew what was happening.

They bowed to each other and then, without any warning, Hamato attacked.

He moved so fluidly that it seemed that he floated over the ground. Rachel was instantly put on the back foot and her arms were a blur as she struggled to block his strikes. Red marks appeared, as if from out of nowhere, on her face and arms, but she managed to avoid being hit hard enough to cause any real damage. She fought stubbornly and started to recover from her initial setback, but never quite managed to take the initiative away from Hamato. She desperately tried a few counterattacks, but all she did was open herself up even more. After only thirty seconds she was sitting on her arse on the floor and breathing hard.

Hamato stood over her, calmly and nodded. 'Good.' He turned to look at Sam. 'Your turn.'

Sam fought back a moment of nervousness and bowed. The old man bowed back and in an instant had closed the distance between them, but Sam had expected it and, instead of retreating, he pressed forward.

Taken a little by surprise, Hamato was unable to take the initiative as he had with Rachel. He struck out, but found his blows blocked and the slight smile on his face betrayed his amusement at finding that he needed to make an effort to avoid Sam's return attacks.

Sam's advantage didn't last very long, though, and Hamato quickly turned the tables on him, his experience far outweighing the enthusiasm of youth. In a matter of seconds Sam was sitting on the ground next to Rachel and breathing hard, one eye bruised and closing slightly.

Hamato smiled down at them. 'Very good.' He drew himself upright, formally, then bowed deeply.

They scrambled around and performed a kneeling bow to him in perfect unison.

'Thank you, Master Hamato.'

They straightened up.

He was gone.

'Wha...?' Sam looked around, but Hamato was nowhere to be seen.

Rachel was smiling at him. 'Your training is over, Sam. It's time to go home.'

Sam was speechless, he didn't want to believe that it was the end of one of the most wonderful and unique periods in his life. He shook his head and was about to protest when he noticed that Rachel was looking at him strangely. 'What?'

'It's time to go home, but first...'

She leapt at him and Sam felt her lips lock to his.

They fell to the ground in each other's arms.

Sam opened his eyes and found himself holding hands with Rachel in his uncle's sitting room. They smiled warmly at each other, keeping the contact between them and taking a moment to acclimatise to being back to their younger bodies.

After a few seconds, Sam turned his head and winked at Andrew. 'I know kung fu.'

CHAPTER 11
OUT WITH THE NEW. IN WITH THE OLD

'I can't believe you lied to me!'

Andrew, of course, had blown his top as soon as Rachel had told him where they had gone.

She shrugged and tried to look innocent. 'It was only an innocent little white lie.'

'But you took him to a bloody jungle on Okinawa! Do you know how many ways he could have died there? The spiders, snakes, the burrowing ants… It's so dangerous there!'

Rachel shook her head in exasperation. '*Everywhere* interesting is dangerous in some way or other, Andrew! The important thing is that he's learnt a *hell* of a lot and he's no longer the wimp he was when I first met him.'

'Hey!' Sam pouted and punched her in the arm, a gesture that had become so natural over the last few years, but had felt so different only an hour ago.

Rachel grinned at him, raising an eyebrow. 'You denying it?' She reached out and squeezed the bicep of the arm that he had used to punch her and which was no longer the large, toned muscle that it had been only minutes before.

Sam looked down at his arm and sighed. 'No. I guess not.'

Rachel chuckled, then turned back to Andrew and continued to argue with him about whether she should have taken him to Okinawa or not.

Sam barely heard them, though, because he was more concerned with rediscovering his body. It was an extremely strange and unsettling sensation to be back to how he had been before he had started training. He was inches shorter, had almost no muscles to speak of, and of course his arm was broken again, or still, or whatever. In addition, he had several bruises and various aches from what he now knew had been his graduation fight with Master Hamato.

He stood up, a little unsteady on legs that suddenly weren't his own. 'Excuse me, I need to go for a walk.'

Rachel and Andrew stopped speaking and watched him curiously as he made his way to the door.

Sam paused and looked back at Rachel. 'Would you come with me, please?'

She stood and followed Sam to the door where she turned and looked back at Andrew. 'We can continue this when we get back, if you feel that you need to.'

'It's alright,' he waved them away. 'Go, you can tell me everything later.'

'You're not really going to tell him *everything* are you?' Sam asked Rachel, a bit worried, as they wandered down the street.

She laughed. 'No, I'm not going to tell him about *that*, don't worry.'

'That's a relief.'

She reached out and took his hand and he smiled at her.

They walked in silence and as the minutes passed, Sam began to get used his body, but it still didn't quite feel like it was his. 'I feel strange, like my mind knows how to do things that my body isn't capable of. Do you know what I mean?'

'Of course. All of us have felt like that at some point.' Rachel nodded. 'It's worse for two of us this time, not just because it's mostly physical training we've just done, but also because we've gone from being children to adults, then back again. Of course, you can do the exercises you've been taught and you're never going to lose the muscle memory from the movements, but, physically at least, you're never going to get back to the same point as you were in the past, mostly because you can't possibly dedicate the same amount of time to training as you did there; you have other things to do. However, even if you don't ever return to being the superman you were in Okinawa, you'll easily get to the point where you'll be able to kick the arse of anyone you meet. Including Quentin.'

Sam smiled finally. 'I *do* like the sound of that.'

Rachel laughed. 'OK, then, why don't we go to the park? I know you're tired, but we can do some basic training and you'll see that things aren't as bad as you thought.'

'That sounds good.'

A few short minutes later they were in the park, with the dirt football pitch and children's playground, where Rafa had beaten Sam up only a few short weeks, but so long, ago. They stood in the bright afternoon sunshine off to one side away from the games going on and started doing some basic stretching. Even just doing that reminded Sam of how much he'd lost and he groaned as he tried to loosen muscles that were a lot tighter than they had been less than an hour before.

'Oh jeez, haven't these guys learnt anything yet?' Rachel pointed with her chin over Sam's shoulder as she stretched her arms over her head and bent from side to side.

Sam bent over to stretch his hamstring and turned his head to sneak a glance without making it obvious. Watching them from the entrance to the park was Rafa. He was accompanied by about a dozen boys, most of whom looked eighteen or older - it looked like he had rounded up every young thug he knew to confront them.

Sam looked at them nervously. 'That's a lot of people… Um… Shall we get out of here?'

Rachel laughed. 'Nah! We came here for you to find out what you can do and I'm fairly sure you already know how to run. OK, I think that's enough stretching, let's do this.'

They straightened up and faced off against each other. Sam had his back to the bullies, but Rachel was watching them from the corner of her eye just in case they approached. She grinned as she rolled her shoulders before lifting her hands into a fighting stance. 'You know, provoking them into a fight would be a *really* good test…'

'Maybe not.'

She shrugged, feigning disappointment. 'Spoilsport. Come on then, let's start with some basics, but slowly, OK? And take care of your arm.'

They started to move, throwing kicks and punches.

Sam tested the limits of his body and winced. 'How did I ever live like this? I'm so weak!'

'I have no idea. Although, I must admit I still found you quite attractive… but not having a six pack is kind of a deal-breaker, sorry.'

Sam laughed while not interrupting his techniques. 'Believe me, that is one of the first things I'm going to work on!'

They circled for a while, throwing casual attacks at each other, not doing much more than warming up. Sam quickly realised that he wasn't feeling nearly as bad as he'd thought he would - his body definitely knew what it should be doing, it just couldn't do it as well as it had before, something he was sure would come with time. He grinned at Rachel. 'Do you feel like kicking it up a notch?'

'Fine by me.'

They started to move faster, getting back into the rhythm that they had found in Okinawa. They were going around in circles as they fought so that they could take turns watching Rafa and his gang and Sam smiled when he next had them in vision; they were starting to look quite nervous. 'I think it's beginning to dawn on them that it wouldn't be a good idea to attack us.'

They switched positions and Rachel glanced at them under Sam's armpit as she dodged a right hook. 'Yep. Looks like they're getting the idea, but I think we need to scare them some more. Do you think you can manage a couple of minutes at top speed? That should finish the job off nicely.'

Sam was somewhat out of breath and wasn't sure he could keep going much longer, but he nodded anyway. 'I think so, but only a couple of minutes; I don't think it would dissuade them much if I puked my guts out like I did that first day after the run.'

'Yeah, I don't think that it would... I heard you, by the way. It wasn't very nice. Very impressive volume and duration though. Thanks for waiting until I got out of sight, I did appreciate it.'

'You're welcome!' Sam would have laughed, but he didn't have the breath to spare. 'Ready?'

'Of course!'

They increased their pace even further until they were moving at a blistering speed that still wasn't quite their best, but not far off.

They could read the intentions of each other so well that they barely needed to look to know what the other was doing, which freed them up to snatch glances in the direction of their audience. Their demonstration was having the desired effect; the bullies were now actively arguing with Rafa and several of them were drifting away. However, while that was certainly satisfying, it wasn't the real reason they were fighting - Sam was rapidly adjusting to his body and he now knew that he hadn't lost everything he had gained in the past. His lack of fitness was a major issue, of course, but the muscle memory was definitely there and with it the techniques he had learnt.

Finally, they stopped and bowed to each other, grinning happily. They were both tired, but Sam was far worse off than Rachel. He was breathing hard and on the verge of collapsing, but he made sure not to show signs of it in case the bullies took advantage of what they might perceive as weakness.

They looked around as a wave of noise from the teenagers playing football in the park washed over them. They had stopped playing to watch and were gaping at them in wonder as they whooped and clapped, most of them with their mouths open.

Rachel smiled and waved at them, causing more than one of them to blush. 'Let's get out of here.' She held out her hand to Sam and together they ran towards the exit.

'See ya, Rafa!' Sam grinned as he jogged past the boy who had caused him so much pain and suffering in the past, but who would most likely never bother him again.

Rafa involuntarily took a step back and the slight look of fear that Sam saw on his face as they went by was immensely gratifying.

They were ravenously hungry, so they sat at a table on the terrace of a nearby street café and ordered sandwiches and cokes.

The sun was going down and the locals were starting to appear on the streets now that the heat was lessening, once more outnumbering the tourists streaming past, going to and from the nearby Park Güell.

'That wasn't too bad, was it?'

'No, it wasn't.' Sam shook his head. 'I'm pretty surprised, actually; I had no idea I was capable of that. I mean, that this out of shape body I have right now would be capable of that.'

'That's the power of a trained mind.'

Their food came and they tucked in, the conversation put on hold for a little while, but Sam had too much on his mind to stay silent for long and there was one especially important thing that he had to ask. 'Rachel, last night in the jungle…'

She smiled; she had known that he was going to get around to it soon enough. 'It was great, but don't get your hopes up; it's not going to happen again, at least not for a while anyway.'

Sam's heart fell. 'Why? Didn't you enjoy it?'

'Yes, of course I did! But you're fifteen, Sam. And besides, you've got no abs so you won't have the same stamina…'

'Hey!' He hit her gently on the arm. 'I said I was going to work on them!'

'Good!' She laughed. 'Seriously, though, I do like you, Sam, a lot, but it's just, I don't know, that this is the real world and things are different here. They *have* to be different here.'

'You mean, like, what happens in Vegas stays in Vegas?'

'Something like that.' She smiled, trying to soften the blow. 'Sam, you and I know who we are, what we are, and exactly how old we really are, but everyone else looks at us and sees fifteen and sixteen-year-olds. We have to act that way, at least for our families. At least for now.'

'Do the rest of your family know what you are?'

'No, no way! They'd lock me up in the madhouse if I started telling them about time travelling and stuff! My parents are... special.'

'I don't know if my family would understand.'

'They seem pretty cool so they might, but you're not allowed to tell anyone about what you can do; Society rules, I'm afraid.'

'That's probably for the best; they'd just worry about me. But I really don't like keeping secrets from them.' He took another sip of coke. 'How do you do it? How do you cope with having two separate lives? One with your family and another as a Displacer that they know nothing about? And having to go to school as well?'

Rachel grimaced. 'Well, my Dad left home long before I got my powers and never came back, so it's been just me and my Mum for years. I've never really gotten on with her, though, or any of her many boyfriends either, so I try to stay away from home as much as I can. And as for school, well, I'm sixteen, so I was able to leave at the end of term and don't have to deal with it anymore, but it's been a nightmare for the last year; I'm as old as most of my teachers, so you can imagine how well I got on with the other girls and as for the lessons, I've learnt so much in the past that I was beyond most of the stuff they teach and because I know exactly what I'm going to do with my life, I *knew* I was never going to need any of the rest... I basically stopped working towards the end and barely scraped enough of a pass to graduate.' She shrugged. 'I guess what I'm saying is that I don't cope, not really - my life in the present has been pretty crap and I spend most of my time looking forward to going back to the past so I can do something more interesting.'

'That's exactly how I felt after I went to Port Royal - I couldn't wait to go back.' Sam frowned as he looked around, taking in the tired and stressed people hurrying past them and the traffic going nowhere. 'And

I guess I feel the same way now; everything just seems so grey in the present… Like nothing's quite real.'

'Don't worry; all of the Displacers feel the same, especially after a long Displacement, it's only natural. The feeling will pass in a few days, you'll see. And in the meantime, you know I'm here for you if you need to talk. About anything.'

'That's good to know, thank you.'

'You're welcome.'

There was a short silence as their hunger resurfaced, temporarily overcoming their need to talk, and they swiftly finished off their Catalan-style sandwiches made with tomato and oil covered bread.

Sam downed the last of his coke and wiped his mouth, hiding a belch discreetly behind his paper napkin, before grinning cheekily at Rachel. 'So… Where are you going to take me next time?'

Rachel raised an eyebrow and barked a laugh. 'Oh, you think I'm going to want to keep Displacing with you, do you? What makes you think I haven't got someone else, a boyfriend… or a girlfriend, who I usually work with?'

'I don't know, I just have a feeling…'

Rachel reached out and stroked Sam's cheek lovingly. It was a surprisingly tender and adult gesture coming from a girl that looked sixteen. 'I would love to Displace with you again, Sam.'

Sam reached up and held her hand to his face and smiled. The moment was ruined, though, when Rachel yawned.

'Oh god, I'm sorry!' She laughed nervously and pulled her hand back to cover her mouth.

Sam laughed too, but then yawned himself; suddenly he was feeling very tired indeed. 'I think I need to go to bed.' He grinned at her again. 'Care to join me?'

She stood up, looming over him and kissed him on the lips, then slapped his cheek gently. 'Naughty boy! Not right now, Sam.' She kissed him again before reaching down to grab his hand and pull him out of his chair. 'Come on, let's get you home.'

It was extremely strange to walk into his house and find it exactly the same as he'd left it more than three years ago; the same papers were on his desk, the same glass of water was by his bed, the drawings that Violeta had been working on were still on the dining room table.

Sam realised to his shame that he had thought about his family only very occasionally while he'd been away and he hadn't missed them at all, except maybe in the difficult times at the start when he had been almost ready to give up. There was just something about Displacing that made you live there fully, as if who and what you were in the present was pushed to one side and almost forgotten when you became someone in the past. In addition the intensity of the training had meant he hadn't had much time to himself to even really think about them. Consequently, he felt very awkward when he walked into the living room and found his parents and Violeta watching a Disney film on the sofa together.

They greeted him casually, perfunctorily, as if they had seen him only that morning and not three years ago, and he had to actively restrain himself from throwing himself into their embrace. He sat on the large armchair beside the sofa; with them, but not really feeling a part of the family, until Violeta stood up and wandered over. She offered him a gummy bear, holding it out to him in a grubby hand, and suddenly he smiled, feeling connected to them again. He popped the sweet into his mouth and she clambered up to snuggle next to him. He wrapped his arms around her and watched the rest of the film with them, then went to bed, happy and once more grounded in the present.

Rachel and Sam had gotten into the habit of training every day in Okinawa and it was natural for them to continue to do so in the present. They ran up the hills overlooking Barcelona every morning, through the woods towards the Tibidabo theme park or the communications tower, before finding a quiet spot among the trees to practice their techniques and fight. Even though the sounds of traffic and other people were never quite gone, they loved to be surrounded by nature for their sparring sessions because it reminded them of Okinawa and helped them to focus. It was also a very good idea not to train where anybody could see them, they were very fortunate in fact that nobody had videoed the fight they had had in the playground on their phone and posted it to YouTube; people their age didn't usually have the level of abilities that they did and it would have called a lot of unwanted attention to themselves.

Despite not being able to spend nearly as much time on training as they had in the past, Sam's level of fitness quickly rose to a level where he could properly and safely use the skills he had learnt. He also made a good start on getting a six pack, which Rachel repeatedly told him was the most important thing for him to recover. She claimed she was just joking, but he wasn't too sure and didn't want to risk it, so he did lots of extra sit-ups at home, although he told himself that he wasn't doing them to impress her, but rather because Master Hamato had continually stressed how important it was to have strong core muscles.

After they had finished training, they would sit and talk while they ate a snack, enjoying the view and each other's company, before they had to head back to the city and the life that still didn't quite seem real.

After a week, Sam's arm came out of the cast. The doctors were surprised at how quickly and well he had healed, but when he commented on it the next day over tea, Andrew just gave him a wink and told him that it was "one of the perks" and said no more.

During that time, Andrew mostly left the two of them to their own devices - he no longer made Sam train constantly and visits to his flat became more like social events. The long summer afternoons and evenings were filled with laughter, Andrew and Rachel's favourite movies and more tea than Sam's bladder could safely handle, but one day Andrew suddenly turned serious and somehow Sam knew that, like his summer holidays, the time that he could enjoy himself without a care in the world was fast coming to an end.

'I've finally been able to get all the members together for a conference call. It's about time we introduced you to them and you officially became one of us.'

'OK...' Sam suddenly found himself quite nervous and he wasn't sure why.

Andrew saw his unease. 'Nothing to worry about, Sam. Just be your usual, charming self.'

Rachel had been in mid-swallow and she coughed and spluttered at the word "charming", choking on her tea.

Sam slapped her on the back, using the excuse to get a small measure of revenge. He nearly knocked the mug out of her hand with the force of his blows and she snorted, doubling over, tea bubbling out of her nose. She stopped coughing but he continued thumping her anyway and she turned to defend herself with a grin easily blocking his strikes with one hand while holding onto her mug with the other.

Sam gave up trying to hit her and pouted, pretending to be offended. 'I can do charming! I charmed you, didn't I?'

Rachel laughed and used the brief respite to put her mug down on the coffee table. 'Yeah, just keep telling yourself that, Sam.'

With a grin she threw a slap at him, which he blocked instinctively just before it hit his face and once more they began hitting out at each other, exchanging a few soft but lightning-fast open-hand blows. However, even though each tried their best, neither of them came even close to hitting the other; so evenly matched had they become.

Andrew laughed at their antics and watched them, amazed, for a few seconds before calling for them to stop. 'Hey! Beat each other up outside of my home, please! I don't want any souvenirs or furniture broken.' He shook his head wryly and tipped his own mug up, but was disappointed when he found it empty. He struggled to his feet and hobbled towards the door; like Sam, his wound was getting better, but not yet fully healed. 'I need more tea. Either of you want another one?'

They shook their heads, Sam rather more emphatically than Rachel.

'OK, suit yourselves. Be right back.'

As soon as his uncle had left the room Sam turned to Rachel. 'I knew that there were other Displacers that I haven't met, but you've never really told me how you're all organised. Do you have some kind of club or something?'

She thought about it briefly before replying. 'I've never really thought about it. We call ourselves a society and I guess it is a bit like a club in a way, although it's only open to people with our powers and it's kept a complete secret from everyone else in the world.'

Sam put a shocked expression on his face, with his eyes wide and his hand covering his mouth. 'Oh god, you're a cult and you've been brainwashing me this whole time… I'm out of here!'

He made to get off the sofa, feigning panic, but Rachel elbowed him hard in the ribs and he collapsed back down, wheezing for breath.

He was still bent over, alternately gasping and chuckling, when Andrew came back a short while later. He raised an eyebrow at them. 'Did I miss something?'

'No, nothing!' Sam unsuccessfully tried to cover his laughter with coughs, 'I just swallowed the wrong way, that's all - I really shouldn't have had that last Jammy Dodger…'

Rachel sniggered. 'Why don't you have some more tea to wash it down? I could go and get you some.'

Sam blanched at the thought of more tea and calmed down almost instantly. He smiled at her, overly sweetly. 'I'm alright now, thank you, Rachel.'

'No problem, Sam.' She batted her eyes at him and he laughed again.

Andrew rolled his eyes before raising his voice to get their attention. 'Anyway... As I was saying... Tomorrow you'll join us for a conference call and you'll officially become a member.'

'Do I get some kind of membership card?' Sam asked innocently and received another elbow in the ribs from Rachel.

Andrew frowned and shook his head. 'We don't have cards as such, but if you want, I can get John to print one for you.'

'No, that's OK, thanks. Just knowing I'm one of the Displacers is enough of an honour for me.'

'As it should be.' Andrew nodded. 'Of course, while you won't get a card, or anything like that, you *will* get a chip implanted in your neck so that we can keep track of you. We use the same kind of gun they use for cats and dogs and I'll do that tomorrow while we're online so everyone can watch. It doesn't hurt *too* much to put it in and I *usually* get it right the first time, but I can't promise anything, sorry.'

Sam opened his mouth to reply, but didn't quite know what to say, so he looked at Rachel quizzically instead.

She nodded, solemnly. 'It's true.' She ducked her head to tap the back of her neck. 'Right here.'

'Yes. We all have one.' Andrew hid his grin behind his hand. 'Don't worry, it won't explode if you drink enough tea to keep it cool.'

'Enough...? Oh...' Sam groaned as he finally got it. He shook his head and stood up. 'I don't think I want to join anymore. I'm going home.'

'Sit down, idiot!' Rachel reached out and pulled him back onto the sofa.

This time Andrew laughed with them, sharing in the joke. 'Seriously, Sam, there's nothing to worry about. Yes, the members will vote as to whether they accept you or not, but it's just a formality and nobody has ever been rejected once their ability to Displace has been determined. More importantly, though, it'll be the first chance for you to get to know the rest of the members and for them to get a good look at you. I know they'll like you and I think you'll like them; they're a good bunch of people, but some of them are very, *very* old and easily annoyed, so best behaviour, please.' He looked pointedly at Rachel. 'That goes double for you, young lady.'

She gave him an innocent "who, me?" look.

'Now, go on, get out of here and leave me to drink my tea in peace. See you tomorrow at six.' Andrew jerked his thumb over his shoulder at the door and reached for another biscuit as Sam and Rachel ran out, hand in hand.

CHAPTER 12
WELCOME TO THE CLUB

Sam spent the following morning with Rachel and, as usual, they went for one of their long runs and sparring sessions in the hills. They took a packed lunch with them and when they had trained enough they sat side by side on the beach towel Sam had brought, with Barcelona spread beneath them, basking in the sunlight and chewing on the Serrano ham sandwiches that Rachel had made.

Rachel closed her eyes and tilted her face to the sun. She smiled. 'I like it here, it's much nicer than London.'

'Have you been to Barcelona before?' Sam realised with a start that he didn't actually know much about Rachel's present day life; all the conversations he'd had with her had centred solely around her Displacing career. Even during the three years they had lived together in Okinawa he hadn't found out a lot about her beyond those experiences.

'No, this is my first time. I never had a reason to come here before, until Andrew asked me to help train you.'

'And your parents don't mind you being here for so long?'

Rachel chuckled. 'My mum barely knows where I am at the best of times; she's too busy with her new boyfriend, going on cruises and taking cheap holidays. Right now I'm fairly sure they're down the coast somewhere near Marbella, so at least we're in the same country.'

Sam winced at the thought of the unlovely, overcrowded and overdeveloped city on the south coast. 'That's not exactly where I would choose to go on holiday.'

'Me neither, and certainly not with them. But they're that kind of people, unfortunately.'

'And your father? What's he like?'

'He left us when I was only three or four, so I only know what my Mum's told me about him. We don't have any pictures either because she destroyed them when he left. I think he was a soldier or something, but I'm not sure. I don't even know if he's alive still.'

'Andrew probably knows more about him, after all, he is your uncle so he must have met your Dad, right?'

'Yeah, Andrew's my mother's brother, but they don't talk to each other much. And they don't talk about why they don't talk, if you know what I mean.' She shrugged. 'I guess he has to know something about my Dad, but I don't really want to find out; he left us, that's all I really need to know. At least right now anyway.'

There was a silence as they chewed on their sandwiches, looking out at the view.

Sam turned to look at her. 'Do you mind me asking you about this?'

She smiled reassuringly at him. 'Of course not; I made my peace with my family situation many years ago. Anyway, now that I'm finally sixteen and I've finished school I can move out for good. I won't need to deal with any of it.'

'Will your mum really let you do that? Doesn't she want you to continue studying? Maybe go to university?'

She laughed. 'Nah! She couldn't wait for me to leave school and she'd dying for me to move out, she's going to spend the money she saves on more holidays and clothes. It doesn't matter, though, because I've already got everything planned; I'm going to go live with Andrew and help him out. We're going to tell my mother that I have a job working for his company, but I'm really going to be helping him with you and the other Displacers. That's one of the good things about being a member of the Society, they always make sure that everyone is taken care of.'

'So you'll live here in Barcelona?' Sam smiled hopefully.

She smiled at his eagerness. 'Some of the time, but you know that Andrew and I are not always going to be here to hold your hand, don't you?'

'Yeah, but…'

'Andrew has to take care of *all* of the Displacers, not just you. Headquarters is in London and the majority of the members live in England, so it doesn't make much sense for him to be here just for you. And when he goes home, I'll probably end up going with him.'

Sam was crestfallen; it hadn't occurred to him that he might lose both Rachel and Andrew - his uncle had been such a fixture of his life for so long that he couldn't imagine not having him there and he'd assumed that Rachel would stay for a lot longer, maybe permanently.

Rachel saw how disappointed he was and ruffled his hair. 'Aw! So cute! You look like a hurt puppy!'

'Gerrof!' He waved away her hand and grinned.

Rachel returned the grin, glad to see the smile back on his face. 'Anyway, even if I'm here, you'll be too busy with school to see me all the time. Don't worry, you'll be coming over to England every so often and you can see me then. Like at Christmas - you see your grandfather, right?'

'Yeah. We almost always stay with him for a couple of weeks or so.' An idea occurred to Sam and he beamed. 'Hey, I could leave school after next year and then I could be with you the whole time!'

She smiled at him fondly and just a little bit sadly, suddenly looking more her real age and not her apparent one. 'That's nice, but you don't know that you're always going to feel this way about me. I know that I'm your first and that's always going to be special, but you might meet someone else...' She laughed, trying to lighten the mood again. 'Besides, I don't think your father, the big shot lawyer, is going to let you leave school early. Or let you even *think* about not going to university!'

Sam groaned. 'You're right, I'm doomed to a life of study.'

Rachel laughed. 'So melodramatic! Maybe you should become an actor.'

'I wouldn't mind that actually, but my parents would kill me.'

'What did you want to do with your life before you knew what you were?'

'I don't know really, I changed my mind so many times that I'm not sure any more. When I was growing up I went through a few phases; like wanting to be a detective after reading Sherlock Holmes, or a pilot after watching Top Gun. All pretty normal childish stuff, I suppose. I even went through a phase of wanting to be a lawyer like my father. Thank god that didn't last long! What about you?'

'I thought about being a doctor for a while, but I just don't have the marks to get into medical school. Then I found out I was a Displacer and realised that I could be anything I wanted to be. *Everything* I wanted to be. Right now I'm just concentrating on being a bad-arse warrior, but maybe I'll study some medicine later; I've got plenty of time after all.'

'I know! I haven't even got close to finishing the list of stuff I'm going to do.'

'That's something you have to look out for: if you're going to be one of us you can't just go gallivanting through time willy-nilly.'

'Wow, "willy-nilly"? Really? That's such an Andrew thing to say!'

Rachel groaned. 'Oh god, you're right. I've been living with him for too long, I'm starting to sound like him. Seriously, though, you should never Displace without running it past Andrew first; it's a basic rule of operation when you become one of us. There are a few dates that are very sensitive, that need almost constant attention and we always need new people to go to them to sort things out, like the nineteen-forties or the early eighteen hundreds. There was so much stuff going on at the same time in those periods in so many different places around the world that the time-line gets spread a bit thin and needs work. It would make Andrew a bit upset if you went sightseeing in those times and then couldn't help out when you were needed.'

Sam nodded, getting the idea. He grinned. 'OK, I'll run it past him before I go off fighting dragons or riding dinosaurs.'

Rachel shook her head and sighed. 'Boys.' She brushed the crumbs off of herself and stood up, offering her hand to Sam. 'Come on, let's head back. You should shower and brush your teeth before the conference call; you want to make a good impression. And try to wear some decent clothes for a change.'

'Yes, Mum.'

He allowed her to help him up and they picked up all their things, making sure they left nothing behind.

They walked back hand in hand in a comfortable silence and when they got to the city they kissed, said goodbye and went their separate ways to clean up before the call.

Andrew led Sam into his study and waved for him to take a seat before going to turn on the computer.

Rachel was already there, sprawled in the leftmost of the three chairs Andrew had set up facing the monitors for the call. She had a leg up over an arm, typing into her phone, and was more smartly dressed than he had ever seen, in black trousers and a white shirt rather than her usual shorts or tracksuit. He even thought he could detect a hint of subtle makeup around her eyes. He chose the seat next to her and she looked up from what she was doing to smile at him.

'Are you nervous?'

'Not much, should I be?'

She shrugged. 'I guess not. You haven't been a Displacer long enough, so you don't know these people or their stories, but some of them are living legends in the Society, *I* still get nervous talking with them sometimes!'

'Thanks, that's really putting me at my ease…'

Rachel shrugged again with a smile, then went back to her phone.

Andrew started speaking as he began clicking a mouse, opening up programs and preparing the conference call. 'Alright. Sam, as you can see I've put tags on the screens so you don't have to remember everybody's name the first day.'

Sam scanned the screens. There were small yellow post-its under each of them with names in Andrew's barely legible scrawl. 'Why have you put the names in two colours? Did you run out of ink?'

'Funnily enough, no. The names in blue, Ralph, Anne, John, Lisa, Julie and Hamish are active Displacers.' Andrew pointed to the labels as he read the names. A couple of screens had two names on them because there weren't enough for everyone to have their own. 'The names in red are the inactive members, what we call "Elders". They are members who can no longer Displace.' He turned on the last screen, then went to his desk and returned to clicking the mouse.

'They're more like "Ancients" if you ask me,' said Rachel with a smile. 'You should be joining them soon, right, Andrew? How old are you now, exactly?'

'Be nice, Rachel, you're not too old to be sent to your room.'

Andrew and Rachel laughed; obviously this was some kind of running joke between them.

Sam wanted to get as much information as he could before the conference call, so he steered the conversation quickly back on track. 'Why are they inactive members? What happened to them to stop them from being able to Displace?'

'Nothing, they just got too old. As we get older we stop being able to Displace as often as we did before; it gets a lot harder and it takes us longer to recover. Then when we hit fifty or so, the toll it takes on our bodies becomes too much and we completely lose the ability to do so. It's known as the "Transition".'

'Another one of those delightfully antiquated names that aren't cool in the slightest.' Rachel added with a grin. The grin disappeared quickly though and she sat up straight and hid her phone as faces started to appear on the screens.

Andrew continued. 'The Elders keep our records, they have the accounts of every Displacement ever reported, records that go back a few centuries and cover hundreds of thousands of Displacements.'

'Some of us don't particularly like to be called that, though; it can be rather insulting being addressed as "Elder" when you're only fifty. Or when you're as young as I am.'

The voice was very familiar to Sam and he looked up in surprise.

On the screen with a tag in red reading "James" was the proudly beaming face of his grandfather.

James was in his nineties, but still sharp as a tack. He was bald except for some remaining grey hair at the back and sides of his head and wore large, old-fashioned horn-rimmed bifocal glasses. He was one of the nicest tempered men that Sam knew, despite coming from one of the roughest areas of London, fighting in the Second World War and having a past as a boxer.

'Grandad! I didn't know you were a Displacer! Why didn't you ever tell me?'

The old man shrugged. 'I couldn't. Nobody was ever sure if you were going to become one of us or not because we were always getting mixed signals from you.'

Sam frowned. 'Mixed signals? What does that mean?'

Andrew broke in before James could answer. 'I'll tell you some other time; it's time to get started.'

Every single one of the screens now showed a face and in a few cases two. Sam was a bit unnerved when he noticed that a couple of them seemed to be scowling at him, especially the man on the screen labelled "Ralph". However, he was comforted in turn by his Grandfather's smiling face and the hand that Rachel sneaked under the arms of their chairs to squeeze his and managed to relax somewhat.

Andrew finished with the computer and came over to sit next to Sam. He faced the webcam that was poking out from a gap in the middle of the bank of screens and addressed the group. 'Thank you for making time to join us this evening. I'd like to introduce Sam to you. You've heard a lot about him and in my opinion he's ready to become one of us.'

'Be sure about this, young man, you don't *have* to join our little group,' the woman with the label "Anne" said in a refined American accent. 'I don't know if you have been made aware of this; some among us don't like to make it too well known, but if you choose not to join our Society we won't be able to prevent you from Displacing and you could easily continue to do so on your own. You will still be able to have adventures, if that's all you really want to use your powers for.'

'But we would, of course, love for you to become one of us,' said an Indian woman, "Lisa". 'We need your help, but we can also help you.'

Sam nodded, thoughtfully. 'Perhaps, then, someone should tell me what it really means for me to be a member?'

'If I may?' said the man who hadn't stopped scowling the whole time.

'Fine, Ralph. Please, go ahead.' Andrew answered with a smile that was obviously forced. There were some very quiet groans from the rest of the people in the chat and Rachel's grip around Sam's hand tightened slightly.

'Young man. Being a Displacer is an honourable tradition and a sacred trust. When called upon you must be ready to...'

'Oh, jeez! Enough with the major boring sh...!'

'John!'

The middle-aged man with thinning hair labelled "John" interrupted Ralph quite rudely and was quickly reprimanded for it by Andrew, but nobody else seemed to mind very much except for Ralph, who fumed in anger. 'I am not boring; I was just about to get to the crux of the matter!'

'Too late, and far too unimaginative, uninspiring and uninteresting!'

Sam chuckled. 'You must be John. I've heard a lot about you...'

'Not all good, I hope.' The man leaned forwards in his chair, closer to the camera, making his head huge on the screen, and smiled at Sam.

'Of course not.'

'Excellent!'

'Excuse me, I'm...' Ralph tried to interrupt, but John was having none of it and continued as if Ralph didn't exist.

'Anyway, it's like this, young Padawan, we've got all sorts of cool secrets, loads of brilliant techniques, hundreds of fab places to go on holiday, and all that jazz, and you'll only get access to those if you join us. All we ask in return is that you put your life in mortal danger every so often to save the world. So, take the red pill, find out how deep the rabbit hole goes and remember: there is no spoon!'

Andrew sighed and turned to Sam. 'Even though John is mixing his movie metaphors, I think you get the idea, right?'

'Just about... I think.' He shrugged. 'Well, I guess I'm in if you'll have me.'

Andrew smiled and patted Sam on the arm before facing the screens and turning serious. 'Are we all agreed that Master Samuel James Vives of Barcelona is worthy of becoming a member of the Honourable Society of Displacers? Are there any objections?' He waited a few seconds in case somebody had something to say. By the continuing sour look on his face it looked like Ralph did indeed want to object, but he managed to hold himself back.

Satisfied, Andrew nodded. 'Then by my authority as head of the Society I declare that our numbers have increased by one.' He looked sideways at Sam with a grin. 'That means that you're in, kid.'

There was a chorus of congratulations from the screens and smiles from most of the Society members and he received an almighty thump on the back from Rachel and a huge smile.

Sam was astounded. 'What? That's it? As easy as that?'

'What did you expect? Secret ballots? Aprons and rolled up trouser legs?'

'No… Well, just a little bit more ceremony, I suppose.'

There were chuckles from some of the screens.

'We don't really go in for that kind of thing, sorry, you'll just have to settle for your own login and the password to our conference calls.'

'Oh. OK.'

There was renewed merriment at Sam's disappointment, but Andrew cut it short to save him some embarrassment. 'Does anybody else have any business? No? Then thank you everybody and see you all soon.' Andrew closed the meeting and everybody signed off except for James, who smiled warmly at his grandson.

'Congratulations, Sam, and welcome to the Displacers. You know where to find me if you need anything, or if you've got any questions. I have a lot to tell you, especially about our family history, but it can wait. For now, trust Andrew, he's a good man.'

James was still talking, but Sam no longer heard him because his attention had been seized by the other screens, screens that had been occupied by mostly unfamiliar faces only seconds before, but which were now showing what he assumed to be the coat of arms of the Honourable Society of Displacers. More specifically, though, his eyes were fixed on the snake that wound through and around the scroll and hourglass on it.

'Trust in the snake…'

Sam didn't realise that he had said the words aloud until he was brought back to himself by his grandfather's raised voice booming urgently from the speakers of the computer and saw the old man's worried face looming large on the last occupied screen.

'What was that, Sam? What did you say? Trust in the snake? What's that?'

'It's nothing, really. Just something that a fortune teller told me in Port Royal.'

Andrew exchanged a look with James before staring intently at Sam. 'You saw a fortune teller in Port Royal?'

'Yes.'

'That wasn't in your report.'

Sam shrugged as he looked back and forth from his uncle to his grandfather. 'I didn't think it was important; what she said seemed like gibberish and to tell the truth I completely forgot about it. It only came back to me now when I saw the snake on the screens.'

James frowned. 'Nothing is ever really gibberish in the past, *especially* where you are concerned, Sam. What else did she say?'

'Um...' Sam couldn't for the life of him remember what the woman had said; he had dismissed her words as the ravings of someone who was at least half-mad and hadn't read any importance into them at the time. He racked his brains, thinking back to that moment in Port Royal when he had left the party that was being thrown in his honour, fleeing from the over-amorous girls who were pursuing him. He pictured himself in the fortune teller's tent in an effort to recall what else she had told him. He remembered the dim light of the tiny lantern that hardly illuminated anything, remembered the feel of the hard stool underneath him, the smell of the herbs hanging over his head. He remembered her eyes most of all - those intense blue eyes shining out of the night black face and the way she had seemed to become someone else, her hands gripping his like a vice and not letting go as...

Suddenly, something sounded in his mind, deafening, like a bell in a church hanging right over his head, and he stiffened as words came unbidden to his lips.

'The time of need is upon us and you have been chosen.

'You must be strong. You will be the rock around which others gather and who they look to in order to deliver them from the coming storm.

'Do not be afraid to lead, even when the path ahead is fraught with danger, for the way will be made clear to you, even if those around doubt you.

'Never give in to your fears and never shy from sacrifice; that way lies destruction as clear as if you had extinguished all hope yourself.

'Beware of those who walk in the light, because they will drag us all into perpetual night if they can, but trust in the snake; it will be your friend and provide you with allies on whom you can rely.

'Above all else, you must find your love and keep her close, for there you will find our salvation and only together will you see us all through this darkest of times and pave the way for the peaceful present that was promised.'

Sam shuddered and gasped in air. He collapsed back in his chair, suddenly feeling very weak, his head hurting, and he squeezed his eyes shut as the room swam around him.

'Sam?'

Familiar calloused, yet soft, hands gripped his and he latched onto them as points of reference to stop the swirling dizziness. A few deep breaths and the fog cleared from his mind enough for him to be able to open his eyes. The light hurt and he winced, but managed to focus, squinting, on Rachel, who had dropped to the floor to kneel in front of him and was looking up at him with a worried expression.

'What... what was that?'

'That, my boy, was prophecy.'

Sam looked over Rachel's shoulder and found his grandfather watching him with a strange expression on his face that was something between pride and satisfaction, but with a touch of something that looked like fear.

'Prophecy?'

'Yes!' James grinned but there was still a slight hesitancy to it and it didn't quite reach his eyes. 'Didn't you ever clean your ears out while you were in Japan, boy? Prophecy! As in fortune telling. As in predicting the future. It's something that you can imagine we come across occasionally, seeing as our job involves travelling in time.'

'So, I'm not going mad or anything?'

It was Andrew's turn to laugh. 'No, of course not! Displacers sometimes bring fragments of prophecies home with them. It's rare, yes, but not unheard of. This is one of those things you'll learn about when you've been one of us for a bit longer, but you won't have to worry about it for many because the Elders deal with all this intellectual stuff so that we can concentrate on the more practical side of the job.'

'Indeed.' James nodded. 'If you want I'll tell you about what the Elders do when you come over at Christmas, but for now just leave this with me. As Andrew said, I'll deal with it.'

'OK, as long as that's not going to happen to me again.' Despite his words, Sam realised that he didn't actually mind whether it happened to him again or not; even though someone or something had taken him over and pushed him to the back of his head, somehow he had known that it hadn't been malicious, but rather the feeling had almost been like an embrace, like his mother wrapping her arms around him to hold him back from danger. He knew that he should have been afraid, losing control of himself like that, but for some reason he had felt almost comforted. Peaceful.

James shook his head. 'It won't happen again; the message has been delivered.'

'Good, because I'm not sure I quite liked it.'

Both of the men laughed at that, but once more their laughter didn't quite seem sincere to Sam.

James leaned forwards to fill his screen again. 'Well, it seems that your trip to Port Royal was rather more eventful than you initially led us to believe! Perhaps in the future you will remember to put little details like this into your report, before they force their way out of you?'

'I'll try.' Sam gave his grandfather a half smile; it was all he could really bring himself to do at that moment.

James leaned back in his chair and straightened his glasses on his nose. 'Well, that was all very exciting, but I'm afraid I have to go; I have a ton of paperwork to take care of. I guess I'll see you and the family at Christmas, Sam. We'll have a good talk then, face to face.' He tilted his head in Rachel's direction. 'You should bring your girlfriend, too!' He gave Sam a knowing smile and a wink and Sam felt his cheeks go hot. The old man laughed, not unkindly, at his grandson's sudden discomfort. 'No wonder your English is so much better; there's nothing like a good woman to motivate a man!'

He signed off before Sam had a chance to protest.

As soon as James had gone, Andrew clapped Sam on the back. 'Congratulations, Sam, you're officially one of us now. Your grandfather will probably be entering your name in the register as we speak.' He leapt out of his chair. 'I think this calls for a nice cup of tea!' He left the room.

Rachel had returned to her seat when James had started speaking and stayed completely silent during the entire conversation, but now that they were on their own she turned to Sam and reached out to take his hands again. 'I won't pretend to understand what just happened to you and I've never heard of anybody doing what you just did, but if James and Andrew say that there's no need to worry, then I would believe them; you know they would never allow you to get hurt if they could help it.'

Sam nodded slowly. 'I know. They're hiding something, though.'

Rachel took a deep breath and eyed the study door. 'Yes, they are. They're not telling you about the prophecy.'

'It seemed fairly self-explanatory to me and it didn't exactly say much, beyond that I'd been chosen for something. Actually, most of it sounded more like advice than prophecy.'

She shook her head. 'The prophecy isn't limited to what you brought back and probably all you did was fill in a couple of pieces of a much larger prophecy that the Displacers have been gathering for at least a hundred years, if not more, from all over history. And it's not *a* prophecy it's *the* prophecy. As in the only prophecy that matters.'

'Oh...' Sam blinked at her. 'So, it's a bit more important than they're making out, then.'

'Definitely.'

'So what's it about, then?'

'Well, basically, there's supposed to be someone special, who is going to come along and make everything alright. Pretty much everyone in the Society is hoping that it's you and after today they will probably be convinced.'

'What about you? What do you think?'

'I think, no, I *know* that you are special, but some kind of saviour?' She grinned and slapped him, none too lightly, on the cheek. 'You're not the Messiah, you're a very naughty boy.'

Sam laughed, recognising the quote from the Monty Python film that he had watched with her and Andrew the week before.

She laughed with him, but he couldn't help but see the concern in the blue eyes that he loved so much, an echo of what had been in his grandfather's eyes.

More than anything else, there was one thing that was really bothering Sam, but he was reluctant to ask, not knowing if he would like the answer. He had to know, though, so he looked into her eyes, holding them as he turned serious. 'Why keep this a secret from me? You had enough chances to tell me, don't you think I should have known about a prophecy that refers to me?'

Rachel looked away, unable to hold his gaze. 'I'm sorry, Sam, I wanted to, believe me, but I wasn't allowed to tell you; the Council of Elders, or the Ancient Know-it-alls as I like to call them, ordered the whole Society not to, not until we could be sure that it was you that the prophecies referred to. James is the head of the Council, by the way, and when I asked him about it he said it was because you had to continue to behave the way you always had, that there mustn't be anything to influence you and push you in one direction or the other. Not like there had been with Quentin.'

Sam nodded in understanding; he had already seen what trying to live up to the impossible expectations of the Society had done to Quentin Price, the way it had found a flaw in his character and twisted him.

Rachel sighed and smiled, almost regretfully. 'I'm really sorry.' She leaned across the arm of his chair and kissed him softly and lingeringly on the mouth. 'Congratulations, Sam, and welcome to the club.' She grinned, stroking him gently on the cheek that she had slapped only moments before, then got up and walked out, leaving him alone with his thoughts.

Sam stared at the wall of screens. They were still showing the crest of the Society, but he barely saw it now; the snake had served its purpose and wasn't demanding his attention anymore. Instead, he was free to think about other things and he replayed the evening's events in his mind, going over what he had been told, but more importantly using Rachel's information to look for what he hadn't been. He frowned at the inevitable conclusion; he trusted his uncle and his grandfather with his life, there was no question of that, but they were obviously hiding things from him and despite himself he couldn't help but feel slightly betrayed, not just by the two older Displacers, but by Rachel as well.

The question was what to do about it, whether to let them decide what was best for him or to take matters into his own hands. The more he thought about it, the more he felt that he needed to know, but he found that he wasn't alone in making the decision; there was something in the back of his mind telling him that he shouldn't leave things until Christmas, that he should press his uncle for answers, that it was important. He suspected that it was the same thing that had taken him over to recite the prophecy, that it was still there, lurking, waiting for something. That didn't exactly make him feel very comfortable, but for some reason he trusted it, whatever it was, and felt he should listen to its advice.

Decided, he slapped the arms of his chair and thrust himself to his feet; it was time to find out what was really going on and, to his utter disbelief, he realised that he actually wanted some tea.

When Sam walked into the living room, he found Andrew and Rachel waiting for him, silently drinking from mugs of tea. There was a third mug on the coffee table for him but he ignored it and stalked across the room to stand in front of Andrew. 'OK, what's wrong with me?'

Andrew frowned. 'Nothing. Why do you ask?'

Sam raised his voice, suddenly angry. 'Don't play innocent with me, Andrew; you know what I mean! I saw the way everyone was looking at me as if I was a freak and I think I even heard John mutter "the one" under his breath at some point. Rachel's already told me that the prophecy talks about some kind of special person, but she doesn't know much else, so I'm going to need you to fill in the gaps. And don't say you'll explain it to me later; I'm getting very tired of that - I want to know now! Not at Christmas!'

'Did Rachel also tell you that we asked her not to tell you?' Andrew shot an incriminating look at Rachel, but she just shrugged and he sighed. 'We really didn't want to tell you about it before we knew for sure, or at least until you had finished training, but after tonight there's not much doubt left, so I suppose now is as good a time as any. James knows more than I do, but sit down, grab a biscuit and I'll tell you what I can.'

Andrew waited for Sam to take a seat next to Rachel on the sofa before he continued. 'Every so often someone brings something back from a Displacement: a hint, or a rumour, or a scrap of paper, piece of pottery, or stone with writing on it, that points at a prophecy of sorts. It's a puzzle that the Society have been trying to piece together since we came together officially as a group in the nineteenth century. However, none of us quite believed in it up until recently. It's likely that what you brought back with you is a part of that, but James will have to study it first to confirm it. Anyway, the prophecy points towards the existence of someone who John does indeed like to call "The One" or "The Anomaly" or something equally silly; someone who can *truly* affect time and not just influence it.'

'John's a bit obsessed with movies, right?'

'How did you guess?' asked Rachel with a grin.

Andrew chuckled and some of the tension dissipated from the room. 'Anyway, this is why we've been tiptoeing around you so much. Everything you've done so far: spontaneously Displacing to Port Royal and stopping Quentin; only needing two weeks between Displacements; the speed with which you can Prepare and Calm, it all points to you being special at the very least and some people were already saying that you could be the person referred to in the prophecy before you did what you did tonight. And remember, this is all based on unproven theories and fragments of hearsay; there is nothing to actually *prove* that such a person could ever exist.' He shrugged. 'I guess it's just that deep down inside most of us want to believe that someone will come along to help us win a battle we've been steadily losing for years.'

'But no pressure, right?' Rachel said with a cheeky grin.

Sam looked daggers at Rachel, but she knew he didn't mean it and her grin only widened, which in turn softened his glare and finally made him smile; there was no way he could be angry at her.

'For now, though, it's best if we continue normally with your training, like we would with any other new Displacer, and not treat you as anything special. After all, look what happened when Ralph started training Quentin - we all got very excited and were sure it was him in the prophecy, just because he tested higher than anyone else ever had. Until you came along, of course.'

'Ralph trained him? Why didn't you?'

'Because even though it should be my job as leader of the Displacers, Ralph is Quentin's father.'

Sam stared at Andrew with his mouth open; of all the things he had expected to learn about his enemy, the fact that his father was still an active Displacer was not one of them.

Without thinking about what he was doing, he took a big gulp of his tea. It was boiling hot and burned his tongue, making him swallow the wrong way, and he spluttered, tea spilling out of his mouth and down his chin. He put the mug back down quickly and coughed, trying to wipe the tea from his t-shirt, cursing.

Rachel hid a laugh behind her hand, but Sam wasn't in the mood for games and he gave her another cold look, which was received in much the same way as the last one had been. He gave up on his t-shirt and turned to Andrew, pointedly ignoring Rachel. 'I got a feeling that Ralph didn't like me very much, is it because of Port Royal? Of how I defeated his son? And why is the father of someone who tried to kill me still a Displacer?'

'Ralph is a valued member and we judge him by his own actions, not by those of his son. As should you. He has repeatedly insisted that he has disowned Quentin, so, in theory, he wants him defeated just as much as the rest of us. And if he doesn't like you it's probably because of me.' Andrew took another sip of tea, carefully considering his words before continuing. 'The leader of the Displacers is always an active member and is chosen by vote, so when the last leader went through the Transition and became an Elder he had to step aside. There was an election with only two candidates - myself and Ralph. I won by a landslide and he has resented me for it ever since. So, the reason he doesn't like you very much most likely isn't because of your dealings with his son, but rather because you're my protégé.'

Sam nodded. 'OK, I guess that makes as much sense as anything to do with the Displacers...'

Rachel tittered and it was Andrew's turn to give her a dirty look.

This time Sam smiled too, but he didn't get distracted and kept his attention fixed on Andrew; he was resolved not to let the chance to finally get some answers slip away. 'Are you sure he isn't still in contact with Quentin?'

'No, he broke off all ties with him when he went rogue.'

Andrew seemed to be positive of that, but Rachel gave Sam a look that said that she wasn't so sure.

Sam took a deep breath. 'So… Am I?'

'Are you what?'

'Special, you know "the one".'

'The vote is still out on that. Don't go getting ahead of yourself, or as John used to tell me: "great, kid, don't get cocky". You have a long road ahead of you still.'

Rachel gave him a sweet grin. 'And I can still kick your arse if your head starts to get too big, just remember that.'

'Are you sure, James?'

'Yes. And Andrew will corroborate.'

James sat at the head of a large rectangular table, facing his fellow Elders. He had called for an emergency meeting at Headquarters and he and the six other Elders who had been able to come at such short notice had shut themselves into the cosy kitchen in the basement, both because it was close to the food and drink, which they were taking full advantage of, but also because it was the easiest place to keep a conversation secret; the door at the top of the stairs was one of the only ones in the building with a bolt lock on it and was far enough away to prevent nosy youngsters from eavesdropping.

He looked from one familiar face to the next, seeing friends and colleagues he had known most of his life, or in a couple of cases, hundreds of years, seeing people whose opinion he respected and whose judgement he trusted. He took note of their varied expressions; shock and doubt were there, as expected, and he could see a couple were still sceptical, but he was pleased to see that every single one of the faces turned towards him was displaying in one degree or other a single emotion, something that had been missing from them for far too long - hope.

He took a sip of Glenfiddich whisky, his favourite, to hide his smile, then spoke into the expectant silence. 'In my opinion it is genuine; it fulfilled all the hallmarks of every account we've ever had of the collection of verbal prophecies. You've all received a copy of what he said and have probably read it as many times as I have - you can see as well as I can that there is more in it than the boy should rightfully know and even though it doesn't give us much new information, it does clear up at least a couple of things. I propose that we admit it to the archives immediately and work on incorporating it into our research as soon as possible.'

The motion passed immediately and Richard, who acted as the secretary at the meetings, made a note in the minutes. The job fell to him as the youngest member of the Council; he was a sprightly fifty-eight years of age.

'Does this mean that the boy is a prophet?'

This question came from Philip and, like every other that had come before it, was directed at James; the other Elders were deferring to his judgement in the matter, not only because he was the oldest of them and their leader, but because he was the only living person who could reasonably claim to be an expert on the prophecy, if anybody could be an expert on something that was as vague and incomplete as it was. He had studied it for most of his life, whenever his duties permitted, ever since one of his first Displacements, when a Sioux Shaman had recited an ancient legend to him that had been passed to him from the previous Shaman, who in turn had learnt it from his predecessor, who had learnt it from his, and so on back more generations than the man knew how to count. James was also the only person on record to have recovered two separate fragments of the prophecy - no other Displacer had ever brought back more than one.

Philip was a curator at the British Museum and as well as being the Society's resident expert on several ancient worlds, including Egypt and Greece, had recently become James' assistant. The old man had begun teaching him everything that he could about the prophecies, knowing that one day, probably quite soon, he would no longer be able to continue his work. James appreciated the new perspective that Philip brought to the study of the prophecy, but knew that the young man, at only sixty-three, still had a lot to learn, which was why he didn't scoff when he answered his question, despite considering it to be rather foolish.

'It's highly unlikely - although something undoubtedly spoke through him today, he wasn't the originator of the prophecy; that was the fortune teller in Port Royal that he neglected to inform us of in his original report. He was merely repeating her words. The time-line took him over to make sure that we got the message, but this will in all likelihood be an isolated incident.'

James looked around the table, seeing agreement and not just a little disappointment; it would have been quite handy to have access to someone directly in contact with the time-line, who could provide them with the information they sorely needed.

He moved on to the next item on the list he had drawn up while he waited for the other Council members to arrive. 'Now, there is one thing in Sam's prophecy that we've never come across before and it is this reference to, and I quote, "those who walk in the light". I don't recall any mention of them in any of the other fragments, have any of you come across the term before?'

Again there was silence; when you lived as long as the people around the table had, you learned that it was best not to say anything unless you actually had something to say.

Richard hadn't quite learnt that lesson yet and he looked up from his notebook. 'Surely it has to refer to whoever is working against us. Could it be Quentin? He was there when Sam recovered the prophecy after all.'

'Somehow I can't believe that it is talking about Quentin; I wouldn't exactly describe him as walking in the light.'

There were laughs at this, but they were short lived and James soon continued.

'I think that it would be naive of us to think that Quentin is our only, or even main, worry; I fear that he may be part of something much larger, something that is perhaps of our own making. Which may be why we have received a warning at this specific moment in time.' He looked around the group, meeting their eyes one by one. 'I hope you have all grasped the significance of the fact that this is the first time that an actual enemy is specifically mentioned?'

This was greeted with utter silence and James nodded. 'Then I believe that we should open up a new line of enquiry and search our archives for any other reference to anything that can possibly shed some light on this, if you'll forgive my pun.'

There were a few chuckles and while Richard made another note the members took advantage of the brief pause to eat or drink; many of them had missed dinner in the rush to get to Headquarters, but as always Richard had brought food from his restaurant and there were plenty of leftovers from lunch. It was not very long, though, before forks were laid aside and glasses were pushed away; not one of them was willing to be distracted from the elephant in the room. However, as leader, it fell to James to broach the subject. 'Does everyone concur with me that this incident is yet another indication that the boy is the one referenced in the prophecies?'

This time the nods came much slower; they had made a mistake before and paid the price, so, despite the weight of evidence, they were understandably reluctant to commit.

'Should we tell him about his place in the prophecies?' The question came from Alfred, a frail old man in his eighties sitting at the far end of the table. He was the second oldest Elder in terms of real years, but he had gone through the Transition in his thirties because of an illness and didn't have nearly as much experience as most of the others.

James shook his head emphatically. 'No. We must have our secrets, at least for now, and it will do him no good to know the danger he is in.'

Not everybody agreed with his decision, but nobody expressed their doubts; they all trusted him to know what was best, especially for his own grandson.

'Thank you.' James nodded his gratitude. 'Well, I think there is nothing much else to say. We all know what we have to do, so I suggest we get to it.'

The members quickly finished off their meals and began making their way from the kitchen, heading towards the attic and the archives, where the prophecies were kept locked up along with the rest of the Society's most valuable treasures.

The last of the footsteps on the stairs faded and James was alone.

Beware of those who walk in the light...

James considered the words carefully as he stared into the dregs of golden fluid in his crystal glass. There was something vaguely familiar about it, something tickling at the back of his mind. However, he knew that there wasn't anything specific in the prophecies, he would have remembered, so it must be something else, something he'd read perhaps...

He downed the rest of the whisky and eyed the bottle wistfully, but he knew that if he drank anymore he would be useless for the rest of the night and it promised to be a long one.

With a sigh he pushed back his chair and stood. He groaned as he followed in the footsteps of his colleagues; the stairs weren't getting any easier and he was far too old to be losing out on sleep like this, but the research was more important and he was supposed to be the expert.

He shook his head and sighed in exasperation; why did the prophecies always talk in riddles? Why couldn't they speak straight for once?

And why did it have to be his kind-hearted grandson who would bear the brunt of the storm that was coming?

CHAPTER 13
BLACKPOOL OR BUST

Sam was impatient to Displace again, but as always there was nothing he could do except wait for his body to recover and, even though he was loving being with Rachel, he was still wishing the days away so that he could go into the past again.

There was no way to make the time go by any faster, though, and it was a full two weeks before he woke up one morning knowing that he was able to Displace again. He leapt out of bed, bolted down his breakfast as fast as he could, said goodbye to his parents, ruffled Violeta's hair and all but ran out of the front door and round to Andrew's place, blurting out the news as soon as he burst into the living room where, for a change, Rachel and Andrew were having tea.

Andrew smiled wryly at Sam's enthusiasm and shook his head. 'Sixteen days. You're a day later than I thought you would be... And good morning, by the way. I'm assuming that you want to get right to it and wouldn't like a cup of tea before you go?'

Sam grinned. 'Yes, please, and no, thank you!'

Andrew shook his head in mock disapproval. 'I keep forgetting you're only half English and can't be expected to be civilised...' He tutted theatrically, rolling his eyes, then leaned forward to push a piece of paper across the coffee table to Sam. 'Right, then, this will be your first solo Displacement, under controlled conditions at least, and it'll serve as your "graduation" - one last test to see if you can go where you're told before I certify you as ready to go on missions for the Society. It's a nice safe place, completely out of harm's way. All you have to do is hit the right time-line, take a look around and bring me back a stick of rock.'

Sam picked up the paper and read the first couple of lines. His eyes widened in disbelief and his mouth pursed in disappointment. 'Blackpool? 1953? Seriously?'

'Yes. Go and see *Morecambe and Wise* at the Winter Gardens. Believe me, you won't regret it; they were at the height of their powers in the theatre before they made the move to TV. It's a unique experience, you'll love it and they're your grandfather's favourite act. He was always crazy about them and he even does impressions of Eric Morecambe occasionally.'

Rachel laughed. 'I like it when he does the paper bag trick!'

Andrew grinned. 'It'll be something you can talk to him about at Christmas, Sam.'

'OK, I guess…' Sam wasn't convinced; he had been hoping for something a lot more exciting.

Andrew saw his nephew's disappointment and became deadly serious. 'Look, we've had enough near misses with you already, Sam. One more and not only do I risk losing my place as the leader of the group, to Ralph of all people, but we could lose you as well.'

Rachel tried hard to keep a serious expression and failed dismally. 'And also you just look stupid going to the wrong places all the time, you'll start to get a reputation. People will start making fun of *you* instead of John.' She poked her tongue out at him.

Sam laughed. 'I really don't want that, do I? Sounds like I'd better go to Blackpool then!'

Andrew smiled. 'That's the spirit! And there's no need to look so glum about it; you'll have a good time, trust me. Besides, you have plenty of opportunities to have adventures in the future. After all, you get to Displace twice as much as the rest of us - I think you can spare one every so often!'

'I guess…' Sam shrugged, then settled back onto the sofa and carefully read the paper that Andrew had prepared for him, letting the details sink in, getting a feel for the destination. It was intuitive, instinctive, he didn't even have to try; the pieces just fell into place like a jigsaw puzzle and when a clear picture formed in his mind he knew he had it.

He had one last thought as he closed his eyes and focussed his abilities. 'I really hope I don't run into Quentin this time…'

When he opened his eyes it was to unexpected darkness. He blinked rapidly, trying to get his eyes to adjust, but it didn't work. Apparently, it wasn't just the dark of night, it was something else entirely - a complete absence of light. He stood in place while he worked out what to do; he didn't want to walk blindly into the darkness because there might be any manner of dangers lying in wait - holes to fall down, obstacles to trip over, low beams to bump his head on, or even, god forbid, spider's webs to walk into or creepy crawlies to step on.

'Hello? Is anyone there?' His voice echoed slightly and he realised that he was in some kind of chamber: a storeroom or possibly an underground cave. He listened for an answer, but he was wrapped in a silence that was as deep as the dark, which was very strange because he didn't think that there would be such a lack of light and sound in a busy seaside town in the height of the tourist season. It was also hot, and not just English summer hot, but much more and it was a dry heat, the kind of heat that Sam imagined you got in a desert country. So either he had Displaced into an underground sauna without any lights, which wasn't particularly plausible, or he was in a completely different country altogether, which, given his previous record, was far too likely.

He cursed silently as he came to the inevitable conclusion that he hadn't made it to Blackpool. He realised that, all things considered, the best thing to do would be to just go home and tell Andrew that he'd missed his destination. Not only did that mean that an entire Displacement would go straight down the drain, but also he was pretty sure that Rachel would never let him forget about it and would probably tease him mercilessly for a long time. Worse, though, it might also hurt Andrew's status in the Society, and, despite only having met the man once, Sam just knew that he wouldn't like having to work under the pompous, self-important father of his enemy.

He was about to close his eyes and start Calming when he realised that the darkness wasn't quite as absolute anymore; a faint, rectangular glow had blossomed to life somewhere in front of him, like a giant television lying on its side. However, as it became brighter he realised that what he was seeing was not a screen, but rather a doorway and the light was coming from somewhere down a long passageway extending past it.

Soon, there was enough light for Sam to make out the rest of his surroundings and he found that he was in some kind of chamber about ten metres square, formed from large blocks of a sandy-coloured stone that had been tightly fitted together. The walls were covered with carvings, symbols which he recognised as Egyptian hieroglyphics. They were smoothed and faint with age, but even so there was something very familiar about them. He frowned and began to move towards them so he could get a better look, but halted when the light suddenly became a lot brighter, dazzling him. He covered his eyes with his hand as the source of the light rounded a bend in the passageway about twenty metres away.

Squinting against the glare, he was finally able to discern the figure of a man walking towards him, holding aloft a flaming torch.

'Are you alright, old bean?' The man called out.

'Old...? What? Sorry?' The man's voice had echoed just like Sam's had earlier and he wasn't sure that he had understood him correctly.

The man came to a halt in the entrance to the passage. 'Didn't see you stop and now I come back to find you standing there like one of those statues we found the other day, except with a bit less personality. You got a spot of heatstroke, maybe?' He held out a small silver hip flask with a lopsided grin, shaking it to make a sloshing sound. 'Here, have a swig of this, it'll sort you out right away!'

Sam shook his head. 'No, thank you.'

The man shrugged. 'Suit yourself.' He took a swig and smacked his lips loudly before putting the flask back in his pocket.

Sam's eyes finally adjusted to the light and he looked at the man slouching in front of him. He appeared to be about fifty years old, sun browned and grizzled, wearing what Sam thought of as "Explorer Uniform": the khaki that you always saw on turn of the twentieth century western explorers in hot places like Africa or the Middle East or Egypt.

Sam glanced down at his own clothes. No wonder he was so hot; he was wearing the same impractical stuff as the man - he should have been in shorts and a t-shirt as well as sandals instead of the huge, heavy boots.

'Seriously, though, old chap, what happened to you? I looked around and there you were. Gone.' He gazed enthusiastically around the chamber. 'Did you see something interesting? Something that hasn't been looted already?'

'Er, no, something caught my eye, but it was only a beetle and then, er, you'd gone and it was dark, and, er...' Sam wasn't quite sure what he could safely say and he resolved to get some advice from the other Displacers about how to turn up in a new time-line without looking like a complete idiot.

'Oh.' He was obviously disappointed. 'Well, come on, then, we've got a long ride into the desert after we're done here so best hop to it.'

He beckoned, turning to go and Sam started to walk towards him.

Suddenly, the man panicked and threw out his hand. 'Stop! Don't step there, for god's sake!'

Sam froze, but it was too late; his foot came down and the floor underneath him depressed slightly.

There was a click followed by a loud *twang* and a dart flew out of the wall on the opposite side of the room.

Sam flinched, instinctively starting to dodge, but he knew it was too late; there was nothing he could do to avoid the deadly weapon.

Time seemed to stand still.

He had thought it was just a cliché, something that was only used in bad films or books, but his life passed before his eyes, bits of it anyway, and he briefly wondered if it was another one of the perks of being a Displacer that Andrew had mentioned before...

It was Christmas and he was seven or eight years old, making a snowman with his father and grandfather in James' back garden in London. His mother was in the window, holding Violeta, only a few months old, in her arms, laughing at their antics and cheering on the impromptu snowball fights that kept breaking out. Even though she and Violeta were separated from them by a pane of glass it was like they were all together, sharing in the fun.

He went back to that last, wonderful night in Okinawa with Rachel. He remembered how she had lain atop him and her face had come down to his in a kiss that had lasted forever, then how afterwards they had fallen asleep in each other's arms under the stars in the summer warmth.

He thought it would be Rachel who he would miss the most, but it was actually Violeta. He saw them sitting on the sofa, playing video games together - it was the time that they had laughed so much that his stomach muscles had hurt for days. Next, they sat together at the dining room table, drawing together, Violeta's tongue sticking out of the side of her mouth in concentration - he saw again the look of satisfaction on her face as she finished and proudly displayed the "portrait" she had done of him. Then he relived the day he'd come back from Okinawa and marvelled at the way she had seemed to know exactly what he needed after his years away had left him feeling alienated from his family.

The memories flew past one after another after another, faster than he should be able to register them, but he saw them clearly, lived them intensely and was surprised to realise that he was actually at peace; he had lived well in a short space of time.

And at least he wouldn't die a vir...

With a clatter, the rusted metal dart flopped to the floor, instantly cutting off his train of thought. It rolled a few times before coming to a halt a good metre short of him.

The man sighed in relief. 'Come on, Vives, buck your ideas up or you'll give me a heart attack!' He fumbled for his flask with a shaking hand, cursing under his breath, and took a long swig before shaking his head and smiling wryly. 'Just as well this tomb's a few thousand years old and the stretch has gone out of the strings, eh? Otherwise that would have been your guts for garters!'

Sam carefully lifted his foot and looked at the floor. Now he knew what to look for, the trap was obvious; a paving stone that was just a few millimetres higher than the others and it only took a quick scan of the floor for him to spot at least three more that were likely the same.

'You feeling alright, old fellow?' The man lifted the torch high and peered at Sam.

'Yes, sorry. I was just... Somewhere else.' Sam deliberately lifted his foot up and stepped over the stone, giving it and all the others a wide berth as he made his way across the room.

The man chuckled. 'Well, mind back on the job, eh? Not on that beauty I saw you with last night... Speaking of which, did you have any luck?'

Sam had no idea how to answer, so he played for time. '"Mind back on the job", didn't you say?'

'Right, yes, of course, old boy!' Mum's the word, what!' The man gave him a cheeky grin and a wink. 'Come on, no use hanging around! These outer chambers were picked clean centuries ago so we're not going to find anything new out here, we have to go deeper. Lead on!'

Sam made his way carefully across the room to the man's side. 'What about the rest of the traps?'

'You've done well enough pointing them out until now, so I'm sure you'll be fine! Besides, it looks like it doesn't matter if you set off any of the dart thingamajigs, but please do be a good chap and don't step on any of the ones that'll collapse the whole place around our ears.'

'Alright, I'll try...' Sam took a deep breath, then led the way along the passage that the man had come down. Thankfully, despite his misgivings at holding their lives in his hands, it was easy enough to spot the traps now that he'd seen one; they were all equally simple.

The passage went down a slight slope, turning back on itself a couple of times before it opened up into another small chambers that had other passages leading off in different directions. There were more hieroglyphics on the walls there as well, but the man didn't stop; he just indicated one of the corridors and waited for Sam to move on; he seemed to have some destination in mind. Sam was still curious as to why the symbols were so familiar, but he didn't want to stop and risk being left alone in the dark again.

Sam's companion didn't say much while they walked, beyond making a few good-natured digs about Sam's constant social activities in Cairo and how they were especially affecting his work that day. The more the man made fun of him, the more Sam began to realise that he had a bit of a reputation as a ladies man in the time-line and he wasn't sure that was a reputation that he particularly wanted to have. However, he knew that if all went well, he'd shortly be on his way home and he wouldn't have to live with it for long, so he shrugged off the man's words with a smile and just carried on with his job.

It was like a maze in the tunnels, but the man seemed to know exactly where he was going, pointing out the passageways that he wanted Sam to take when there was more than one choice. They came across a couple of skeletons as they went, men who hadn't been as lucky as Sam and had fallen victims to the metal bolts traps while they had still been effective, hundreds, or maybe more than a thousand years ago. Sam blanched when he saw the twisted positions they were in and hastily looked away; the projectiles had obviously been poisoned with something quite nasty that had made their victims writhe in agony before they died.

After about half an hour of carefully picking their way past traps and an occasional collapsed wall, they came to a dead end in a small chamber that was about the same size as the room that Sam had found himself in when he had arrived. This one, however, was completely bare of any ornamentation and the stones that formed the walls were undressed and rough. To Sam's eye it almost seemed as if the builders had been trying to make it look as nondescript as possible in order to hide something and he suspected that that was why the two of them had come there.

The man halted in the middle of the room. He took out his flask again and sipped from it while he eyed the walls.

Sam was on the point of asking him what he was looking for when the man cried out in triumph. 'Ah ha!' He leapt forwards, the torch guttering and almost going out in his haste and knelt down next to the wall. 'Take the torch, would you, old man?'

Sam did as he was told and, as soon as his hands were free, the man bent down close to the ground and slipped his fingers into a rectangular hole at the bottom of the wall about a thirty centimetres long but only a couple wide that Sam hadn't even noticed was there, so well was it camouflaged.

'Hmmm... No. No... Ugh, that was probably a beetle. No. There!' There was a click as the man finally found what he was looking for. He grunted as he pulled and a panel in the wall - a cunningly hidden door - swung gently open with a crunching, grating noise. It was a huge slab of stone, fully two metres high, four or five metres wide and a good half a metre thick, but the man moved it with one hand as if it were just a revolving door in a hotel.

When the opening was wide enough for them to pass, the man stopped pulling and the door slid to a halt by itself. He brushed his hands off and stepped towards the gap. 'Well, then! Let's see what we've got!'

Sam followed him through but then stopped short, gaping in wonder at what the light from the torch revealed.

It was a large chamber, easily ten times the size of anything that they had passed through, and it was covered from top to bottom by carvings and paintings of all shapes and sizes - a veritable treasure trove of ancient Egyptian culture, incredibly well preserved.

'Blast!' The man's voice echoed in the cavernous space and for a second Sam had no idea what he was swearing at; but then he realised that, while he had been staring at the walls, the man had been looking at the floor - while the room's decorations were still intact, the same could not be said of its contents and the shattered remains of jars and statues were scattered everywhere - it looked like not a single thing was still in one piece.

The man picked his way carefully through the debris. He bent down every so often to pick something up, but invariable laid it aside again after a quick glance. He sighed, shaking his head. 'I thought we were on a winner here when the boys from the museum couldn't find the main burial chamber, but it looks like somebody else got here first.'

They made their way to the far side of the chamber, where there was a plinth with a stone box on it. The box, a sarcophagus, was cracked and split, with pieces chipped from it. What was probably its lid was laying on the floor next to it, shattered. The man ran his hand over it and sighed again. 'This was probably quite magnificent, but the barbarians have stripped it of everything of value... At least the mummy is still here, although it's looking a tad worse for wear.'

Sam leaned over the box. Inside were the remains of a mummified corpse, but with the sarcophagus broken open it had been exposed to the air and the bandages had almost completely rotted away, leaving only the decaying body behind. He could see where the hands and fingers had been broken to remove any jewellery it had been wearing and its head was twisted to one side, most likely for the same reason. It was fairly gruesome, but he didn't want to look away; he was pretty sure he'd never get another chance to see an actual mummy in its original tomb in Egypt.

'Bring that torch over here!'

Sam realised that in his fascination with the mummy he hadn't noticed that the man had moved off and was crouching some metres away, near the back wall of the chamber. He hurriedly moved to his side and held the torch up to shed some light on what looked very much like just a pile of rubbish.

'Ah ha! Looks like the museum will get something out of this after all!' He lifted a small statuette out from under some rotted wooden chests, followed by several more. They were mostly intact, protected from harm by the litter on top of them.

Sam frowned. 'What are those?'

'Mummified cats! Not particularly rare or valuable, but visitors do like them and a set like this will bring them flocking in, which will keep the museum happy for a while.'

There were a dozen of the stylised cat figures in the end, in various states of disrepair, and the man set about wrapping them in straw and packing them in a bag he had brought with him to carry any finds. When he was done he stood and hefted the bag carefully onto his back. 'Well, we really should be going; places to be and all that. I've delayed us too long, but I knew the museum boys had missed something and I just had to have a nose around before we leave it to them to catalogue.' He waved for Sam to lead the way and they began to retrace their steps.

They soon found themselves back in the room where Sam had arrived. It turned out to be very near the entrance to the complex and the corridors beyond it were increasingly clogged with sand. The last few metres they had to drop to their hands and knees and crawl through a hole that had obviously been recently excavated and propped up with wooden boards. There was enough light coming from up ahead to see by, so Sam stubbed out the torch, relieved that he didn't have to crawl and try to hold a live flame at the same time.

After only about ten metres the tunnel came to an abrupt end and Sam was blinded by sudden brilliant sunlight, seemingly coming at him from all directions as it reflected off the golden sand.

The heat hit him at the same time, like an almost physical wave, and he gasped for breath. It was far hotter in the open than it had been inside the tomb and it felt like the moisture was being sucked right out of him. He tried to remember the phrase his mother liked to use during Spanish summers about Englishmen and mad animals or something - he couldn't remember exactly how it went, but it would probably be highly appropriate at that moment.

When he finally managed to open his eyes, what air he had managed to drag in was immediately snatched away again by the incredible sight that confronted him - enormous pyramids loomed over his head, rising above the heat haze and the gentle dunes of a wide plain, so close that he felt like he could reach out and touch them. There were a few smaller pyramids and several other buildings nearby, but they were almost insignificant compared to the towering majesty of the three main pyramids.

He'd seen photos of the Giza pyramids, but they didn't come anywhere near to doing justice to the real thing and he couldn't take his eyes off the gigantic buildings, which was why it took him a good few seconds to realise that he was being watched - half a dozen men in white robes were squatting about twenty metres away, taking shelter from the sun however they could. They were accompanied by a dozen camels, half of which had saddles, while the others were laden with baggage; it was like something out of *Lawrence of Arabia*.

'Excellent! It looks like Francis has the gear packed and the bearers assembled and ready, so there's nothing holding us back! We've got about three hundred miles to travel into the middle of nowhere and the sooner we get going the better.' The man took a long drink from his flask, evidently that was how he coped with the heat, then gestured at the camel train with it as he stood, gently swaying, next to Sam. 'I hope you've made friends with your camel already, because she's going to be the only female you see for a few weeks!' He laughed and upended the flask again, but scowled as he found it empty.

Sam laughed with him, but his heart wasn't really in it; now that they were out of the tomb he had to decide what he was going to do, whether he was going to go home or not.

Seeing the pyramids like this, up close and alone, before the area was flooded with thousands upon thousands of tourists, would have been a wonderful Displacement if he had planned it, but the fact was he had missed his destination by a whole continent and who knew how many years. Again. Now the man was expecting him to ride off into the middle of the desert, and a long uncomfortable journey on a camel in such heat wasn't exactly his idea of fun.

The choice was easy, so he closed his eyes, took a deep breath that almost burned his lungs and started to relax. With the sun beating down on him and the oppressive heat it was going to be a bit harder than usual to Calm himself, but there probably wasn't any water nearby, so he was just going to have to try.

His concentration was broken almost immediately, though, when the man grabbed him by the shoulder and started walking him to the camels. 'Come on, Vives, stop dozing! Time waits for no man and I'd hate to have that bloody Price bounder beat us to it!'

CHAPTER 14
TAKING THE TABLETS

Sam's eyes flew open and he immediately forgot about going home as his attention shot back to the man. 'Did you say Price? Please don't tell me you mean Quentin Price.'

'That's the fellow, a jolly bad egg, or my name's not Bertram Campbell. Uses up natives like nobody's business. He gets the job done, alright, but it's just not cricket!'

Sam trailed behind the man, Bertram, as he stomped across the sand towards the camels. He handed the bag with the cat mummies in it to one of the bearers in white robes. 'Get this to Fidwick at the museum, would you? Carefully, please! Then catch up as soon as you can.'

The man performed a shallow bow, then took the bag and climbed easily onto one of the camels and went trotting off towards the city that could just about be made out in the distance - Cairo.

Bertram watched him go, wincing. 'Don't know how anything remains intact with the amount of bouncing around these blasted animals do...' He turned to grin at Sam. 'Just as well I bought several extra cushions for our saddles, eh?'

He laughed, then clambered awkwardly up onto his camel, which struggled just as gracelessly to its feet. 'Well, what are you waiting for, Vives? Come on! Tally ho and all that!' He kicked his camel into action and it loped away, closely followed by the rest of the party.

Sam pulled himself up into the saddle of his own camel, barely getting settled before it stood up with an almighty heave, almost throwing him off over its head in the process. He took a last wistful look at the pyramids, then spurred his mount forward, grimacing at the jolting in certain parts of him that promised a very uncomfortable journey.

He soon caught up with the others and reined the camel in to a walk, which thankfully proved to be far more comfortable than the trot, and fell in beside Bertram, who was singing under his breath in time with the gentle swaying of his own mount. 'Uh, Bertram?'

'Yes?'

'I think you were right and I must be suffering from a bit of heatstroke after all. Either that or I'm a bit forgetful because of a rough night after all my, you know, socialising and stuff. Would you remind me what we're doing, please?' Sam pantomimed being dizzy, putting his hand to his forehead, while all the time hating that he had to confirm the man's low opinion of him.

The man laughed. 'Certainly, old chap! I knew something was wrong! Let's get you up to speed, then, because I'm going to need you as sharp as a tack and on top of your game when we get to the oasis.'

'The oasis?'

'Yes, the oasis.'

Sam gave him a sheepish smile. 'Maybe you should start from the beginning, that way I'll be sure I'm not missing anything.'

'You really did hit the sauce a little too much with that bit of stuff last night, eh, old mucker?' Bertram grinned and raised an eyebrow. He upended his flask over his mouth, having apparently forgotten it was empty. He swore as he put it back in his pocket, then reached down to pull a full bottle out of his saddlebags, which clinked suspiciously. He uncorked it and took a long swig, then waved it around to punctuate his speech, which was becoming noticeably more slurred as time went on. 'Lord Carnarvon, our esteemed boss, has commissioned us to go to Bahariya Oasis, that's in Egypt as well, by the way, if you'd forgotten that too.' He took another swig of whisky before going on. 'His Lordship's chief tomb robber, your friend and mine, Mr "Hoity Toity" Howard Carter, discovered a tablet there. Well, he *claims* he discovered it, but I'm pretty sure the locals just showed him where it was; that's how he usually makes his big finds. Anyway, he believes it might be a marker stone pointing the way to a legendary forgotten treasure that's supposed to be in the area somewhere. Unfortunately, he can't read hieroglyphs and he didn't have anyone with him who could, so he doesn't know for sure if he's right or whether it's just some ancient Egyptian shopping list or something. He hasn't got time to go back and decipher it either, because he's had to get back to work - he's supposed to be in charge of Lord Carnarvon's excavations in the Valley of the Kings and if he doesn't make an appearance once in a while he doesn't get paid. Which he can't afford, by the way, because of the size of the bar bill he's racked up since he left the Antiquities Service!' Bertram chuckled and shook his head; he seemed to be in admiration of the man's drinking prowess, if not his skills as an archaeologist. 'Anyway, that's why it's us who are off on this little jaunt into the middle of nowhere. We're going to take a little look at the tablet for him and if it turns out to be directions then we'll see where they lead us.'

'And Quentin? What's he got to do with all that?'

'Ah, yes. Well, the dastardly Mr Price was hanging around the hotel bar in Cairo where I was talking to Howard about the marker stone. It didn't twig at the time, but he usually frequents the more salubrious joints in the red light district, so he must have been there just to spy on us. Although, how he knew I was meeting Howard at that time, I really don't know.'

'He has his ways...'

'You know him, then?'

Sam nodded. 'Oh, yes. We've had our run-ins in the past and let's just say I'm not exactly happy to find him here.'

'Ha!' Bertram barked once with laughter. 'I'll drink to that!'

Sam waited for him to lower the whisky again before continuing. 'And what about the treasure? Does Carter have any idea what it is?'

'Of course not; he never has any idea about anything unless he's told by someone else and even then he's likely to get it wrong. It'll probably be the usual Egyptian stuff, you know; mummies and burial masks, maybe some gold or whatnot, if we're lucky and it hasn't been looted, like the tomb back there. I'm hoping that there will be at least some kind of written history or lost knowledge, it would make a really nice change and something to tell the folks back home about. Imagine finding a stuffed Sphinx or a document describing precisely how to build a pyramid!' He laughed. 'That would really make our names!'

'I guess we'll find out when we get there, then.' Sam smiled; despite the man's evident drink problem he was very likeable and seemed like a decent person.

'*If* we get there; we've got to find and decipher that tablet first.' Bertram took another long swig of his whisky then stashed the bottle back in his saddle bags. 'And then we have to make sure that the vile Quentin Price doesn't bump us off so that he can keep all the goodies for himself, which wouldn't be very nice at all.'

'You seem to know him quite well.'

'He's been hanging around the dig sites for god knows how long, several years at least, snatching finds from under our noses - he's never made a discovery of his own that wasn't based on somebody else's research or downright stolen from them.'

Sam was pleased to hear that Quentin's backstory was far worse than his. It was also interesting that it was once again very much in keeping with the young man's actual character, much like his persona of Jack Swallow had been. 'Why hasn't anybody done anything about him?'

The man blinked, as if the idea had never occurred to him, which, if Quentin had only turned up recently, it probably never had. 'I'm not really sure, actually... but I guess it's because, even though he's a damn bounder, we don't turn on our own; he's still one of us and an Englishman to boot, even though he's a disgrace to the name.' He shrugged. 'I think we've all just hoped he'd be bumped off by an angry native or he'd stumble into a trap or step on a snake long before we actually had to do something about it.'

Sam smiled wryly; he certainly sympathised with the man - Quentin's death would solve more than the British archaeological community's problems with the man, it would do the Society a pretty big favour as well.

It was strange, but, except for the stuff about Quentin, which had been completely new to him, Sam realised that he had known everything else that Bertram had told him and he belatedly remembered what Andrew had said about turning up in a time-line knowing what you would know if you actually belonged in it, just like he'd known how to captain a ship back in Port Royal.

And with that the floodgates opened and Sam was inundated with all sorts of knowledge, including the year: 1907, and the fact that he was an Egyptologist from the Ashmolean Museum in Oxford, which he had never heard of, was in his mid-thirties and had recently arrived in Cairo to be immediately contracted by Lord Carnarvon to aid Bertram in this job, which had been thrust on him at the last moment. He was also quite surprised to find that, despite retaining his Catalan surname, he was one hundred percent English; apparently the time-line had completely disregarded half of his ancestry, probably to make him fit in a bit better in a world that was dominated by the British Empire.

Unfortunately, though - or perhaps fortunately, he wasn't sure how he felt about it - he had no memory of the supposed "beauty" Bertram said he had "been with" the previous night. He didn't mind though; it wouldn't have been real and it would have made him feel like he'd cheated on Rachel, even though he hadn't done anything. However... since the event was part of his backstory and everything in it was real until he left, did that mean that he *had* in fact done something? Did it truly matter that he hadn't actually arrived until *after* the deed was done? It was still him who had done it and if he met the woman now she would remember having been with him, at least he hoped that it had been memorable enough for her to do so. But if...

He quickly cut off his train of thought before it tied him in knots, like it had so many times before; no matter how many times Andrew or Rachel explained things to him, he still couldn't get his head around the intricacies of time travel; it was just beyond him. He was just going to do what he always did - take things as they came and trust what was in his head as much as he could; he knew that he hadn't actually done any of the things that the people here believed he had and that was what really mattered to him.

However, none of his newly surfaced memories helped to explain how he had ended up in the same time-line as his enemy once more.

Andrew had told him that it should have been impossible for him to have crossed paths with Quentin in Port Royal and yet here he was. There was obviously something strange going on, but he couldn't for the life of him work out what it was. It didn't really matter though, because apparently it was the job of the Elders to figure this stuff out while his job was to do the time travelling stuff, which he had to admit he liked a lot more, and having said that, it looked like it hadn't been a totally wasted trip after all; it was his duty to find out what Quentin was doing in the time-line. Even better, it might even mean that it had been beyond his control and not his fault that the Displacement had gone so wrong - at least he hoped that the rest of the Society would see it that way.

Feeling much better with his situation, Sam turned his attention back to his unusual surroundings.

They had left the pyramids of Giza completely behind now and were passing another temple complex with the ruins of another pyramid. There were surprisingly few people around; Sam had known that there wouldn't be any tourists, obviously, but he had expected there to be more archaeology things going on. Instead, the entire plain seemed deserted and the only signs of life he could see were a few dozen goats grazing near the edge of a line of trees up ahead.

They soon left even this second set of ruins and headed into the welcome relief of the shade between the trees, scattering the goats.

Through the gaps in the sparse forest Sam noticed yet another ruin, columns and statues worn down by the elements, but, before he could get a good look at it, that too was left behind them; the camels were faster than they looked.

Suddenly, they broke through the trees and came out on the bank of a wide river - the Nile.

Here they found the first real signs of life: there were boats on the river, several other camel trains and thousands upon thousands of goats.

One of the Egyptian bearers spurred his camel forward until he was beside the two Englishmen. 'Our conveyance is waiting for us, gentlemen, if you please. My brother is the captain of a humble ship and he has given us an excellent price for such short notice!' The man spoke in an educated English accent, which surprised Sam somewhat and he was ashamed to find that he had been prejudiced by the native clothing that he wore, a mistake he swore not to make again.

'Thank you, Francis, well done! Ride on ahead, will you, and make sure everything is ready.'

'Right you are, sir!' The Egyptian sped his camel ahead towards one of the boats pulled up at the bank of the river.

Sam looked at Bertram quizzically. 'Francis? That's not a very typical Egyptian name, is it?'

'He was brought up by Catholic missionaries, who sent him on a scholarship to university in England, hence the accent. They gave him the name because they couldn't pronounce his real one, or were too lazy to learn it. He prefers it, at least he tells me he does. I'm afraid I don't know what his real name is. Very intelligent man and he should be a curator at the museum, not in charge of the porters, but he's never had the chance to prove himself. All because he's not white.' Bertram spoke with more than a hint of shame in his voice and Sam's opinion of him rose a bit more.

Francis' brother turned out to be a toothless and sun-browned man with a dirty turban, but despite his appearance the boat turned out to be an impeccably maintained barge with a large triangular lateen sail and plenty of room for the men and animals. Sam and Bertram had been allocated a cabin to share, but in the end they didn't use the room for sleeping because it was far too hot, instead they just stored their baggage in it and slept on deck under the stars in the cool of the constant breeze.

It was a little more than a three day journey up the Nile to where they would disembark and head into the desert and the time passed very peacefully. There was nothing else for him to do, so Sam spent the days on deck with his companions, in the shade of the huge sail. He refused the whisky that Bertram continually offered, did some exercise when he could and enjoyed the scenery as it drifted past. He even tried to learn some Arabic from Francis; he knew that the language could come in handy at any time, in any time, but it was incredibly difficult and he didn't do very well. Even so, he persisted, figuring that he could impress Rachel with it when he got home.

The further up the river they went, the more Sam got the feeling that they were travelling back into the past. The modern steamboats gave way to boats, like the one they were on, that had been built the same way for hundreds of years, but they thinned out over the course of the first day until they had almost completely gone. The people, with their camels and goat herds, disappeared along with the boats, replaced by wildlife that included an unbelievable amount of crocodiles, and soon they were going hours on end without seeing any sign of another human being.

For a city boy, the quiet and the isolation were a bit strange at first, but Sam quickly grew used to it and began enjoying what was the first real rest he had had in his life, away from the distractions prevalent in the modern day.

It would have been perfect if it hadn't been for the shadow of Quentin Price looming over him.

They docked in the morning of the fourth day on the boat and unloaded the camels and gear in a town next to the river called Samalut, which was much closer to their destination than Cairo, but still over a hundred miles away. They replenished their water then turned their backs on the river to start the long ride to the Oasis.

Every step took them further and further west into the deep desert where nothing lived. While the journey by boat had been pleasant and restful, the journey into the desert was a nightmarish test of endurance.

The ground was hard packed beneath them, monotonous and unchanging in its flatness all the way to the horizon, reflecting the sun's brilliance, hurting their eyes with the glare and surrounding them with a dry, baking heat that sapped their energy.

Once, in the afternoon of the second day, Sam glanced backwards towards where they had come from, longing for the cool comfort of the river, and thought he saw shadows following them - a dozen or so dark and indistinct figures on camels that wavered in the heat haze. He mentioned it to Bertram, but his companion just dismissed it without even looking, saying that either they were in his mind or were mirages of things that were probably hundreds of miles away. Sam wasn't too sure about that, but didn't have the energy to protest and in any case the shadows were gone by the time he looked again. His struggle with the heat soon pushed the riders from his mind and he forgot all about them as he returned to his constant private misery.

Surprisingly, Bertram seemed to take the harsh conditions in his stride, steeling himself with what appeared to be an endless supply of whisky stored in his saddlebags. With nothing else to ease the boredom, Sam would often watch him swaying in his saddle, moderately drunk and gently snoring, but somehow still staying in the saddle. He didn't know if it was just the whisky, the famous British "stiff upper lip" or whether the man was really immune to the conditions, but whatever it was, Sam wished some of it would rub off on him to relieve some of his discomfort.

The Egyptians didn't seem as perturbed by the heat either, taking it stoically in their stride. Sam was envious of their loose white robes. He hadn't worn his jacket during the day since the very first moment on the boat; taking it off had been the first thing he'd done when he'd had the chance, but that hadn't done much to relieve the general unsuitability of the rest of his clothing. Francis saw his discomfort and took pity on him. He lent him a headdress, a keffiyeh, which helped to block the sand from his nose and mouth as well as providing some protection from the sun, and he showed Sam how to use it as a mini tent when they stopped during the noon heat, with the stick used to control the camel as a pole to prop it up. Sam politely refused the spare set of robes he was offered, though, knowing that Bertram wouldn't cease poking fun at him and that he probably wouldn't be able to wear them in a dignified manner, no matter how comfortable and appropriate they were for the desert.

In stark contrast to the days, the nights became much colder and with nothing to fuel a fire they huddled together, wearing everything they had brought with them, keeping close to the camels for warmth. Sam wasn't too bothered by the cold, though; he had been taught ways of dealing with it during the careful training he'd received in Okinawa, rather it was the heat of the day he struggled with - summers in Barcelona had in no way prepared him and there was no escaping from it like there was in the overly air-conditioned modern world.

It was during the long periods of wakefulness in those long nights that Sam got to know his travelling companion, Bertram Campbell. Campbell had been in Egypt for the last twenty years, having come out from England in 1883 as an apprentice with something called the Egypt Exploration Fund, fresh out of the University of London and bringing with him a young wife. When the rest of the expedition had gone home they had stayed on to live in Cairo so that Bertram could continue to work. Because most of the archaeologists of the time would only come for short stays, usually a single dig at a time, then go back to England to present their finds, this had given him a distinct advantage and he had been present for most of the major finds of the early days of excavations, although the credit had always been taken by the lead archaeologists.

He had worked hard for many years, becoming more and more highly regarded, until finally, in late 1901, he had been given control over his first site - a minor discovery in Luxor, some four hundred miles south of Cairo. It had only been a small commission, but it was an important step towards finally gaining recognition.

The dig had gone well and he'd made discoveries that had revealed that the find was actually far more important than had been first thought. His time there was extended, which meant that he was still up the Nile in Luxor in the summer of 1902, when Cairo had suffered an outbreak of cholera and his wife and their two children had died. The tragic loss had destroyed him emotionally and he had turned to drink for comfort. As a result his work had suffered. He was replaced by the sponsors of the dig and sent back to Cairo in disgrace.

In the following years he had gotten a couple of small commissions, but, as his drinking continued, his reputation and good name had all but disappeared, until he was reduced to taking what jobs he could and the last five years he had been working in the shadow of better-known men, like Howard Carter. A week before, when he had been offered the chance of seeking out a previously unknown find, he had jumped at the chance to redeem himself, but, knowing his own shortcomings, he had asked his sponsor, Lord Carnarvon, to hire Samuel Vives as his apprentice. Which was why they were on what could very well be a wild-goose chase, heading out where no European had ever been - into the inhospitable deep desert of Central Egypt.

Right from the start they were on short rations of water. Sam's mother was always telling him that he didn't drink enough water, but they were now surviving on much less than even he usually drank and after just two days he began to feel the effects. His skin felt dry, his mouth was struggling to make saliva and he was thirstier than he had ever been in his life, perpetually craving water. He suffered in silence, not complaining, although sometimes he thought that the only thing keeping him from emptying his waterskin every few minutes was the discipline that he had learnt from Master Hamato. He couldn't completely ignore the thirst, though; it was a constant aggravation, preventing him from being able to concentrate on anything else.

On the third day it became too much.

The camel train had become strung out over about a hundred metres during the day and in the early afternoon Sam found himself riding next to Bertram, who was snoozing as always. He was trying to think of anything to take his mind off of his thirst, but every time Bertram's camel took a step there was a sloshing noise. At first he could block it out, bolstering his discipline by going through martial arts techniques in his head and daydreaming about his time with Rachel, but the noise of liquid moving around in the glass bottles was constant, an unceasing torment. It was slowly driving him crazy and in his heat-addled state it never even occurred to him that the simplest solution would be to just move out of earshot. Eventually he snapped.

He snarled and opened his mouth to shout at Bertram, to bawl him out, maybe even to take those stupid bottles out of his saddlebags and throw them into the desert or, better yet, grab them and smash them over his...

He caught himself just in time.

He closed his eyes and clenched his fists around the reins, gritting his teeth while he fought violent animal impulses, which he hadn't even known he had, for control over his body. He recovered very slowly and when he could think rationally again he slowed his camel so as to fall back a little, away from his friend, ashamed at how close he had come to betraying everything he believed in.

Sam had a hallucination on the fourth day - he glanced to the side and discovered Rachel riding a beautiful white horse next to him. In a daze he smiled at her and she smiled back, flashing her perfect white teeth at him. He started to say something, but the words caught in his throat as she changed before his eyes. The skin began to pull back from her teeth, her face started to dry and wrinkle grotesquely, and her lush blond hair turned grey and fell out in ashen drifts as she aged. Her body shrunk as the moisture left her completely, until all that was left were her mummified remains and the smile that he loved so much had become a horrific rictus that was more gaps than rotted brown teeth. He couldn't bear to see her like that, even if it was just the memory of the mummy in the tomb several hundred miles back resurfacing in his fevered mind, so he closed his eyes and ignored the horrible vision, hoping that it would go away quickly.

Long afterwards, when he was at home writing his report and thought back to the journey across the desert, he wasn't sure if the vision had been brought on by the thirst or the heat, or whether it had come from some dark place deep inside of him that was still troubled by the age and experience gap that existed between him and Rachel. Whatever the cause had been, it hadn't exactly been pleasant and it made him wonder if he should see a shrink; although, he supposed that if he told a psychologist about any of his Displacements they would probably have him locked up in a heartbeat. He idly wondered if any of his new colleagues was a trained psychoanalyst; it would certainly be very useful in their line of work - he himself had only been on a handful of Displacements and had already gone through things that haunted his nightmares; he hated to think what the others had gone through. Or what had given Andrew his terrible scars.

As they got closer to their destination, the solid flat desert gradually gave way to soft sandy dunes. For a while it was a nice change from the monotony of before, but then the wind got stronger and the loose sand started to fly up to sting their exposed skin and Sam found himself wishing for the boredom of before.

The dunes grew steadily larger over the next couple of days and it became harder and harder for them to make any progress. They were forced to struggle up the steep faces of the dunes, slipping back almost as far as they climbed, then all but slid down the backs of them. They pushed on ahead doggedly, though, until finally, a couple of hours after the noon rest on the eighth day after leaving the Nile, Francis rode up to join them. He touched his finger to his brow and bobbed his head, grinning widely. 'Excuse me, sirs, but we are almost there - Bahariya Oasis is just on the other side of this next dune.'

Sam squinted, trying to see past the glare of the sun, looking for some sign of the truth of the man's words, and spotted a multitude of birds wheeling in the sky ahead - there hadn't been any in the deep desert beyond the occasional vulture and he knew that seeing so many of them was a sure and welcome indication of more hospitable conditions. He smiled. 'Thank you, Francis.'

Francis smiled in return and nodded, then turned his camel around and fell back to re-join the rest of the bearers following them.

Sam and Bertram exchanged a grin, then as one they spurred their mounts ahead excitedly, racing each other to reach the top of the slope.

The camels showed no reluctance now; they were more than keen to forge ahead, their nostrils flaring as they detected the presence of moisture in the air.

They halted at the top of the dune and looked down on the oasis. It was nothing like Sam had imagined it would be; he had fully expected to see what was in the movies - a small pool of dirty water and a few palm trees surrounded by sand, but instead it was a sea of green that covered the whole of a huge valley; the complete opposite of the seemingly endless sand of the lifeless desert on which they were still standing. There was a small village with a couple of dozen huts next to what he could only describe as a lake that glistened in the sun and there were goats wandering everywhere. In the distance, past the abundant life, there were some low rocky hills and beyond them the desert began again.

Francis reined in by their side as the rest of the caravan caught up with them and pointed across the valley. 'The stone tablet was found in a cave in those hills. We can stop to fill our water on the way and there is plenty of time to have afternoon tea, if you gentlemen wish, and still get to the cave before the sun starts to go down, sir.'

'Jolly good show! Well, let's get cracking, shall we?' Bertram kicked his camel into motion and rode off down the side of the dune, all elbows and legs, somehow full of energy.

'Tea, there's always tea...' Sam sighed to himself; he wanted much more than just a cup of tea, he wanted to go to sleep for a week and soak in the oasis for a few hours to ease his aching muscles.

He gave Frances a wry smile and a nod of thanks, then got his own camel moving and followed Bertram at a more stately pace.

They got to the oasis half an hour later and, while the bearers filled the waterskins, Sam drank his fill from the pool, kneeling down next to a camel that was doing the same thing. The water wasn't exactly clean by modern standards, but he was far beyond caring and it was now more a question of survival that he replenish his body's moisture, rather than just a simple one of what was best for him according to his mother.

For the first time since leaving the boat they were able to make a fire to heat water for Bertram's tea and he drank several mugs of it, downing it with an enthusiasm that was comparable to how he devoured whisky. Afterwards, he insisted on a snooze and Sam didn't complain; it was very pleasant by the oasis, with plentiful shade, and it was fairly cool, which was a relief when compared to the open desert.

He washed his face and body as best as he could, fended off the amorous advances of a couple of goats, then laid down in the shade of a palm tree, removed his boots and was quickly asleep.

Bertram woke from his nap after a couple of hours and chivvied them all into action.

Sam stretched and yawned, scaring away a goat that had been nibbling on one of his boots. He was somewhat surprised at how refreshed and full of energy he felt, but the truth was that the journey hadn't actually taken very long, they had been well-provisioned and they hadn't had to go to any extremes to survive. On top of that, he had been in good physical condition when they had started out, so he would probably completely recover after a good night's sleep and plenty to drink for a couple of days.

The camels were bad tempered and reluctant to move away from the water, but the bearers eventually got them going and they soon left the pool behind, starting the short trek through the trees towards the hills. They reached them in only minutes and, as they climbed, Sam twisted in his saddle to gaze back at the oasis; it was fascinating to him how such a thing could exist in the middle of such desolation. Just as he was about to turn his attention back to the trail there was a flash of light from somewhere near where they had rested. He frowned and searched for the source, but it didn't come again, so he assumed that it had just been the sun reflecting off of the water of the pool and thought nothing more of it.

The cave they were heading for was half way up a hill and not actually very far from the oasis. It had been very well concealed, hidden behind a thick row of thorny bushes, which was why it had remained undiscovered until fairly recently. It had only been found after one of the shepherds from the village had lost a goat amongst the thicket and come across the opening by chance. He had cut back the bushes so that he could use the cave as a shelter and in his explorations of the tunnels behind it had come across the tablet leaning against the wall in a side chamber about a hundred metres in. He had told his companions about it one night while drinking around the fire, then had promptly gotten himself killed when, in his drunken stupor, he had mistaken a snake for a stick when he'd gone to gather firewood.

The other shepherds had naturally taken that as a sign that the cave was cursed.

That had been fifty years ago and they were still avoiding the place in superstitious awe, but when Howard Carter had arrived, following rumours and hearsay in search of treasure, one of them had got together enough courage, fuelled by cold hard cash, to take him there. The bushes had grown back over the entrance, but it had been a simple matter to cut through them and expose it again, at least according to Francis, who had been in Carter's party, and that was how Sam and Bertram found it.

None of the bearers would enter the tunnels because of the curse, except for Francis, who didn't hold with such things, although he nonetheless kissed the silver cross that he had around his neck and said a quick prayer before entering the cave, so it was just him, Sam and Bertram who entered. Bertram and Francis held aloft flaming torches while Sam had their one lantern. The light frightened away the numerous rats and they used the torches to burn away the spider's webs that liberally covered the place.

It didn't take long to find the tablet. It was just over a couple of metres tall, almost a metre wide and covered with a light layer of cobwebs and dirt that had accumulated on it in the few weeks since Carter had been there, obscuring the carvings that covered it. Francis immediately stuck his torch into the ground and began to clean it with a soft brush, expertly using techniques he'd obviously learnt previously on dig sites. Once he'd finished he stepped back and the two Egyptologists moved forwards to peer at the symbols.

'Wow,' said Sam finally. 'What does it say?'

'How should I know?' Bertram raised an eyebrow and gave Sam a slightly bemused look. 'I can read a bit, but you're supposed to be the expert. That's why I brought you.'

Sam was about to tell him that he couldn't read the hieroglyphics, but then Rachel's laughter echoed in his mind and it dawned on him that he was being an idiot; if Bertram had brought him along specifically to do things like this, then he must have told either him, or more likely Lord Carnarvon, that he could read hieroglyphics, which in turn meant that he'd learnt to do so somewhere in his backstory. It was also why the writing on the walls of the tomb had looked so familiar.

With a sigh he told the teasing voice of Rachel to be quiet and concentrated on the carvings. They were certainly familiar, but at first they stubbornly remained the indecipherable pictographs that they would have been to him at home.

He had to be able to read them; it was a skill he needed, so the time-line must have given it to him.

At least that was what he hoped - he had no idea if that was how it really worked.

It wasn't working, though, and he glanced to the side, to where Francis and Bertram were watching him expectantly, waiting for him, depending on him to tell them whether the hard journey had been worth it or not.

Looking at their hopeful faces, he realised that if he failed to read the symbols then he would be letting down more people than just himself. And what could he possibly say to them? That he'd lied to them? It would be the same strange circumstance as before - he himself wouldn't have lied to them, but the Sam in his backstory would have.

Admittedly, he'd gotten to know the talkative Bertram much more than the quiet Francis on the journey, but he still considered both of them to be friends and he really didn't want to disappoint them.

It turned out that he needn't have worried, because as soon as he turned his attention back to the tablet it suddenly became clear as if a switch had been thrown in his head. Sam blinked in surprise. 'I can read it!'

'You had me worried for a minute there, old bean; it would have been a bally waste of a journey if you couldn't!' Bertram took a swig of whisky to celebrate. 'Well? What does it say then?'

Sam found that, while he could read the hieroglyphs without any problem, he was getting several options for most of them. It was like having *Google Translate* in his mind; each symbol could be interpreted in many different ways, and it was happening in his head as he looked at them. It was quite confusing, but he did his best to sort it out. 'Er, well, it seems to be some kind of story or legend. As far as I can tell it says: *Many years ago, soon after the wise ones left, the Demigod Nasus smited...*' Sam frowned and turned to Bertram. 'Um, what's the past tense of smite? Smited? Smote?'

Bertram sighed. 'I'm not sure it matters, old chum; we get the idea.'

'Oh, right.' Sam grinned sheepishly. 'Um... *He smited the ground with his rod that was huge,* no that's not quite right, *over-sized?* Or perhaps *needlessly large* would be a more accurate translation? Yes, that's probably it. Anyway, *he smote the ground so hard that it cracked and opened a,* I'm not sure about this. A *valley?* Actually, that's probably *rift, in which he declared that the Pharaohs should entomb their most valuable riches and their greatest knowledge. There it would remain, safe for all time, until one who has travelled,* uh, *some time?* That's not quite it: *a long while* perhaps? *comes for it. Our greatest treasure, The Secret of the Ancients, is for him and him alone.*'

Bertram had been taking notes as Sam read the symbols, seeming to make sense of Sam's confused rambling. 'Good, good. Treasure, knowledge, secrets, all nice… What else is there?'

Sam quickly scanned the rest of the stone. 'Well, it goes on a bit more. It's actually quite interesting, but it doesn't say anything else about the treasure or give any directions, it basically just says to make sure not to tell anyone about this on pain of, well, on pain of a painful death, and to have slaves or minions do all the building and dirty work. Nothing much of use really.'

'Right, well that's not very helpful. It's worth taking note of, obviously, and it'll certainly be worth coming back to study some more, but it doesn't do anything to help us find that valley or the treasure, now, does it?' He frowned. 'Are you sure that's all it says? I thought there would have been directions or something.'

'Hang on, there's something else here…' Sam had spotted something carved into the very bottom of the tablet, still half-buried in the ground. He borrowed Francis' brush and knelt down to finish cleaning it off, to his surprise working just as expertly as the Egyptian had.

He sat back on his heels and frowned at it. 'This one's actually quite unusual, I'm not sure what…' The symbol he had exposed was clearer than the other ones on the tablet; being covered had protected it somewhat, but even so he was struggling with it - the translator in his head wasn't providing him with a definitive answer, instead it was popping words into his head, none of them quite right, as if it were searching for the solution. It was dizzying and quite disconcerting and for a moment he wondered if he'd get stuck like that if he couldn't find the correct meaning, but then he laughed as the right one finally floated to the forefront of his mind and stuck there. 'Oh! It means "P.T.O.". You *really* don't see that very often!'

'P.T.O.?' asked Francis, mystified. 'Please, sir, what does that mean?'

Bertram stepped forward and, with a nod to Sam, they both grasped the sides of the tablet near the top. 'It means "Please Turn Over". Grab the top when you can, will you, Francis, old boy?'

Even with the three of them lowering it as gently and as slowly as they could, it still landed on its face with an almighty thunk. Thankfully, the ground was soft, otherwise it might have broken.

At last, the back was revealed and the three men crowded around it.

'Wow…' exclaimed Francis in his curious British accent.

'You can say that again.' said Sam.

'Er... wow?' Francis frowned, not understanding.

'Never mind.' Sam smiled. He squatted down and used the brush on the tablet again, clearing away the few cobwebs that had gathered on its back.

Carved into the back of the tablet were a few hieroglyphs here and there, but the vast majority of the space was taken up by what looked at first glance like random squiggly lines.

Sam knelt down next to the tablet to read the symbols, pointing them out to Bertram as he went. 'This is the hieroglyph for oasis and this is the one for the Nile...'

Bertram squatted beside him. 'My word, it's a map! This must be the way we have to go, then.' He traced his hand along a straight line that ran from the symbol for oasis until he found another one. 'And this, what does this symbol mean?'

'That's the same as the one that was on the other side; the "Rift" or "Valley" that it talks about, and I guess this is what's there; some kind of temple or tomb maybe.' Next to the hieroglyph was a drawing of columns flanking a rectangular doorway with a triangle on top.

Bertram rubbed his hands together in glee. 'Wonderful! So now we know what we're looking for and the way to get to it. Let's get a copy of this down and get cracking!'

Sam took out his notepad and joined Bertram in scribbling down his own version of the map, just in case. When they had finished they each compared their efforts with the original on the tablet. Satisfied with the results they grinned at each other, coming up with the same idea at the same time; simultaneously they bent down and worked their fingers under the top of the tablet.

'Give us a hand with this, would you, Francis, old bean?'

Together the three men lifted the tablet back to its original position, then Bertram made sure that the hieroglyph at the bottom was covered again and the floor around it look undisturbed, trying to make it seem as if they had never moved the stone.

Bertram surveyed his work and nodded in satisfaction. 'That should keep Price guessing for a little while.'

They dusted themselves off and retraced their steps out of the chamber and back through the tunnels.

Egypt seemed to be a land of extreme contrasts: from the utter darkness in caves and tombs to the blinding light of the desert; from the heat of the day to the cold of night - there didn't seem to be any comfortable middle ground and, as they neared the entrance of the cave, Sam was half-blinded by the sunlight once more.

Bertram and Francis didn't have any problems and went out to where they had left the camels, but Sam stopped in the shade of the mouth of the cave. He put a hand up to protect his eyes from the glare and blinked at the ground while he waited to adjust, which was why he had no clue that anything was amiss until he heard a familiar and unwelcome voice calling out.

'Ah, Bertram! There you are! Looks like we're neck and neck!' It was Quentin Price, sounding just as smarmy and self-important as ever.

'Actually, Price, we got here first, so I'd say that puts us in the lead.' Bertram answered dryly.

Sam took his hand away from his eyes and squinted at the tense scene taking place just outside.

Quentin was accompanied by about a dozen of the ugliest, toughest-looking men Sam had seen outside of a movie, dressed in black, despite the heat. They surrounded the mouth of the cave in a semi-circle, corralling Bertram's bearers and preventing anyone from leaving. Their rifles looked both well used and well taken care of and, while they weren't yet pointing them at anyone, they were nonetheless holding them at the ready - a clear threat.

Sam barely saw any of that, though, because something else had captured his attention: sitting on the camel next to Quentin's was one of the most beautiful women he had ever seen. She looked like she was in her late teens or maybe young twenties and had long dark red hair that fell down her back and incredible green eyes. She and Quentin were both dressed in khaki explorer garb, similar to Sam's and Bertram's, but hers just fitted her *better* somehow.

She turned her head to look at him. Their eyes met and an almost palpable shock ran through Sam. He hastily looked away from her, but not before the half smile she flashed at him made his heart race.

Quentin was about to say something else to Bertram, but he stopped when he saw the direction of his companion's gaze. He squinted into the darkness of the cave, looking directly at Sam. 'Who have you got back there, Campbell? Another of your educated savages?' He sneered at Francis before calling out. 'You there! Come out here where we can see you!'

Sam took a step forwards into the light.

He watched, fascinated, as Quentin's face turned white with shock, then slowly went through several shades of angry red until it was almost purple with fury. He smiled inwardly when he saw Quentin's hand lift involuntarily towards his forehead; his greasy hair was slightly longer than it had been in Barcelona and it now reached almost to his eyes, effectively hiding the scar that Sam had given him and that the man was obviously still very conscious of.

Sam chuckled, enjoying the moment as much as he could. 'Hi, Quentin. Nice to see you again.'

'Vives!' Quentin snarled Sam's name, barely getting it out between clenched teeth. The hand that had gone towards his forehead now twitched towards the huge pistol holstered at his side, but he froze when he noticed that the girl was watching him intently with a smirk on her face. He drew himself up in the saddle and smiled widely, somehow managing to sneer at the same time. 'Going native are you, Sammy? I didn't recognise you with that ridiculous thing on your head! What the hell are you doing here?'

Unlike Quentin, Sam had enough self-control to stop himself from reaching up to finger the keffiyeh that he was still wearing. 'Well, I heard you were in the neighbourhood and thought I'd pop by to see how you were.'

Quentin looked like he was about to blow his top and order his men to start shooting, but the girl reached out and put her hand on his arm to calm him.

'Now, now, Quentin, remember your manners! Aren't you going to introduce us?' Her voice was smooth, silky, like liquid chocolate, but the smile she turned on Sam was cold and didn't quite reach her eyes; the smile of a predator looking at their next meal. She slid smoothly down from her camel and walked over to Sam, coming to a halt in front of him with her hands on her hips. She was as tall, or rather, as short as he was and had a frank way of looking at him that caught his attention and made him blush. After a few seconds that seemed like an eternity she held out her hand and he automatically took it.

'I'm Diana, Diana Birch, pleased to meet you, Mr…'

'Vives, Sam Vives.'

'Mr Vives.'

'Call me Sam.'

'Very well.' She nodded graciously and smiled at him, but once again it didn't quite make it to her eyes. She held his hand and his gaze equally and there was an awkward moment that went on just a bit too long as everybody watched them in silence.

The spell was eventually broken by a cough from Quentin. 'If you're quite finished playing with your food, Diana, we have important matters to discuss with Mr Campbell.'

'Yes, of course. Sorry, Quentin.' She spoke without taking her eyes from Sam's, raising her eyebrow in slight exasperation at her companion's impatience. 'A pleasure to meet you, *Sam.*' She finally released his hand, letting it slide sensually from hers, and turned, sashaying back to stand by Quentin's camel.

Sam blinked and shook himself back to life - at the very least the woman was hypnotic. And the way she had purred his name… He shuddered.

'So. Bertram, *old man.*' Quentin put emphasis on what he knew was a verbal tick of Bertram's, twisting it and turning it against him, taunting him. 'Are you going to tell us what you found, or are you going to make us take it from you?'

Bertram was defiant, even in the face of superior forces. Typically British. 'I'd like to see you try!'

Quentin smiled evilly and was about to reply, but again Diana interrupted him.

'Why don't we just go and look at the tablet, Quentin, I'm sure that we can decipher it for ourselves, just as well as they can. There's no need for violence.' She winked at Sam. 'At least not yet anyway.'

Quentin grumbled, but reluctantly agreed. He leapt down from his camel and stalked over to the three men who had come out of the cave. He snatched the torches away from Francis and Bertram with a growl and thrust one at Diana for her to carry.

'Watch your back, Vives,' said Quentin with a sneer, brushing past him and disappearing into the cave.

Once more Sam couldn't help but compare Quentin to Rafa; they had used the exact same words when threatening him. The difference was that Quentin was far more capable of carrying out his threats and he suspected that if he did it would mean much more than a simple beating like Sam had too often received from Rafa.

Diana paused next to Sam as Quentin went into the cave and gave him a smile. 'Be seeing you soon. Sam.' She followed Quentin into the darkness accompanied by two of the black-clad thugs.

Bertram whispered to Sam. 'Come on, let's get out of here before they come back and change their minds.'

They hurried to their camels, mounted up and quickly left the cave behind, all too conscious of the rifles at their backs.

They rode as fast as they could away from the hills and back past the pool, pausing for a couple of minutes to replenish what little water they had used in the short journey to the cave before moving on. It was only after they had crossed a couple of dunes and the oasis was far behind them that they relaxed their pace and took a moment to look at the map. It was fairly clear which way they had to go - south-west and even deeper into the desert. Bertram took out a compass, quickly got a bearing and they set out, skirting the edge of the valley.

Francis heard them talking. 'There is nothing south-west of here, sirs, there is just empty desert for hundreds of miles. Nobody goes out that way, or if they do, they never come back to tell the tale.'

Bertram saluted Sam with his whisky. 'That's encouraging. What do you say, Sam, old boy?'

'Sounds like the perfect place to hide treasure to me.'

CHAPTER 15
THE RIFT

They rode further into the deep desert.

There was some grumbling from the bearers because of the way they were heading, but Francis had a word with them and they quietened down, not exactly happy, but thankfully not rebelling either.

The first time they stopped for a rest, Sam looked at the map in his notebook, checking it and rechecking it against the picture he held in his mind of the back of the tablet, constantly wondering if he'd made some error. Bertram's copy was the same, though, and Sam came to the same conclusion every time, but that didn't stop him from taking out his notebook again the next time they rested and poring over it again.

If the map was to scale, which he hoped it was, then, extrapolating from the relative distances from the Nile to the oasis and from the oasis to the "Rift", the journey was about three hundred miles, which was about three times longer than the previous trek. However, it was something that they could make in less than a week by pushing the camels, something that they hadn't done on the way to the oasis, but would do now because of having Quentin in pursuit. The only problem that he could foresee was missing their destination; if it was small enough they might just walk right past it, never knowing it was there and keep wandering out into the desert. But even then, they could just turn around and go back to the oasis to refill their water then try again. They didn't want to have to do that, though, because it would open the door to the possibility of Quentin beating them to the Rift.

Sam didn't know if it was because he was getting used to the conditions, or whether it was because the prize was in sight, but the second leg of the journey was proving to be a lot easier than the first. It was hot, yes, and they still had to shelter from the noonday sun, but they had plenty of supplies and the camels never seemed to tire, despite the faster pace.

With those hardships all but gone, his greatest problem became boredom - the dunes had petered out during the first day and the landscape had returned to the flat, hard-packed plain. It was day after day of endless sand under an endless blue sky and a relentless sun, not being able to talk much because of having to conserve moisture and with little to do except stare into the distance. For the first time in his life, Sam found himself really wishing that he had a book to read. He wasn't exactly a big reader, he read what he had to for school, of course, but he had always preferred spending his free time playing video games or watching television, at least until Rachel had come along and he had started training with her. However, in an effort to conserve weight, neither he nor Bertram had brought any reading material with them. The only books available, in fact, were the small copies of the Quran that the bearers carried with them wherever they went, but, while Sam would have been very interested in reading one of the copies, if they would let him, they were in Arabic and he was having enough trouble learning how to speak the language, without trying to comprehend the writing as well. So there was nothing for it, except to struggle on, alone with his thoughts and the monotony of the surroundings.

It was an immense relief, therefore, when, on the morning of the sixth day, the perfectly straight line of the horizon, slightly off to the right in front of them, became uneven. They eagerly adjusted their course towards it and over the course of a few hours the irregularity slowly resolved into a chain of low hills, seemingly planted in the middle of the desert.

The way they rose out of the otherwise empty plain reminded Sam somewhat of *Montserrat*, the mountain range that was not far from Barcelona, but on a much smaller scale.

As they got closer, the smooth sand they were travelling across became spotted with half-buried boulders. They were large, the smallest the size of a camel, and had been made smooth over the ages. Bertram stopped to examine the first one that they passed, but declared that there was nothing special about it - it was just a rock.

Over the course of the next hour, the boulders became successively bigger and closer together, until eventually they were unable to keep a straight path and were having to weave between them. It became harder to progress and a few times they found their way blocked and had to backtrack. Eventually, though, they came to the foot of the hills themselves and were surprised to see that they were, in fact, just more chunks of rock, only far larger - bigger than a house or even the apartment blocks in Barcelona.

Sam frowned at them. 'I thought we were looking for a hole in the ground?'

'Yes. Indeed we are, old man.' Bertram grinned at him, seemingly encouraged by the sight. 'But let's say a god came along and hit the ground with a big stick, like it says on the tablet, what do you think would happen?'

'You'd get a hole.' Sam blinked, not understanding.

Bertram just smiled wider. 'Ah, but what do you also get when you dig a hole?'

'I don't... Oh!' Sam finally realised what his friend was getting at. 'You get a big pile of dirt as well as a hole!'

'Or in this case, a big pile of rocks!'

It was Sam's turn to grin as he realised the implications of what the man was saying. 'We've found it, then!'

'Looks like it, old chap! Come on, one little climb and we're home and dry!' He tipped his flask up and gulped down some golden liquid before turning to wink at Sam. 'Well, not exactly *dry*, but you know what I mean.'

Like the smaller boulders, the desert had done its best to reclaim the larger rocks and in a few thousand years more it might succeed, but so far it had only been able to round them off and ground them down, packing sand into places that it hadn't got around to weathering yet, making them easy to climb.

It was still a couple of hours before noon, but the day was already sweltering hot when they got to the summit of the closest hill and gazed down on what lay beyond it.

Bertram stared, astonished. 'My word! It's like someone's ploughed the bally desert!' His mouth opened and closed a few times, but he couldn't seem to find anything else to say.

The hill that they were standing on formed part of an elongated oval of irregular rock formations, several miles in length, with a valley between them. However, it wasn't the ring of hills that was what had rendered Bertram speechless, it was the long hole, perfectly straight, that had somehow been dug into the floor of the desert below, like a ditch or a trench - the Rift or Valley that the tablet had spoken of. It was deep enough that its bottom was completely lost in shadow, making it look like a long black line, painted on the brilliant yellow sand.

Bertram hadn't taken his eyes off of the chasm, except once to glance at his flask before stowing it in his pocket, and his voice was hoarse with wonder when he finally found it again. 'What could have done this? It's solid rock!'

Sam grinned at him. 'Maybe it really was made by a god?'

'Pshaw!' Bertram scoffed. 'Don't tell me you believe in such rubbish as higher powers and all that?'

'Sometimes, I suppose...' Sam shrugged; he wasn't exactly sure what he believed. Neither his mother or father were very religious, so he hadn't been to church much while he was growing up and he hadn't had it forced it down his throat like some of the children at his school had by their parents. He was fairly sure that he didn't believe in "God", at least not the way that most people did, but he sometimes thought that there might well be something else, a "higher power" as Bertram had put it; there seemed to be too many coincidences and fortunate happenstances in his own life, especially since he'd become a Displacer, for them to be completely random.

Bertram laughed. 'Even if there was something up there watching over us or playing marbles with moons or whatever, I doubt he or she would bother coming down here and hitting the ground with a big stick. This is either man-made or just a fluke of nature.'

Sam nodded, thinking that he was probably right, but then he caught sight of Francis, who was astride his camel on the far side of Bertram. He had a sly smile on his face, as if he knew different, but it disappeared as soon as he saw that he was being watched. Sam raised an eyebrow at him, but the man just gave him a shallow bow and turned away to go to the other Egyptians.

Bertram pointed down the hill to the left. 'Well, I think it's pretty obvious that we're supposed to go down there.'

Sam hadn't spotted it before, because it had been fairly well camouflaged from where they were standing and his attention had been elsewhere, but a few hundred metres away, down at the foot of the hills, was the start of what could only be described as a ramp leading down into the dark abyss. It looked like the ramp into an underground parking garage, but one so big that a dozen cars could drive down it side by side and still have room to manoeuvre.

He smiled. 'That's convenient.'

'Yes it is!' Bertram laughed. 'Would you mind having a look to see if the tablet had anything useful to say, old bean? Like what we're supposed to be looking for down there?'

Sam tore his eyes away from the extraordinary view and took out his notebook. The difference between his copy of the map and Bertram's was that he had taken down the translations of the symbols on the tablet as well, whereas Bertram just had the lines of the map itself. Even so, there wasn't very much information to go on, just a vague implication that whatever the map pointed towards was somewhere in the chasm. He shrugged. 'It doesn't say much, actually. I think we're just going to have to explore.'

'Old school! I love it!' Bertram kicked his camel into a walk with a huge grin on his face and headed down the hill.

The group descended the ramp and Sam shivered when they passed into the shadow and the heat was sucked out of the day.

The walls swiftly rose up on either side of them, sheer on both sides, as if they had been cut from the rock, just like the slope had been, and Sam could easily see how whoever had carved the tablet in the cave had believed that a Demigod might have struck the earth and opened it up; it certainly didn't seem natural, it was far too straight and regular for that.

The way down was fairly steep, but it was smooth and flat and the camels easily coped with it and after about ten minutes, when they were about a hundred metres under the surface of the desert, the slope levelled out as they reached the floor of the Rift itself - they were still descending and the walls were still rising, but the gradient became barely noticeable.

They rode slowly, taking their time. They had arranged that Bertram and Sam would take a wall each and inspect it as they went, so as not to miss any possible clues, while Francis rode in the middle of the canyon keeping an eye on the ground for the same reason, but there was nothing to see - no writing, no holes, no doors. Nothing to give a clue as to any treasure hidden anywhere nearby.

The image of the trench walls towering above them and the wall at the end steadily approaching was a familiar one to Sam and he kept half expecting to find some kind of exhaust port in the middle of the floor, but there was nothing, only a few loose rocks that had fallen from the cliffs overhead.

They went further down into the earth and the walls loomed ever higher over them, casting them into deeper shadow with every passing minute.

It was almost two hours before they finally reached the point where the Rift ended at a vertical rock face and, unable to go any further, they brought the camels to a halt and stared at it, mystified. It loomed above them, fully two hundred metres tall, blank, without marks or signs of any kind, exactly the same as the walls.

They were in the right place, there couldn't be any doubt of that; it was highly unlikely that there were two such geological features in the desert of Egypt, but the Rift remained curiously void of any trace of whatever the tablet had pointed them towards.

Bertram sipped from his flask as he looked up at the wall above their heads. 'Do you think we have to climb up? There doesn't seem to be anything down here.'

Sam eyed the smooth rock face, sceptically. 'I don't fancy climbing that and, besides, there doesn't seem to be anything up there either.'

With nothing else to do, they left the camels and walked away from the end, retracing their steps, gazing around the whole time, searching the walls and the floor for anything that they could possibly have missed. Sam took out his notebook and they read through his copy of the inscriptions on the tablet again, but there was no new information to be gleaned, nothing that could help them.

Francis joined them. 'This has been your wild goose chase after all, perhaps, friends? A practical joke played by long-dead people with a peculiar sense of humour.' He shrugged and smiled apologetically. 'We should go; there are many other places to explore - I can take you to pyramids and tombs that have not been entered in thousands of years, you will see. No need for disappointment; I will show you wonders that will more than compensate! Come, let us go, the bearers are nervous, they don't like this place, they are a very superstitious lot.' He beckoned to the bearers to bring the camels.

Bertram and Sam looked at each other and shrugged. Bertram took a swig of whisky and sighed. 'Oh well, you can't win them all. But let's take a more roundabout route on the way back, so as not to tip Price off that there's nothing here; with any luck he'll get lost in the desert.'

Sam grinned. 'One can only hope.'

'Although, if you want, we can see if we can find them; I saw the way that Birch girl was looking at you! She was a bit of all right, wasn't she? I bet that if she wasn't with Price you'd make a move on her, wouldn't you, you devil!' Bertram winked and sighed wistfully. 'One of these days you're going to have to share your secret, tell me how you do it. Oh, if only I were twenty years younger…'

Sam shook his head with a smile and turned away from him.

They were just about to mount their camels and leave when the sun started to reach its zenith. It poked its way above the rock walls, and beamed directly down into the canyon, rapidly heating the air around them.

It wasn't only the temperature that changed, though; the light, which had previously only been shining on the top of the wall at the Rift's end, now illuminated its entirety from almost directly above. Protrusions and indentations on the lower half of the rock face, which had been in near darkness, created shapes with their shadows that sharpened as the sun cleared the top of the wall, until finally they resolved into two blocks of hieroglyphs set one above the other.

And at the base of the wall itself a deeper shadow was revealed…

'My word! That looks like a door! Quick! Before it disappears!'

Bertram ran towards the dark rectangular shape at the base of the wall, but Sam was too busy gazing up at the hieroglyphs. Without taking his eyes from the symbols he took out his notebook and started to take notes. A few of the hieroglyphs were hazy, the rock outcroppings forming them eroded over the years, which made it slightly harder for him to recognise them, but, compared to the tablet, the language was simple and once he worked out what the symbols were, he was able to understand it without much difficulty.

Here within resides the treasure of pharaohs, riches to satisfy the greed of any man. However, the wise will know that true wealth lies not with worldly goods, but often with what appear to be the most worthless of items.

Sam smiled; Master Hamato had always insisted that knowledge was more valuable than gold and it seemed that at least some ancient Egyptians agreed with him, but when he translated the second set of hieroglyphs his face fell and a shiver went through him, which was nothing to do with the cold radiating from rock walls that were almost perpetually in darkness.

By the time Sam had finished, the sun had almost reached the other side of the canyon. The markings were evidently only visible for a few minutes each day when the angle of the sun was just right, probably only at certain times of the year as well, and he frowned as he realised exactly how lucky they had been to arrive within minutes of the phenomenon. His mind drifted back to the conversation he had had with Bertram and he wondered if this was further evidence of the existence of a "higher power" helping him out, but he dismissed the thought almost before it was formed and turned his attention back to his work.

As the sun was eclipsed by the wall, the shadows became distorted and elongated, unreadable once more, then all at once they disappeared completely as the bottom of the Rift was plunged back into semi-darkness.

It was too late, though; the wall had revealed its secrets.

Sam completed his annotation of the last section of the wall just in time and reread it with a sigh as he made his way over to join Bertram at the foot of the wall. 'Um, Bertram…'

'Look! It really is a door, old boy! I can't believe we didn't see it before!' Bertram was running his hands over the rock face, feeling the minuscule cracks in it, marvelling at how well they had been concealed. He had used a piece of chalk to mark the outline while the door had been revealed and those white lines were now the only visual indication that anything was there at all.

'Bertram…'

'Come on, help me pull it open!'

'Bertram!'

At Sam's shout the man stopped what he was doing and turned to look at him. 'What is it, old bean?'

'The hieroglyphs on the wall above us.'

'Instructions? We don't need them! We've already found the door!'

Sam shook his head. 'They're not instructions; the first bit essentially says we're in the right place…'

'Then why so glum, chum?' Bertram said with a rather childish chuckle. He seemed to be more giddy from excitement than he'd ever been from drink.

'Because it's the second part I'm worried about, it was a pretty clear warning.' Sam glanced down at his notes, wanting to get the words exactly right. *'Do not enter unless you are convinced of your worth, for inside are traps for the undeserving, the unwary and the ignorant. Those who bring with them only malice or avarice should prepare their souls for the afterlife.'*

'Pish and tosh!' Bertram interrupted, waving away Sam's concerns. 'These places always say they're cursed.'

'This one doesn't say anything about a *curse*. It specifies *traps*.'

'And no instructions on how to get past them?'

'No. I suppose if this were a, uh…' Sam almost said "movie" because he was thinking about *Indiana Jones and The Last Crusade*, but he stopped himself just in time. '…an adventure story, then there would be helpful clues scattered around to help us get past the traps, but no such luck, I'm afraid.'

Bertram shrugged. 'It would have been jolly helpful, but I'm not surprised, actually; there was probably some kind of guardian or priest here and that kind of information would have been handed down verbally, so that they could tend the treasure or live inside without killing themselves. They'll all be long dead by now and the knowledge lost, but it really doesn't matter; any traps that there might have been will have rotted away a long time ago. And besides, we're not here with malice or avarice, are we? We're here for science and knowledge, so we'll be perfectly safe! But if there's some gold in there as well, we won't say no, right, old man?' Bertram winked then jerked his thumb over his shoulder at the door. 'Now come on, let's get this open!'

Sam could see that Bertram was determined to face whatever was lurking behind the door and quite frankly he was keen to see what was inside as well, no matter the danger. He couldn't help but be worried, though; the way the symbols had been written on the rock wall above them spoke of a level of ingenuity that was far beyond anything that the makers of the traps in the tomb had demonstrated and he was certain that anything designed by them would be cunning and deadly and not likely to rot over time.

It didn't take more than a second for his sense of adventure to completely swamp his misgivings, though, and he stepped forwards to help Bertram.

Francis was looking extremely glum; he must have heard them talking about the traps, but he nonetheless joined them and Bertram arranged them around the door so they could all get as good a grip as possible on the shallow handles, which were little more than indents in the stone for their fingertips. 'On three! One, two, thr…' Together the three of them pulled as hard as they could and stumbled backwards as one when it swung open smoothly and without a sound.

Bertram grinned, brushing his hands off on his jacket as he peered into the pitch black of the tunnel that had been revealed behind the door. 'Well, that was easy! Bodes well, wouldn't you say?'

'Not really; it was too easy,' thought Sam with a frown.

They went back to the camels to get torches, then forged into the dark.

CHAPTER 16
TRAPS

The tunnel was perfectly rectangular, exactly the same shape and size as the door and as perfectly smooth and straight as the Rift had been. Bertram led the way with his torch held high, but the dark was so deep that it didn't illuminate more than five or six metres in front of them.

They walked very slowly, pace by pace, in silence, scanning the walls and floors for traps as they went, but there was nothing to be seen; the walls and floor were solid, not made from cut stones or paved and there was nowhere to hide pressure plates or other simple traps.

After a couple of long minutes Bertram put into words what Sam had been thinking for a while. 'This doesn't feel right; there are barely any cobwebs, the floor is almost dust free and where are the snakes? There's always snakes!'

'Maybe this place was just so airtight that the dust didn't come in and the spiders and snakes couldn't breathe?'

Bertram looked at Sam as if he was crazy and rolled his eyes. 'Can *you* breathe?'

'Uh, yes?'

'Then it obviously wasn't airtight. Smell the air - it's almost fresh. I've opened enough tombs that had been sealed for hundreds of years and, believe me, you want to give them a few hours or days to ventilate before you go in.' He shook his head. 'No, this place has been entered recently. And by recently, I mean in the last decade or so.'

'If robbers have already been here, then maybe it would be best to leave...' Once again, Francis was the only one of the Egyptians who had agreed to come with them, but, judging by the frown on his face, he wasn't very happy to be there.

Bertram chuckled and patted him on the shoulder, reassuringly. 'Where's your stiff upper lip, Francis, old man? We've come too far to leave without having a look around. And if the treasure's gone, then so be it; I'm sure there will be plenty of items of archaeological interest still here.'

Bertram's confidence faltered slightly, though, and he came to a halt when, ahead of them, what feeble light the torches had been shedding ended abruptly, as if it had been cut off or extinguished somehow. He shared a glance with Sam and together they moved forwards, going slower and taking even more care than before.

Sam wasn't sure what he expected to find in the black abyss, but he could never have imagined the sight that confronted them when they reached the end of the tunnel and the light from the torches was suddenly magnified and reflected back at them.

'Whoa!' Sam gaped at the spectacle with his mouth open.

They were standing in the middle of a gigantic geode: the circular floor had been polished flat, but the walls had been left in their natural state and millions on millions of crystals of all shapes and sizes formed a dome that peaked only a dozen or so metres overhead.

Sam couldn't take his eyes off of the play of light on the crystals, which was making them sparkle and scatter a multitude of rainbows as the flames from the torches flickered and flared, reminding him of the diamond he had briefly had possession of in Port Royal, just on a vastly larger scale. He sighed. 'It was worth Displa... uh...' he cut himself off just in time.'...worth *the journey* just to see this...'

Francis gave him a funny look, but said nothing.

Bertram didn't feel like hanging around to admire the view, though, and he started across the smooth floor. 'Come on you two, no time for dawdling - there will be plenty of opportunities to come back and gawk later. Sam, there are more passageways over there and I think there's some writing above them that you'll have to translate for us.'

Sam reluctantly followed his friend across the room. He supposed Bertram was right, this incredible cavern wasn't going anywhere and he had a job to do before he could enjoy it.

There were three doorways cut into the wall about twenty metres away on the other side of the room, directly opposite where the tunnel had come out and, as Bertram had said, there was a row of hieroglyphs above them, formed of black stone inlaid in the crystal.

Bertram went to each opening in turn and peered into them, holding his torch aloft to try to see as far as he could without crossing the threshold.

Sam, meanwhile, read out the writing. *'Three paths await the unenlightened. Two will take fools to their deaths while only the truly centred will choose life.'*

Bertram took a swig of whisky and smacked his lips. 'Well, that's jolly cheery. How do we choose?'

Before either Sam or Francis could reply, they were interrupted by a metallic click that echoed around the room - the sinister sound of a pistol being cocked.

'Three doors, three of you. To me that seems incredibly convenient.'

They spun around to find Quentin standing in the entrance to the room, pointing the largest pistol Sam had ever seen at them. A moment later he was joined by the beautiful young woman, Diana Birch, and a half-dozen of his vicious-looking black-clad bearers, who rushed to surround them with their rifles at the ready.

'Hello, Sam. We really should stop running into each other like this; people will start to talk.' Diana's silken voice filled the room.

'A pleasure to see you again, Miss Birch,' Sam said cheerfully. 'I wish I could say the same for you, Quentin.'

'The feeling is mutual, believe me, Vives.'

'You managed to find the map, then.'

'What map?'

'The one on the back of the tablet.'

Quentin and Diana looked at each other and shared a grimace.

Bertram chortled. 'Oh, that's rich! You didn't even find the map, let alone decipher it! Some Egyptologist you are, Price!'

'Unlike you, I have never claimed to be an Egyptologist, Campbell. I am here for the treasure, pure and simple, and I don't care how I get it. I couldn't give a damn about any of the other academic crap you keep whining about.' Quentin grinned, pleased with himself. 'We let you lead us here; it wasn't hard, we just had to follow the trail of empty whisky bottles. Anyway, I'm bored with this conversation, as I was saying, there are three of you and three doorways, pick one each and start walking.' He waved the pistol, gesturing at the tunnels.

Diana laid her hand gently on his arm. 'Quentin, dear, we'll need Sam just in case there are any more hieroglyphics to be read, why don't you just send in Bertram and the funny looking one? If one of them comes back we'll know that's the way to go, if neither of them does then we know it's door number three.'

Bertram was angry. 'I don't think any of us feels like doing anything for you.'

Quentin swung the pistol around to point squarely at him. 'You can either walk through a door or I'll shoot you in the leg and you'll have to crawl.'

'I'll go.' Francis said gently, trying to forestall any more argument. He began to walk towards the doors.

'Francis, no!' Sam tried to pull him back, but Francis stopped him with a beatific look.

'It's alright, sir; my God will protect me.'

'Fine, fine, yes, yes, that's lovely. Now get a move on before I start shooting people!' Quentin waved his pistol towards the doors, indicating for Francis to go. 'You've got two minutes and then it's Campbell's turn to try his luck.'

Francis kissed his crucifix and looked at the doorways. He chose the one on the left and walked towards it.

'Wait!' Sam called out.

The Egyptian man halted, but it was Quentin who answered, the pistol once again swivelling to threaten Sam. 'And why should I do that?'

Sam's mind was racing, trying to find anything to say or do that would stop Quentin from sending one or both of his friends to their deaths. He instinctively knew that there had to be something that he was missing, some way to know which was the correct doorway; the builders were too insistent on visitors being worthy, or in this case enlightened, and just being lucky proved nothing.

Suddenly, he knew what needed to be done; the clue was in the awkwardly worded inscription above the openings.

He grinned at Quentin. 'Because I know how to choose the right door. You don't need to send any of us to our deaths.'

Quentin laughed. 'Yeah, right, you've just this second, coincidentally, all of a sudden, right when it mattered, had some kind of epiphany.'

'Not quite. More like a bright idea, actually.'

Quentin glared at him. For a second he seemed to consider whether to listen to Sam or not, but eventually gave him a curt nod. 'If you're wasting my time, though, I might just have to shoot your friend anyway.'

'I'm not.' Sam smiled, but inside he wasn't feeling as confident; he thought he knew how to find the right door, but, until he tried, he couldn't be sure and if he was wrong it would certainly provoke Quentin into violence.

'Alright. Hurry up and choose, then.'

'Thank you.' Sam gave Quentin as polite a nod as he could, trying to appease him as much as possible. 'I need all the torches.'

When he had added Bertram's torch to his own and collected the two that Quentin's men had brought with them, then, with the only source of light, he started to walk away from the doors.

'Vives...'

Quentin's warning growl made him stop and he turned. 'Give me a minute!'

He waited and after a few seconds, with a snarl, Quentin nodded.

Sam turned and went to the centre of the cavern, searching the floor as he went; searching for something that he hadn't seen as he had crossed the floor earlier, but desperately hoped was there.

He grinned as he found it; sometimes X really did mark the spot - in the exact centre of the room there was a cross-shaped opaque crystal embedded in the otherwise translucent floor. He had missed it before, not only because it was small, only six inches across, but also because it was incredibly hard to see unless you were looking for it; there was nothing to differentiate it from any of the other crystals in the floor, apart from the way it reacted to the light in Sam's hands.

Sam stood on the cross and faced the doorways, holding the torches in front of himself. Seeing nothing, he slowly started to lift them higher, above his head.

'Vives, what the hell are you...?'

Quentin didn't complete his sentence because he and everyone else had suddenly noticed what was happening as Sam raised the torches. They watched, spellbound, as dozens of rainbows, refracted by the largest of the crystals around the room, slid across the walls and floor, all moving inexorably towards the three doorways. When Sam was almost at full stretch they converged on one of the openings and the multicoloured rays combined to form a white light that in turn caused a layer of crystals around the frame of the opening to luminesce with a brilliance that hurt their eyes, signalling the way forwards.

Sam was relieved to see that it was the same door that Francis had chosen to go through and, even if he hadn't worked out the riddle in the writing, his friend would have been safe. He sighed with relief that he had gotten the riddle in the writing right and lowered the torches,

allowing the dazzling light to die out, then went back to join his friends
and enemies.

'Oh, jolly well done, Vives! Well done indeed!'

Bertram's praise was effusive, Francis beamed and even the woman,
Diana, clapped gently, a half-smile on her face, but, predictably,
Quentin wasn't impressed. 'Don't celebrate yet, Vives; we're still going
to send your man in first, just in case you're wrong, and I'm sure there
will probably be plenty more chances for you to mess up and kill one
of your friends later on.'

He smiled evilly, then turned to Francis and gestured with the gun
for him to go through the doorway.

Francis took one of the torches from Sam with a smile. 'Well done,
sir.' He nodded in respect, then turned and went through the opening.

The light from the Egyptian's torch revealed another tunnel beyond
the opening that looked identical to the one that had led to the crystal
chamber. It stretched on and on, and before long Francis had gone so
far that the darkness had completely swallowed all trace of him.

A minute passed and there was no sign of him.

Another minute went by and finally Quentin shrugged and gave
Sam a sarcastic smile. 'I think that's long enough, don't you, Vives? It's
too bad about your friend, looks like you got it wrong after all. Your
turn Campbell.'

Quentin motioned to his men and two of them stepped forward
and started to frogmarch Bertram towards one of the doorways.

'I say, steady on!' Bertram tried to free himself from their clutches,
but it was useless and in seconds they had positioned him in front of
the opening and were preparing to throw him in.

'Look!' Sam wasn't sure, but he thought he could see a faint light
coming from the tunnel.

At a signal from Quentin, the men stopped pushing Bertram and
they all watched the doorway.

Sure enough, the hurrying figure of Francis appeared. He came out
and spoke breathlessly to Sam, pointedly ignoring Quentin. 'There is
another chamber about a hundred metres away!'

Quentin sighed and shook his head in mock disappointment. 'What
a shame; it looks like you're in luck this time, Campbell, but your friend
Francis here is going to run out of his at some point and then you'll get
your chance. Lead on, Franky.'

Francis led the way back down the passage followed by Bertram
and then Sam, Quentin followed close behind, his pistol poking Sam
in the back.

Sam turned his head to eye the gun and raised an eyebrow. 'I could probably make a comment about over-compensating for something, but that would be far too obvious and there *is* a lady present, after all.'

Quentin said nothing, but answered eloquently by snarling and hitting Sam in the back with the butt of the pistol.

Just as Francis had said, the passage soon opened out into another chamber. This one wasn't quite as big or nearly as impressive as the previous one had been; it was plain rock, the same rock as the Rift walls, cut into a rough cube with the entrance in the middle of one of the sides. In the faint illumination from the torches they could just about make out another doorway, only one this time, directly opposite them, about twenty metres away. There was a black line on the floor, five metres from the entrance, that went from one side of the chamber to the other and beyond it the rock had been replaced by large tiles made of a shiny red stone. The tiles were square, about a metre each side and set out into a diamond pattern that covered the entire width of the room and stretched for five or six metres before ending at a second black line.

By unspoken agreement, everyone stayed well away from the line on the floor and the red tiles that gleamed like wet blood in the flickering light; it seemed patently obvious that, if there was a trap, it would have something to do with them.

There were symbols on the floor directly in front of where the passage had ended, written in black stone, just like the line. Quentin prodded Sam with the pistol and jerked his chin at them. 'Get to work, then.'

Resentfully, Sam walked to the line and peered down at the writing. 'It says, *seek celestial guidance and tread carefully, like a cat.*'

'Celestial guidance?' Quentin laughed. 'Pray to God to get across safely? A cat god?'

'Of course not...'

'But it basically says to have faith and be careful where you step, right?'

Sam frowned; much as he hated to admit it, Quentin was correct and he couldn't see another way to interpret the words. 'I guess...'

'Well, that's really bad luck for Franky, then, isn't it? Let's just hope he's more cat-like than he looks!' Quentin laughed again, then looked pointedly at Francis and jerked his head at the tiles, indicating for him to start across the floor.

Francis walked to the line, moving like a condemned man. Sam joined him and together they looked at the diamond pattern. Sam knelt and inspected the tiles, putting his head right down onto the line, taking care not to cross it but getting as close as he could. He couldn't see any way to distinguish between one square and the next - no difference in size, texture or even the amount of dust on them. There were no footprints to follow, neither was there anything to indicate where any possible danger would come from. He stood up again and shrugged. 'I can't help you, sorry.'

'Do not worry, Mr Vives, I will be safe.'

'Call me Sam, please, Francis.'

'I would be delighted to. Thank you, Sam.'

'Enough with all the touchy-feely stuff already! Get on with it!'

Quentin was losing what little patience he had and Sam cringed as the pistol once more lifted to point at them.

He turned back to Francis and stuck out his hand. 'Good luck.'

The Egyptian shook his hand with a smile, then turned to the line. He looked beyond it to the red tiles and Sam could almost see the debate going on inside the man's head. Eventually, though, he just had to choose, and he did so, seemingly at random. He lifted his foot and held it out in front of him, hovering briefly over one of the tiles, but then he changed his mind and put it down again before moving to stand in front of a different one.

Sam watched him, clenching his teeth in anguish. He couldn't believe that Quentin was going to send Francis into danger without at least making an effort to solve whatever riddle was in the writing. In the end his conscience won out over the threat of Quentin's gun and he reached out to pull the Egyptian back from the line. 'Hang on, Francis.'

Quentin glared at him. 'What now, Vives? This is getting very tiresome!'

'At least give me a chance to work out how to get across safely! Please!'

A slow smile spread across the young man's face and Sam could tell that he was going to refuse, but once again the girl intervened, providing the voice of reason playing counterpoint to the young man's impatience and disregard for human life. She put her hand on Quentin's arm and batted her eyelids at him. 'Why not give him a few minutes, Quentin? I'd quite like to see what he comes up with.'

Quentin looked at her, then looked down at her hand on his arm, then back up at her. His face softened almost imperceptibly and he gave her a curt nod. 'Very well. Vives, you've got two minutes, no more.' He took a large golden watch from his pocket and glanced at it pointedly.

Sam frantically began trying everything he could think of. He read the writing again, checking his translation, then examined it from several different angles to see if there was some kind of optical illusion. Next, he inspected the tiles, even going so far as to hold the torch close to several of them to see if there was any reaction from the flame-red tiles to the heat. He walked the entirety of the line, trying the same thing with the black rock, wondering if there would be some indication of a starting point at least.

Nothing.

Sam threw his head back and growled in frustration.

There was an answering laugh from Quentin; he was very obviously enjoying himself immensely. 'Thirty seconds, Vives, and then we do it my way!'

Sam was about to go back to read the writing again, when something caught his eye and he paused - the plain rock of the ceiling wasn't quite as bare as it had first appeared to be. 'Celestial guidance...' He muttered to himself. Suddenly, he grinned, excited; "celestial" didn't necessarily mean "divine" it could also mean something that was actually in the sky. Astronomical.

'Everybody, hold up your torches! As high as you can!'

'What is it, old chap?'

'Look at the ceiling, Bertram; there's something there.'

'I can't see anything... Wait... You two!' Bertram pointed to the two black-clad men holding torches in turn. 'You go down that end of the line and you go the other end.'

He tried to direct them, but the men stared at him, uncomprehending. It wasn't until Francis called out to them in their language that they understood and started moving.

With the two men in place the ceiling was more uniformly illuminated and it was far easier to see what Sam had only just managed to catch a glimpse of.

Bertram clapped him on the back. 'You've done it again, old chum!'

Embedded in the ceiling, high above them, were dozens of large golden disks. They were almost the same colour as the yellow rock and were only visible because they reflected the light differently than the rest of the ceiling. They were joined by thin golden lines and set out in three groups, side by side, extending out over the tiles, each one of them beginning above the closest black line on the floor and ending over the other.

'Why,' exclaimed Bertram. 'They look like...'

'Constellations.' Sam finished Bertram's thought with a grin.

'Wonderful!' Bertram returned Sam's grin, but then gave him a puzzled look. 'But, how does that help us?'

Sam consulted his Egyptology knowledge and found some handy information in the back of his brain, courtesy of the Displacement. 'Well, many of the constellations were the same then as they are now and, if I'm reading the clue right, we're looking for a cat.'

'Leo, by god!'

Sam nodded. 'Quite right.'

Bertram looked from one of the groups of disks to the other. 'Which one is it then, old man? I'm afraid neither my astrology nor my astronomy are particularly up to scratch.'

Sam smiled at him, but inside he felt like raging and weeping. 'I have absolutely no idea. I was hoping you would know.'

'I know.'

The voice was silk and it came from directly behind them.

Diana had been listening to them from only a step or so away, uncomfortably close, and she smiled at their surprised faces. 'Oh, gentlemen, did you think I was *just* a pretty face?'

'No, I, uh, not a, uh... Never!'

While Bertram stammered and stuttered, Sam met the girl's beautiful green eyes, flaring like emeralds in the torchlight, and felt his cheeks go the same colour as the tiles, the same colour as her hair. 'Please, could you tell us which one is Leo, Miss Birch?'

'Certainly. And please, call me Diana... Sam.' She pointed to the one in the middle. 'That one.'

Sam smiled at her. 'Thank you.'

'You're welcome.' She returned his smile and gave him a nod, then stepped back to the side of the scowling Quentin.

Sam exchanged a glance with Bertram and received a wink and a knowing leer in return, then, sighing, he looked upwards. 'Well, it looks like we have our path mapped out for us, but where do we start from?'

'Well,' said Bertram. 'I'm guessing here, but I reckon we simply start on the tile that's below the first star in the constellation.'

'Of course!' Sam chuckled. 'It looks like it's *my* turn to congratulate *you*, Bertram.'

Bertram nodded. 'Thank you.' He pulled out his flask and saluted Sam with it before tipping its bottom towards the ceiling and the constellation of the lion.

'Oh, will you just get on with it?' Quentin's voice echoed around the room, making them jump.

Bertram gave Sam an exasperated look, but he nonetheless put away the flask and looked back up at the ceiling. He tilted his head and squinted, almost comically. 'Alright, so, if that one's Leo, then it's... *that* one we have to start with.' He pointed at a tile on the floor and marched towards it with every intention of stepping onto it.

'Bertram! Wait!' Sam ran after him and pulled his friend back before he could cross the black line. 'What are you doing?'

'I'm going to put my money where my mouth is, old bean. Come on, you know it makes sense for it to be my head on the line, so to speak.'

'If anyone should go it should be me; I'm the one who may have mistranslated the writing.'

'Nonsense! Anyone can see that that hieroglyph is supposed to be a cat, even if they can't read them!' Bertram's voice dropped and he leaned in to whisper to Sam so that nobody else could hear them. 'And besides, I don't know if we can fully trust that girl and, if she was lying, Francis is going to need you alive to stop Price from sacrificing him needlessly next time.'

Bertram again turned to step on the tile, but this time it was Francis who reached out and grabbed his arm to stop him.

'Please, sir, it should be me.'

'Nonsense, Francis! No need to be a martyr.'

Francis smiled. 'I'm not planning to be, sir - I have faith, but I am not stupid. I believe in you and Mr Vives... *Sam*, and I know in my heart that you are right.'

Bertram looked the man in the eyes for long seconds before he seemed to come to a decision and nodded. 'Very well.'

Bertram stepped back and glared at Quentin before deliberately turning his back on him to watch the Egyptian.

Francis went to stand on the line in front of the selected tile. He turned his head to smile at Sam, then stepped forwards.

The group held their breath as one, waiting for something to happen. Two seconds passed, then five, then more and there was a collective sigh as it became evident that nothing was going to happen to him.

'All right, all right, good choice, well done. Now get a move on and do the rest; we haven't got all day. And you, Campbell, take this and mark the safe tiles.' Quentin threw a piece of chalk to Bertram who, grumbling the whole time, crouched down to draw a cross on the edge of the square that Francis was standing on.

Sam saw that it was actually the same tile that Francis had chosen before and the words "higher power" once again rang in his ears. However, this time he also heard the voice of his grandfather, quoting one of the old man's favourite sayings, "God helps those who help themselves", reminding him that the Egyptian's luck was bound to run out at some point, that one mistake would cost him his life, and it was best that Sam apply himself to making sure he took the right path.

He turned his gaze to the golden disks embedded in the ceiling, determined not to let his friends down. He walked back and forth along the line, looking from the stars to the ground and back again from every possible point of view. The lines that connected the stars made the job a bit easier, giving him an angle between steps and a relative distance, but because the ceiling was so far away it was actually quite hard to work out exactly which tile was directly below which golden disk.

He deliberated over the next move as if he were playing chess, just like James had taught him, taking his time to make absolutely certain that his one, all important, piece wasn't stepping into danger. Finally, he realised he was as sure as he was going to get and he told himself that he had to stop dithering and tell Francis what to do, before Quentin took the decision out of his hands. 'The second square should be the closest one to you, forwards and diagonally to your left.'

Sam crossed his fingers as Francis moved to the tile he'd pointed out, but again nothing happened and he let out the breath he hadn't known he'd been holding.

Feeling much more confident that they had gotten the riddle correct, he exchange a brief smile with Bertram, then looked back up at the constellation and began going through the same laborious process as before of choosing the next step.

It was very slow going and Sam could see that Quentin was becoming more annoyed and frustrated with every passing minute, but he wasn't willing to go any faster just to appease his enemy.

Finally, though, the patience that Quentin had been steadily losing, completely ran out. 'This is utterly ridiculous! There aren't any traps - this is all just to frighten the weak-minded and make us waste time in here. Well, I'm not going to spend hours in fear. Let's go!'

He waved his men forward.

A couple of the black-clad thugs stepped over the line and onto two of the tiles that Bertram hadn't marked as safe.

The reaction was immediate; as soon as they placed their weight on the tiles it was as if the floor underneath them ceased to exist, so quickly did they plunge downwards. Their screams were quickly cut off as gouts of flames shot up out of the gaps and Bertram, who was kneeling nearby on one of the safe tiles, had to shield his face from the intense heat coming from just a short distance away.

A few seconds later the tiles reappeared from below and there was a faint scraping noise as they slowly moved back into place, leaving the grid exactly as it had been before, as if nothing had happened.

The remaining black-clad thugs looked at each other, for the first time showing signs of nervousness and reluctance. Even Diana was looking somewhat whiter than her usual pale self and Sam wondered if maybe she didn't quite have the stomach for Quentin's callous tactics.

Quentin swallowed. 'Maybe we should proceed with some caution after all…'

'You think?' Bertram's face was red, both with the heat from the flames and anger at the stupid loss of life.

Quentin pointed the pistol at him. 'Shut it, or you'll be changing places with Francis. Keep going.'

Sam returned to his task. He was tempted to take even longer over it, but thought that it was probably not the best of ideas to provoke Quentin any more than was necessary.

Francis had barely looked around as the men died and he continued to say nothing while Sam called out his next moves, he just stepped from one tile to the next with the same stoicism as before. After what seemed like an eternity, but what was in reality only ten or fifteen minutes, he reached the line that marked the far side of the grid and safety. He stepped over it, staggered a few steps as his legs all but buckled beneath him, then dropped to his knees, bowing his head and closing his eyes as if praying.

'Well? What are you waiting for?' Quentin motioned for Sam to follow Bertram and Francis across.

Now that the path was marked out it was easy enough to cross; the tiles were so wide that Sam could just stroll over, there was no way to lose his balance. The irrational part of him told him to stick to the dead centre of the tiles though, just in case, and he hopped from one to the other, staying as far away from the edges as possible. He joined Bertram at Francis' side and they waited patiently until Francis had recovered.

The Egyptian stood up and smiled at them. 'You both look very serious, what's the matter?'

Bertram and Sam shared a glance, then burst out laughing. Bertram pulled out his whisky and offered it around.

Francis took a small sip and even Sam wet his lips, Bertram of course took a long gulp.

'Ah! That's the stuff! You can't beat it, at least when you haven't got time to make a decent cup of tea anyway.'

'If you are quite finished?' Quentin had joined them and he prodded Sam again with the pistol.

Sam glanced down at the gun. 'You know, you're doing that quite often... I'm pretty sure Freud would have something to say about it.'

Quentin snarled and pulled back the gun to hit him again, but was stopped by a chuckle from Diana, who had evidently been quite enjoying the exchanges between the two of them.

He glared at her, then lowered the pistol to his side and leaned forward to snarl at Sam. 'Your smart mouth is going to get you in trouble one of these days, Vives. Am I going to have to shoot one of your friends to shut you up? Just get moving.'

Sam didn't really know why he was antagonising someone who could have them all shot with a word, but he thought that, since he was going to try to kill them anyway, whatever he said or did, he might as well have some fun while he could. He gave Quentin a cheeky grin, flashed a wink at Diana and then turned back to Francis. 'Are you alright to continue?'

Francis smiled at him. 'Yes, I am fine. Thank you, friend.'

Without another word, Francis walked through the doorway and they followed him down the next connecting passageway.

After less than a minute they arrived at a third chamber. This one was pitch black and, at least as far as Sam was concerned, it was just as spectacular as the crystal cavern had been.

It was entirely made up of black volcanic rock, obsidian, which completely absorbed any light that was shone on it. It would have been impossible to tell the shape of the chamber if it wasn't because the uniformity of the obsidian was broken by dozens of thick white bands that stretched across the ceiling clear to the far wall, showing that the roof was semi-circular, some four or five metres at its highest point directly above them. It reminded Sam of one of the old train stations, like *Estació de França* in Barcelona, or any of the big terminus stations in London - ones that had a single high, curved shelter and opened up at the end where the trains entered. Something didn't seem quite right, though; the white lines were off centre and the general effect was that of looking down a tunnel that bore to the left.

Looking up at the ceiling was making him slightly dizzy, so he looked down at the floor instead. There was a line drawn across the floor marking a limit of some kind, similar to the last chamber, with hieroglyphs underneath it. Both the line and the symbols were white marble, contrasting starkly with the black rock. Beyond the line, the floor was a black abyss and, with no white bands to show its shape, there was no way to tell if it was just that it was the same black obsidian as the rest of the chamber or if there wasn't a floor at all.

While Sam had been occupied by the ceiling, Quentin's attention had been drawn greedily to what was on the other side of the chamber; about twenty or thirty metres away, it was impossible to accurately gauge the distance, was their destination - a huge doorway, flanked by two tall columns and topped by a large triangular pediment. It was made of a white stone that seemed to glow with a ghostly light, in contrast to the absolute black around it, and looked exactly like the carving of the temple or tomb on the back of the tablet they had found at the oasis.

'That's where the treasure is, right? Finally!' Quentin made to walk straight across the room to it, but Diana clapped a hand on his shoulder to stop him and pointed mutely down at the writing and the line on the floor. He looked down at it and fumed, completely out of patience. 'Oh, come on! How many of these stupid games do we have to play?' He stalked up to the writing and looked down. 'Well, Vives?'

Sam joined him and read the symbols, 'it says: w*alk ahead, walk in the middle, walk straight, walk true. Only the strong-minded will pass.*'

'Only that?'

'Yes.'

'Sounds simple enough.' Quentin grinned, rubbing his hands together, gleefully. 'Well, seeing as this will probably be the last of these idiotic tests, there won't be any more stupid symbols to decipher. So I think it's time that you took your turn and led the way.'

'I don't mind…' Francis started to speak, but Quentin turned on him, shoving his pistol in his face.

'Shut it or I'll send you to your God. We don't need *you* at all.'

Francis put his hands up and backed away.

Quentin turned the gun on Sam. 'Crunch time, Vives. All you've got to do is walk, apparently.'

Sam looked at the gun and then at Quentin. There was no pity in the young man's eyes, no sign of any weakness, no sign that he would back down; there was no getting out of it - this last trap, if it was a trap at all, was his to deal with or die trying.

He went to the row of hieroglyphs and used them as a reference to make sure that he was in the exact middle of the room, like they said. Then, fully expecting to fall to his death, he took a deep breath and stepped forward over the line and into the unknown…

His foot hit rock and he almost toppled over in surprise before he caught himself. He bent down and laid his palm on the floor. It was the same obsidian as the rest of the room after all. Even close up he still couldn't see it, he only knew it was there by the feel of it - smooth and cool and very real. Apparently, thankfully, there was no third trap, no final test.

He sighed in relief and started to move forward carefully, but with a bit more confidence.

He kept his eyes fixed on the faintly glowing temple doorway directly ahead of him, trying to walk in a straight line, just in case, but his eyes were constantly being drawn to the bright white bands overhead and his brain was being fooled into thinking that straight ahead was actually off to one side. With every step he could feel himself drifting to the left in sympathy with them, his balance shifting to that side, pulling him away from the true path…

He stumbled to a halt, swaying as the room swam before him and squeezed his eyes tight shut against the sudden vertigo.

This, then, was the nature of the trap here - it was a test for those who had a strong mind, just as the words had said - the weak would topple to one side, stepping from the centreline of the room and into who knows what.

Sam doubted if he had the discipline needed to be able to focus on the temple without the white bands disorientating him; he had never been able to concentrate on anything for any length of time and it showed in his marks at school. He briefly considered dropping to all fours and crawling, but knew that the builders would likely have thought of that and it probably wouldn't be a defence.

He realised that there was one thing that he could do, though.

Keeping his eyes shut, Sam relaxed. He reached out to that place within himself where his powers resided and felt the energy grow. His mind sharpened, but instead of sending his thoughts homeward, he focussed them on the temple in front of him.

He opened his eyes and smiled as the doorway shot into perfect clarity and all dizziness vanished. There was nothing to stop him now.

'Oh no you don't, Vives! You're going to stay here until you've witnessed my triumph!' Quentin's shout reverberated around the chamber, but was immediately drowned out by the deafening sound of a shot.

The shout and the sound of the shot broke Sam's concentration instantly, just as Quentin had intended, but that wasn't the main cause of his downfall.

The bullet ricocheted from the ceiling above him and his eyes automatically shot to the puff of white powder above his head as it destroyed a part of one of the white bands. Realising his mistake, he tried to change his focus back to the temple, but merely moving the direction of his gaze had thrown off his balance and he had an attack of vertigo as his brain tried to tell him that down was a different way to the one that his body was insisting was correct.

His vision blurred and he wobbled, feeling suddenly nauseous. He started to topple, unable to recover his equilibrium and his foot went out to the side, trying to compensate, reaching for a solid floor that wasn't there…

Suddenly, somebody caught him and pulled him back, centring him with a gentle downward pressure on his shoulders. An accented voice whispered in his ear. 'I've got you. Close your eyes and breathe, feel the floor beneath your feet.'

Sam did what he was told. He closed his eyes, feeling the floor, solid beneath his feet, grounding him. The nausea faded rapidly and his head gradually cleared.

'Now walk. Don't open your eyes, just walk straight ahead.'

Sam placed one foot in front of the other. He didn't know why, but something in him told him to trust Francis and he didn't feel at all afraid as he walked forward blindly, with death so close on either side.

In seconds it was over and the Egyptian squeezed his shoulders before releasing him. 'You can open your eyes now, Sam.'

Sam found himself in front of the temple door. It was actually much smaller than it had seemed from the other side of the room and the dark opening was no larger than the door of his bedroom back home; another clever optical illusion from whoever had built this whole amazing complex.

Bertram, Diana and Quentin had followed closely behind them and Quentin now turned and beckoned to his men to follow them.

The four remaining thugs were understandably unsettled; they had lost a couple of their friends already and the sight of this new strange room had frightened them further. Quentin took a step towards them and levelled his pistol as a threat. Mumbling discontentedly, they followed in Sam's footsteps, coming single file towards them.

Everything looked fine until the first man wobbled. He staggered another step then stopped, managing to regain his balance. He started walking again, but once more he wobbled and this time he teetered off balance. He tried to compensate, exactly like Sam had, by moving his left foot out to transfer his weight, but his foot hit empty air and he toppled. He reached out and grabbed at the man following immediately behind him, desperately trying to pull himself back on balance, but succeeded only in dragging his companion with him and they both fell, screaming.

The torch the second man had been carrying fell with them and as it dropped below the level of the floor the construction of the chamber was finally revealed to be as Sam had already guessed - a very narrow walkway crossed the middle of the room and surrounding it was the blackness of a pit, seemingly without a bottom, invisible, deadly.

The screams echoed on and on, for many seconds, fading as they got further and further away until, very sharply, they were cut off.

The two remaining guards stood motionless, staring downwards into the pit for a couple of heartbeats after the screams had ceased, then they turned and bolted, luckily remaining on the centre path, and disappeared back the way they had come.

Bertram smiled sweetly at Quentin. 'It looks like the two of you are on your own now, Price.' He pulled out his flask, raised it to him, then took a big swig, smacking his lips noisily.

Quentin snatched the flask from his hands. He took an equally deep swig and smacked his lips in imitation of Bertram, but, instead of handing it back, he sneered and threw it over his shoulder. He held Bertram's gaze until the clanging and banging of the tin flask bouncing around the bottom of the pit had faded then smiled, just as sweetly. 'Yes, but I still have a gun. Get inside.'

CHAPTER 17
THE TEMPLE

The first thing they saw as they walked through the entrance and the two remaining torches lit up the space beyond was the figure in the glittering golden throne, sitting in pride of place opposite the entrance, staring down at them like the statue of Abraham Lincoln in Washington - the wrapped mummy of a Pharaoh, with two black sceptres crossed on its breast, wearing white robes made yellow by age with intricate embroidery and a golden death mask that looked somewhat like the famous mask of Tutankhamen.

'Now, that's more like it!' Quentin gazed hungrily at the mummy's mask, transfixed for a moment, but then he frowned as he noticed the distinct lack of anything else even remotely valuable in the room. 'What the hell? Where's all the rest of the treasure? Where's my gold?!?'

Sam gazed around the chamber. Like everyone else he had been so awestruck by the sight of the sarcophagus that he hadn't seen anything beyond it. Aside from the sarcophagus on its throne in the centre of the room, the rectangular space was bare, apart from a dozen or so torches in sconces. As Bertram went around lighting them, more and more of the room was revealed and they discovered that the walls were covered in writing, carvings and pictures. It was a riot of colour, very well preserved considering how old the temple must have been.

Sam walked to the wall next to the entrance and began to read, completely forgetting about Quentin, in his eagerness to study the temple.

He didn't get to read more than a couple of hieroglyphs, though, before he was grabbed from behind and forcibly spun around. He barely had time to react as Quentin swung the pistol at his head and all he could do was twist and take the strike on his shoulder instead. It was a heavy blow and it knocked him completely off balance. He stumbled, knocking his head against the wall and falling to the floor, stunned, blood already soaking into his shirt from the deep cut where the foresight of the gun had gouged him.

Quentin stood over him, furious, his face red in the flickering torchlight. 'I've had enough of your interference in my business, Vives.' He gestured angrily at the empty room. 'This is your doing, I know it is. I hope you said goodbye to your Displacer friends before you came here because they're the only ones who are going to remember you.'

Quentin pointed the pistol at him, ready to take the shot, but suddenly Bertram was there. He grabbed Quentin's hand and started wrestling him for control of the pistol. Bertram was a drunk and had a very old fashioned way of talking that made him sound foolish sometimes, but there was nothing weak about him. He forced the gun up and away and Quentin's shot went wide, chipping stone from the wall a couple of feet above Sam's head. He forced Quentin back and would have taken the pistol away if it hadn't been for Diana's intervention. She appeared from nowhere behind Bertram and with a quick squeeze, which to Sam looked rather like a Vulcan nerve pinch, managed to incapacitate him long enough for Quentin to free himself.

Snarling, Quentin levelled the pistol again. 'Goodbye, Vives.'

Quentin's finger tighten on the trigger and time slowed to a crawl as Sam found himself staring into the black hole of the barrel.

His life didn't flash before his eyes this time, but he did have a powerful sense of déjà vu as he looked beyond the gun and into his enemy's face - it was ugly, twisted in hatred, exactly as it had been in Port Royal on the two previous occasions that the young man had tried to kill him.

He willed his limbs to move, wanting to roll, or jump, or kick out, or anything, just as long as it got him out of the way of the coming bullet, but he couldn't move; the blow to his head as he'd fallen had left him stunned and his body refused to work.

The trigger shifted and the hammer of the pistol pulled back...

'No!' Suddenly a white-clad figure flashed into view - Francis, his shout coinciding with the deafening bang of the pistol, had placed himself between Quentin and Sam, deliberately blocking the path of the bullet.

The Egyptian stood motionless for what seemed an eternity while the echoes of the shot faded, his arms flung wide in his attempt to cover as much of Sam as he could.

Everyone had frozen in place to watch this tragic tableau, but then, as his arms dropped and he collapsed to the floor in a heap, a red stain spreading slowly on his chest, the spell was broken.

'Again! What is it about you? WHY WON'T YOU JUST DIE?!?' Quentin screamed at Sam, almost hysterical in his rage, and he lifted the pistol once more, but this time he didn't get the chance to fire; Bertram had managed to free himself from Diana with the distraction of the shot and he came out of nowhere, slamming his fist into the side of Quentin's head, knocking the man to the ground and sending the pistol spinning from his grip.

Bertram scrambled to seize the gun, but he didn't use it, instead he just kept hold of it as he ran to Francis and threw himself onto his knees next to him.

Sam at last managed to regain some control of his body. He crawled over to join Bertram at Francis' side and together they lifted the Egyptian into a sitting position. He was still alive, but only barely; the front of his robes were soaked in blood and there was a pool of it spreading across the floor below him. Despite all that he smiled and opened his mouth to speak.

Before he could, he was interrupted by Quentin. 'One of these days you're going to run out of friends to die for you, Vives. Oh, and by the way, you lose!' He held up the golden mask that he had grabbed from the figure on the throne and laughed insanely, before turning and shouting to Diana, who was still staring in shock at the bloody figure of Francis. 'Come on, let's get this to the Master!' He left, racing out of the door without waiting to see if she was following.

Diana didn't immediately follow him, though. 'I'm sorry...' she whispered, taking a half-step forward, as if to help them. She met Sam's eyes and he could see the torment and indecision in them, but he just stared coldly at her, making her know that she wasn't welcome. With an understanding nod, she turned away and raced after Quentin.

Bertram growled. 'Take care of Francis, would you, I'm going to kill that bastard!'

Sam was shocked at the look of pure rage on his friend's face as Bertram leapt to his feet and rushed out of the temple, brandishing the pistol.

He was about to call him back, but was halted by a hand that clutched weakly at his clothing.

'Don't stop him, please. Let him go... I must talk with you. Alone.'

Sam looked down at Francis. The man was very weak, but he was using his dying breaths to try to tell him something - the least he could do was listen, so he let Bertram go.

Francis was smiling still, despite the pain. He was struggling for breath, but there was a light in his eyes, a knowledge and a strength that was keeping him conscious and talking. 'I know what you are... All of this... is for you. And anyway, the mask is a fake.'

He laughed at Sam's surprised face, but stopped quickly and grimaced in pain as specks of blood appeared on his lips.

Sam frowned at him in concern. 'Don't speak, save your strength. We'll get you out of here, get you to a doctor...'

The Egyptian smiled again, showing reddened teeth. 'We both know that is not going to happen; we are a very long way from the nearest hospital.' He coughed, gasping for air, but stubbornly kept talking. 'I haven't got much time, so just shut up and listen to me. The back wall, find the symbol that means "prophecy" and push it. Bring me back the vase within - you'll know which one.'

'What? How do you know...?'

'Just do it. And hurry, please.'

Sam gently laid Francis back on the ground and stood. He was still somewhat shaky from hitting his head, but he went as fast as he could towards the back of the room, skirting around the throne and the mummy, which was now mask-less revealing the desiccated corpse beneath.

He scanned the wall, knowing that he would recognise the symbol when he knew it, but wondering if it would actually be there - a large part of him suspected that the dying Egyptian's fevered mind was making him hallucinate a familiarity with the temple that he couldn't possibly have, but there was at least a little bit of him that remembered the man's luck with the traps, and the strange looks that he had been shooting Sam throughout the journey, and realised that it would explain a lot if Francis had indeed been in the temple before.

He wasn't surprised, therefore, when, down near the bottom right-hand corner of the wall, he found what he was looking for. He knelt down and ran his finger around it, inspecting it from every angle, but there was nothing to differentiate it from any of the rest of the symbols.

'Hurry!' The voice of Francis floated across the room, little more than a croak and far weaker than it had been only moments before and it was only the sheer silence and the acoustics of the room that allowed Sam to hear it at all. Sam stabbed at the large symbol with his finger, feeling it give a little. He pushed again, this time using the palm of his hand and heard something click.

Next to him, a section of the wall popped out as if on a spring and he slipped his fingers into the gap. He pulled and an entire section of the wall, fully four metres wide and three high, swung silently open, just as easily as the door back in the Rift had done.

The room revealed behind the door was the same size as the chamber with the mummy, but it was nowhere near as empty; everything that Quentin had been expecting to find in the main room had been hidden away in there - the light from the torches in the main room didn't reach far, but it was more than enough to reveal countless golden statues, plates, tiaras, chests of coins, jewels. Every treasure imaginable was represented in just the small sample that Sam could see. However, it was the object that sat in pride of place on a pedestal a few metres into the room that caught his attention: a vase made of plain, dark-brown pottery, undecorated and sealed with an off-white wax stopper, about a foot tall but only a few inches wide. There was no real reason why it should be set apart from the riches in the room, but, just like the Holy Grail in that *Indiana Jones* film, it stood out for its sheer, apparent worthlessness. Sam was certain that was what Francis had asked for, so he grabbed it, ignoring everything else, and ran back to the Egyptian, praying that he would still be alive to explain just what was going on.

Francis was as white as a sheet and his eyes were closed, but when Sam rushed up and fell to his knees next to him, they fluttered open weakly and blearily focussed on him.

'Francis, I have it, the vase.'

'Good. Very good. Now listen carefully, my friend, for I fear I will only be able to say this once - I am the guardian of this place, the last in the long line stretching back thousands of years and the last that it will ever need, now that it has served its purpose, now that you are here and have this.' Francis reached out and laid his hand gently on the vase in Sam's hands. 'Sealed in here is our most cherished treasure - a scroll, one of the earliest writings of my people. It contains a prophecy that talks of one who will come in the hour of our greatest need, who travels through time and who will alter the time-line and put history back to how it once was and should always be.'

He coughed again and Sam could see that he was fading fast, but somehow he found the energy to continue. 'I believe, no, I *know* that *you* are that person. You must take it back with you. Decipher it and use the knowledge that it contains to protect this world...'

Francis stopped suddenly, wracked with pain and cried out. His face, which had been white before, now had a very unhealthy-looking waxy sheen.

'One… last… thing.' He lifted his arm weakly and pointed to the wall above him. 'Press… "death"… and… run…'

His eyes fixed on Sam one last time, and he caressed the side of Sam's face briefly, gently with his raised hand. He smiled, forced out the words 'thank you', and died.

Sam gently closed Francis' eyes, then folded his arms over his chest. Contrary to the violent manner of his death, he looked peaceful and contented.

He ran the man's dying words over in his mind as he stood up to scan the section of wall that the Egyptian had pointed to, quickly finding the symbol for "death". It was obviously the trigger for some kind of mechanism that destroyed the temple complex and, if Francis had told him to run after pressing it, then the process would undoubtedly be quick. He grimaced as he looked back down at his friend's body; he was loathe to leave it behind, but there was no way he could carry it and run at the same time. He considered taking it out of the temple first and then coming back, but realised that he had no way of knowing whether Quentin and Diana were waiting for him outside in the Rift, ready to pounce on an opportunity to come back in with reinforcements.

In the end, he decided to just obey Francis' last wish - he would press the symbol and run, leaving the body behind, after all, what better place for his friend to be buried than in the temple that he had dedicated his life to guarding?

He went to the wall and inspected the symbol from up close. Just like the one for "prophecy", which opened the door on the other side of the room, there was nothing to distinguish it from any of the other thousands upon thousands of hieroglyphs.

He took a deep breath, then reached out to push it.

A hand dropped on his shoulder and pulled him back.

He spun in place, ready to defend himself from Quentin or Diana, and came face to face with Francis.

'You shouldn't do that, my friend.'

'You… you're alive!' Indeed the man looked positively healthy and there was no sign of any blood, either on his clothing or on the floor.

Francis looked slightly puzzled for a second and was about to reply, but then he saw the vase in Sam's hand and an expression of understanding spread across his face. 'Ah! The time-line has changed, has it not?' He chuckled. 'So, I died, did I? Well, I hope it didn't hurt too much!'

At that moment Bertram wandered into the temple. Instead of a gun he was holding an unopened whisky bottle and was fighting with the cork, trying to open it. 'Here we are! My last bottle, believe it or not! Sorry to make you wait, but we just *had* to have something to wet our whistle while we worked on writing down all the hieroglyphics in here. It was damn clumsy of me to drop my flask down that bloody great hole!'

Francis put his finger to his mouth and whispered so that only Sam could hear. 'Our little secret, alright, friend?'

Bertram looked up from the bottle and saw the vase that Sam was holding. 'What the dickens…' He then caught sight of the wide open door at the back of the temple. The bottle slipped through numb fingers and smashed on the ground, but he barely noticed; he only registered the glitter of gold in the torchlight. 'Oh… my… word.' He splashed through the puddle of whisky that was slowly spreading across the floor and ran towards the hidden chamber. He paused and looked up at the mummy on the throne and a puzzled look passed over his face. 'Shouldn't that have a mask?' but then he shrugged and moved on, heading for the room and the wealth of items waiting to be catalogued. He disappeared inside and all that could be heard was the occasional "my word" or "golly".

Once Bertram was safely in the treasure room and out of earshot, Francis turned back to Sam. He took him by the arm and led him out of the temple, back to the obsidian chamber.

'I don't know exactly what has happened, but I suspect that good has won over evil, at least this once. And now it is time for you to go home, my friend. I hope that I will remember you, I have a strange feeling that I will, but even if I don't I will see that the prophecy is gone, so I will at least know that I, and the hundreds of guardians that have come before me, have finally fulfilled our destiny and can rest.'

'I hope you will remember me, I *certainly* won't forget you.' Sam smiled, then took a deep breath and started to Calm himself, but then something occurred to him and he paused. 'Um. Just out of curiosity, what would have happened if I'd pressed the "death" hieroglyph?'

Francis laughed. 'Then you would have had to run very fast, or risk finding out which would happen first - the ceiling falling on your head or the lake of lava rising up and roasting you alive from the feet up.'

'That's nice.'

'It happens fairly slowly. You probably would have had time to get out.'

'Probably?'

Francis shrugged. 'As you can imagine, we've never actually tested it. It's a one-shot kind of thing.'

'OH MY GOD!' They both looked back into the temple as Bertram's scream of joy filled the space, echoing over and over in the rock chamber.

Sam chuckled and shook his head. 'Right... I should go. Please look after Bertram.'

'I will, don't worry.'

They shook hands and Francis nodded, then disappeared back into the temple.

Sam closed his eyes, concentrated...

...and woke up back in Andrew's living room.

He opened his eyes and looked at Andrew and Rachel. They were smiling at him, expecting him to tell them how much he'd enjoyed the *Morecambe and Wise* show after all, but once again he was going to have to report to his uncle that things hadn't exactly gone according to plan.

He hesitated, unsure how to start, but before he could, Rachel cried out. 'You're bleeding!'

Andrew noticed the blood seeping into Sam's t-shirt from where Quentin had hit him with the gun and his grin instantly faded. 'Oh god, what happened this time? Please tell me you just heckled too much and got thrown out...' He sighed as he saw Sam go red. 'Rachel, hand me the first aid kit, please.'

Sam glanced down at his shoulder. He'd completely forgotten about his injury; so much had been happening so quickly since Quentin had hit him, but now that all the excitement was over it was starting to sting and he winced. 'It's not bad, it can wait.' He held up the vase. 'I've got a lot to tell you and we need to get this to the Elders.'

'So, you did it again!' Rachel laughed as they ran up the hill towards Collserola and the Norman Foster designed communications tower - Andrew had dismissed them after Sam had told them about his Displacement, saying that he needed to talk to the Elders and that they might as well go and do their exercise for the day.

'I still don't understand how it happened; I'm sure that I had the right destination in my mind, I could *feel* Blackpool in 1953, but then at the last second I got a flash of Quentin and everything went wrong.'

'Whatever you did, if you do it much more then Andrew's going to stop you Displacing ever again!' She grinned at him as she jumped over a fallen tree with a completely unnecessary flying kick.

'Show-off.' Sam mumbled, returning her grin as he vaulted over the tree in a more functional, but far less impressive manner. 'Well, maybe he should; every time I do, somebody gets killed or almost killed. First Smithy, then Jock, then Francis... I just get people hurt! Maybe I'm jinxed.'

Rachel pulled up short and Sam stopped with her. She dragged him around to face her, turning him sharply by the shoulders and holding him in place, staring him aggressively in the eyes.

'Don't you *ever* think that! It is not your fault that bad things happen when you Displace. If you must blame someone for Smithy and Francis then blame Quentin, and as for Jock you were in a *battle*! In one of the most violent episodes in the history of the world! What did you think was going to happen? Besides, Smithy and Francis were OK after Quentin left the time-line, so no harm done!'

'I can't help thinking that it *must* have had some effect on them, on their souls or something... I mean, Francis *died*! You can't tell me *that* had no consequences whatsoever!'

'Sam, Displacers have had this debate over and over, it's one of the Elders' favourite topics, but the truth is we just don't know. A few Displacers believe that, when somebody dies, the soul escapes to wherever it goes, heaven or whatnot, but when they come back to life the soul can't come back with them. However, most of them just think that they were never dead because it didn't actually happen.' She shrugged. 'That's what I believe, anyway.'

He nodded reluctantly. 'I suppose that makes sense...' He wasn't entirely convinced, but he realised that it was the kind of philosophical question that better minds than his had debated and if they hadn't come up with a satisfactory answer, then what chance did he have? He wasn't particularly happy about it, but he guessed that he was going to have to accept that bad things happened all the time - he just had to make sure that he didn't do anything to get Rachel hurt; he wouldn't be able to take that.

Rachel shook her head. 'Don't worry, you'll get used to this kind of thing, just give it time.' She gave him one of her lopsided grins. 'Now come on, we've got a few miles left to do.' She wrapped him in her arms and gave him a long kiss on the lips, then turned and sprinted away. 'Race you to the tower! First one there chooses our next Displacement!'

Sam had been so distracted by the kiss that he didn't react for a good few seconds. Then what Rachel had said finally sank in and he sprinted after her. 'Not fair!'

He laughed, not at all upset and rather enjoying watching her running in front of him.

EPILOGUE

As soon as the front door had closed behind Sam and Rachel, Andrew rushed straight to his study and turned on his computer.

The best way to contact the Council of Elders was through Skype; some of the members spent most of the day connected, busy with research or deep in discussion with people all around the world in various academic fields, so he could always count on at least a couple being online. Those Elders would then begin the process of contacting the others, by whatever mysterious and arcane means they had, probably landlines, and the word would spread until there was a quorum for a meeting.

It was all very slow and a bit old-fashioned compared to the usual high-speed pace of modern life and normally Andrew quite liked it; he found it comforting that not everything had changed to suit a human race which was suddenly in such a hurry, but today he wasn't in a patient mood. Today, the news was too urgent.

For the umpteenth time since he'd taken over the job as head of the Society he made a note to make it a requirement that the Elders had a smartphone; he didn't have a WhatsApp group to coordinate with them like he did with the active Displacers because there was no point - most of them didn't own smartphones and the ones that did probably wouldn't know how to use the App anyway. But there had just been too many things happening over the last year or so that it was becoming more and more important for him to have a way of contacting everyone instantly for situations exactly like this one and he resolved to see to it that everyone was issued with a Society phone and taught how to use it as soon as possible.

His computer finally turned on and he frowned when he saw that there were far more Elders online than usual and there was a conference call already in progress.

He joined the call and the faces of almost a dozen Elders filled most of the screens on the wall in front of him. They immediately fell silent as they noticed him, the heated discussion that had been going on abruptly cut off.

Feeling observed and far more young and inexperienced than he had a right to be, he nodded in greeting. 'Excuse me for interrupting, ladies and gentlemen.'

'What's the matter? Is Sam all right?' This was from James - as always his first concern was the well-being of his grandson.

'Sam is fine, James. He's a bit shaken up and has a pretty deep scratch on his shoulder, but he's fine... um, it's just he's...' Andrew shifted uncomfortably in his seat, feeling the eyes of the Elders burning into him. 'Well, let's just say he's had another unexpected adventure - and a second run-in with Quentin, this time in Egypt, 1907.'

Andrew was surprised when James sighed in relief, rather than being angry at him for letting yet another of Sam's Displacements go wrong. 'Are we to assume that my grandson has once again prevented some attempt at mischief by the wayward Mr Price?'

Andrew nodded. 'Indeed.'

'Well, that explains a few things; we felt a significant change in the time-line a little while ago and were trying to work out what had happened when you joined us.'

'He didn't just defeat Quentin again, though, this time he also brought something back with him.' He held the vase up and rotated it slowly so that they could see it.

'What is it?' asked James.

'According to Sam it contains a scroll with a fragment of prophecy. It was given to him by the guardian of some kind of temple complex in Egypt, in the desert somewhere south-west of Bahariya Oasis.'

'That's not possible; there isn't anything south-west of Bahariya Oasis.' This came from Philip, the Society's expert on all things ancient Egyptian. His job as a curator at the British Museum also allowed him to use their facilities to examine and evaluate items brought back by the Displacers, in secret, of course. 'There are *no* dig sites and *no* archaeological finds out there as far as I recall. It's just open desert. He must have been mistaken.'

'It's not particularly important *where* the find was, Philip, just that it exists. According to Sam there was a bit of a *Last Crusade* thing going on down there with elaborate traps, a temple and quite a lot of treasure.' Andrew frowned. 'He went there with someone called Bertram Campbell, who he left behind to catalogue the find. Perhaps that will help you pin it down in the museum's records.'

Philip snorted. 'Not likely! My great-grandfather and namesake, Philip Fidwick, knew Campbell in Cairo; he did some work for the museum every so often. I think I remember reading in his journals somewhere that the man was a drunk who never amounted to very much. He disappeared into the deep desert on a wild-goose chase in 1907 with a case of whisky and was never heard of again.'

Andrew stared pointedly at Philip, waiting for the penny to drop.

It took a good few seconds of silence, but Philip eventually realised what he'd been saying. 'Oh my god! So it wasn't a wild-goose chase after all, he actually did find something out there!'

Andrew nodded. 'It seems that way, but if there is no record of the find then something must have happened - Quentin and his associates might well have gone back after Sam left and plundered it. I think we should send someone to find out exactly what they've done and see if they can do anything to stop them.'

Philip nodded. 'Lisa is the obvious choice, she's been helping me out at the Museum recently and has paid a few visits to the general area. She has the knowledge necessary to get to the bottom of it.'

'Fine, but for now we have this.' Andrew held up the vase again. 'Sam was told by the guardian that the whole point of the temple was to get this into *his* hands, that they were waiting for *him.*'

'John's going to love that…' James, like Andrew, wasn't a big fan of John and his movie-based vocabulary to refer to the prophecy and Sam.

Andrew grinned. 'I'll let you tell him, shall I?'

'Have you or the boy opened it?' asked Phillip, interrupting impatiently.

Andrew returned to the matter at hand and held up the vase again, closer to the camera this time so that the Elders had a better view. 'Of course not. As you can see, the seal is unbroken. Sam knows better than to crack open something this important to the Society and I really didn't want to find out what damage exposure to the humidity and pollution in Barcelona would do.'

Philip was relieved. 'Thank god for that, I can't imagine what damage a teenage boy's sticky fingers would have done to it. Send it to me as soon as you can and I'll sneak it into the Museum for a proper look.'

'Will do.' Andrew looked around the group. 'I assume you don't need me to inform you all of the possible implications of Sam's discovery and the revelations that may come from it?'

The Elders, as one, shook their heads and he nodded in satisfaction. 'Well, let's try to keep this secret, then, please; we do not want Quentin and friends finding out about it.'

'You are a disappointment and a disgrace.' The Master's disguised voice sounded tinny coming from the laptop's inadequate speakers, but it still had an authority to it that made Quentin cringe at its disapproval.

'But I got the mask!'

'The mask is a fake! It is lead covered with gold leaf and as worthless as you are. Whatever the real treasure was, you ran away before you found it.'

Quentin stared at the blank screen with his mouth open, not believing what he was hearing.

He was sitting in a nondescript hotel room. Bright sunshine streamed in through a gap in the curtains, illuminating the messy, unmade bed and the remains of a McDonald's meal strewn across the low table next to the laptop. The contents of a suitcase were scattered on the floor around him.

'That's impossible… Diana must have switched it for the real one before she gave it to you!'

'Don't be ridiculous, Price, and do not question the loyalty of people who have proven themselves time and time again to be far more trustworthy and worthwhile than you. And far less expendable.'

A cold sweat broke out on Quentin's skin as he realised that he might have gone too far for once. When he had left the Displacers he had sworn never to apologise for anything ever again, but for the second time in just over two months he found himself doing so. Because of Sam Vives. 'I'm sorry, sir.'

There was a grunt from the Master, but to Quentin it sounded more like he was trying not to laugh than an acknowledgement of his apology. He clenched his fists as his anger returned in full.

The distorted voice once more sounded from the laptop's speakers. 'Give me one good reason why I shouldn't replace you with someone more reliable for the operation this December?'

Quentin gritted his teeth. 'Because you know there's nobody better than me.'

'Except Sam Vives, apparently.'

'He's gotten lucky twice, next time I'll kill him.'

'*If* there is a next time… Come back to England, immediately. Leave Vives and his family *alone*, that's an order! Continue your training, do your research *properly* this time, and then maybe I'll let you go on the mission. In the meantime, write up a full report of your most recent failure so that I can send the twins to try to clean up your mess and bring back what they can.'

Quentin dropped his head, shamed, but still furious. 'Yes, Master.'

'Watch yourself, Quentin. One more failure and you may find yourself retired. There are plenty of others willing to step up and take care of Sam Vives and the Displacers for me.'

Before Quentin could protest, the Master broke the connection.

He snarled in anger and frustration and in a fit of rage he grabbed the gun from the sofa next to him and shot the laptop.

The foam darts bounced harmlessly off the screen without doing any damage, but he nonetheless felt much better. A couple of them went wide of their target, though, and he scowled, resolving to spend some time on a shooting range when he got back to London; next time he had Vives in his sights he would make sure not to miss.

ABOUT THE AUTHOR

Simon Brading tried his hand at many things before it occurred to him that he might have a few stories to tell. As well as the odd novel he writes screenplays and also does some acting every so often.

www.simonbrading.co.uk

For news of special offers, upcoming releases, exclusive content, competitions and events, please follow me on social media.

Instagram - @sibrading
Facebook - Simon Brading Author
Tiktok - @SimonBradingAuthor

ALSO BY SIMON BRADING

The "Displacers" series - a young adult time travel adventure series for all ages.
The Time Traveller's Nephew
The Secret of the Ancients
The Whitechapel Plot
The Price of Greed
The Time for Vengeance

The "Misfit Squadron" Series - a Steampunk series set in an alternate World War 2.
The Battle Over Britain
The Russian Resistance
A Misfit Midwinter
The Lion and the Baron
The Maltese Defence
Tales from the Second Great War
The Siege of Gibraltar
The King's Mission
The Home Front
Taking to the Skies
The Invasion of Britain

The "Twin Ambitions" series - ballet books for children ages 7 and up.
Fight to Dance
Back to Basics

The "Ni Hon - The Two Books" Series - a young adult series set in a dystopian future Japan.
The Black Book

Others
Public Enemy
Empath
The Lifeboat at the End of the Universe

www.ingramcontent.com/pod-product-compliance
Lightning Source LLC
Chambersburg PA
CBHW051305210726
48287CB00002B/673